Fate's Highw

By Christine D. Shucl

Elaine —
Thank you so much for hosting
me here in Dublin!

Christine

Standalone
The War on Drugs: An Old Wives Tale
Get Organized, Stay Organized
Winter's Child
Short-Term Rental Success

Watch for more at christineshuck.com.

Also by Christine D. Shuck

Table of Contents

First World

August 30th, 1886

Within the cloistered walls of the Arbre Genealogic, in the oldest part of Zurich, a dozen children ran through the halls, their dark hair disappearing into the folds of their robes, black shoes tapping out like gunshots on the stone floors and ricocheting off of the stone-hewn walls. Several jockeyed for position, intent on leading the charge through the doors in front of the others.

A glyph hanging in the air near the door, however, changed everything. Instead of boisterous talking, or a few girls pushing to the front, the children quieted, slowed their steps, and fell silent. The door opened, massive yet silent, and they filed inside.

Bridget Oriel was waiting for them and she smiled serenely as they quietly entered the room.

"Draw closer and listen, my children." The willowy and tall raven-haired young woman beckoned to the group of children and they moved as one, settling themselves upon the floor at her feet. Her robes were intricately embroidered, dazzling golden and silver filaments on a backdrop of black. The room was cold and the hard stone floors hardly welcoming, but the children seemed not to notice.

"I will tell you the story of our people, and of humans, but first you must understand the beginning of all of it." She continued, as the last child slipped into position, their eyes fixed on hers.

"Billions of years ago, when our solar system was new and a hundred planets circled the sun, one very important planet formed. In the vast darkness of space, it spun fast, faster than it does now. It was nothing like the world we see today. Instead, it was a red hot, boiling sea of molten rock - a vast magma ocean. Like countless others, it had been formed by the violent collisions of smaller bodies of space rock."

The children were silent, their raven black hair and piercing green eyes fixed upon her words. The woman continued, "Before anything more than a thin layer of crust could form on this new world, another smaller planet, not so much different in size than the red planet we call Mars, hurtled through space towards it. The two planets collided with such cataclysmic force that pieces were ejected, forming the Moon and the asteroid belt."

"And the energy from that collision also tore a hole through into a new dimension, sending a large chunk of the mass from both planets to the other side, forming Grote and Min, and coalescing into Fyrsta Heim."

"Our real home." A quiet voice from the rear of the group spoke up.

The woman turned to the child and smiled, "Yes, Zenobia, that's right. Our world, Fyrsta Heim, and Earth, connected through one ancient collision, but forever apart." Her face became solemn, "This collision caused a fracture, a tear if you will, and that has had consequences that threaten us to this day. The schism divided us not just geographically, but also in other ways."

She turned, murmured under her breath, and an image of Earth appeared in the air above them, gold outlining the continents on a background of roiling smoke. "Here we have Earth. Much like Fyrsta Heim, yet very different." She murmured again and an image of Fyrsta Heim, whole, with its continents outlined in silver. "And here is Fyrsta Heim, our home."

A collective sigh rose from the children as they gazed on a home that they had never seen and most likely never would.

"Our home was where we evolved, where our magic is strongest, and it is where we were meant to live." She waved her hand and the two worlds vanished, tendrils of smoke rising up and dissipating until the last remnants were gone. In its place, following another whispered command, there appeared the images of scores of raven-haired people dead and dying, with survivors fleeing as the ground shook and bucked. "Our forebears made a terrible mistake and we continue to pay the price to this day. A cataclysm destroyed much of our world, fracturing it through a combination of geological upheaval and wild magic gone wrong."

"The Brams." A child in the middle whispered, eyes rapt on the scenes that hung there in the air, switching now to a massive volcano erupting and raining down rocks and debris.

"Not just the Brams, Branwen, but the violence of this world so close to the barriers between Fyrsta Heim and here. That blood, that violence, combined with the wild magic that only a Bram could produce - they fed each other - and the cracks that had already been with us for billions of years ripped and tore. It was called the Great Dissolution, but it was more than that."

Her fingers flicked and the sibilant whispered command was barely audible. The scene changed to a battlefield filled with the dead and dying, a village filled with smoke, and scores of human soldiers and peasants running in panic.

"For every ten inhabitants of Fyrsta Heim, nine perished. The survivors fled, they had no choice, but in the chaos of those final moments, humans from this world were pulled through the World Walls by the last of the wild magic, even as most of the Brams died, their magic was fierce and dangerous in this world. As they fled and fell, as our people entered this foreign battleground, the magic the Brams possessed flared and turned, creating a boomerang effect that sent humans into our world. The rift was sealed by the Protectorates in order to protect this world, its human occupants, and the last, ragged survivors from Fyrsta Heim. At least here we were alive, back home there could only be death."

She sighed, and the children sighed with her, a collective release of ancient suffering and loss.

"Our world was shattered, broken into pieces that seem to fit onto this world loose, like the skin of an onion, and without mooring. The world itself calls to us, yet we cannot return."

"Not ever?" Zenobia asked, her tiny chin trembling.

"No, my child. Not ever." The woman said gently, "Only the Protectorates, those who guard the World Walls and serve Fyrsta Heim can return. The World calls them, pulls them through in moments of need, and only for as long as is necessary to serve the World's needs before they must return. We lost the chance to return home a millennia ago. Our magic, at least the deep, true stores of magic we would need for such a task, are all stored in Fyrsta Heim. This world is limited, *we* are limited and we are trapped here."

What You Ask of Me

Tuesday, June 14th, 1930

The child kicked inside of her. Zenobia placed her hands over her belly, feeling the tiny foot move again, sliding along the wall of her uterus. It wouldn't be long now. She had done what she could, eaten sparingly, and altered her clothing to conceal the burgeoning belly. She created spells that hung in the air, sliding around her, giving the illusion of a far smaller belly to the world. She had become so good at it that even she was fooled. Anyone who saw her would think she was perhaps four or five months along at most. Her stomach growled with hunger. Another spell made her face rounder, the bones less prominent. No one must suspect.

She caressed her belly. Her fingers found his head and stroked it. She would not lose him. Not this child, not again. It had been two years now and she still felt sick at the memory of it. Her hands around her firstborn son's tiny neck, squeezing before he could draw a second breath in the world. It had felt wrong, so wrong, and she would never let it happen again. She had sworn to die childless rather than risk bearing a son on Litha or Yule again. But fate, and the Arbre Genealogic had other plans for her.

"You must bear a child, your World will require a Protectorate." The instruction had been clear. It had to be her. They had ample examples of what happened when the World lost its Protectorate. It could not happen here. It would destroy everything. And Zenobia was the only daughter among one son and one Regional. There was no one else to do this. And so, she had allowed herself to be bred, yet again.

The boy's head moved, sliding slowly under her fingers as he rotated in the ever-diminishing space her womb provided. He was a boy, she was sure of it. Greta had confirmed it, her thin, bony fingers pausing when she had touched Zenobia's womb. Her rheumy, clouded eyes narrowed in confusion at the taut, rounded skin. Zenobia had held her breath, prayed to the Goddess that the old woman was too addled by Zenobia's magics to recognize how far along she was.

"He says his name is Conor," the old woman had croaked. "You don't have long, my dear, perhaps a week or two? Is it summer yet?"

"Yes, Greta, just one more week." Zenobia had answered quickly, "But it is nearly *August* now."

Greta frowned for a moment, "But wasn't it Beltane, just a while ago?"

"Oh Greta, how I wish it were so early in the year. I have so much to do before winter, and the days have already begun to shorten." She laughed, her heartbeat speeding up. The baby kicked inside of her, responding to the fear that ran through her.

The old woman's eyes couldn't be fooled by spells, for she was blind, and had been for two years. Her mind wandered too. Their people lived far longer than most, but after nearly 125 years of age, Greta was pushing the upper limits. It was precisely why Zenobia had kept her close. If she was required to keep a far-seer, she would have one that was virtually ineffective. Anything to keep the secret.

"But I thought..."

"Greta, dear," Zenobia lay a hand on the old woman's shoulder, forcing her tone to remain calm, even concerned, "Are you feeling well? I know you were ill during Litha. It took so long for you to feel better, but perhaps you need to rest again."

"I was ill during Litha?"

"You don't remember feeling ill, Greta?"

"Well, yes, but I..."

"We were all quite concerned. I mean, my goodness, it was nearly six weeks before you were able to get out of bed!"

Greta blinked, her rheumy eyes unfocused, film covering them. Zenobia refrained from shuddering.

"I thought it had only been a few days."

"Oh Greta," Zenobia paused and sighed, "Although I can certainly see how you might have thought that. But it was weeks and weeks. Perhaps you need more rest. Here, drink this."

She gently placed the cup of tea she had prepared for the old woman. Her finger drew a glyph that hung for a moment in the air, twisting and wet, before sliding down the inside of the teacup and disappearing within the dark liquid.

That would buy her a week of peace, possibly more. It was a powerful dose, and considering the old woman's age and condition, she was tempting fate. She watched the old woman as she sipped at the tea, her old face still brooding and confused.

A handful of minutes was all it took for the tea to take effect. Greta spasmed, slipping from her seat, with Zenobia instantly at her side, calling out for help.

She hid a sigh of relief as two of the house staff lifted the old woman in their arms and carried her out.

No, Greta would not be a problem.

A week later, in the darkest hours of the night, Zenobia slipped out of a side door, her belly rippling with contractions. She gasped as the sharp twisting pains shot through her. The dappled horse stood in the corral, his back bare of any saddle. Zenobia never used such contraptions. She preferred the smooth hide between her legs. Here, far from any neighbor, she lived as she wished. She had been riding daily, preparing for this possible outcome for weeks now.

She slid the plank that covered the opening to the corral to one side. The horse huffed softly, his breath steaming the night air, visible now that the moon was full and high overhead. He sidled closer to the fence and Zenobia climbed up onto it beside him before slipping one leg over his flank.

The maneuver was difficult, and made worse thanks to the frequent contractions. She had so little time, but she knew she could do it. She leaned forward, sliding the rest of her body into place, breathing through the pain, and whispered a command only the horse could hear. He nodded, tossing his head, and exited the corral, heading into the valley to the east at a steady pace.

The first rays of sunlight were stealing across the desolate land by the time they arrived at the tiny isolated cabin. There in the window a lamp shone, the flame flickering and dancing as the Santa Ana winds forced their way through the cracks. Zenobia tethered the horse and made her way to the door, her teeth gritted as another strong contraction hit. It wouldn't be long now.

"Senora, you came by yourself? All this way?" The woman was in her mid-30s, but looked older. Her hair was streaked with gray and her mouth already showed deep weathered lines. It seemed that the land here was not kind to women, no matter their profession.

Zenobia ignored the midwife. The pain was excruciating now and her water had broken seconds before, coursing down her leg and the side of the horse as she had slid off of him and collapsed in a clumsy heap on the ground, bruising her hip. Now as the next contraction hit, so soon after the first, she knew her labor could be measured in minutes. "It's time, the baby is coming."

She could see everything was prepared. The woman had followed her instructions to the letter. In the corner was a chubby, full-breasted young woman, still in her teens. She was tucking in the corners of a sheet that fit over a narrow bed. Her eyes never met Zenobia's and her hands twisted in nervousness over her deflated, yet still-protruding belly.

Zenobia's eyes closed in concentration and she fought the urge to squat there on the threshold and begin to push. Just a few more steps. She tottered to the bed and the midwife put her arm out to support her weight, slowly lowering Zenobia onto the edge of the bed.

"Mas almohadas. Date prisa!" The midwife snapped at the girl. The girl skittered away to the opposite end of the small cabin, reaching into the cabinet on the wall for more pillows. The older woman reached for Zenobia's skirts, pulling them up as Zenobia groaned in pain.

"Ah Senora, your water has broken. Such a risk for you to ride the horse here!"

"Dolores, please stop. The baby is coming, I need you to..." Her thought broke as the contraction continued, intensifying. She screamed then, and bore down. Her stomach rippled.

Hours later, she slid onto the horse, her belly sore from the contractions and empty of her child. Now came the task of hiding in plain view. She had spent the past few hours holding Conor. He was tiny, far smaller than her first son had been. But then she had been so certain of the girl that she had to be carrying that she hadn't had to starve herself and hide an ever-burgeoning belly.

"He is so very tiny, Senora. But do not worry, Maria has plenty of milk. She will feed him until he is fat and round. Don't you worry." The midwife had reassured her as Zenobia bore down and passed the placenta in one last great gush of gore. In the corner, Maria had stared at the baby with a mixture of longing and desperation. It was the second hardest thing Zenobia had ever done, leaving Conor in that girl's arms. But it had to be done.

The dappled horse smelled the coppery scent of blood on her. She had washed her body afterward and changed into a fresh set of clothes, but the stallion could still smell it. His eyes rolled, but he held still as she mounted, and soon they were heading back to the ranch. The rays of the sun lit the early evening sky in a myriad of reds and blues as the ranch drew into sight. Figures came running.

"Protectorate! I was ready to send a search party out for you." Her foreman, his face and arms reddened from the hot California sun, held the horse's mane in his large hand. "You have been gone all day! And in your condition..."

Zenobia arched an eyebrow. "My *condition*?" Honestly, Robert."

Robert had the decency to look embarrassed. "My apologies, Protectorate Saronica." His keen eyes flitted down to her belly, and Zenobia resisted the urge to look as well. She had practiced weaving the spells for months. First those showing a smaller belly, hiding the taut roundness of it these past few weeks. And now, the spell to push it out beyond what it now was. Hiding the emptiness would take work as her uterus contracted back to its normal size.

All would be well as long as she played the part. *Just your average run-of-the-mill pregnancy. Nothing to see here.*

She just had to keep it up for six more weeks and then sneak the girl Maria back in with Conor. His tiny size would work to her advantage. In six weeks he would be larger, but not *that* much larger. A carefully placed spell or two, and no one would be the wiser if she were to have suddenly gone into labor in the middle of the night. No time to call for help. After all, she had given birth before and second children often came quicker than expected. Her baby boy would be "born" on Old Lammas. Not a Bram, not a danger, no need for him to die.

She had it all worked out, every contingency planned for.

Except for one.

Eight weeks later, after the "birth" day passed and the girl had handed Conor back over to her, sobbing quietly, Greta had proved to be the failure point in Zenobia's carefully crafted plan.

She had chosen the old woman purposefully. Her mind eroded and broken by the dark visions of impending disaster, she should have been the perfect choice. Breeding Protectorates were always assigned far-seers to help mitigate any potential disaster of a Bram being allowed to survive his birth.

We are so afraid of our sons, so fearful that they cannot be contained, that we are forced to murder *them.*

Zenobia had never questioned it. Not until after she held her firstborn child in her arms and was ordered to end him. Doing that, taking that step, and living with it afterward, was what had changed her mind. *Never again.* When the Arbre Genealogic had again sent Jacques to the estate, Zenobia had not welcomed him. Barely a year had passed. She could not imagine risking birthing a son on Litha or Yule again.

Trust a Beshuzer to woo her. Damned if they hadn't sent him on purpose.

Njerez men had a fraction of the power of most women, but in Jacques it manifested as the perfect mix of empathy and sex appeal.

And one thing led to another.

"Protectorate, I must speak with you." Greta's small, hunched form filled the doorway. Her clouded eyes stared unblinkingly, seeing nothing. *Nothing in this realm, perhaps.*

Zenobia rose from her desk. "Greta, come in, please come in." She felt her heart rate increase. "Would you like some tea?"

The morning air held a chilly nip. Soon the sun would warm the land and the chill of night would be a mere memory. The Santa Ana winds had taken a rather uncharacteristic break two days before, and the air was still. Zenobia's breath fogged out, and her thoughts turned to Conor. He lay under a warm blanket, peacefully sleeping in a crib in the corner.

Greta shuffled into the room, one crabbed hand clutching a shawl around her thin, bowed skeleton. Until ten years ago, she could well have been mistaken for a woman in her early seventies. The Zradce far-seers lived a long time, but they courted madness with each premonition they experienced. Zenobia was surprised that Greta was sane at all after the sights she had seen. The old woman made her way into the expansive room and sank into a chair.

"No, no tea."

Zenobia sat down across from her. "What is it you needed to speak with me about, Greta?"

The old woman stared at her, the sightless eyes, clouded and rheumy, focused on her as if they were able to see clearly.

"I know what you have done, Zenobia."

"I'm sure I don't know what you mean, Greta."

"I am old, but my mind is not gone."

"Of course not. But I fail to understand what you mean."

The aged woman's voice hardened, "Do not play games with me girl. I know you gave birth to that boy on Litha. I know what he is."

Zenobia felt her heart skip a beat. She had made sure that the girl and the midwife would never tell anyone. The money had kept them quiet and the poison had made sure they didn't change their minds. She was safe, her son was safe. No one, save the old woman in front of her, had any suspicion.

"You know the law, Zenobia. The child cannot be allowed to live. No Bram may be allowed to live. It is too dangerous."

Zenobia let a long moment slide between them before she said, "I will take him to Fyrsta Heim before his twenty-first birthday. This world will remain safe, his magic will be contained."

The old woman cocked her head. "It can't be done. Only a Protectorate can pass between the World walls."

"Yet I have done it, Greta." Zenobia smiled, "Yesterday, I passed through the World walls with Conor in my arms."

"It isn't possible." Greta said, shaking her head.

"Yet, I did it." She allowed a note of steel to creep into her voice. "I can and will keep my son. He will grow up here, in this world. And when the time comes, before his powers vest, I will take him through the World walls, where he will inherit his birthright." Zenobia reached forward and grasped Greta's bony hand. It was cold, the old woman's skin paper-thin. "We did not always kill our male children, Greta. Once, before we found ourselves thrust upon these alien shores, we allowed our Bram sons to rule the World with us, manipulating time and space. We were powerful, and we were *free.*"

"And what would you have me do?" Greta asked.

"Say nothing. Trust me. I will take him there long before he ever manifests. It will be safe. This world will be safe, and Conor can grow up to embrace his powers in our home world, where his abilities are not a threat to this world or to us."

Greta pulled her hand away. "What you ask of me, Protectorate. It is..."

"Just consider it, Greta. Please. He is my son. He isn't a threat." Zenobia kept her voice calm, non-threatening, but she could see the future written plainly on Greta's face even as the old woman spoke.

"I'll...consider it."

"And you will tell me when you have come to a decision?"

"Of course, Zenobia." The old woman hesitated, "I do know how difficult this is. My cousin, she is a Strega. She mourned her son for years afterward. It is not easy living here, in this human world. Such sacrifices we must make."

Slowly the woman levered herself into a standing position, the curve of her back pronounced, the long years so evident upon her bony frame.

Zenobia knew it then. There would be no warning, no answer. Once Greta left this room, her freedom, and her son's life, would be measured in hours. At most, days. She watched Greta hobble out, slow. Zenobia stood as the woman began to head for the wide stone steps that led down to the main level of the house.

The ornate iron railing, the smooth stone...

Nine months later...

"He's quite handsome, Zenobia, congratulations! I am sure that Marta was disappointed he wasn't a girl and born on Litha, though. By the Goddess, but that woman can be difficult to deal with." The younger woman sighed, shifted the sleeping toddler in her arms, and sat down next to her. Zenobia smiled at her young friend.

"Analeigh, so good to see you! And this must be Castor, yes?" The little boy, born on Ostara in late March was twice the size of her son. His round, chubby face was framed by black curls and Castor held his mother's shirt in a plump little fist. "My goodness, I fear I am underfeeding Conor, or waiting for a growth spurt that should happen any day now. Such a difference!"

"Oh, enjoy it while you can," Analeigh laughed ruefully, "What I would give for Castor to be that small again!" She shifted the boy in her arms, and stretched gingerly. "He was born on Old Lammas, wasn't he? That's my birth day as well. It seems you will have someone to care for your fields before you know it."

"You seem to forget where I live, my dear Ana," Zenobia laughed. "The only thing to grow there are cacti and sagebrush. It is a barren place compared to this lush paradise."

Conor shifted, his eyes opening, blinking in the filtered sunlight. He peered up at the tree above them, a small bit of drool dribbling from a lip. Several teeth had been fighting their way through in the past two weeks and he had been cranky all morning.

"I was so sorry to hear about Greta," Analeigh added, bouncing her son on her knee, "Such a terrible end. It is hard to believe she would have celebrated one hundred and twenty five years on Samhain."

"Oh yes, it was horrid." Zenobia leaned over Conor, her fingers threading in his fine baby hair, moving a lock of it from his eyes.

"To tell you the truth, I have nearly fallen down those steps several times over the years, and Jacques very nearly did the other day as well."

Analeigh's eyes lit up, "Ah, Jacques is back so soon?" A smile danced over her lips.

Zenobia sighed, "You know how the Arbre Genealogic is. Marta hid her disappointment well, but insisted on sending Jacques to me on Ostara. We are nothing but breeding stock to them."

Analeigh's eyes tracked down to Zenobia's stomach. She was showing, and Eryka, Greta's daughter, was due at the estate any day now. She would verify what Zenobia already suspected.

"Do you know yet?" Analeigh asked, a hopeful look in her eyes.

"No, but I'm sure this one is a girl. And she will be born on Yule."
Zenobia allowed her lips to curve into a small smile, "The Arbre Genealogic
will have the future Protectorate they are so insistent upon. And as for me? I
will be left in peace."

Analeigh laughed, "From what I have heard, Jacques isn't *that* bad."

"Well, I wouldn't be one to kiss and tell." The two women shared a laugh
and held their young sons. Zenobia breathed a sigh of relief. Her secret was
safe. Her son was alive. She felt the tiny girl inside her kick then. A flutter of
fairy wings now, the next Protectorate of Fyrsta Heim. Her fingers smoothed
her son's dark hair and breathed in his clean baby smell.

The Call

Monday, May 26th, 1997

M The phone rang once, then twice. Sarah rushed from the hall into the study and answered it before it could ring again.

"Hello?"

"Mrs. Aaronson?" A young woman's voice sounded tinny in her ear.

"Yes, this is she."

"Good afternoon, Mrs. Aaronson, this is Candy, from Highland Park Cemetery."

Sarah closed her eyes. Finally, she could get to the bottom of this mystery. "Yes, Candy, I've been expecting your call." She could hear the girl shuffling paper at the other end of the line. "What did you find out?"

Candy cleared her throat, sounding nervous. "Well, I'm sorry Mrs. Aaronson, but we have not been able to identify the origin of graves you were inquiring about in Lot 62."

"What do you mean? You must have records of who is buried in your cemetery. I mean, don't you?" Sarah asked.

"Well, yes ma'am, we have records and the cemetery has only been here for sixty or so years. It's just that, well, our records don't show any graves in that location."

15

Sarah snorted, "Well, you must have missed something. There are four headstones there. And they all have my, well, the last name of Edmonds, which is my maiden name, on them. So there has to be a record somewhere."

The poor girl sounded embarrassed. "I'm sorry ma'am, but we don't know where those headstones came from. It is possible that they were placed there as an odd joke. I mean, people do the weirdest things in cemeteries! Why, just the other day..."

"Surely you have checked to see if there is anyone buried there."

"Oh yes, well. My supervisor said something about removing the headstones and..."

"Wait!" Sarah felt a sharp panic rise in her, "You can't do that."

"I'm sorry?"

"You can't do it. You don't understand, I think my dad is buried there and his family that died in 1962."

She stopped, realizing how bizarre she sounded. "Look, you just, you can't do that."

There was a long silence from the other end of the line. "Mrs. Aaronson, your father was Dean Edmonds, right?"

"Yes, that's right."

"And he passed away," she paused and Sarah could hear papers shuffling, "the 13th of May, right?"

"Yes."

The girl said nothing for a moment and the silence stretched out over the telephone line. When she spoke again, she seemed to choose her words with care. "But my records show your father interred next to Mrs. June Edmonds, in Lot 580."

Sarah willed away the urge to scream with an effort, "Yes, I know where he is. Look, it's a long story; could I please speak with Mr. Wilkins?"

"He's currently in a meeting, ma'am." Candy said it with practiced ease. *Sure he is in a meeting. Right. He's probably standing over you right now pantomiming hanging up the phone, desperate for you to get rid of the crazy lady.*

"Well could you have him call me when he gets out of the meeting?"

"Of course, Mrs. Aaronson." Candy's voice held that artificial cheer that conveyed in the most clearest of terms that there would be no call back.

"Well please do that. And..." Sarah took a deep breath, "Don't do anything to those headstones, *please*."

Sarah hung up the phone. None of this made sense. None of it. She closed her eyes, trying to will away the headache that was forming. Ever since Betty had told her the story, she had struggled to quantify it, to find a reasonable explanation for it all. But she couldn't.

After they laid Dad to rest, after the private ceremony and very public reception, as they had washed dishes and the men had disappeared out back with bags of trash to drink beers - Betty had told her a story filled with different lives and impossible things. It had made Sarah's head hurt as she tried to keep track. What made it worse were Betty's spotty memories from that time. Which wasn't surprising, she had only been four years old, and Sarah hadn't even been born.

Danny would have remembered. He had been six at the time, but Danny was gone. He had died in Khe Sanh, on Valentine's Day 1968, just two months past his 22nd birthday.

Sarah brushed away the tears that formed in her eyes. She missed her mom, and even more, she missed Dad. They had all known where it was headed with Mom and there had time to prepare for the inevitable. But with Daddy, it had been so quick, so final. None of them had the chance to say goodbye. And where he was found, there in the graveyard, in front of those four headstones. Sarah shook her head, it didn't make any sense at all.

Theo knocked on the door frame and walked into the room. "Is everything okay, sweetheart?" After more than twenty years of marriage his light brown hair was heavily sprinkled with gray. The laugh lines made him even more attractive.

Sarah tried to muster a halfhearted smile, failed, and then shook her head. "I just don't know what to think. The copy of those half-filled out commitment papers in Mom's files. That crazy story Betty told me, and Daddy gone." She choked back a sob, "I miss him so."

Theo pulled Sarah into his arms, and stroked her hair. "I do too. Both of them were so good to me, but especially your dad." Theo sighed heavily, "Your dad was the best. He treated me like a son."

Sarah kissed her husband's shoulder and nestled against him, "He thought of you as a son. He really loved you, Theo."

"So was that was the cemetery on the phone?"

"Yes. They say they can't find any records of those gravestones. How insane is that?"

Theo continued to stroke her hair and his warmth soothed her like it always had. From the moment they had met in Psych 101, Theo had remained a constant, reassuring presence in her life. Safe in his arms, Sarah thought about her girlfriends and their endless struggles to make relationships work. She didn't know a single one who wasn't on their second, sometimes third marriage. Theo and she may have started out young, but despite her mother's initial disapproval, it had worked out. He had won them over quickly, showing his commitment to her and his new role as a father just six months later.

It was Theo's love for her that made the loss of both of her parents within days of each other bearable. He spoke then, his warm breath tickling her neck.

"This might not be the best time to have dinner with Michael then."

Sarah pulled back, "What do you mean?" Michael had graduated with his Bachelor's, returning home in time to hold his grandmother's hand and say goodbye to her. And he had stayed by her side during both funerals.

"Why wouldn't it be all right?" she asked.

"He said he was bringing a friend." Theo pulled back and looked at her red, puffy eyes. "I could ask him to reschedule. It will be several weeks before he goes out to New York to visit that girlfriend of his."

Sarah shook her head, "No, no, I want to see him. I'll suck it up." She managed a small smile. "We hardly see him as it is. And I don't know about you, but any chance I get, I'm taking it."

Theo smiled at her and lifted her chin with a finger. "Red, puffy eyes and all, you are the most beautiful woman I have ever married. Honestly, you are my favorite wife."

"Silly," she said, giving him a playful smack, "I'm your *only* wife."

He didn't miss a beat, "That is beside the point."

"Help me with dinner?" Sarah asked.

"Of course." He chopped the broccoli and then the chicken. They danced around each other in the small kitchen. Theo took advantage of the close quarters to pull her close and steal a kiss once they were done. Sarah felt a current of desire run through her and smiled. *After more than twenty years, we still have the chemistry.*

"Mm..." Theo's mouth grazed her neck, his five o'clock shadow tickling her skin. She squirmed and laughed, pushing him away.

"We have time for a quickie."

"Oh no we don't!" Sarah said, holding her husband away, "You need to run to Gomer's and get us a bottle of wine!"

Theo pulled her close. "Five minutes. You know I can't resist it when you wear that perfume."

Fifteen minutes later Theo whistled as he walked out the front door. Sarah tucked her hair back behind her ears and straightened her skirt. Michael would be here soon.

The sun's rays sent bright sunlight through the kitchen window. A breeze blew the curtains. The beautiful spring weather was holding for now, but soon it would be time to close up the windows and doors and turn on the air conditioning. Summer was just around the corner.

Michael's favorite dinner was cooking in the oven and Sarah mixed together a fruit cobbler for dessert. She heard the front screen door open.

"Hey, Mom! Dad? We're here!" Michael's voice called out. "Oh man, it smells amazing in here. What's for dinner?"

Sarah turned the corner wiping her hands on her apron, "Chicken broccoli bake, of course. It's still your favorite, right?"

He grinned, "With the crunchy onion bits on top?"

"Of course."

"Still my favorite!" His lanky arms enveloped her in a big hug and Sarah leaned into it gratefully. Michael had always known when she needed a hug. He was gentle and sweet like that. A young woman stood behind him. She hung back, looking nervous.

"Mom, this is Julie."

Sarah beamed, "Julie, I had no idea you were in town! I have heard so much about you, my dear!"

"Hi, Mrs. Aaronson, it's nice to finally meet you." The girl was tall and slender. Her blond hair fell in curling waves and Sarah could sense a kindred spirit behind the girl's stunning crayon-blue eyes. Sarah hugged her and took Julie's hands in hers.

"You are absolutely beautiful, just as Michael described you." She felt smooth metal under her right fingers, and looked down, her eyes widening. There was a simple gold band encircling Julie's ring finger, a small round diamond at its center. She looked back at Julie and then Michael, her mouth forming a small "o" of surprise.

"Damn it, Mom, you ruined the surprise!" Michael said, shaking his head. He turned to Julie, "I should have known she would beat us to the grand announcement. It was impossible to pull anything over on her when I was a teenager. I swear, I just gave up and toed the line. It was far easier that way."

Julie laughed ruefully, "So much for your grand speech." She turned back to Sarah, "He was practicing it all the way here."

Sarah hugged Julie again, harder this time, and then wrapped her arms around her son. Tears shone in her eyes. "Daddy always said nothing got past me. He said I had the mind of a writer. That I watched everything, noticed the details."

"High praise, indeed, Mrs. Aaronson. I've read several of Mr. Edmond's books, 'Touched by Light' was my favorite," Julie enthused.

"Mine as well, right next to 'A Life Relived.'" Sarah dabbed at her eyes, "Oh my goodness, I just can't get over it. I knew it was serious when he went to New York for Christmas." She laughed then. "Your dad and I were guessing it wouldn't be long. But when in the world did this happen?"

Michael glanced at Julie, who smiled and blushed.

"Last night. I had been planning it for months, but then with Grandma and then Grandpa." He looked down at the ground, "I wasn't sure if now was even the right time to tell you. Dad said you were still trying to get answers from Highland Park, and..."

He looked up and shrugged his shoulders, his eyes a stormy gray of worry, betraying the calm exterior, "Surprise?"

Sarah could see how important her approval was to her son. "Oh honey," Sarah's eyes filled again, and she hugged Michael close before reaching out a hand and pulling Julie in as well, "Welcome to the family, Julie. I can't wait to learn more about you."

She's Not for You

Friday, March 18th, 1949

"She's not for you, Conor." Zenobia stood in front of her son on the brick path near the campus cafeteria.

He blinked at the impossibility of it. Mother was in California. She never traveled. At least, she never traveled in *this* world. How could she be here, in New York, when her post was in Los Angeles?

Her appearance was normal. She had exchanged the customary robes for a knee-length dress that peeked out of a gray wool coat. The shoulders of the coat squared. There were two rows of buttons which ran down the length of it beneath the sharp, pointed lapels. Her raven-black hair pulled back in a severe bun.

"Mother...I...what..." Conor searched for the words, unsure what to say. Had Mother been watching them? Had she overheard them talking?

The promises he had uttered just moments before, rose in his mind. What had Mother heard?

His eyes scanned the quad. Maggie was already gone, having disappeared in the distance. She was no longer visible. Her thin form had blended into a scattering of students at the far end of the campus square. She had been hurrying because she was late for her class. Maggie hated to be late, yet she

23

had risked it to meet with him. And she had finally told him why she had been so quiet recently, so reserved.

Conor had seen it in her eyes. She had been so scared, afraid he would reject her. But he hadn't. How could he? He was in love with her.

"It's time to come home, Conor." His mother added, her sharp green eyes boring into him.

"You said I still had time." He protested; panic sending icy tendrils down his spine. "I have another three years. Why are you here?"

"A child, Conor, you made one with that slip of a girl." Zenobia looked at him, her brilliant green eyes dark with fury, "We do not mate with humans. You know this, yet still you disobeyed."

"Mother, why would you say that?" he asked, stalling for time. Perhaps he could run. Perhaps he could slip away, get to Maggie, and just keep running.

"You would deny it, Conor?" She snapped, "Stand there and lie to me, will you? Do they teach you to lie here? If so, you are a terrible student. Your face shows your deception."

"She just told me. Just now. How could you know already? I didn't even know!"

"I could see it, the child growing inside of her. It is obvious." She shook her head.

Conor broke eye contact with his mother, casting about, his mind churning. It was just a few hundred steps to Maggie.

They could go to New York, lose themselves in the millions of people who lived and worked there. Or even catch a train to Kansas City. No, not Kansas City. Definitely New York. There the human population could hide them well.

Her eyes watched him as he took a step backward. Her mouth crimped into a flat hard line, noticing his small movement. He stilled, and her eyes cut into him.

"Conor Saronica, I bind thee to me." Zenobia's voice was hard and full of power. Behind the voice, under it, ran a river of magic, full of energy he wished that he had at his disposal now. But he would not see his manifest until his twenty-first birthday. At the hour and moment of his birth, his power would surge. And that was more than two years from now.

Conor could feel his legs and body stiffen in response.

"Please Mother. I love her. I want to marry her! We could take her there, you know we could. Humans are there, as well as here. Please..."

Zenobia moved a finger, muttered something under her breath and his tongue fell silent. He stared at her, hurt beyond words. *How could she do this to me, ME, her only son?* Mother had never treated him this way before. In his entire existence she had never once used her considerable powers against him.

"You will follow me now."

Conor wished he could scream, but no sound escaped his lips. He raged in silence, impotent, and helpless as his limbs moved of their own accord. He fell in beside Zenobia and the two of them walked along the sidewalk, a thin layer of ice crunching under their feet. Conor felt his feet moving and his body turned in unison with his mother's, heading for his dormitory.

Around them, students walked, passing the mother and son, oblivious to Conor's inner struggle. He continued to resist, a tiny drop of sweat beading on his brow despite the chill in the air. If only he could break his mother's control. No one noticed the two of them; no eyes fell upon them and stuck. Nothing he tried made a difference. He couldn't so much as twitch a finger without her consent. There was a brief moment of hope when Fred Gathers, nodded and waved at him. They were in the same Biology class.

"See you at the library tonight, Conor!"

Conor felt his hand come up and wave as they passed, his head bobbed in a nod towards Fred, a grin creeping over his face. All under his mother's control.

"I'm disappointed in you, Conor." Zenobia spoke in a low voice, pitched so that only her son could hear her. "You knew the rules. You know them now. Yet you broke them. You consorted with a human girl and you are fighting me even as I speak." Her voice was tight, full of anger. "I should never have allowed you to leave. Such a risk! And especially with you being who you are. What was I thinking?"

They approached the stairs of his dormitory taking the steps in unison. Inside of the main doors, the large entry hall stood. Next, it was up two more flights of stairs, again without so much as a step out of turn.

"You are in room 305, yes?"

Conor's head nodded and at the top of the second flight of stairs they turned left. The hallway was empty and Zenobia muttered again as they approached Conor's dorm room. The door swung open.

His roommate Castor, psychology textbooks strewn about him, was absorbed in his studies. "Did you forget your History book ag..."

Castor froze in mid-sentence, his eyes widening. He stood, books clattering to the floor in his haste. Zenobia and Conor entered the room. The door clicked shut behind them.

"Protectorate Saronica, you honor us with your presence." He bowed to Zenobia, his eyes meeting Conor's. His face filled with concern and no small amount of fear.

Conor felt his mother's power ebb from his body. His limbs were his again, his mouth, his tongue free from his mother's power. He glared at his friend.

"You told her, didn't you?"

Castor's eyes glanced away, towards Zenobia, then back to Conor.

"I had to. You know the law."

"The law? The *law*?" Conor spat. "I trusted you, Castor. It isn't as if you haven't dallied yourself."

"Dalliances are one thing," Castor began.

"Shut up!"

Conor put one foot forward, a fist clenched. He could feel a flush of heat in his cheeks and the fury rising inside him. In that moment, he felt capable of true violence. He stared at his friend and imagined hitting him, again and again. In his mind, he longed to see the blood spurt and hear the crunch of bones beneath his fist. Castor had been his companion, and his friend, for longer than he could remember. But this betrayal, it was unforgivable.

"Conor, I am warning you." Zenobia's tongue dripped icy cold threat. He could feel her power, centered on his spine. It curled there, threatening a repeat of the indignities he had just experienced.

A wave of despair washed over him. Mother was here to take him home. And home was over three thousand miles away. Maggie would come by tomorrow to see him, and he wouldn't be here.

"Mother, please, let me talk to her. I could explain."

"What exactly would you explain, Conor? There is nothing more to say." She looked around the room. "Castor, you will pack up Conor's things and send them back to Los Angeles for me. You are to stay until the school breaks for spring. At that time you will return to your family."

Castor's shoulders sagged. He nodded, his eyes still on Conor. "Yes, Protectorate, I am yours to command."

"Mother, please!"

"This experiment is over Conor. I will see that the girl and her child are both cared for. I promise you that."

"Mother, if you would just let me see her."

"No more, Conor, no more. It is time to leave." Zenobia turned on her heel. The dormitory door sprang open at her command and she strode through it.

Conor had one brief second to contemplate escape and then her influence fell over him again. He managed a single look of loathing directed over his shoulder at Castor. Then Conor found himself marched out of the dormitory. He fought, to no avail, as they left behind the college, New York, Maggie, and his unborn child. The door slammed shut behind them.

The following day, Conor and Zenobia exited the sleek silver jet. Here in Los Angeles, the weather was already warm and inviting. There was no hint of the icy cold or late winter storm that had enveloped the coast as they left. It was a clear day, cloudless, and there was a slight breeze.

It should have been reassuring, even welcoming, but it was not. Here in the city that he had called home his entire life, something felt wrong. Conor's mind was working away, wondering what Zenobia had in store for him.

Did she think he would agree and accept his fate? Could he expect she would become complacent and then he could make his escape?

He wondered how to go about it. There were cars at the compound, any of which he could use to escape. It would have to be at night, so he could get a decent head start.

He looked up and saw his mother watching him. Perhaps he had given himself away already. Perhaps she was assessing the threat that he had become to her, and to the rest of their kind. He forced a weak smile to his lips.

An hour later they drove along the twisting road deep into the foothills. Right now they were green with life, covered in wild grasses and bunches of scrub brush and new trees.

In a few months that would all change as the Santa Ana winds took hold and dried out the life of the land. The grass would turn brittle, and lose its vibrant green color.

Even the trees would suffer, desperate for water after weeks of exposure to the hot, dry winds. What was now green and soft would turn to a harsh crunching brown mass underfoot. Then they would all hold their breaths as they courted disaster. Just one cigarette butt tossed out of a window at just the right spot would set the hills alight.

Conor had seen it several times over the years. He stared out of the window, dreaming of Maggie. The baby growing inside of her. They had made it together, in love. What would she think when he didn't meet her today at their usual place?

What would Castor say to her? Would he even answer the door? She would think he had abandoned her? That he had run away? His heart ached, she would think he had rejected her and the baby.

"It is so beautiful here in the spring." Zenobia's voice was kind. He turned to see her stern, careworn face smiling at him. He tried to remember that he was angry at her, but Conor couldn't help but smile in return.

"Just wait until you see the view on the other side," she added and placed her hand on his shoulder.

He didn't have time to process her words and understand what they meant before it hit. There was a twisting sensation, both from deep within his body and in the air around him. A shimmering that became a blur of bright, white light. And just like that, the landscape changed. Everything looked different.

Instead of the bright Los Angeles sun, it was overcast and gray. The air was cold, damp, and there was a strong smell of salt and fish. The view of trees and grasses had changed to a severe rock face, stretching up out of sight in the mists above. On the other side, a sharp cliff hung over the pounding surf. A profusion of greenery poked out of rocks and cropped up along the edges of the roadway. Thick vines inched their way up, hugging the rock wall. They displayed brilliant bursts of yellow and red flowers. The track was narrow, almost too narrow for the car, which had remained with them.

In the distance, he could hear a bell tolling. It rang thirteen times. The soft throaty sound bounced off of the walls of the cliff face.

"Welcome to Fyrsta Heim, my son," Zenobia said, her mouth softening as she let the car coast to a stop on the road.

"My god," Conor breathed, staring in shock, "It's *real*. And it is so different from what I imagined. I always imagined it looking like Earth, like the foothills of Los Angeles."

He took a look at the small village in the distance and the walls of the great stone castle in front of them.

Then it dawned on him, "Mother, how am I here? I thought that only a Protectorate could travel through the World walls."

Zenobia nodded, "As did I. It was a fluke. A cat hitched a ride once. I had been petting it when the World called and we both came through. I tested it with a dog after that, then a child from the ranch, just to be sure. Later I brought you here when you were small. Although I doubt you remember it. Come," she said, stepping out of the car and onto the cobblestone road.

"I want to show you the castle. I know you took an architecture class and I thought you would want to see it. The workmanship is exquisite."

Conor felt a small tendril of unease begin to coil inside of him, but her happy smile disarmed him. Besides, if he behaved, she would let down her guard and then he could slip away and return to Maggie. And the sooner the better, right?

They entered the castle through wooden doors. They were enormous and stood at least twenty feet tall. They hung on massive iron brackets and groaned when opened. Conor thought they sounded like a wounded beast forced to open its mouth. They walked inside and he sucked in a breath at the sight before him. At regular intervals, massive torches blazed. They were housed in metal sconces mounted on the stone walls.

The floors, walls, and ceiling were all the same dark gray stone. Much of it carved in intricate detail. Softening the carved stone were wall hangings. The lush tapestries that depicted scenes filled with landscapes, castles, and people. He could have spent hours staring at them. The tapestries were also enormous. He had read about how tapestries were created in his Medieval

Studies class last semester. The skill it would have taken was dwarfed only by the thousands of hours of work entailed in such a task. In many ways, tapestries were far more complex than an oil painting could ever be.

Beneath their feet was a thick carpet over ten feet wide and running the entire length of the giant hall. There were many levels above them. Walkways, doorways and more opened up, at least a dozen, possibly two dozen stories above them, all with a view of the hall below.

"It's...enormous," he breathed in wonder.

At the top, a massive stained glass skylight sat. He could see the beams of colored light dancing on the floors below.

"Indeed," Zenobia said, her mouth twisting in a small smile. "I've wanted to share this with someone else for a long time. Ever since I stepped onto the path behind us forty-three years ago. From what I can tell, this entire castle was carved out of the granite mountain."

"How is that even possible?" Conor asked. His eyes ran over the carved portico. His mouth dropped open as he tried to imagine how long it must have taken. Years, decades, maybe more. If only his professors could see this.

Zenobia didn't answer, pointing instead to a far wall.

"That tapestry there is particularly fascinating."

Conor stepped forward, moving ahead of his mother. The tapestry his mother had pointed to was different. He squinted at it. Was it actually moving? As he drew closer, the figures began to change, swirling on the fabric. He could see a figure resolve, the man in it was pounding on a clear glass wall. Beyond it, just feet away, the figure of a woman, stood.

He advanced, closing the distance so that he could see the details. As he stared, his entire focus on the tapestry, he felt a change in the air behind him. Then the man in the tapestry turned. It looked so out of place from the rest of the tapestry. And then he realized why. A sick dread twisted his guts and he turned on his heel, panicked. Beyond the thick sheet of glass, his mother stood. Zenobia's eyes locked on his, her green eyes full of pain.

"I am sorry, my son, but this is how it has to be."

"Mother, let me out of here." Conor struggled to keep his voice calm. "I'll do as you say. I will stay at home. There is no need for this."

"Oh Conor, how I wish that were true." Zenobia shook her head, "From the moment I birthed you, I knew what you would be. I chose to flaunt the law. But in exchange, you and I both know this was always your future."

"My fate, you mean? In this prison?" Bitterness crept into his voice.

"This isn't a prison," Zenobia fired back, affronted by the thought, "It is our home. It has always been our home. Here we didn't have to kill our most powerful male children. Here we didn't have to hide when our sons were born on the Solstice." Her lip trembled, "I couldn't do it, Conor, not again, and not to you. I loved you. I did it once. I let the Fer Complir have their way. I had loved that child, wanted that child, and yet I took the life I had just bore into the world. It was the law. But with you, when I knew what you were, what you would be, I couldn't do it."

"Let me go back and get her, Mother." His hands smudged the thick wavy glass. He pushed, wishing again that his powers had manifested, that he didn't have nearly two years to wait. The glass wall did not budge.

Zenobia's eyes filled with tears. "No, my son, already I have done too much. There will be questions. They would come for you if they could. Here you are safe. Only a Protectorate of the Saronica lineage can cross the threshold. Here you will be safe for as long as I draw breath."

"Mother, please don't do this." Conor pleaded, his fingers knuckle-white against the thick glass. They curled into fists, his heart racing. "I don't belong here."

Zenobia smiled and stepped backwards, "This was always your future, Conor. It was this or my hands about your neck. And I love you too much for that. I will see you soon, my son."

She turned and walked away. Conor screamed after her. The walls echoed his cries, distorting them and sending them back down. It was a perverted echo that laughed in the face of his pain. He beat on the glass until the skin on his knuckles split and blood marred the glass wall.

Tribunal

Wednesday, March 31st, 1949

The image of Conor's stricken face had haunted her all the way back through the world walls. She had not stopped at the ranch, although she knew they would be concerned. Instead she had turned the car around and set it on the long drive back to the bustling Los Angeles airport. A few hours later, Zenobia boarded the flight to New York. She landed as the last rays of the sun dipped below the hills, the sky on fire in orange, pinks and streaks of red.

There was no time to admire it, however. The ship was waiting.

When the letter from Castor had arrived, she had set into motion the plans she had laid out years before. She knew what she needed to do. Protect her son, put him back in the world where he belonged, where they all belonged. After that, well, the future was clouded.

The voyage across the Atlantic had taken eight days and Zenobia had left her tiny stateroom a handful of times, electing instead to prepare herself mentally for what would lie ahead.

Rotterdam's port was bustling with energy, as was the rest of the city. As she walked from the port, the air was filled with the sound of hammers, saws, and industry. The city remained mostly in ruins. Mountains of decimated buildings stood side by side with new ones. Stone and fresh timber filled with shining glass windows stretched up towards the sky.

Zenobia could see scaffolding surrounding the massive St. Lawrence church near the city center. It had been one of the oldest buildings to survive the Blitz nine years earlier. The entire city appeared to be under varying states of reconstruction.

She found herself momentarily distracted from her own delicate situation as she took in the vast amount of devastation. She had not seen Rotterdam since her confirmation as Protectorate of Fyrsta Heim in 1927. The city had looked quite different then, before the war, before the German bombings and invasion. The streets had been lined with trees, the city crowded with ornate stone architecture, and bustling with commerce.

She had heard that, above ground, the ancient stone edifice that had housed the Primera Veu had been blasted to bits during the bombing. Yet their history, the library and records of the Arbre Genealogic, along with other important documents, were all saved, buried deep in the secret tunnels below. The building above had been rebuilt, of course, and she had seen a photo of it. Although nothing like the medieval beauty that was lost, the new home for the Primera Veu provided all of the latest modern comforts.

She passed a group of boys playing ball in a vacant lot, a plain two-story housing structure that consisted of concrete and glass, minimalist and lacking any detail, was behind them. One of the boys yelled as he was blocked by another, the ball slipping from his hands and escaping to bounce in front of a small truck loaded with fish. The driver honked at the boys, waved a fist, and drove on.

Zenobia shifted the suitcase from one hand to the other. She hadn't seen any cabs. Then again, she had been one of the few passengers on the ship, which had been loaded with needed supplies destined for the busy port. Before the war, there had been cabs, along with a trolley car, plenty of transport into the city for visitors. However, with the landscape so drastically changed, she had not known where to look. A car slowed in the road to the left of her, pulled up to the curb and a man leaned, "U dient een rit, missen?"

Zenobia looked over. The man was middle-aged, clean, with graying hair and a worn coat. He smiled at her.

"Ja, harelijk dank."

He pointed to the back door and she opened it and climbed inside. The leather seat was worn and patched.

The man turned back to the road, "You are from America?"

"Yes." She smiled, "Is it that obvious?"

The man laughed, "Perhaps." He drove down the block and they passed a large skeleton of a building, metal girders clawing at the sky.

"I need to go to Jan Evertsenplaats. Are you heading that way?"

His face had changed when she told him the street. She had glimpsed it in the rearview mirror - a look of recognition. He covered it up quickly. "Yes, yes. I need to make a delivery at Meent and Coolsingel. It is on the way."

He swerved to avoid a dog and they drove in silence for a moment before he spoke again. "The bombings, they destroyed so much."

"Yes, I can tell. I was here in '27. It was very different."

"We, how do you say, remake?"

"Rebuild?"

"Yes, yes, rebuild. So much work. For your people, for mine."

The last sentence hung there in the air. *Your people.* She should have expected it. Secrets are difficult things to keep. No matter how circumspect the Primera Veu had been, there were those who noticed the tiny details one tried to keep hidden.

"Indeed." Zenobia remained non-committal. *He certainly doesn't mean American. With the exception of Pearl Harbor, there hadn't been anything to rebuild after the war, unlike Europe.*

"I have three grandchildren now. My daughter and her husband, they were caught in the bombing in 1940. My son-in-law, he had been delayed, and my daughter would not leave without him. I was sure I had lost them. Instead they were taken in. A group of three women, all of them with raven black hair and green eyes like yours, they took them in, brought them underground, where it was safe. My daughter survived, while hundreds perished." He said it, his eyes flitting from the road and back to the rear-view mirror.

"She was pregnant, and the baby, my first grandson Viggo, was born in the tunnels, after a hard labor." His hands tightened on the steering wheel, "She very nearly died, and the baby with her. But those women, they saved my daughter Marieke. She began to bleed, hemorrhage. They lay their hands on her and she says that they performed a miracle. They saved her, protected her and little Viggo, and her husband Frederik."

Zenobia remained silent. At an intersection, the old man slowed the car down, waited for a lorry filled with steel girders to pass in the opposite direction. He met her eyes. "Since they climbed out of the rubble and escaped to the hills where it was safe, a city burning around them, I have not forgotten this kindness. And Marieke has had two more children in the years since."

They drove in silence then, their time together measured in three short blocks, before the old man pulled up in front of a modern building, filled with glass and concrete.

"Dank u." Zenobia said, reaching out and clasping the man's hand. "Your name?"

"Christophe Meijer."

"Zenobia Saronica."

"Be well, Christophe."

"Be well, Zenobia Saronica."

She exited the car, suitcase in hand, and entered the nondescript building.

The front entry was small, plain, and there was a raven-haired girl sitting behind a desk. She looked up at Zenobia with curiosity and a glimmer of recognition. Her mouth formed an "o" of surprise when she finally put together exactly who was standing before her.

"Protectorate Saronica," she said, standing and bowing slightly, "I apologize for not recognizing you. I had not been told to expect you."

Zenobia nodded at the girl, struggling to remember the girl's name.

"I'm Martha Rowan."

"Ah, yes, your mother is Ruth, correct?"

"Yes, ma'am." The girl brightened, "I'll let them know you are here." She leaned over a small speaker and pressed a button. "Protectorate Saronica is upstairs, ma'am." The response was too quiet for Zenobia to hear. "Yes ma'am, right away." She nodded to Zenobia, her eyes straying to a nondescript door behind her. "If you will just go through that door, Protectorate, the Council is expecting you."

The door led to a short hall and another door, which buzzed when she approached it. Zenobia grasped the handle and turned it before the buzzing stopped. Another short hallway, complete with four doors, all unmarked.

An intercom mounted in the ceiling crackled, "Second door on the left." She approached the door and opened it when it buzzed.

There was a tiny landing, concrete steps surrounded by rock, and stairs descending deep underground. They banked right and disappeared around a corner. Before the war, the steps had been hand-cut, the walls etched with symbols, runes and draped with tapestries. The way down hadn't looked like this at all. Not a bleak, modern, minimalist feel.

Instead it had been steeped in tradition - not just their people's tradition, but an older one as well. The humans, most certainly, but ones who, in what must have been Neolithic times, carved elaborate tunnels far beneath the surface of the land, with only torches to light their way. Whatever had caused them to abandon or forget the small labyrinth of tunnels and rooms was a mystery, but the Primera Veu had set up their headquarters here in the first years of this millennium. Still reeling from the Great Dissolution, they had formed a home base in the long-forgotten tunnels and here they had stayed.

There were rooms filled with art, books, and records produced by the Protectorates. They chronicled the world that they had lost, one that was only accessible now in tiny, isolated pieces.

Zenobia wondered where her records were. She kept accounts which faithfully recorded each visit to Fyrsta Heim, her fragment of their home world. The copies were sent here, and added to the large dusty tomes that every Protectorate in training eventually had to read through. She began to descend down the stairs and felt relief when the precise concrete finally gave way to worn stone. Some things needed no modernization, they were sufficient in their imperfect, timeworn way.

The walls showed no signs of repair. Had the bombings caused cave-ins? If so, the Primera Veu remained incredibly secretive. A triad of three women, they kept their own counsel, and would have said little, if anything, of such inconsequential things.

All three members of the Primera Veu were Protectorates, despite having no portal to protect. With a few whispered words the caverns would have been restored to a state better than they had been before.

The stone steps continued to turn, and along the way, torches would flare into flame at intervals as Zenobia approached them. Behind her, she could see the torches dim and sputter out after she passed. The passage continued down, circling farther, the walls close. Occasionally a glyph would appear, twisting, turning in the air. Invisible to any human, they served as protection from human intruders. A human would see a wall, a dead end, if they saw anything at all in the blackness since the torches on the walls would not respond to their presence.

Finally there were no more steps, only a smooth stone floor lining the long dark passageway, intersected with dozens of doors. At the end of it stood a woman, her raven hair disappeared into a velvet-lined hood and long robe that revealed only the tips of her shoes.

"Zenobia, it has been a long time." Her voice held little warmth.

"Anna," Zenobia nodded to the woman, and approached her. "Congratulations are in order, I see."

Anna had served in the Maiden position of the Primera Veu for fifteen years before ascending to Mother less than a year ago. Almira Dean had held the Crone position for decades before passing the torch to Branwen Tecio by quietly passing away in her sleep at the age of 112 years. Zenobia had heard that Anna had been less than excited over her new position. Not surprising really, considering

Anna had never been considered particularly maternal. She had given birth and promptly handed the child over to be raised by others, meeting the criteria of Mother in name only. There was nothing maternal in those sharp green eyes, nothing but hard edges and judgment.

Anna did not respond. Instead she dipped her head, a hard-edged look settled over her features and she pursed her lips, "We have been expecting you." She held out her hand and ushered Zenobia into the room beyond.

The room was lined with intricate tapestries, which appeared to move and shift of their own accord. The scenes woven upon them were of places that few had ever seen. As Zenobia's eyes traveled over them she saw familiar images, the cliffs of Behel, the village that lay below the great stone palace, and the ocean beyond it.

If I stare long enough, will I see Conor?

At the center of the room was an enormous table. It was shaped from a large, ancient tree trunk, the rings clear beneath the highly polished surface. Originally round, a lightning strike had cleaved a v-shaped divot in its enormous girth. That was where the penitent would stand, where she must stand. The table was so massive that it could easily seat thirty people and still have room for more.

On the sides of the table she could see the heavily burled wood, a rich dark brown, and it took her breath away. This was the fabled Tree of Judgment. It had come from Fyrsta Heim in the decades after the Great Dissolution.

The magic it had taken to bring it across had to have been incredibly difficult, a collaborative effort that would be impossible now in their divided state. Along its massive edge she could see hints of glyphs twisting and turning, etched into the wood. This tree had served for more than three millennia, on Earth and on Fyrsta Heim, as a place of judgment.

Already seated at the table were Branwen Tecio, who served as Crone. Anna Verndari, who had led the way, had seated herself in the Mother position. Against the wall, judging from the rather unhinged look on her face, was a far-seer.

Of course, they knew I was coming.

Behind Zenobia, Hannah Suisser slipped past and assumed her seat at the table. Zenobia had heard of her. She was the Maiden, the position that the girl at the front desk, young Martha Rowan, would someday take. They all stared at her in silence.

Branwen, whose seat was directly across from Zenobia, pointed to the divot, "Approach, Protectorate Saronica."

Despite her years on Earth, and her experience as Protectorate of Fyrsta Heim, Zenobia felt a tremor pass through her. She had known this day was coming for nearly twenty years. She had dreamed of it, tried to imagine some way out of it, but there was no avoiding it. She had betrayed her people, broken one of their most sacred laws and now she had to face their judgment for it.

She stepped forward, her shoes clicking on the stone floor. In the preternatural quiet of the room they sounded like gunshots.

Anna spoke next, her words formal and measured, "The Council will now come to order. We pray that we may judge sincerely, without anger, without personal motive, and serve our people to the best of our ability." She paused, "Who serves as Crone?"

"I, Branwen Tecio, serve as Crone."

Hannah spoke next, "Who serves as Mother?"

Anna answered, "I, Anna Verndari, serve as Mother."

Branwen spoke next, "And who serves as Maiden?"

"I, Hannah Suisser, serve as Maiden."

Anna asked, "And who comes before us? Who stands accused before the Crone, Mother and Maiden?" Her face was a cold, impenetrable mask.

Zenobia's heartbeat had increased, she felt it difficult to breathe for a moment and placed her hands on the expanse of wood before her. The power of it was palpable, a heavy stillness of years gone by.

"I, Zenobia Saronica, First Protectorate of Fyrsta Heim, stand before the Council today and submit to your judgment."

Branwen nodded to the woman on her left. Her nails were bitten to the quick and the woman stared at Zenobia as if she were able to see straight through her. It left little doubt in Zenobia's mind as to her identity. This had to be Greta's daughter, Ursula.

"And who comes before the Council to give evidence?"

Ursula stood. To a mere human she appeared to be in her mid-twenties, but the far-seer had seen more than half a century. Her hair hung in greasy black strings and her eyes were filled with madness.

"I, Ursula Zradce, stand and give evidence against a traitor in our midst."

Spit flew from her mouth as she uttered the last words, and she trembled.

Zenobia wasn't sure if she trembled with anger or fear. She had heard that Ursula was one of the strongest far-seers they had ever seen, eclipsing her mother's visions in both number and clarity. She had collapsed the day before her mother died, felled by a catatonia that had robbed her of speech for nearly two years. Zenobia couldn't help wondering what she had seen. If Ursula had seen her mother's death, she had said nothing for nearly twenty years.

Was that about to change?

"The Council awaits your evidence, Far-seer Zradce," Branwen said.

"There is no need," Zenobia said, "I am here to confess."

Anna's sharp green eyes narrowed, and she leaned back, "By all means, Protectorate." She waved a hand at Ursula, "You may be seated."

On the long journey to Rotterdam, Zenobia had spent most of it trying to think about anything but standing here, before the Council. Nevertheless, there were moments when it caught up with her and she had tossed and turned in her cramped stateroom, dreams filled with Conor's anguished face caught behind thick glass. Waking always brought her thoughts square and center to this moment, standing before the Council and admitting what she had done.

Zenobia sucked in a breath. All of the stone - below her feet, the walls, even the ceiling - felt as if it were closing in around her, stealing the oxygen. Despite the tall ceilings and large room, it created a heaviness in the air around her. Another deep breath as she tried to focus not on the memory of Conor's face, but here in this room, and on the faces of the Council before her.

"I, Zenobia Saronica, First Protectorate of Fyrsta Heim, have broken the laws of our people. Nearly nineteen years ago, on Litha, I gave birth to a Bram, in full violation of the laws set forth by the Council since the years after the Great Dissolution. I did this with full knowledge of the law and at the price of three lives. Two human, one Njerez."

Ursula sat in her seat, shaking, a tear sliding down her cheek. "You murdered her. You murdered my mother."

Zenobia swallowed, trying to clear the tightness of her throat and nodded wordlessly.

Hannah, new in her role as Maiden, asked softly, "Please continue, Protectorate."

"I hid my pregnancy, gave birth to Conor on Litha with the help of a human midwife and arranged for a wet nurse to care for him until Lammas. Greta was blind and easily misled as to the date. But afterward, after I had collected Conor and dispatched both the midwife and wet nurse as humanely as possible, she confronted me and told me she knew the truth."

Ursula sobbed out loud as Zenobia continued, "I made it look like an accident and she passed before she could betray my secret."

There was silence then, a long moment punctuated only by Ursula's distress and her hissed words, "*Murderer, murderer, murderer, murderer.*"

"You took the lives of two humans, *murdered* one of our own, and betrayed your people. And then you hid him away before coming here." Anna's voice was sharp, her words like knives. "Where is the Bram, Zenobia? Where have you hidden him?"

"Where he can never harm anyone," Zenobia answered defiantly.

"There is no place on Earth that is safe from his power when he comes of age," Branwen replied, "You know that."

"Which is why he is no longer on Earth."

"No longer on Earth? Do you truly expect us to believe that? No one but a Protectorate can travel through the World Walls. And certainly no one who is not already keyed to that World. That is impossible." Anna said it flatly, stating facts that everyone had known for centuries.

"Look on the tapestry behind you. The Cliffs of Behel, the village below, and Conor there in the castle. If it is so impossible, how do you explain his presence in Fyrsta Heim?"

In unison, the Council's attention focused on the tapestry on the far wall. Ursula shook her head, "I told you Anna, but you would not believe me."

Branwen peered at the tiny figure on the tapestry, touched it with one finger and murmured under her breath. The scene changed, zooming in, until Conor's face was clear. He was asleep in a bed, still wearing the clothes he had on the day she took him into Fyrsta Heim. His hair looked lank and greasy, and he had lost weight.

Zenobia sucked in a breath. Had he been eating enough? Asleep, his face was relaxed, and he looked younger than his nearly nineteen years. She couldn't help wondering what his powers would be like there.

Fyrsta Heim was where they all belonged. She believed that with all her heart. They could go back, she was sure of it, and Conor was the key to all of it. He held the power over time and earth. Together, they could heal their home world and return to it. If only he hadn't gotten distracted with that human girl. She never should have let him leave for that ridiculous college. What a fool she had been!

"I didn't think it was possible," Hannah said, her eyes locked on the tapestry. "Who else has been able to do this?"

"No one." Branwen said, "Ever."

They turned as one and stared at Zenobia. Anna spoke first, "You will show us. I will travel back to the portal with you and you will take me through."

"I will not."

Anna gaped at her, "What did you say?"

Zenobia stared back at her, her eyes calm, "I will not take any of the Council, or any other of our people through the portal. None of you will ever be allowed near my son. He has the right to live in a world in which he can be free. A place where his life is not forfeit."

Branwen sputtered, "He cannot be allowed to live! Have you forgotten your history? Brams are the *reason* we are here! Everything they touch, they destroy!"

"He is where he belongs and I will fight for him and his life with every fiber of my being," Zenobia said, her eyes steely, "You cannot have him."

Branwen hissed, "Then his life and yours are forfeit. You have betrayed your people Zenobia and the Council will see that justice is dispensed."

She stood up, the heavy carved wood chair falling to the floor and leapt onto the massive table with a grace that belied her advanced years. As the Crone, it was her place to dispense justice, her place to take a life. She moved swiftly, closing the distance between them, her robes swishing, shoes clicking on the wood, a shining dagger in her bony hand.

What happened next left the members of the Council and Ursula Zradce dazed and disoriented.

Zenobia muttered an incantation under her breath, her right hand tracing a glyph that hung in the air, twisting for a brief second before exploding in a blinding wash of light. Moments ticked past, the flare of magic blinding them all. When they could see again, Zenobia was gone. No manner of searching the corridors yielded success, and young Martha Rowan, on duty at the only entrance and exit, had not seen her. Zenobia Saronica had disappeared.

The Council sent several Fer Complir, their own internal version of police, to the sprawling ranch in California, hoping to find her there. To no avail.

It would be years until Zenobia's daughter, Mona, who was only fifteen, would be able to assume her mother's role and enter Fyrsta Heim. Conor was safe, for now, and Zenobia's whereabouts remained a mystery.

The Crash

Wednesday, May 13th, 1953

"Dean, she's getting worse," his wife's voice cut through the babble of the television in the den. "And I can't reach the doctor, the storm has knocked out the phone line again."

Dean said nothing in response, his frustration rising despite the two fingers of Scotch he had tossed back with his dinner. June had stared at him from across the dinner table, her mouth set in a tight line. She hated it when he drank in front of the children. It wasn't as if they noticed. Betty was in bed and Danny had been too busy stuffing his face with fried chicken to care.

He had ignored her look of disapproval and kept drinking.

She has no idea the hell of a day I have had. Sitting there, staring at me, sanctimonious and judging.

The morning had started off with a bloody scene at the factory, the first accident in almost two years. Some young fool just three months on the manufacturing line hadn't been paying attention. If he was lucky, he would keep the three remaining fingers on his right hand.

Doyle, the operations manager, had called with an update before Dean left the office. "Two of the fingers had to be amputated. The thumb was almost crushed and his hand is broken."

Dean swore under his breath. "Make sure the family knows we will cover the medical bills and keep him on at full pay until he recovers. After that, perhaps he will work out in sales, there's an opening now that Simmons has retired."

"Already done, Mr. Edmonds," Doyle had answered. Doyle, along with Howard, had been with the company since the early days. They knew the business better than anyone. Better than Dean, for that matter. After all, they had worked for Dean's father, Arthur, from the beginning. They had been handling situations like this since Dean was still in short pants.

It was the most expensive hit the company had seen since the 1951 floods. At least with that, they had seen it coming. Dean could still remember them struggling to get the paperwork and lighter equipment off of the main floor before the flood waters had risen. Nevertheless, the disaster had shut down their operation for a full month. Many of the plant's employees, most of whom were residents of Armourdale, were not as lucky. Many of their people had lost everything in that flood.

"Dean, did you hear me?" June's shrill voice interrupted his thoughts. God, he hated the sound of her voice these days. "Betty can't breathe. This is the worst attack I've seen yet. We need to get her to the hospital."

Dean closed his eyes. June's voice annoyed him, even her soft snore at night annoyed him. He wished he could just sit in his armchair and be left alone. His daughter's asthma was just the latest in a string of domestic matters he didn't want to deal with. Not on top of work at least. How much domestic nonsense did he have to endure on top of providing for his family? Next she would expect him to cook and clean. It was ridiculous. He thought of his mother, then. Helen Edmonds had been a quiet woman. She had even died quietly, without fanfare. There one minute, gone the next. In contrast, June was loud, abrasive, and Dean wondered if she spent her days looking for some transgression or another to complain about.

The rest of the day had seen one catastrophe after another. The production line had struggled to recover from the delays caused by the accident. The men were always off-kilter after such incidents. They had lagged behind, the production of an already overdue order still not completed by the end of the day. Worse, this was a new client. Dean was sure that, after receiving the part a full two weeks later than promised, the client would not be returning.

As he had struggled to explain the delay to the client, his new secretary had spilled coffee all over his desk. Rattled, she turned and dropped the carafe, the glass breaking into sharp shards he would be finding for months and coffee spilling everywhere. This was, of course, during the phone call to the same client.

"What the hell is going on over there, Edmonds? What kind of a side show clown car business are you running?" The man had demanded.

Dean held his tongue until he hung up, then turned on the girl and described to her in detail why she was unfit to hold the job. She had disappeared, sobbing, from his office. An hour later she was gone from her desk, a letter of resignation on her chair.

On the way home, it had begun to rain. Not a gentle, easy rain, oh no. This was a violent downpour. The gusts of wind rocked his solid-built 1948 Ford Woodie. He had forgotten his umbrella, again, and his coat had been soaked through in the dash from his car to the house. Two hours later, the storm was still in full swing.

And his wife wanted to go out in that.

"Dean."

"Damn it, June, I heard you the first time. Stop your damned nagging!" He levered his body out of his easy chair.

He ignored her dagger stare and turned on his son, "Turn the television off, Danny."

Danny didn't move. Instead, he began to whine, "But Captain Video just started!"

"You heard your father, turn it off, *now*." June's voice was hard, angry.

"It will just take a few minutes to watch! Why can't I stay here?" Danny made no move to flip off the television, his face intractable, stubborn.

"Damn it, boy." Dean shouldered Danny out of the way, flipping the television knob to the "off" position. "When I tell you to do something, you better damn well do it."

Danny looked sullen. He glared at his father.

"Get your shoes and coat on." When Danny made no move to obey, Dean added, "Or don't and damn well drown in the rain for all I care."

June threw up her hands, her anger written on her face. She clenched her teeth together and muttered under her breath as she wrapped Betty up in a blanket.

With the television off, Dean could hear Betty's wheezing clearly. She sounded bad, worse than he had ever heard. And of course, it had to happen on a Friday night. The emergency room would be full up. *Everyone gets sick on a weekend and ends up in the emergency room.*

Dean sighed in resignation, reaching into the front closet for his hat and raincoat. The umbrella bent under the hammering of the rain as they ran to the car. A few minutes later he was backing the car down the drive. Behind him, Danny kicked the back of the car seat. Through flashes of lightning in the rear view mirror, Dean could see his son's small face screwed up in an angry scowl.

"You and your stupid asthma," Danny glared at his sister, "You ruin everything."

Betty said nothing, focusing all of her energy on breathing.

"Daniel Arthur Edmonds!" June said, shocked.

Dean shot a look back at his son. "The world does not revolve around your spoiled and inconsiderate little self, boy. I've a mind to give you a hand in remembering that."

Danny folded his arms over his chest, glaring out the window, his foot continuing to kick the seat in front of him.

The rains pummeled the car. It was dark out, earlier than normal thanks to the storm, and the wipers did little to clear the view of the slick road ahead of them. Dean peered through the fogging windshield. He cursed his wife, the weather, and even the labored whistle of his sick child from the back seat as Betty struggled to breathe.

Dean wished he were home, comfortable in his easy chair. He would have to work tomorrow, despite it being Saturday. He would need to oversee a skeleton crew that would get them back on schedule after all the delays. The damned hospital would take forever to see them, he was sure of it.

"Dean," June said, while she pointed to her right, "take Lansing, it's quicker."

Dean swore under his breath. Everything she said or did these days irritated him. It had been this way for years. Especially since his father had died and he had assumed the job of running Edmonds Manufacturing. The days were long, the work demanding. Having to work those long hours had been bad enough. But it felt as if he worked all day just to come home to a wife who was critical and demanding.

And children who are spoiled and rude.

It ate away at him.

He had found himself flirting with the pretty receptionist at the front desk. He had even considered having an affair, before catching himself.

As if that would make domestic life better, then I would have two *women carping on me instead of just one.*

"Damn it June, I know how to get to the hospital."

His father had managed it. He had maintained a string of mistresses through the years. And Dean's mother none the wiser. Or perhaps she had known and chosen to ignore it. Dean wasn't sure.

Hell, for all I know, I have a half-sibling somewhere out there.

He could feel June's eyes blazing holes in him, but she said nothing. Instead, she straightened her shoulders and stared out at the heavy rain. In the backseat, Betty's breathing alternated between whistles and tiny gasps. Danny continued to kick the seat while he scowled in Betty's direction. The foot shifted. It connected with Dean's back, near his kidneys, a sharp, knifing pain. Dean saw red.

"Danny, you stop that damned kicking right this minute!"

Growing up, it had only taken a scant handful of whippings with a birch rod by his father to keep him in line. Danny was different. June's interference had coddled and spoiled the boy far too long. Dean was going to put an end to his son's misbehaviors the second they had Betty in the hospital. He would show that boy once and for all that his behavior was unacceptable.

June harrumphed at her husband's language. Betty was too busy struggling to breathe to be her normal whiny self. Spoiled by June because of her asthma, Betty made a career out of whining and crying to get what she wanted.

Danny stopped and Dean could hear the boy muttering under his breath, resentful of the rebuke. The road ahead was populated with trees, branches weaving a thick canopy above. One side of the road was a high wall of rock, the other a sharp slope into wooded darkness. Disoriented in the darkness and heavy rain, Dean turned right twice and found himself on an unfamiliar road.

"What does that sign say?" he barked at June who peered through the window. He was hard pressed to see anything but rain and trees whipping in the wind.

"It said, Shh-something, maybe Schicksal...Shicksal *Turnpike*?" she answered. "I think we have gone the wrong way. I *told* you that you should have taken Lansing."

Dean clenched his jaw, and reached out with one hand to clear the fog from his side of the windshield. As he sat back, Danny's foot slammed into his kidney, sending a sharp wave of pain through his back and side.

"Damn it, Danny! I'm going to give you licking of your life if you don't stop that. I've had enough, do you hear me?"

He turned in his seat, glaring at the sullen child sitting behind him. In the darkness, Betty's pale face was lit up from a set of lights on the road in front of them. June screamed, hands reaching for the steering wheel, body turning away from what was coming.

Dean whipped his body back, his attention returning to the road in front of him.

It was too late.

In front of them, the blinding lights of a large truck bore down on them in their lane, its horn blaring a frantic alarm. There was no escape, no room to maneuver, brace, or avoid. And for one terrible long moment, there was nothing but light.

Bright light.

June and the children's screams, and then...

Nothing.

I'm Sorry

Wednesday, June 10th, 1953

Dean was alone in the darkness. Within it were random disconnected sounds. A slow squeaking, a wheel in need of oiling perhaps. The squeak stopped just a few feet away. In the distance he could hear murmurs, indistinct voices speaking. The smell of bleach offended his nose. He heard footsteps approaching. They came close, a door groaned on its hinges.

"And how are we today, Mr. Edmonds?" It was a woman, her voice warm and comforting. "Any words for me today?"

There was a short pause as she waited for his response. It seemed to Dean that he had heard her voice before, many times. In some ways he felt as if he had been climbing through the dark for a long time, listening only to her. It kept drawing him closer. There was a richness to the tone, a feeling of safety and security in this place.

"Well I have to say, Mr. Edmonds, or perhaps I could call you Dean?"

Her breath felt warm on his skin. She leaned close, the scent of lavender washing over him as she adjusted his pillows.

"My floor supervisor Ms. Green would write me up, she would indeed. She says we are not on a first name basis with our patients, but I can't see how it hurts."

51

"In any case, I have to say that I think it is high time you woke up now. You have had plenty of rest, you know. And from what I hear from Mr. Jenkins, who visits you nearly every day, by the way, you have a company that needs running. I think that it would be best for all involved if you were to wake up soon, you hear?"

The pillows fluffed, Dean now felt her delicate fingers on his wrist, along with silence. She sat there for a full moment and then moved away from his side, a pen scratching on paper.

"Well your pulse is steady and you are going through these IV fluids like no one's business."

"The doc says your reflexes are fine and your right leg seems to be healing, although I imagine it hurts. Does it hurt much, Mr. Edmonds?"

He tried opening his eyes. The darkness held him, smothered his voice, and hung like lead over his limbs.

He felt her touch again as she patted his hand. "I'll tell you what. I sense a reader in you. Am I right?"

He struggled to answer, his tongue held fast.

Her voice continued, unaware of his efforts. "In any case, I'm reading a fascinating book right now. It's by Steinbeck. 'East of Eden,' perhaps you have heard of it? I bring it with me everywhere. I never know when I might get a chance to read. Here it is in fact."

He could hear the shuffling of pages, "I'll read you a small bit."

His throat worked, his tongue began to move.

"'And this I believe: that the free, exploring mind of the individual human is the most valuable thing in the world. And this I would fight for: the freedom of the mind to take any direction it wishes, undirected. And this I must fight against: any idea, religion, or government which limits or destroys the individual.'"

"It certainly makes you think, doesn't it?"

Her hands straightened his sheets. "In any case, if you wake up, I will make sure you have a copy of it to read. How does that sound?"

"Uh..." In his mind, he could visualize a full sentence, but his tongue would not cooperate.

The woman's voice paused. "Oh, my. That was you, wasn't it?" She was silent for a long moment. "Mr. Edmonds?"

"Mm…"

"That was you! You wait right there. I'll be right back with the doctor!"

The next hour was a bustle of activity. Over the course of it, he managed to open his eyes, wincing at the flood of bright light.

The doctor was a stout man with bushy eyebrows. His breath reeked of raw onions as he peered into Dean's eyes. He clucked his tongue at intervals, his mouth working away as if he were still busy chewing.

Dean found his gaze straying to a petite blond nurse standing nearby. It was her warm voice which had guided him back to this bright world.

The doctor spoke, "Good to see you have rejoined us, Mr. Edmonds."

"Uh…wh…" Dean struggled to speak.

"Easy now," the doctor smiled. "You have been in a coma for almost four weeks, Mr. Edmonds, since the car accident. Do you remember it?"

Dean shook his head. That simple motion took enormous effort and he felt wrung out, limp.

They had raised him in the bed, the pillows allowing him to look around the room from a better angle. He could see his right leg encased in a cast. It hung in traction. His ribs ached, protesting each time he took a breath in and his arms were covered with an assortment of healing cuts and burns.

"Nurse, I'll want follow up x-rays. We need to see how your leg is healing, along with those ribs." He clapped Dean on the shoulder before he left, oblivious to his patient's pained wince. "Hang in there, Mr. Edmonds, you will be up and moving around before you know it."

The next morning Dean's voice and thoughts were more cooperative. His nurse, the one he had seen the day before, the one who had read to him, pushed her little cart in through the door. Her trim white nurse's uniform was pristine. Her blond hair peeked out from under the jaunty cap on her head.

"Good morning, Mr. Edmonds. I didn't get a chance to tell you yesterday how good it is to see you awake."

Her smile was warm and reassuring, a perfect match to the voice he had heard while he struggled to escape from the darkness.

Her name was sewn in neat script above the left breast pocket of her uniform.

She reached for the empty IV bag, replacing it with a new one.

"Maggie." His voice didn't sound right. It was rusty, unused.

"Yes, Mr. Edmonds."

"I was in an accident. The Doc, he said that much." It was exhausting, the effort it took to talk.

"Yes, you were." Her eyes were a brilliant blue and filled with compassion.

"My family, they were in the car too."

"Perhaps I should get the doctor to speak to you," Maggie began to step away from the bed, looking toward the hallway.

"My wife June, and my boy and girl, they were in the car with me. I remember now." It had come to him in the night, the images sharp, the sound of his wife and the children's screams still lingered in his ears.

"It will take me just a moment to find Dr. Ridley."

Dean's hand caught her wrist. "Please tell me."

Maggie looked away, "It isn't my place to discuss these things. I can fetch the doc..."

"Tell me."

Her eyes met his, the brilliant blue of them darkened to a gray, "I'm so sorry, Mr. Edmonds, really I am. Your family, they didn't make it."

"None of them?" His lips felt numb, coldness spreading over him.

"I'm so sorry, Mr. Edmonds."

"Are you sure, Nurse? He struggled to remember her name. "Maggie, I mean. Could you, could you check?" He took a deep breath, willing this moment to be anything but what it was. A bad dream, surely. "There was my wife, June and my two children, Betty and Danny."

He could still hear their screams - surely they had been hurt, perhaps like him they had been in the dark.

Maggie's eyes met his, "Mr. Edmonds, truly, I wish I could tell you something different. You were the only one to make it to the hospital. Your wife and your children were all killed instantly."

His hand fell away, his mind spinning. He didn't feel any great surprise. If they had made it, if June had survived, she would have been here. For better or worse, she would have been by his side. But the children, he had told himself that they had been fine. They had been in the backseat, after all. There had been some space between the impact and them.

The thought of them gone too, that was what hit him the hardest.

In the middle of the night, he had woken up, struck by the image that was now seared into his brain. The bright lights of the truck had lit up the inside of the car. He remembered June and the children screaming. It had all ended, in an instant. No time for do-overs, no time to turn the wheel. They had died, and he had not. *Why me?*

"Let me call the doctor, Mr. Edmonds."

"No. Please don't." Dean turned away from her and closed his eyes.

"He could give you something to..."

"I don't want anything. I don't deserve it." There was nothing left, no one he cared for or who cared for him. Their marriage had been no picnic, but there were no second chances, no way for him to ever make it right or be the husband and father his family had deserved. He had failed to protect them.

Maggie stood there watching him for a long time. Dean did not move but he could feel her presence. Finally she slipped out of the room, leaving him alone to deal with his grief and loss. Slowly he sunk into a hazy sleep filled with the faces of his family admonishing him before walking away into the darkness.

The curtains were drawn and he could see the lightning playing through the dark clouds as the sun set. Beside his bed was a small book, a piece of notepaper tucked inside it.

Dear Mr. Edmonds,
Something to while away your time here. I hope that it helps.
Sincerely,
-M-

He could see other small ragged slips of paper at intervals. He turned to one and began to read.

"Your children are not your children. They are the sons and daughters of Life's longing for itself."

Dean's throat began to close and his voice broke, "*They come through you, but not from you, and though they are with you, yet they belong not to you. For their souls dwell in the house of tomorrow, which you cannot visit, not even in your dreams.*"

For Danny and Betty, there would be no tomorrows.

Outside of his window, the last rays of the sun disappeared beneath the horizon and thunder rumbled, shaking the building as the storm continued to advance. Dean read on.

"If you would indeed behold the spirit of death, open your heart wide unto the body of life. For life and death are one, even as the river and sea are one...and when the earth shall claim your limbs, then shall you truly dance."

Dean heard the door to his room open. He looked up.

"Kahlil Gibran." Maggie stood in front of him, her purse in hand. "My shift is over but I just wanted to check in on you."

Dean set the book down. "Thank you for this."

He tapped the book, "The images that the words convey, are..."

He searched for the right words for a moment before giving up, "Well, you know."

Maggie nodded, her eyes more gray than blue at the moment. Dean wondered if her eyes changed color with her mood.

"I read it when I was going through some rather challenging moments. It helped."

"Indeed. Thank you, Maggie."

"Of course." She glanced at the window, "Shall I close the curtains for you?"

"Please don't."

She paused, looked at the floor, and brushed at one eye. "Well, I will see you in a few days, Mr. Edmonds."

He nodded and closed his eyes, listening to her footfalls receding down the hall.

Outside in the black of night, the lightning strobed and the thunder spoke. If he listened close he was sure he would hear their voices in the storm.

An Accounting

Saturday, June 13th, 1953

Dean opened his eyes the next morning and found his plant manager, Howard Jenkins, hunched in a chair.

Howard was in his late fifties. His brown hair receding, leaving a wide swath of pink, shiny skin that caught the lights overhead. In his lap were a pile of reports. The man was jotting notes, oblivious.

"Howard."

The man started, his pen skittering sideways on the paper as his head jerked up.

"Dean, I," the pile of papers on his lap tilted, and Howard grabbed at them, losing his pencil in the process. He stood up and put the pile on a nearby table.

"Sorry. You were asleep when I arrived and I wasn't sure if I should stay or not. They called and told me you had woken up. I came as soon as I heard."

"Is everything going okay at the plant?" Dean asked. As the words left his mouth he realized he didn't give a damn one way or the other.

Why had he even asked it?

"The plant? What? Oh yes, yes." Howard waved his hand in dismissal. "Everything is running on time. We caught up, even finished ahead of time on several projects. I was just here because, well. I've been here every day but then my wife wasn't feeling well, and…" He stopped again, running his fingers through his hair. "Dean, I'm so sorry." The man looked a decade older. "I hope, I mean, I made the arrangements. For the funerals, caskets, everything. I made sure," His voice broke, and he stared at the floor, struggling.

"Thank you, Howard." It came out wooden, expressionless.

"My wife, Doris, you met her at the Christmas party."

"Yes."

"She helped pick out the, the…"

"Please tell her thank you."

"I will. I just wanted to tell you how sorry I am, Dean."

Dean could see that Howard was searching for the right words to say. The older man had two children of his own, one was in his late teens now. A son, if Dean remembered right. His wife, Doris, was a short, round, mousy looking woman. Despite her plain appearance, the few times Dean had seen her, it was obvious that Howard doted on her. Howard was everything Dean's father had never been - a devoted husband, an involved father and leader in his son's Scout troop. It was no wonder he looked so tormented over Dean's loss.

Dean changed the subject, "How has that fellow who had the accident on the line been doing? What was his name?"

"Jimmy Tannenbaum," Howard answered.

"Yes, right. How is Tannenbaum doing?"

Howard smiled, "The hand is still in a cast, and we put him on the sales team. You would not believe it, Dean, the kid is a natural. He pulled in a major account last week. A new bomber Boeing is calling the B-52. They need subcontractors for a few of the parts. The contract has the potential of *doubling* our sales for next year."

Howard rattled on and Dean nodded, saying little but asking questions each time the man seemed to run out of steam. It was a diversion of sorts, listening to talk of work meant he didn't have to think of June and the kids, at least for a few minutes.

A knock sounded at the door and Maggie peeked in, pulling her cart in behind her.

"Good morning, Mr. Edmonds. Good to see you as well, Mr. Jenkins. I thought I heard voices coming from this room." She smiled at them, eyes scanning Dean, taking in his haggard expression.

"Good morning, Miss Aaronson," Howard smiled, "Dean, this young woman is phenomenal. She spent hours reading to you, although I'm sure you don't remember it.

Dean nodded, "I remember some of it." Her voice had led him back from the darkness.

"Well, I do hate to interrupt Mr. Jenkins, but we need to do a couple of tests on Mr. Edmonds." She stood there, a friendly yet firm look on her face.

Howard appeared to take the hint and stood up, "I've talked long enough. I'll check back in tomorrow. If you need anything, you just have the hospital call and I'll come right away."

Dean nodded, "Thank you Howard."

Maggie waited until the door had closed before she began to move about the room. "Mr. Jenkins has been here every day."

"He's run the plant for over twenty-five years."

"He seems kind."

"Yes."

The room fell silent. Maggie checked his IV, changing out the bags and then plumped his pillows. Dean winced as he shifted position. His right leg, encased in the heavy cast, ached.

"What tests do you need to do?" he asked, after watching her move around the room.

"What?"

"You told Howard you needed to run tests."

Maggie pursed her lips, "Oh, that. It looked like you needed a break from business talk."

"Was it that obvious?"

"It's my job to notice when my patients need their rest."

"That isn't it. I have had more than enough rest."

Her eyes were steady on him, "I know."

"The accident was my fault." The words, now uttered, sounded matter of fact. As if he was commenting on the weather.

Maggie paused in clearing the bedside table of the dead flowers.

"Your daughter, Betty, you said she had an asthma attack that night, didn't she?"

"Yes. We were on the way to the hospital."

"Did you somehow cause your daughter's asthma attack?"

Dean paused, he could see where she was going with this. "I allowed myself to become distracted."

"In a downpour? With a truck in your lane?"

"I was miserable." There, that was the truth of it. "I was married to a woman I no longer loved. My children weren't angels. They were self-entitled, greedy, rude little creatures." Dean laughed then. It was a short, bitter laugh, devoid of mirth. "So much for not speaking ill of the dead."

"Mr. Edmonds..."

"Call me Dean."

"Dean, then. I have found that, no matter how hard we try to make it otherwise, life is not black and white, evil or good. Children are rarely perfect angels, nor are they irredeemable hellions."

The dam inside of him, he could feel the cracks opening up. "But all of this, it was my fault. I have no one to blame but myself. For the crash, and even before that. I was miserable. I hated my job, I let my relationship break down and I wasn't a proper father to my children."

Maggie stared at him. "I wish I knew what to say to you, Dean." Her hand touched his arm, warm and gentle. "I think that, no matter what memories you hold of your family, you still must reconcile this loss. It isn't easy, no matter how you look at it."

He took a deep breath in and then released it.

"Thank you."

"For what?"

"Thank you for not uttering useless platitudes about my children being in God's arms." He looked down at her hand on his arm, "I have never found it reassuring or honest in any way."

She nodded, a small smile on her lips. "You are welcome." She paused as if unsure what to say next.

"So, it looks like you will be with us a while, especially with that leg and those ribs still needing to heal."

"Yes," Dean grimaced, shifting gingerly, "So I've heard from the good doctor."

"I brought you something that might help pass the time."

"Oh?"

Maggie walked to the door, where her cart stood. "I brought another book for you to read. I found it fascinating. And I thought you might enjoy it."

"I used to think I would die if I didn't read every day," Dean mused. "It has been years since I've sat down and read anything but sales or production reports."

Maggie handed him the book, "Well I hope this will keep you entertained."

"My God, I loved this book!" Dean said, staring at a copy of *The Fountainhead* by Ayn Rand.

"Oh dear, you've read it already then," Maggie's face fell, "But of course you have. It came out ten years ago, after all. I just recently found it at a rummage sale." She reached out her hand to take it back from him.

"Oh no, please, I would love to read it again. I found it...inspiring." He stared at the book in his hand. "The thought of being true to one's dreams, despite adversity and even scorn. It spoke to me."

He said nothing for a moment and then added, "I was still in college, and dating June at the time. It was my second year at William Jewell. I dreamed of changing my degree from Business to English. I wanted to become a writer."

"Did you really?" Maggie smiled, her lips curving up, tiny laugh lines appearing near her eyes.

"I guess you could say I was a dreamer. Even after working for my father's company after school and every summer I still dreamed of earning a living writing books. I must have started writing half a dozen stories, possibly more."

He stared at the book, his thoughts eight years in the past.

"My father insisted that I major in Business Administration. I hated it, it bored me to tears. He had never finished college, and I guess he figured my degree would take us to the next level. The business would move into the big leagues, you know?"

"And did it?" Maggie asked as he sat there, staring at the book for a long moment.

"What? Oh, yes, I guess it did. My grades were high." He straightened, "I graduated with honors. Within three years business had doubled."

Dean sighed, "But I still dreamed of something different. I filled my days alternating between those tedious textbooks and reading Rand, Orwell, and Hemingway. I think they kept me sane. Reading some of the textbooks made me want to jump out a window. Anything but have to read another marketing strategy."

"I almost told him to stuff it." He held up two fingers, "I was this close to telling him I was changing majors."

"You didn't, though." Maggie's voice interrupted his reminiscing.

"No. I didn't." He paused, "I got engaged instead."

"She wasn't keen on marrying a writer, was she?"

"No, I guess she wasn't."

Maggie cocked her head to one side. Unlike his wife June's curly locks, Maggie's was straight, and her eyes were a stunning blue instead of light brown.

"And this is where we avoid speaking ill of the dead." She said gently.

Dean's heart gave a painful thump. "That would probably be for the best."

Maggie was quiet for a moment. "My favorite author is Kahlil Gibran."

"That book you brought me to read, *The Prophet*, it was amazing."

"Isn't it, though? There is another poem he wrote that has stayed with me over the years. I actually memorized it I loved it so." She concentrated for a moment, "'*Half a life is a life you didn't live. A word you have not said. A smile you postponed. A love you have not had. A friendship you did not know. To reach and not arrive, work and not work, attend only to be absent.*'"

Dean sighed, "I think I need to read that one as well."

Maggie smiled. "I have the rest of my rounds to make, but I do hope you enjoy re-reading the book. I'll see if I can't find something in the hospital library later today for you."

"Thank you, Maggie," he turned the book over in his hand, "This was thoughtful of you. I appreciate it."

She smiled at him, "It isn't too late to follow your dreams, Dean. After all, all we have is time. Why waste it being unhappy?" Without waiting for a reply, she slipped from the room.

For You

Wednesday, July 8th, 1953

"Your soul is often a battlefield, upon which your reason and your judgment wage war against your passion and appetite." Dean read from the slim book.

"Back to Gibran, are you?" Dean looked up. He hadn't even heard her come in.

He smiled and set the book down, "It helps pass the time. He has a way of conveying imagery along with the words."

"That he does."

Four weeks had passed since he had first opened his eyes in the hospital and Dean had nearly recovered enough to be released. Howard visited him daily, as did Maggie. Day after day, as she made her rounds, she brought him books. Each time he smelled the delicate lavender scent of her perfume he had felt his spirits lift.

Alone in the hospital, it was all he could do not to think of June and the children. In some ways, it still felt overwhelming. It caught him at odd moments. How had he survived when they had not? More and more, he returned to a vortex of conflicted emotions. How could he actually feel relief at their absence? What kind of monster was he? There were moments when he was actually *thankful* that he no longer had to hear the rude, whiny comebacks from the kids. No more endless squabbling over what show to watch on the television.

With survivor's guilt came relief as well that there would be no more arguments with June. There would be no more nagging or hostile stares from her direction. Each time he felt that sense of relief, he felt renewed guilt. If only he had been a better husband, a more involved father. Why had he lost his temper with Danny that night? If only he had paid better attention to the road.

The would haves and could haves ran through his brain each night in the darkened room as he struggled to fall asleep.

The cycle of guilt seemed endless. It was a parade of conflicting emotions marching through his brain as he lay in the hospital bed.

What kind of a man am I? What kind of man is relieved that his family is no longer eating him alive with their needs, complaints and dissatisfaction?

Maggie seemed to sense it. Their talks ranged from philosophical discussions to religion, and even to the metaphysical. And always they had circled around books.

He had given Howard a list of titles to buy - Salinger's latest book, *The Crucible* by Miller and the newest from Hemingway. He tore through them. He breathed in the words and consumed them. The stories distracted him mostly, although in quiet moments he found himself comparing the characters in the stories with his own life. Beside his bed, a stack of sales reports and contracts to review had been ignored and remained untouched.

When he had finished with a book he would set it on the side table for Maggie. By the time he handed her the third one she had laughed.

"I fear I don't have as many free moments to read as you do, Mr. Edmonds, I'm only two chapters in on the one you gave me a week ago!"

Dean smiled, "Start a library of your own then. That way you will keep all of your patients occupied and out of trouble."

The doctor had visited daily as well, checking on his progress. His ribs had healed well and his leg would soon be relieved of its heavy cast.

"You'll be released soon," Maggie had said, after she watched Doctor Ridley jot some indecipherable notes on Dean's chart that morning and nod curtly at her as he headed out the door. "Maybe even tomorrow."

She handed Dean a small cloth-bound book. "I'm sorry, it isn't much, but I thought it might get you started." She patted her pockets, "Oh, and this goes with it. Everyone is writing with ballpoints these days." Maggie handed him a slim, inexpensive pen. "I do hope you will find a way to put some of those words floating about in your head on paper."

Dean opened the book. She had given him a blank, unlined journal.

"Thank you," he said. She nodded and gave him a brief smile before hurrying out of the room.

He hadn't seen her again. It had been the last day of her shift, and he was discharged the next day.

Howard had driven him home, silent after a few attempts to engage Dean in a discussion about the quarterly sales report.

It had ended once Dean declared, "You have handled it better than I could, Howard. Keep at it. In a few more weeks I will do a thorough review if you want. But for now, make my mind up for me. I trust you will make the best decision."

Howard had straightened his shoulders and nodded, turning onto Grand Street where the car made its way up the driveway.

"Will do, Dean, you can count on it."

The crutches cut into his armpits as he slowly hobbled up the front path. The cast on his leg would be removed in another week. Meanwhile, it felt as if it were made of lead, it was so heavy.

"Several of your neighbors have taken turns cutting the grass." Howard held the front door open, "And my wife said the refrigerator is full of meals."

"Thank you, Howard. And please thank Doris for me, the angel food cake you brought on Monday was delicious."

Howard smiled, "She will be happy to hear that. It is a family favorite."

Dean's leg ached. Despite lying in bed for weeks on end, the effort it had taken to leave the hospital, and even to sit upright in the car, had been exhausting. He could feel the weariness washing over him. At the moment, all he wanted was to fall into his own bed. He stood there, trying to figure out a way to get Howard to leave so that he could finally be alone.

"If you need anything, don't hesitate to call me, day or night." The older man frowned, "I hate to leave you here on your own, especially with that cast still on. Are you sure you won't come stay with us?"

Dean tried to imagine staying in Howard's house, four walls filled with laughter, children, and love. He had visited it on a few occasions, usually just giving a honk in the driveway when Howard's car had been in for repairs and he needed a ride to work. He had never been inside.

It was a smaller home, located a few blocks south of Independence Avenue, on a quiet street. The lawn was always well-kept and Howard's wife had a small vegetable garden on the east side. Once, Howard's son had come out and handed Dean a sack full of fresh donuts, still warm and glistening with sugar.

"Good morning, Mr. Edmonds. My mother said to bring these out to you and tell you my father will be out momentarily."

The boy's hair had been slicked back, pants pressed and shoes shined. He had been wearing the khaki uniform and necktie of the Scouts. Dean's mouth watered at the memory of the yeasty sweet smell of the donuts in the bag.

From the few details Howard had shared, Dean knew the Jenkins house was as different as day and night to what his own family home life had been like growing up. Where Dean had endured a cold, distant father with a loving but nervous mother - Howard shared stories of the family camping adventures.

Dean couldn't recall *ever* going camping with his father. Arthur Edmonds had been far too busy working to ever be involved in Boy Scouts or other activities.

And hadn't he done his best to repeat that with June? The only difference being that she had hamstrung him every time he tried to be strict.

He shook his head no. Right now, the last thing he needed was a reminder that he was completely alone in the world.

"I'll be fine, Howard, thank you for handling all of this."

Howard turned to leave, his face worn, eyes troubled, and "If you need me to stay."

"I'll be fine."

The door closed behind him and Dean stood in the living room, waiting for the sound of Howard's car to drive away.

When it did, his shoulders sagged and he hobbled to the base of the stairs. He began to hitch his body up one painful step at a time. The house, despite being empty for two months, was immaculate. There wasn't a speck of dust or a single cobweb in sight. It felt almost dreamlike.

The walls covered with the familiar art and family photos, the furniture the same as when he had left it - yet it felt alien, as if it belonged to someone else. Had he changed so much? Was he so different that the familiar no longer felt like home? Had it ever really felt like home? He sifted through his memories, trying to remember something good, some kindness or moment of laughter.

They were there, he was sure of it.

He reached the top of the stairs. He was out of breath, the muscles in his back gripping and twisting, little fingers of agony moving their way from his ribs to his back and down his right leg. He made his way down the long hall, his gait slow and awkward. He paused to rest against the wall several times.

The first open door was Danny's room. It was pristine, which was rather shocking. His son had been an absolute slob.

The neighbors must have tidied it up.

He moved on and stopped again at Betty's room. The bed was made, everything in its place.

Dean was panting now. It took a great deal of effort to move his body forward and he fought off a wave of dizziness.

This has been more exercise than I have had in months.

He limped into the master bedroom.

The pillows were arranged neatly on the bed, everything in its place, or nearly so. He could see that June's perfume and ephemera had been moved, probably when they were dusted, and then placed in a neat line.

He wondered who had done it. Howard's wife perhaps? He had met her several times, once when she had brought Howard his lunch that he had forgotten at home. She was a quiet, nervous woman who never met his eyes, preferring to stare at the ground. She was competent, though. He could imagine her wiping down surfaces, making Betty's bed, and picking up Danny's toys.

He would have to thank her the next time he saw her. Or send word through Howard.

Dean let out a breath and hitched his way over to the bed, sitting down on it. It was June's side and he could smell her unique scent mingled with

Chanel No. 5 rising up to greet him. Some part of her still lingered here, reaching out, haunting him.

He couldn't bear to lie down in their bedroom. Not here, not in this bed he had shared with June. With effort, he stood up again and made the return journey down the stairs.

He briefly considered going into his office. The door was closed, as it had been when his wife and children had been alive. The office was not a place where they were welcomed, it was a place where the work from the day continued, if only to avoid negotiating the children or June. He turned instead and went to the living room.

The couch will work just fine.

By the time he had settled on the couch, Dean's face was dripping with sweat. The lunch he had eaten at the hospital lay in his stomach, a hard greasy lump that defied digestion. It didn't help that the house was warm, muggy.

The intense summer temps were at their apex in July and August, and it was now the middle of July. He sat for a moment, gathering enough strength to get up once more and then turned on the air conditioning in the window. He sank down on the couch, exhausted. The camel-colored tweed fabric was rough under his hands. Even here he couldn't shake the feel of them. The ghosts of his family surrounded him. Danny had always chosen that spot over there, too close to the television. He would sprawl there, eyes glued to the screen, with his mother insisting he scoot back.

"You will ruin your eyes staring at that thing!" Danny would move back a few inches, regaining them the moment June turned away.

Betty had preferred the sofa. He could see her now, June would sit in her smaller chair to the left of it. Dean stared at his easy chair, resting at an angle to the couch on the right. He had always sat there. But nothing felt comforting or familiar any more.

This house, Dean felt the cold air from the window unit begin to wash over him, *it isn't home*.

Perhaps it never had been. But in this moment, with his mind full of memories and ghosts, he was sure it never could be again.

Words and Dreams

Friday, July 31st, 1953

Dean sat in the tiny beach-front cottage and read from his own copy of *The Prophet*. "Work is love made visible," he read aloud, his words hanging in the air, with nothing but the seagulls and sand crabs listening. "And if you cannot work with love but only with distaste, it is better that you should leave your work..."

The fishy smell of salt and sea wafted through the air. A gentle breeze slipping through the half-open windows, disturbing a fly. It buzzed past his head.

It had taken two days for Dean to flee the house. As he had limped his way through the rooms he felt as if *he* were the one who was dead. Every room held reminders of June and the kids. He could see them everywhere. He saw it in the gouged wood frame of Danny's bedroom door. The boy had exacted his revenge over being sent to bed without his supper last fall. There was the stain on the carpet in the living room where Betty had thrown fruit juice in a fit of rage.

And of course, there was the lingering smell of June's perfume in their room. He had slept on the couch, and used the hall bathroom rather than stay for more than a moment in the master bedroom.

Even the words he had said to her when they had fought – the memories hung there waiting for him to walk past and relive them all over again.

His neighbors had been kind. When they learned he had come out of his coma, they had cleaned out the rotting food in the Frigidaire. The stacks of casseroles and desserts ensured he wouldn't need to cook for weeks. If he had stayed, that is.

Instead, he had holed up in the President Hotel until he could work through it all and get his head on straight. He needed something different, he could see that now. It had taken him sleeping for several stretches of twelve hours or more before he felt more like himself again. Afterward, he had walked down to the lobby of the hotel and placed a few calls.

The following Monday he walked in the front door of Edmonds Manufacturing. Edna, who had served as the receptionist for the past twenty years, stood up, walked around the tall desk and flung her arms around him. Her perfume filled his nose. Joy, by Jean Patou. His mother had worn it. The last Christmas before she had died he had given her a bottle.

Edna's voice rasped in his ear, "Oh, Mr. Edmonds! It is so good to see you up and moving around!"

Dean stood there, unsure what to do. Finally he hugged her back.

She was the first to step back, brushing an invisible crease from her blouse and dabbing at one eye. "I was there at the funerals, Mr. Edmonds, we all were."

"Thank you, Edna. I appreciate that."

She sniffled, stepping back and resuming her professional mask once again. "If there is anything you need, Mr. Edmonds..."

"Thank you, Edna."

Howard Jenkins was in his office when Dean entered, stacks of reports covering his desk. His intense look of concentration was replaced with surprise.

"Dean, it's good to see you!" Howard's eyes had slipped for just one moment, staring at the walking stick in Dean's hand, before looking away. "Please, sit down, sit down. How are you doing?"

"Fine. I guess. As well as can be expected." He sat down in the wood chair. It had been in Howard's office for as long as he could remember.

Howard nodded and looked down at the stacks of paper covering his desk.

"Actually, I was hoping to speak with you and Doyle about the business. Would now be a good time?"

"He's down on the line. They had a small hiccup with a new part, but I think he probably has it worked out by now." Howard spoke into the intercom unit connected to Edna's desk, "Edna, could you please have the office girl find Doyle and ask him to come to my office?"

Dean heard the intercom burble back, "Yes, Mr. Jenkins."

"Thanks Edna." He turned back to Dean. "He should be here momentarily. Let me get you a coffee."

"Thank you."

Dean sipped at the steaming black liquid and listened to Howard update him on sales numbers until Doyle Laurel had joined them a few minutes later. He didn't waste time with pleasantries and instead laid it all out.

"I want to sell Edmonds Manufacturing." The two men looked at him in consternation. "I'm hoping you two will buy it, and I'm prepared to work out a deal which would benefit us all."

There was silence at first. Howard and Doyle glanced at each other, back at Dean, and then at each other again. Howard was the first to speak, "Dean, this is a big change, and you have been through a terrible experience. I wouldn't want you to make a hasty decision."

Dean smiled wryly. "If there is any good thing I can take away from the past few months it is the realization that this," his hand encompassed the room, "was never my dream. It was my dad's. I think that it is your dream as well. A person should do what they are fit best for, don't you think?"

The two men exchanged a glance. Doyle nodded, "I've spent my entire career here at this company, Mr. Edmonds, I'm proud of what we have built."

"As am I." Howard added.

"Then let us come to an agreement that allows all of us to move forward on our appropriate paths." Dean said.

By the end of the week the three men had hammered out a deal that benefited all of them. Business was booming and it was the perfect time for Dean to walk away from the manufacturing business his father had been so invested in. Dean signed the necessary papers, his name resting next to theirs.

Doyle and Howard had stood side by side with his father and helped create the successful business. He knew it would be in good hands.

Signing the papers lifted a weight off of his chest. He wasn't defined by or tied to a business that had dogged his steps for more than two decades. He was free from it. He had also hammered out a deal that left him so well off that, if he lived simply, he would never have to work again.

And now, three weeks later, as he stepped out of the simple beach cottage in Florida, the sand slowing his steps, Dean knew that this isolated stretch of beach wasn't his future either. For now, he could live a quiet life, finish healing and find his passion.

The cottage was in a sleepy beachside town on the west coast of Florida. As a child, he had visited here once with his grandparents. The town looked exactly the same now as it did then.

Each day he would make his way into town, eat lunch at the local diner, and pick up something simple for dinner. That afternoon at the general store, he added a scoop of pecans to a small bag and selected a small nutcracker from the rack. A tin of Spam and two oranges joined them. He made his way to the register.

"There's a storm rolling in, Mr. Edmonds." The young cashier smiled at him.

"Yes, I noticed that." He struggled to remember her name. Was it Vera? Vinny? Wait, Vinita, yes that was it. He had felt the storm before any hint of clouds had appeared in the western sky. His knee had woken him up, aching and stiff. If it hadn't been for his dwindling supply of canned foods, he would have stayed in the cottage.

"Papa says that the Farmer's Almanac is predicting the first week of August to be the worst yet for storms." Vinita continued as she rang up his purchases. "You want the chipped beef too? It just came in and I haven't had time to get it out on the shelf."

"Yes please, Vinita." She smiled then, exposing a set of large buck teeth, pleased that he had remembered her name.

"Your total is three dollars and sixty-two cents, Mr. Edmonds. Shall I put it on your tab?"

He smiled and nodded at her. "Add a chocolate for yourself as well."

The girl giggled and looked down at the counter, "Thank you, Mr. Edmonds. I'll have Anton deliver your groceries later today."

He signed the slip of paper she slid across the counter towards him and gave her father a nod as he left. The old man said nothing, lines etched deep into his brown skin, a battered straw hat upon his head. He never spoke to Dean. Whenever he heard the man speak to his daughter, Dean struggled to remember what little Spanish he had learned. Cuban Spanish was different though. His limited vocabulary was no match for the quick stream of words that would rush from the old man's lips. He could feel the girl's moon-calf eyes centered on him as he left the store.

Despite the pain from his damaged leg, Dean walked down the length of the street. Since arriving in town he had walked further and further each day. He was slowly strengthening the atrophied muscles. All of the weeks of lying in a hospital room had taken their toll. He still used the walking stick, but it was becoming easier to move around each day.

He nodded to several others as he passed them. He knew only one of them by name. Dolly, a tiny woman with gray hair owned the small cafe where he usually ate lunch. She smiled, her teeth stained yellow, an incisor missing.

"Mr. Edmonds, good to see you today. Mind you head back soon, though, looks like we will have a spot of rain coming down the pike."

The wind had already picked up and he nodded. "Just a little more and then I'll head back."

Dolly patted his shoulder as she walked away, heading towards the cafe. "Mind that you do. From the way my knees are aching, it's gonna be a big one."

He tipped his hat in response and continued on. The last of the shops lay before him. After that there was the town's lone gas station. And beyond that were small houses with peeling paint and dry wood. Dean stopped in front of the last window. A matte black typewriter with shiny black and red keys caught his eye. The sign in the window read Perkins Printing and Office Supplies.

Dean stepped inside of the store.

"Good afternoon, sir." The store clerk was older, his dark hair sprinkled with gray. "May I help you find anything?"

The store was clean and smelled of ink. Dean could hear the solid thump of machinery emanating from the back. "That sounds like a printing press."

The clerk nodded, "Yes sir, the town newspaper prints their weekly here."

"I used to work at one of the smaller circulars when I was younger," Dean remarked, breathing in the acrid scent of ink and paper. "Just for a few weeks in the summer, mind you. I helped set the print face."

He had been so determined not to be sucked into his father's manufacturing business. He had loved it – the smell of the ink, the paper when it was hot off of the press and the ink still wet. Dean's mouth turned down, frowning, as he remembered that day when Mr. McAteer had come down from his office and told Dean to go home.

"Your dad's been telling me he's got a place for you at the plant, son." He had thumped Dean on the shoulder. "You'll never see that kind of pay working here in this office. Gotta know when to make choices that make sense, ya know?"

Dean moped through the rest of that summer, despite earning twice what he had while sweating over the printing press. The work was empty, unfulfilling, and at night he had dreamed he was working the press. The metal letters formed words that danced from his lips in the early morning, long before the sun had come up. He had written some of them down, for weeks on end, before the summer had ended and it was time for school again.

"Sir? Were you needing some printing services? Or perhaps you should sit down, rest a spell?" the store clerk had come closer, noting the walking stick, a look of concern spreading across his face.

"Sorry," Dean forced his lips into a tight smile. "Something in your window caught my eye."

The clerk brightened, "I'm happy to hear that. What can I help you find?"

Dean gestured at the front window, "I saw you have an electric typewriter in stock."

The clerk nodded, his back straightening as he turned and walked across the room, "Yes sir, we do. That one in the window is a top of the line model, made by IBM. We have a show model over here on this table."

Dean looked at the machine, noted the price tag and clucked his tongue, "Hmmm."

"As you can see, the carriage return is this red button here. Having an automatic carriage return will give your secretary a 35% increase in productivity." He pointed at another button, "And the Tab Set button will streamline her typing practice even more. This reduces the need to count the spaces..."

"Actually, this typewriter will be for me."

The clerk looked startled, "Oh, but of course, sir." He paused for a moment, "Are you a writer?"

Dean didn't know how to answer that question, so he ignored it. He wasn't a writer yet, after all.

"And how heavy is it? Is it portable?"

The clerk shook his head, "Well, it is rather heavy. It weighs, let's see..." He consulted a small facts sheet next to the typewriter, "Ten pounds, three ounces."

"I'll take it. Please have it delivered to Penny Coast Cottages tomorrow."

The clerk nodded, pleased, "Of course, Sir. If you will just step over here, I'll write up the ticket."

The next day, the typewriter had arrived in a large wooden box, nestled in excelsior. The ruddy-cheeked, damp-haired delivery boy struggled to lift it out of the wood shavings. The rain had ended just moments before. It had poured all night, thunder cracking open the sky, lightning flashes revealing a dark, angry surf that roiled and pitched. It had continued into the morning. And in a blink of an eye, it had gone away, the clouds clearing, leaving nothing but blue sky. Large swaths of seaweed, shells and driftwood now cluttered the beach. The seagulls swooped and screamed, finding plenty of prey to catch their eye on the sand as well as at sea.

"Here, let me help you with that," Dean offered.

"It is quite heavy, sir."

"Yes, I can see that." Together they lifted it to the table and the boy scuttled under the table to plug the machine in. Dean reached out and flipped a metal lever on the side and the typewriter began to thrum.

Dean handed the boy a shiny dime, "Take the box with you when you go."

"Thank you, sir!"

He sat down in front of the IBM, pulled out a piece of paper, fed it into the machine, and stared at it. He could feel the reassuring thrum of the machine through the heavy desk, down the legs, into the floor. It tickled the soles of his feet.

For days now he had felt the need to write. The words he wrote by hand in the newest journal, they hadn't been enough to meet the need. It had risen and become a swell within, which grew with intensity and strength each day. Words, phrases, ideas – they floated through his thoughts. They had pushed him to buy this electric monstrosity that now hummed in front of him.

"What am I doing?" Hearing the words spoken out loud was startling. They cleaved the air, muting the distant roar of the surf and the seagulls squabbling over a fish on the beach nearby.

He tried again, "What is it that I want to write?"

His words bounced off of the thin glass window and echoed in the small space.

A wave of words crashed inside, fragmenting, phrases, and thoughts tossed about like so much flotsam. Dean realized with a stab of panic and fear that he didn't know. After reading countless books, sitting for weeks in a hospital room, and selling his company; here he was. He was hundreds of miles from home, alone, without a clue. *Who am I to think I can just suddenly become a writer? What kind of cosmic joke or early midlife crisis is this?*

He closed his eyes. Maggie's words came back to him, "It isn't too late to follow your dreams, Dean. All we have is time."

That was something that he had plenty of. "This isn't Edmonds Manufacturing. There are no deadlines here. All I have is time."

He felt his body relax. Just hearing those words spoken aloud had given him permission to move forward in his own way and at his own pace.

He opened his eyes and turned to the map on the wall near the door. It hung on a hook within easy reach. Each day he walked farther, moving inland only when the beaches were impassable or too rocky. He had passed the cove where the fish were caught in drying tide pools and held his breath at the rank smell. He had marked on the map where the dolphins preferred to breach. He could see them well while standing on the tall cliff to the north and watching them with binoculars. He stood up, removed the map from its hook, gathered some supplies and headed out the door. A long walk was just what he needed.

The Storm

Saturday, August 1st, 1953

The breeze was strong, whipping the thin, wispy white clouds away, and pulling the dark gray line at the horizon closer. Perhaps he wouldn't have as much time as he had thought. The weather was so changeable, erratic, now that hurricane season was upon them. Small wonder that most of the beach-dwellers and vacationing families had left last week.

Dean's feet sunk into the sand as seagulls cartwheeled through the clear blue sky. They screamed over scraps of fish, diving into the surf. They seemed a little desperate. Perhaps they sensed the next storm coming and were eager to feed. Especially now, while they could still fly.

He moved along the beach, barefoot. The sand was still damp from the rains, and he felt it slide between his toes. The skin on his feet had become tough, roughened by the constant exposure to salt and sand. He could feel the small journal that Maggie had given him bumping in the sack on his back. It was that, a canteen of water, and a fancy new ballpoint pen. He had run the other out of ink two days ago.

The journal was full of ideas. He had filled the margins with scribbled additions, considered names, even fleshed out characters. His mind passed over the main character he had been outlining. He mentally reviewed the notes he had written over the past two days. His mind had been jumping ever since he had awoken from a particularly vivid dream. The story that he wanted to write, it was in there. He just had to figure out how it would come to the page.

The clouds on the eastern horizon were building again. They stretched as far north and south as he could see and occasional lightning flickered. Dean had spent long enough on the coast to know he had a few hours at most before the maelstrom descended.

Just a mile, maybe two, until I have to turn back.

The beach was empty of anything except Dean and the seagulls. He wondered if the dolphins would be near the cliff outlook today. They weren't always there, but especially after a strong storm, they seemed to find better offerings. Perhaps the fish were stunned by the ferocious pounding of the sea against the rocks. It would take him almost an hour to reach the cliffs, but why not? All he had was time. Maggie's words still echoed in his thoughts.

Ahead in the distance he could see someone. He couldn't make out the details. The further north he walked, the less people he usually saw. The sandy beach became populated with sharp, unwelcoming rocks. This was not attractive to the tourists who gravitated towards the swimming beaches and gentle sandy stretches. Nor was it compelling for the fisherman for that matter, since the rocks tended to jut out and catch at the fishing lines. The only time he saw anyone this far north was when the tide ran out and there were hordes of tide pools to pick through. The ocean life caught in the shallow pools were easy pickings. It seemed that only the locals knew that little secret.

However, right now the tide was not out, much the opposite, and Dean's curiosity increased as he closed the distance.

A solitary man stood there, gazing out at the sea. He glanced over as Dean approached.

"It looks as if we aren't quite done with those storms," the man said.

"Indeed. I imagine we have a couple of hours before it hits." Dean replied.

The man had jet black hair and green eyes. His thin lips curved into a half-smile as he glanced down and noticed Dean's bare feet.

"Live around here?" he asked.

"I'm just visiting," Dean answered. "An extended stay, but I'll head home in a few months. Just in time for winter, I imagine."

The raven-haired man nodded, "Midwest?"

"Is it that obvious?"

The man laughed, "I study languages. My focus is on the Far East. In college, one of my professors made a point of identifying every student in his classroom. He could manage it right down to their particular county or city. I picked it up and now it is habit."

His eyes narrowed and he stared at Dean for a moment. "St. Joseph? No, wait, Kansas City. Am I right?"

Dean smiled, "That's a pretty good trick, and you must be popular at dinner parties."

"I imagine I would be if I ever went to them." The man extended his right hand, "I'm Adolphus, by the way, Adolphus Suisser." He pronounced the last name with precision, emphasizing each syllable *soo-wee-sir*.

Dean shook Suisser's hand, "Dean Edmonds. It's a pleasure to meet you."

Adolphus smiled, his white teeth gleaming. "When I'm not studying languages, or teaching linguistics to foolish and inattentive college students, I like to travel. I've never been to Florida. I've been to Tokyo, Beijing, Nice, Rio de Janeiro, and dozens of other destinations around the world, but never here. In fact, much of the United States seems to be rather uncharted territory for me. My own backyard, if you will, and I haven't explored it at all!"

"I know what you mean." Dean stared out at the dark storm clouds to the east. "Except for the annual vacations when I was a young child. I haven't seen much. It is a situation I hope to rectify soon."

Adolphus' eyes traveled to the walking stick in Dean's hand. "I noticed your fine stick when you approached."

"Have a look at it if you wish." Dean held the stick out to him. He had bought it recently in town at a local shop that catered to the tourists. The intricate carvings had attracted his attention. The artist had created smooth polished dolphin bodies suspended in surf in the gleaming wood. Tiny waves curled in an infinite froth around them.

Dean realized that wasn't really what Suisser was asking. Instead it was an inquiry. One that gave him an easy out if he didn't wish to explain.

"I broke my leg in a car crash earlier this year," Dean said as Suisser examined the walking stick. "I don't need it much anymore. Only when I'm tired or I've walked too far."

"Such detail. I must get one for my sister, Hannah. She is quite fond of dolphins."

"The shop in town may still have some left."

"I will have to make a stop in town, then." He handed the walking stick back to Dean. "I'm sorry to hear of your injuries. I understand they are introducing legislation that will require newer car models to have a restraint system in place. It's supposed to save lives."

"I had not heard that, but it is good to know."

Too late for June and the kids.

"May I ask what happened?"

Dean looked away, "A truck came into my lane. It was raining and I was distracted. There was no time to get out of the way." He said nothing more. He didn't want or need a stranger's sympathy.

He could feel Suisser's eyes on him. Instead of returning his gaze, Dean stared at the dark clouds. They roiled, moving towards the shoreline. A particularly large bolt of lightning carved its way through the gray and he could hear the low grumble that followed. The storm was still a distance away. The wind was picking up and he could feel the humidity rising. It didn't look like he had two hours at all. In fact, he would be lucky if he made it back to his cottage before the storm hit.

Suisser made a clucking sound. "A truck, my word, and in your lane, no less! Whatever brought them there, I wonder?"

Tension began to coil inside Dean. It had been a long time since he had been near anyone else, much less idly passing the time of day. He was unused to it. Unused to people in general. He felt like a rusted garden gate that objects anytime someone walks through it.

Why did I even stop to talk to this man?

"It was raining. The driver swore there was a man in the road, but in that downpour? Not likely." Dean bit back any other words. This was not the time or place to share his loss. "In any case, I had better be heading back. The storm is moving faster than I had first imagined."

"Indeed," said the man, turning back to stare at the dark clouds scudding towards them. A bolt of lightning lit the sky, reaching down, fingers of energy crackling, spiking down into the ocean. "I've kept you long enough, Mr. Edmonds. I fear it is high time we both headed back to our respective shelters. Good day to you, sir." He bowed and turned to the north.

Dean turned and did his best to walk faster. The storm was getting closer, and he could already feel a fine mist of rain drifting down through the air.

Funny, I've not seen any beach houses to the north.

The highway wasn't in that direction either. It veered inland, avoiding swampland, before gently flowing back to the coast. Still, the man had definitely headed in that direction. He mulled over it for a moment and then dismissed it. He could feel the story he wanted to write moving within him, it was high time he put it to paper.

His leg ached in protest as he pushed his way through the sand. He dug the walking stick in deep, using it to propel himself forward. The wind was now whipping with a frenzy, the boom of the thunder growing louder. As he closed the distance, his beach front cottage in view, the heavens opened. There was no gentle start, but a drenching downpour instead.

Mere yards away, he saw the brilliant pulse of lightning splitting the sky, the air, and Dean could smell the ozone. The hairs on his arms stood on end. The Farmer's Almanac sure did seem to be spot on for August. The storm had taken less than an hour to arrive. He stepped inside of the beach front cottage. Water poured off of him, pooling in a large puddle on the floor around his feet. He shut the door behind him and began to strip, shivering. As he stood there, fighting with his sodden clothes, the lights flickered and then went out.

So much for using the typewriter.

He used the lightning flashes to guide him as he located the kerosene lamp and matches on a shelf.

More than a mile to the north, on a high cliff, a man and woman stood. Around them the storm raged, but in a tight circle there was nothing but the lightest breeze. Their clothes remained dry. Lightning forked through the sky and the surf below pounded against the tall rocks.

"I hear there are dolphins that feed here," Suisser said, addressing the tall, raven-haired woman who stood there.

"The dolphins fled to deeper water when the storm approached." She said, barely acknowledging his presence. "Your report?"

"Ah yes, straight to the point. The Primera Veu, and the Council itself, is not known for dissembling." The woman's brilliant green eyes narrowed in response. Adolphus gave an obsequious smile and bowed again, "My apologies, I meant no offense."

"You and your family have much to answer for, Adolphus." Behind her, the lightning spiked, striking the stone cliff. He could feel the power thrum through the stone. "There are those with the Fer Complir who suspect you conspired to hide Conor's birth."

Adolphus barked out a short, bitter laugh. His lip curled in disgust, "Believe what you will. I had no part in my aunt's subterfuge. The news was as shocking to us as anyone else. In truth, I would think that the Arbre Genealogic would be the ones the Fer Complir should be looking at more closely. Were they not responsible for attending each birth?"

The woman said nothing, but her jaw tightened as her hands moved in time with the lightning. Adolphus was sure she was egging it on, enjoying the violence of it, even as she maintained the bubble of protection around them.

How it must gall her to no longer have The World call to her, he mused. Perhaps that is why Anna acted as she did. Perhaps it was not enough to serve in Council as Mother. To be without a world, to never have the chance to see their home world, it ate at the world-less Protectorates. His mother had been much the same.

"Well? You have met Edmonds. What do you think?" She asked, jarring him out of his thoughts on magic and closed portals to a home world he would never see.

"He knows nothing."

"How can you be sure?"

"He doesn't believe the driver's account of why the truck crossed into his lane."

"So he saw nothing else? Nothing of Conor? Nor Zenobia?"

"No." He paused, frowning. "I thought that we had confirmation. Hasn't Mona been claimed by Fyrsta Heim?"

"Yes, Mona Saronica was confirmed as Fyrsta Heim's Protectorate last year. But we haven't found Zenobia's body."

"Ah, I see. And Conor..."

"Is still missing. We will find him. It is only a question of when."

"And time is on *his* side."

The woman gave a small snort, "I suppose you could say that." She relaxed, her shoulders slumping. The lightning slowed, as did the wind.

"As it should be." Anna said to him, turning to leave. It was obvious the conversation was over.

"Quod ut is mos persevero futurus," Adolphus answered.

Anna gave a brief nod and walked away. The storm followed her.

Hours later, in the tiny beach house to the south, Dean worked away. The storm had ended as suddenly as it had begun, and the power had flickered on moments after the last rumble of thunder died down. In that moment, he had found himself seized by it, that feeling he had been waiting for and hoping he could find. It was a moment of clarity - a crystal clear image of the story that had been hovering about in the back of his brain. As if unlocked by the storm, the plot had revealed itself. He knew it, whole and encompassing, an idea which begged to be put to paper.

Words and dialogue crashed wildly through his thoughts. And riding the wave, he sat down at the table, stared at the typewriter and turned it on. It rewarded him with a steady hum. Dean slipped in the first piece of paper and began to type. His fingers wanted to fly, like his thoughts, but he was still unused to the key positioning. Still, he typed for hours. The ideas surged. The twists and turns of the plot clawed at him.

Anyone passing by the small beach cottage would have heard it. A steady tip-tap, tap-tap, as his fingers sought out the keys, creating magic.

Tour de Force

Saturday, May 8th, 1954

"The depth of the characters, the richness of their lives and language, is seconded only by the breathless ride that Mr. Edmonds takes us on in his debut novel, *At Winter's End*." The speaker was a short, rotund man with a shiny pate of skin reflecting the light overhead. Gripping the edge of the podium, he continued to spout praise.

Dean wondered if the man had somehow gotten his book confused with another. He could not possibly have written the book that this man was describing.

When the words had begun to flow, there had been no shutoff valve, no way to stop the characters who took root in his heart and mind. He had felt them clamoring to be released while he ate his bacon and eggs in the morning. During his mid-afternoon walk down the beach, the waves pounding the sand, the characters defined themselves, took on personalities, opinions, and desires. At night, mixed in with his dreams of June and the children, the characters spoke to him, crafting themselves out of stardust.

His fingers ached at the end of each day. Summer had faded into fall, and fall into winter. Not that winter in Florida amounted to anything more than a few chilly days here and there. It was nothing compared to the dry, bone-chilling winters in the Midwest. While his neighbors had packed up and disappeared, leaving the beaches and small cottages empty, save for a few local fisherman, he had stayed on. The beach cottage was not built for winter guests, and he could feel every breeze that found its way through the walls from the gray, frothing sea outside.

Each day the typewriter keys click-clacked, interrupting the seagulls with a sound of industry and unspoken dreams. The pile of papers had grown, slowly, surely. Those few, rare jewels of writing classes he had managed to sneak in as electives - they came flooding back. Words dripped from his mind, taking shape on the page.

Dean had written stories as a teenager, before his father had insisted he turn his focus toward business. When he had emptied his parents' house out, preparing it for sale as he had his own house just days before, he had found them. As he paged through the round hat box, dusty and faded from the sun that peeked in the lone attic window, he was surprised. He had expected the writing to be terrible, adolescent and awkward, lacking in depth. Instead, he found that his teenage self had possessed a talent for description. He had lost himself in those papers, stopping only when the movers had come to pack up the last of the boxes and place them in storage.

The hatbox had sat in a corner of the rented cottage. In the few instances when the story that was surging through his mind came to an abrupt halt, or he had trouble with a certain scene, he would pull out the old writings and read them again.

He filled the small clothbound book that Maggie had given him. He had filled it with a myriad of thoughts. Everything from a character and his attributes, to a memory of his last days with his wife and children. There had been no theme; instead it had been a catharsis of sorts. It had been Dean's path towards reconciling the man he had been. He had been, undoubtedly, a terrible husband and father. He knew this. He had fallen out of love with June years ago. He knew it was in great part because he had been unhappy working for his father's company, but that hadn't been a good enough reason to stop trying everywhere else.

"After Dad died. I could have stopped. I could have sold the company then, but I didn't. I just kept doing exactly what was expected of me." He wrote in his journal. *"And what is the definition of insanity? Repeating the same thing over and over and expecting a different result."*

The days, weeks and months had marched on - and Dean had only had the seagulls to keep him company. There had been several letters from neighbors. Howard had written, updating Dean on the company's transition and progress. His mousy little wife, Doris, had even sent a letter inquiring after his health and informing him that the sale of his parents' house was almost complete.

As the stack of finished pages grew taller the days grew shorter. The hours of daylight reduced until his mid-afternoon walks were graced by the setting sun in the west. The red rays sinking behind the sand dunes as he returned from the small town.

Half of the stores were closed for the winter. A local tavern was still open, and it served the typical greasy spoon fare. When he grew tired of his standard bacon and egg breakfast, sandwich lunch and canned dinner, he would head over to the tavern for a bite to eat and to drink a beer. The first time he had stopped at the establishment he had ordered a scotch. One sip and he had pushed it away, his guts twisting.

That night he had had trouble sleeping. Tossing and turning, he had remembered the two fingers of Scotch he had gulped down, then another, the night of the accident. Had that been the cause? Probably not, the scotch hadn't put the truck in his lane after all. But it sure as hell hadn't helped. It had slowed his reactions, even if just for a millisecond. It had been enough to kill his wife and children. One sip was all that it had taken to bring those memories flooding back.

Further introspection had brought home the realization that he had used alcohol to deal with his frustration and disappointment - over his life choices and more. Even the beer that passed his lips felt wrong. *Not* drinking in the tavern was not an option. So he would order one beer and sip it while eating his meal.

These months with only his own thoughts to keep him company had given him time to visualize a future. The future would not contain running a business, he had already made sure of that. And between the sale of the two homes as well as Edmonds Manufacturing, he didn't need to worry about money for a long time. He lived a simple existence, had little or no expenses, and this kind of life could continue for as long as he wanted it to.

But the truth of it was, as December marched on, and Christmas grew nearer, he found himself missing Kansas City more and more. He dreamed at night of the Plaza, lit up for the holidays, wreaths and bows on each of the streetlights.

It had been a traditional destination for the entire family. Danny and Betty had loved seeing the lighting ceremony each Thanksgiving. June had insisted on viewing the latest fashions, and usually buying one at Harzfeld's. The kids and Dean would window-shop at the local stores and then Betty would beg to go to Putsch's Cafeteria for a hot chocolate.

Kansas City was his home, despite the bone-chilling cold of winter. It called to him in his dreams.

After a time, he made the arrangements, settling on a room for rent in the Northeast, before putting together his finalized manuscript and mailing it to Viking Press.

The winter had been exceptionally cold, and his Christmas lonely, although the spinster who lived downstairs had invited him to join her for dinner. She had lived in the house most of her life, moving there as a small child with her uncle, aunt, mother and grandmother. Ms. Abney lived on the main floor, and let out the rooms above, four apartments in all, while working as a teacher at a local teacher's college.

It was there, in early January, when the wind rattled the windows and his room took on an icy chill which only vanished when he lit a fire in the small stove, that he received the letter. It had led him here, to this lecture hall, waiting in the wings.

"But I could go on and on, ladies and gentlemen." The man said, "And you didn't come to see me talk about this amazing book, you came to meet Mr. Edmonds for yourselves. Please welcome this Kansas City native to our beautiful windy city of Chicago!"

The audience clapped, the auditorium filled with a sea of faces as he walked out on stage.

He waited for the applause to die down. "Thank you for coming. Although, I'm sure that I'm not the author who my gracious host just introduced." He made a show of looking around, "Perhaps Ernest Hemingway is on the docket and they have confused our books?" The audience laughed.

"No? Well, I will go ahead and read a passage to you from Winter's End."

He cleared his throat, sipped from the glass of water there on the podium and began to read.

"Cloaked in a darkness so thick and deep, Liv lay there, unsure of where she was, of what consisted of her body, her dreams, and her very existence. She felt unmoored, lost in the thick grip of mystery, surrounded by the black. Part of her wished nothing more than to stay here, forever, in this quiet place."

A few hours later, his hand sore from signing, he shook hands with his host. Just three months after publication and his tour schedule had gone from a handful of cities to a long, rather exhausting list.

"Mr. Edmonds it has been a pleasure having you here in Chicago," Charles Loring enthused, "Where are you off to next?"

"Actually, I'm taking a few days to enjoy the spring weather in my home city," Dean answered. He didn't want to explain that the one-year anniversary of the crash was next week. He would visit the graves and take some time to try and recover from the constant grind of the book tour. He doubted he would be given the chance to rest at all. His landlady, Ms. Abney, had called his agent, Scotty Abernathy, and asked Scotty to let Dean know that the letters were stacking up in his room on Tenth Street.

After weeks on the road, Dean needed a break, anyway. There had been so many faces, and just as many questions. *And it hadn't just been run-of-the-mill signings, oh no.* There had been interviews, both on radio and television.

Scotty had also informed him that he would be meeting with Walt Bodine, a radio personality with WDAF while he was back in Kansas City.

No matter how many microphones he had stuck in front of his face, Dean was sure he would never become accustomed to fame. He kept his voice steady, his tone measured, but he usually felt nauseous by the end of each interview.

"Well thank you again, Mr. Edmonds. I was so honored to be able to introduce you and welcome you to our city." Mr. Loring continued, grasping Dean's hand in his own. The man's hands were soft, as were most of those he encountered. He was used to the work-roughened hands of his employees.

Well, former employees.

"I was happy to come by. Thank you for having me, Mr. Loring." Dean let the man pump his arm, his wrist aching from the hour of book signing he had just completed. "I look forward to returning with my next book."

The man's face turned rapturous, "That would be excellent Mr. Edmonds, and I anxiously await it!"

Dean slowly edged his way out of the building, a cab already waiting to take him to the airport and back home. Late that evening, another cab deposited him at the front door of the tall brick home. The street was dark. There were no lights lit on the main level. Ms. Abney had undoubtedly retired for the evening. The front porch planks creaked as he made his way up the wide stairs, the recent rain had wet the rich loamy earth and it smelled of spring. Perched on the thick banister rail which curved around the side of the house to his left were several planter boxes, and the rich perfume of the flowers filled the air with a sweet, heavy scent. It was already quite humid. He let himself in the door on the right designated for the apartment residents and slowly climbed the stairs.

His room was to the right, with a small jog to the left at the end of the hall. The two other doors on this end of the hallway held two double rooms, and the doors on the other end of the hallway opened into one single apartment, which consisted of a tiny room and a fair-sized bedroom and living space. They all shared a single bathroom, the water closet separated from the bathtub and sink space.

His room was the smallest apartment in the house, but he didn't need much. A single bed, a small stove that he could cook a simple meal on, and of course, his typewriter which occupied one end of a small table. What more could he want? As he fumbled with the key, unable to see it well in the dark, the door next to him opened.

"Oh, it's you." Nora Middaugh's voice quavered. She peered through the cracked door at him.

"Good evening, Miss Middaugh." Dean removed his hat, bowing slightly. "I'm so sorry, did I wake you?"

"No, no, not at all." She stood there staring at him.

"Oh, well, good night then." Dean said, realizing what she wanted. He went inside his room and shut the door, locking it. After a moment, he heard her door creak open, then her shuffling steps in the hall, before the bathroom door closed and locked.

Ms. Middaugh was uncomfortable broaching certain subjects, one of which included the fact that she needed to use their shared facilities at least three times each night, often times far more than that. She would never say it though, and it had taken Dean a few interactions with the aged spinster to finally catch on.

He was the only male boarder. In the other double room lived two spinster sisters and at the far end of the hall, a young widow and her infant daughter. Dean shook his head. Ms. Abney had remembered the story of the crash and the loss of his family from when the story had been covered in the newspapers. As soon as he had uttered his last name, she had known exactly who he was. Perhaps this was why she had relaxed her steadfast rule against single male boarders.

The view from the four windows was better than any of the other views. He had set up his bed in one corner so that he could push the small desk and typewriter which doubled as a dining table over to the windows. Here he had found that the words flowed well, when he wasn't being sent off to more stops on the book tour.

Dean stretched out on the bed. He was tired, but needed to use the restroom as well. He settled in for a long wait. Ms. Middaugh was at least seventy-five years old. And at that age, she didn't do anything with haste. Lying there in the dark, fully clothed, his eyes slipped closed.

Lost But Not Forgotten

Thursday, May 13th, 1954

Dean knelt down in the grass. It was already growing thick and green, no sign of disturbance, not the raw earth he had seen last year piled around the large stone and the two smaller ones. The headstones were smooth-edged and rough-faced, a gray black in color. The center headstone, June's, had a vase built into the base and he placed the flowers inside it, removing a handful of dried and withered stems.

Who had put them there?

He had only visited twice, but each time he had, there had been flowers, even in the winter. Just days old by the look of them.

The day was beautiful, sunny, and the dampness from last night's rainstorm had already evaporated into the air. Dean wondered if the summer would be a scorcher, like last year had ended up being. Danny's headstone was on the left side of June's and Betty's on the right, each flanking their mother. The large stone was apparently for both June and Dean.

"June Larabie Edmonds Born June 12th, 1925 Died May 13th, 1953" was etched on the right hand side, on the left, "Dean Arthur Edmonds Born September 15th, 1925."

The rest was blank of course, but at the time of the funeral, he had still been in a coma. Seeing his name there, only the death date left off, Dean realized how close he had come. He reached out to the left and felt the granite cool under his fingertips, despite the warmth of the air.

A smiling nurse, a tiny squalling baby wrapped in a soft white blanket, a blue knit cap on its head.

"Here is your son, Mr. Edmonds, would you like to hold him?"

He had nodded and held out his arms, trying desperately not to shake, and stared at the tiny, red face nestled in a sea of white, his pale blue cap covered the bare wisps of brown hair. This tiny creature, a fusion of his cells and June's, appeared red-faced and angry at being evicted from his warm and comforting home. A tiny hand flexed and then fisted tight, waving with a random anger at a world that was far too bright and colder than he was used to.

"He's going to be a handful, this one is!" The nurse had exclaimed. "Do you have names picked out yet?"

"Violet if it is a girl, and Daniel if it is a boy." He had answered, distracted, his focus centered on not dropping the tiny creature in his arms. He had helped make this. Half of him was contained in this tiny, angry little body. The baby continued to shriek.

"Daniel is a lovely name," she said in response, her eyes were gray and matched the strands of hair peeking out from under her cap. "It means 'God is my judge'. I'd best get this one off to the nursery for his first meal." She took his screaming son from him with gentle, competent hands. "You can go and see your wife now Mr. Edmonds."

He had released his hold on the baby, relieved.

Dean's lips stretched into a smile, before disappearing again. *It never really got any better than that.*

His right leg and knee ached in the lush grass.

"Mr. Edmonds, how good to see you here."

A shadow fell over Dean and he started at the woman's voice. He looked up, peering to see the face haloed by the bright sun.

She smiled, "I'm Doris Jenkins, Howard's wife."

"Oh yes, of course, Doris! I apologize, I was just lost in thought." Dean scrambled awkwardly to his feet, dusting himself off. He towered over the tiny woman.

Doris smiled up at him, fresh flowers clutched in her hand. "I visit my daughter every week and I usually have extra. I was just coming over here to put them in and saw you. How are you, Mr. Edmonds?"

"Please, call me Dean. I'm doing well. I just, well it has been a year, so I thought I should visit them, and..." His voice petered out.

"And you don't know what you are doing here, do you?"

This was not the mousy woman he remembered meeting a scant handful of times.

"No, I guess I don't." Dean glanced back at the graves. "I don't mean to offend, but I can't figure out what I'm doing here. They are gone and I don't believe in heaven or hell or that they are in the arms of Jesus right now. They are just *gone* and I can't make it better."

"And is it about making it better, Dean?" Doris asked softly.

"I don't even know that."

She nodded, "Will you walk with me?"

"Of course."

Around them, the trees had fully leafed out and birds were singing. The air was warm, heavy with moisture from the evening rain and promising more to come.

They didn't walk far before arriving in a small mix of trees and a family plot and tomb that read Belvedere across the top. Near the crypt were more recent stones, including a tiny one. Doris stopped at it.

"You probably didn't know that I was married before. Tom and I were childhood sweethearts and we married straight out of high school."

Dean watched Doris' face as she spoke. Her lips curved up in a smile, her eyes dreamy and faraway.

"Tom loved to sketch. And he was so good at it! His sketch of a roseate spoonbill was so detailed that Audubon purchased it for their magazine cover in 1919."

She glanced up at Dean, "I often wonder what Tom would have done if he had come back from the Great War. He was drafted the same week we learned I was expecting a baby."

Doris' hand caressed the small stone. She knelt and removed the withered flowers, placing the bright blue bachelor's button in the tiny vase.

"He was so talented, so full of life and love. The gentlest man you have ever met, as well."

Dean read the inscription on the stone.

"Ella Belvedere, beloved daughter of Tom and Doris Belvedere. If I had a flower for every time I thought of you...I could walk through my garden forever."

And below that, one date, "February 6th, 1918."

Doris sighed, "He was able to visit once, she had just begun to move in me, and he was able to feel it. The look on his face."

She turned away for a moment, "He would have been an amazing father."

Dean waited for her to collect herself, and she breathed out a long sigh.

"I went into labor on the fourth of February. They say the first ones usually take the longest, but even the doctor became concerned. When she finally came, well, the doctor's face said it all. She was so tiny. Her hands couldn't even wrap around my smallest finger, her eyes were closed, and her skin was pale."

She looked up at him, met his eyes, "They were so kind. They gave her to me, wrapped in a soft white blanket. I held her against me and told her how much she was loved. And for just one tiny moment, she opened her eyes and I saw Tom in her, the same perfect color of brown that I loved and missed so much. She took a couple of breaths, and then, she was gone."

"I'm so sorry, Doris." He asked gently, "And Tom?"

"The Battle of Soissons in July, just five months later. His division was under French command. It was a victory, but at such a price."

Her small, plump hands twisted at the buttons of her blouse.

"Howard was Tom's friend and was there next to him when he died."

Doris reached out, took Dean's hands in hers, and met his gaze.

"Sometimes life's mountains seem too big, too impossible to overcome. In those months that followed, I didn't want to live. My love was gone, and the child that we had made together. I had no one and nothing to hold onto. One day, a few months after the war had ended, Howard came to see me. He knocked on the door, introduced himself, and of course I recognized his name from Tom's letters."

She gave a rueful laugh, "I was so angry. I was even angry at Tom for not coming back to me. I told Howard to go away. But he was patient. He stayed at a boarding house, found work, and visited me every day, and eventually one thing led to another. It took years for me to hold another child in my arms. But when it happened? The loss and grief I had felt over Ella and Tom changed. The wounds in my soul healed.

"You think that June and your children are lost and forgotten, but they aren't, Dean. As long as you draw breath, so do they. They live in your memories. But don't you dare live in the past. Remember the love, forgive the bad, and do the absolute best thing that you can do in these circumstances. Live your life."

She gave his hands a squeeze and released them.

Dean felt a wave of sadness wash over him. "I just wish that, I mean, my marriage wasn't like yours. I wasn't…"

Doris smiled, "You weren't perfect? You didn't say the right things? You weren't the best father or husband that you could be?"

"Yes, all of those."

"Oh Dean, even if you had done everything right, how would that matter in the face of this? There are no do-overs, no perfect marriages. Do you really think that it would have changed the here and now? We are at the mercy of fate. Joy and sorrow, they are one."

The words awoke a memory.

"I was given this book, it says that joy and sorrow are inseparable, that 'when one sits alone with you at your board, the other is asleep upon your bed.'"

Doris laughed lightly.

"And it is true. All these years, Ella is never far from my thoughts. She would be grown now, possibly even a mother herself. I will always mourn the fact that she didn't get that chance. I come here and visit her and Tom, but my life with Howard and our sons is a good one. I mourn what could have been just as I recognize that the person I was then, is not the person I am now. From what I have heard of you, Dean, it sounds as if you are embracing the opportunity for change as well."

"My book."

"Indeed. I've read it, you know. The copy you sent Howard is quite worn and well-used." She laughed, "Once Howard finished with it, I read it, and then it was the book of the month for the ladies book club I belong to.

Imagine, Dean, if you had not had the situation you were dealt, would you have ever become a writer?"

"I don't know." He thought about it, imagining June's objections, and the kids' constant fighting and distractions, "Probably not."

She knelt down and gently touched the small stone. "Never forget them, but don't let the loss of them hold you back from making your life a good one."

"Thank you Doris."

As he left Doris Jenkins to spend time with her infant daughter and young husband, her words, and her story, stuck in his thoughts. He walked through the headstones, the grass thick and lush under his feet. Memories of Danny, his favorite toy a six-shooter and holster that buckled around him, and Betty and that cloth doll she was never without slid in as well. His first book had borrowed heavily from his memories of his family, but there was more that he could say. The writer in him began to draw the shapes of characters, a snippet of storyline arising, the beginning of a new book stirring in the gray folds of his brain. Overhead, the sun was high in the sky and the slow wind felt heavy and wet.

The Work Never Ends

Monday, May 24th, 1954

Walt's grip was strong. It had been only a few moments from Dean entering the studio of WDAF and sitting down before Walt had walked through a door on the left, smiling broadly and reaching out to shake Dean's hand. "Mr. Edmonds, it is a pleasure to meet you. How are you today?"

"I'm fine, thank you."

He had woken up late. The hands on his wristwatch had informed him it was past nine a.m. in the morning. But that was merely a confirmation to what his eyes had already told him. The sunlight poured into his windows, heating up the room, promising another early, and wretchedly hot, summer day.

The first anniversary of the crash had come and gone. Despite his talk with Doris in the cemetery, it had hit him two days later, a slap in the face, and he had spent two weeks in his room, brooding alone, rarely leaving. This mood had been broken with a letter from Scotty Abernathy. The excitable New Yorker had been driven crazy by Dean's miasma. Letters had begun to roll in daily, demanding Dean call him. It seemed that *At Winter's End* was continuing to climb the New York Times list.

The last missive from Scotty had included a rather long-winded diatribe on how Dean could not be complacent, and how important it was for him to call.

"Excellent. Let's go on back to the studio and get you set up." Walt Bodine ushered him through the studio door.

"My landlady had quite a lot to say about you, Mr. Bodine," Dean said.

"Oh, really? And please, call me Walt."

"Yes. She's a professor at a local women's college. She teaches speech and promotes proper elocution techniques."

Walt's head snapped back, "Oh my, what did she say?"

Dean laughed, "Really she was quite impressed. She said you had managed to eliminate the Midwestern twang fully and that your vocabulary was larger than any other radio personality she has listened to of late."

Walt looked relieved, "Good to hear. You mentioned she is a professor?"

"Yes. Dr. Louise Abney."

"My goodness, yes, I've attended one of her speeches before!"

"Well, I guess that explains it then."

"Indeed!" They turned left and then right, the building a maze of doors and hallways. Dean was hopelessly lost by the time they reached the recording studio.

"Here we are. You will sit here. Can my girl here get you some water? Or would you prefer tea or coffee?"

"Water will be great, thank you." Dean sat down in the seat, the large microphone centered in front of him.

Walt sat down across from him. Beside him was a copy of *At Winter's End*. The slipcover was creased and there were scraps of paper sticking out at intervals.

Walt smiled, "I can't tell you how much I enjoyed this book, Mr. Edmonds."

"Why, thank you, Walt. Hearing that never seems to get old." Dean said. So many of the interviews he had done had been slipshod, pretentious and unimaginative. He had been feeling rather jaded of late. Certainly the book was popular, but the radio show hosts he had dealt with had relied on assistants who had read the book for them, giving them tips on what questions to ask. For some reason, he was sure that Walt Bodine had not done that. He truly had read the book and enjoyed it.

"Well, I call them how I see them. I found myself lost in the characters and the story, eager to see what would happen next. And this truly is your *first* novel? Are you sure you don't have a stack of novels hidden about waiting to be published?"

Dean laughed and shook his head, "No, sorry to disappoint, but it will be a while until the next one comes out."

Walt looked let down, "Ah well. I read it twice, by the way, and then insisted my wife read it." He smiled at Dean. "She was captivated by it."

He had a list of notes in front of him. "We have a few minutes before we go on the air, I hope you don't mind if I just double-check the information I have for you. And let me know if there are any questions you wish for me to strike from the list."

Dean nodded and Walt ran through his questions which were the standard background - where he had lived, his career up until recently, and Walt gently approached the death of his family.

A few minutes later and they were on the air.

Walt moved through the regular introductions, pointing out that Dean was a local author and mentioning that the book was still climbing the New York Times bestseller list.

Walt smiled at him, "I must admit that I read your book twice. I was absolutely drawn in by it, Mr. Edmonds. The characters, the setting, it was truly compelling."

"Why, thank you."

"I understand that your book is now number fifteen on the New York Times bestseller list," Walt glanced at his notes, "Edging out Joseph Hayes' book, *The Desperate Hours*."

"Yes, I received word of that yesterday from my agent."

"Quite impressive for a debut novel." Walt continued.

"I owe it all to my family," Dean answered.

"Reviews have called your book 'visually stunning' and there have been some who have said that your world, while beautiful, could never truly exist. What do you have to say in response to that?"

"Well Walt, my novel is fiction." Dean answered, choosing his words carefully, "Despite this, I can't say I agree with those critics who would sell the human spirit and experience so short. I think that we are capable of so much more, it lies within each of us, waiting only for us to access it."

Walt asked, "In the end of the book, you mentioned your family. And you said just now that you owe this book's success to your family. Could you tell us more about that?"

By now, he had found ways to respond to it, although the ache could still be felt in his chest, each time he had to answer. "My family, my wife and my two young children, died last year in an automobile accident. Their deaths were my wake-up call."

"Could you tell me what you mean by that, Mr. Edmonds?"

"That all we have is this moment. That our dreams of something different should be listened to, followed, before it is too late. It took losing my family to learn that lesson. I would not be here today, if not for the crash that cost them their lives, and I very nearly lost mine as well. I cannot get them back, and make amends, make our relationships better, or watch my children grow into adults."

Walt let a moment of silence slide by, allowing the radio listeners some time to digest this. "I am sorry for your loss, Dean. And yet, you speak so honestly in the book, and paint such detailed descriptions of your characters. It feels as if your family has been given life within these pages."

Dean nodded and realized it didn't translate over a radio. "Yes, I did borrow heavily on my memories of them for this story. I wanted them to live again, at least in some form. But at some point, reality ends and fiction takes over. Honore is not my wife June, nor am I the Antoine described in the story. Perhaps a hopeful wish of who I should have been, who I would have liked to have been, but not the me who was June's flesh and blood husband."

"We are often consumed with regret." Walt said.

"Indeed."

The interview continued for half an hour and he was waylaid twice on the way out of the building as several employees eagerly asked for his autograph in their newly purchased copies. The day was far from over, now he had a book signing to go to a few blocks away.

"Should I call you a cab, sir?" A pretty young girl at the reception desk asked.

"I'll just catch the streetcar, thank you, Miss." Dean said, tipping his hat. Outside the sun was shining, but Dean could feel the moisture in the air. There would be another storm tonight for sure.

He reached the stop for the streetcar just in time. The round-domed, cream-colored trolleys always reminded him of the butter cream frosting his mother had lavished on his birthday cakes over the years. She had passed away in 1950, just a couple of months after Betty was born.

Dean stepped aboard and paid the five cent fare. The trolley was nearly empty. This was surprising, Dean remembered riding it in his youth. Day or night, the cars were full of passengers. But now, in the middle of the day, the car held him, the driver and just two others.

The ride wouldn't take long, and although it was humid, the cooler spring temperatures were still holding. He settled back in a seat and thought of his mother.

His father, Arthur, had been strict and very distant. Clara Edmonds, on the other hand, had been loving and affectionate. He had been the only one of her children to live, after all. A string of miscarriages had culminated in only two live births. He remembered the birth of his sister. Her short life remained indelibly printed upon his memory. He had been three and she, born far too early, had struggled to live. He remembered standing next to her crib, reaching to stroke her hand, crabbed and red. Her tiny body had twitched, desperately fighting for each breath in. Irene Edmonds had lasted for nearly two weeks, before fading away. Afterward, his mother had cried and cried, retiring to her bed and refusing to eat.

There had been no more pregnancies or babies after that. And the giant house, with three of its bedrooms standing empty, was far too large for a small boy to grow up in alone. Despite this, his parents never bothered to look for another, even after their dreams of a large family to fill it had sputtered and died.

Doris Jenkins had written him when it sold and told him that the family, a well-off lawyer, his wife and six children, had put an offer on it after their first visit. It was a relief. He had held onto the house for far too long. Knowing that there was a family living, laughing and growing up within its walls had been some measure of solace. He didn't miss his boyhood home, or wish to live in it, but he felt as if it deserved some happiness now.

When the conductor called out "Eleventh Street, coming up!" Dean straightened his jacket and pulled the string. As he emerged from the streetcar, he scanned the buildings for the bookstore and located it quickly.

As he walked in, a young salesgirl looked up and smiled, "Welcome to Glenn Frank Books. May I help you find anything?" The store was busy, bustling with customers.

"Yes, I'm Dean Edmonds, I'm here for my book signing."

The girl jumped from her perch and came around the corner, "Oh, Mr. Edmonds! Mr. Frank is expecting you, right this way."

Dean found himself led to a large room in the back. Already a crowd had gathered. Dean's book had appealed to both women and men, judging by the sea of faces he saw staring at him expectantly. He checked his watch, fifteen minutes to spare. A tall, lean man noticed Dean come in and advanced, his right hand held out.

"Mr. Edmonds, thank you for coming!" He beamed down at Dean, shaking his hand with a bone-crushing grip.

"Mr. Frank, I take it?"

"Yes, indeed! Please, come this way," he said as he ushered Dean to the podium. "You will be here. I'll be back momentarily with a glass of water." The man hurried away.

There were stacks and stacks of *At Winter's End* on a table near the back and, from what he could tell, most of the sea of bookstore patrons already had one in their hands. It seemed that a home grown author was big news.

Dean set his satchel on the floor and pulled a worn copy of his book out. It was marked at places with slips of paper - these were his favorite passages. The buzz of voices was loud, although there had been a lull as he took his place at the podium. A moment later, Mr. Frank was back with the promised glass of water, setting a pitcher down on a nearby table before clearing his throat.

"Ladies and gentlemen, if you could kindly take your seats."

The crowd quieted.

"I am honored to have one of our own, a Kansas City native, and talented author of the book *At Winter's End* here this afternoon. Mr. Edmonds will be reading passages from his book and then will be available for book signing directly after." Mr. Frank cast a glance down at his notes, "And I've just received confirmation that *At Winter's End* has now risen to *thirteenth* on the New York Times bestseller list, having outperformed Samuel Shellabarger's book *Lord Vanity*!

The audience erupted in applause and the bookstore owner waited for a moment for the noise to die down before he continued.

"Not many debut authors make such a large impression as Mr. Edmonds has in just a few short months. His characters have been described as compelling and his prose throughout *At Winter's End* is both vivid and concise." He looked up from his notes and smiled at Dean standing at the podium, "But why take my word for it? Here is Mr. Edmonds himself. He is here to take you on a journey into a world you will never want to leave."

He shook Dean's hand and walked away from the podium while the audience clapped again. As Dean began to read the excerpts to his audience a few minutes later, there was absolute silence. By the time he had finished with his readings, the room had filled with even more people. It was standing room only and they hung on each word he uttered.

After the applause for his reading had died down, Mr. Frank had asked those who wanted autographed copies to line up along the wall. It snaked around all sides and out of the door. Dean signed his name over and over, his hand aching. Slowly the line dwindled down to a handful of patrons.

Dean reached for the last book. He noted that the hand holding it was slender, feminine, and hidden in a pair of white cotton gloves. He looked up at a familiar, smiling face.

"Hello Mr. Edmonds, I see you got around to writing that book." Her face held the same, warm smile that he had looked forward to each day in the hospital.

"Maggie! What a wonderful surprise!" He stood, "I'm so glad to see you!" His hands enveloped hers, the others in the room forgotten.

"You remember me, then."

"How could I forget? I looked forward to your shift every day. A spot of light in my otherwise dark day. How are you?"

It felt different, seeing her here. She wore a simple, flowered dress with a gathered neckline. Her honey colored hair was pulled back in a demure bun and she had a touch of blush on her cheeks. Her eyes were the same lovely shade of blue he had remembered. She was a beautiful young woman. He couldn't help noticing it.

"I'm well." She looked somewhat nervous, "But, I shouldn't keep you. I just saw the notice last week that you would be here. I wanted to hear you read from your book. I had the day off, so I had no excuse not to come and see you."

"I'm so glad you did." Dean realized he was still holding both of her hands in his. He dropped them self-consciously, shook his head, and smiled at her. "Forgive me, here I am just staring at you like a country bumpkin. Let me sign your book."

She smiled at him, and he could smell her perfume. It was a gentle scent, reminiscent of the hedge of lavender his grandmother used as a border in her front yard.

He signed inside of the cover with a flourish and handed it back to her.

"Thank you so much, Mr. Edmonds, I look forward to reading it."

"Please, call me Dean." He held her gaze for a moment.

She bit her lip, but managed a small, warm smile before she broke eye contact.

"Well thanks again, Mr...er...Dean."

He nodded at Maggie. Her face and voice had filled far too many of his dreams over the past few months. He watched as she turned and walked away. Her skirt swished as she moved, her heels clicking on the wood floor.

The owner of the bookstore stepped forward, "Mr. Edmonds, I am so glad that..."

Dean was not listening. His eyes remained fixed on Maggie's retreating form. He watched as she approached the cash register. She paused then, digging into her boxy purse and removing a slim wallet.

Without a glance at the bookstore owner, Dean walked away, everything else graying out except his focus on her. He drew near as Maggie pulled a tattered dollar bill out and began to dig for coins.

"Here," he said as he set down a five dollar bill, "It's on me."

Maggie's cheeks reddened. "Mr. Edmonds, I have enough, I do." Her gloved hand snatched up the five-dollar bill and handed it back to him. "As a writer, you won't ever make any money giving away your books!"

Chastened, he took the money back from her. A sudden longing washed over him. He wanted to talk with her again, to share his thoughts with her on the latest book he was reading, a disturbing, yet fascinating book by William Golding.

Maggie was beautiful, but what fascinated him beyond that was her quick wit and literary enthusiasm. He watched as the cashier took her money, wrapped the book in paper and twine and thanked her.

Her bright smile washed over him again, "It was so good to see you again, Mr. Edmonds."

"Yes, Maggie, likewise. I hope you enjoy the book." He ended lamely, wincing as he did. *Could I sound more ridiculous?*

"I am sure I will, Mr. Edmonds." The salesgirl was still watching them. "Well, goodbye then."

He watched her walk away. She stepped out of the store, turned right, and climbed into a trolley that had just rolled to a stop. Within seconds she was gone from view, lost in the crowd.

"Dean Edmonds, you are a fool."

"Sir?" The salesgirl looked confused.

He blinked, smiled and shook his head. "Sorry, just talking to myself."

The girl flashed a huge smile in return. Her teeth were twisted, crowded in her small narrow mouth. "I do that all the time."

Later, as he headed back to the small rented room on Tenth Street, he thought about Maggie. She had been the only one to see him as more than just a business owner. She had shared with him her ragged collection of books and guided him back to his love of literature.

Why didn't I tell her that?

He thought to himself as he heated a can of beans up on the stove.

And why didn't I ask her out to dinner?

Kismet

Saturday, May 29th, 1954

Dean settled back in his seat on the trolley. It was mid-morning and he had shopping to do. This time he was going further than the corner market. Ms. Abney had recommended a nearby business when he asked after a good butcher shop.

"I would suggest L&C Meats, down on Eighteenth Street," she had answered, "I buy a roast from them once a month."

He could have walked it, but the day was already warm, and he was moving through his book at a rapid pace. He had found himself stuck in the doldrums, unable to focus on his new manuscript and tired of the endless book tour for the first one.

Let's face it, I need some down time.

He relaxed into the seat, he figured he had at least five minutes to read. His lips spoke the words quietly as his attention dipped back into the text, "What are we? Humans? Or animals? Or savages? What's grown-ups going to think?"

"Mr. Edmonds, what a surprise!"

A familiar voice brought him back to present. The trolley slid forward, shaking slightly. Dean looked up surprised to see Maggie standing in front of him.

113

"Maggie! What a pleasure! I didn't know you lived up north." He slid over, opening up the aisle seat, "Please, sit down, sit down."

Maggie was wearing a pretty yellow dress with red piping and starched cuffed short sleeves. It fit her form, flattering her small waist. The dress swirled gently as she moved, sitting down next to him.

"Thank you."

Her cheeks held the slightest hint of blush and her Yardley English Lavender perfume washed over him in a gentle breeze.

"I actually live south of here, but I make a special trip to this little bakery on Independence Avenue every once in a while." She held out a brown paper bag, "They make the perfect beignet. Would you like one?"

"I don't have a clue what that is, but sure, why not?" Sitting this close to her, he felt tongue-tied all over again.

Get a grip on yourself, man, you are gawping like a school boy.

She handed him a pastry and he examined it for a moment. It was square in shape and dusted liberally with confectioner's sugar. He took a small bite and a puff of sugar blasted away, dusting his trousers. Inside, it was filled with a rich chocolate paste.

Maggie stifled a giggle and handed him a napkin. He shook his head, smiled back, dabbing at the sprinkles on his leg.

"What did you call it?"

"A beignet. It's practically a food group in New Orleans."

"I've never been to New Orleans."

"I went to visit my aunt Beulah one summer as a child. She lived in this tiny shotgun house on Dublin Street."

Dean took another bite and growled in frustration as a cloud of sugar dusted his pants. Maggie giggled again.

"If this wasn't one of the most delicious pastries I've ever eaten, I would be rather put out right now."

"Well I suppose there is that." He had seen her eat one as well, yet her clothes and hands were free of mess. "How did you eat that without it ending up everywhere?"

"We walked down the street to the local bakery every morning of my visit, except on Sundays, and had them for breakfast. I guess I learned the trick of eating them along the way."

Her smile warmed him. The other occupants of the trolley, even the scenery rolling by, faded into the background, lost to a set of crayon blue eyes and lips which held a hint of gloss.

"Kismet."

She tilted her head at him, "What?"

"It means fate." Dean explained.

"I know what it means. It also comes from the Arabic word, qisma, which is portion, or lot."

He winced, feeling rather foolish. *Of course she knows what the word means, you pompous fool.* "I was just thinking that it was kismet seeing you here today."

"Ah, I see." Her eyebrows arched, "I'm glad to see you too."

Dean looked away from Maggie as the trolley jerked to a stop.

The driver called out, "Thirteenth Street!"

An old woman and two children disembarked, the old woman steadied on each side by the boy and the girl. Her grandchildren, possibly? A bevy of young teenage girls spilled up the steps, giggling. The doors closed and the bell clanged three times before the mammoth green and butter yellow machine jerked and then began to advance again, sliding down the street at a steady pace.

Maggie broke the silence, "So where are you headed?"

"To the butcher out on Eighteenth Street, L&C Meats. My landlady, Ms. Abney, she told me that their cuts of steak are the best quality."

"Really? Did she say anything about their roasts?"

"Actually, yes, she did. She buys one every first Saturday of the month. She mentioned that they were small, but definitely high in quality."

"I had been headed home, but perhaps I will come and see this butcher. Do you mind?"

"Not at all!"

The trolley lurched every so often and Dean breathed in the delicate wash of lavender each time Maggie moved. She pointed to the book that Dean had shoved into his satchel when she sat down. "Lord of the Flies?"

"Yes, by William Golding." He pulled it out and handed it to her.

"I've never heard of it."

"It's new, and there aren't any reviews yet." He watched as she looked over the front and back cover.

"It looks like a children's book."

Dean laughed, "Believe me, it's not. There is some pretty heavy stuff in it. My agent wants me to read it and write a short review for the guy, he says the book has only sold a few hundred copies, and he owes him a favor."

"Is it good?"

"Yes, but it is more disturbing than anything else. I've not finished it, but it seems to be headed down a dark path."

"Interesting. I might need to check it out." She handed it back to him and her fingers brushed his.

Dean sucked a breath in. "Indeed." Her eyes met his for a brief moment.

The trolley lurched to a stop and the driver called out. "Eighteenth Street!"

"And this is our stop." He stood up, satchel in hand, and Maggie stood with him. "The shop is down the street, a block from here, according to Ms. Abney."

They disembarked, climbing down the steep trolley steps, crossed the street and walked along the sidewalk, still damp from the morning rain. The heat of the late spring day had evaporated most of the puddles, the air was still heavy and thick. It would be a muggy day and, looking at the sky, Dean expected it would be another wet, stormy night.

"No wonder I didn't know it was here, that's a pretty small sign,"

Maggie commented as they approached the store front. The glass was etched with the letters, *L&C Meats, est. 1948.*

The display window showed steaks and pork chops, cut thick, and nestled on a bed of lettuce.

Inside, the wood floors were spotless, despite the damp outside, and the walls were bare except for a handful of pictures of charts - the outlines of cattle, sheep, goat with precise lines indicating which cuts came from where. The counter was clean, and the gentleman behind it had just finished ringing up a customer.

He nodded and called out, "I'll be with you in a moment."

Dean held the door, first for Maggie and then for the customer who was leaving.

The butcher wiped down the counter, and his hands, drying them on a thin white towel when he was done.

"How may I help you today?"

Maggie spoke first, "I would like a roast, please."

A few minutes later, the butcher had wrapped a small beef roast for her and then showed Dean some of the steaks.

"I have a thicker cut in back if you would prefer, sir."

"This Kansas City strip will be just fine, thank you."

The clerk glanced over at Maggie and then back at Dean, "Will you be needing any more, sir?"

"No, this one will do." Dean said and handed the man cash.

The heat hit them with a blast as they stepped outside. Dean pulled out a handkerchief and wiped his brow. "The summer didn't waste any time getting here, did it?"

Maggie smiled and shook her head, shading her eyes from the glare of the sun from overhead.

"I had better get home," she said, and glanced across the street. A trolley car had just pulled away down the street. "And it looks like I'll be waiting a while."

Dean felt the moment slipping away from him, it was now or never. "Maggie, wait, I..."

How long had it been since he had asked a beautiful woman out? Since college?

"Yes?"

"Could I buy you lunch?" He laughed self-consciously, "I know we both bought meat, but I know this deli off of Independence. It makes the best Reuben sandwiches I have ever eaten.

"I couldn't."

"Please, I could use the company." He smiled at her, "Besides, I've hardly eaten all day. You would be doing me a favor."

Maggie sighed, and looked up at him. "I can't."

Dean flushed red. "Of course. I do apologize, I've been presumptuous and overstepped."

He turned to step away, half embarrassed, half mortified. What was he doing? She had been his nurse, after all. He wanted to tell her how much her words had meant to him during those dark days in the hospital. How many times had he thought of her in the months since? Her smile and gentle touch?

Maggie reached out her hand and stopped him.

"Mr. Edm...Dean...I'm sorry. I didn't explain myself well. I would love to have lunch with you. It's just that..."

Her words petered out and he could feel the warmth of her touch through his shirtsleeve.

Dean turned back towards her.

"It's just that I have to pick up my son from my neighbor. And that's why I can't join you for that Reuben, which sounds fantastic by the way."

A son. But no ring. Not on either hand. He stood there, and it all fell into place. Of course.

"Would you...would you care to have dinner with us instead?" Maggie blurted out, her fingers falling away from his sleeve.

Dean smiled. "I would like that."

A Dinner In

Saturday, May 29th, 1954

Dean wrote down Maggie's address and returned to the rented room on Tenth Street. The wind had picked up and he stretched out on the bed near the open window. The street was filled with children playing, their shouts echoed as they ran up and down the sidewalk and the solid *thwack* of a ball and bat coming together originated from the paved alleyway behind the large house.

A cool breeze ruffled the curtains.

He thought of Maggie and wondered if he was making a mistake. *Getting involved with a single mother, with June and the kids gone just a year.*

It's only dinner, he told himself.

An hour later he stepped into the cab.

"Where to?"

"Seven-oh-one East Twenty-Seventh Terrace, please."

Maggie's house was five or six blocks away from the hospital and an easy walking distance from her work. He wondered what she did in the winter months. *Did she still walk to work? Or did she have a friend who she could share a ride with?* He had found his mind wandering to mundane questions like this, ignoring the telegram from his agent Scotty asking him to call immediately. The excitable New Yorker could wait, he had other things occupying his mind right now.

The house was a narrow, two-story affair with shutters at the windows and a small, tidy yard. It sat on the corner of the street and there was a young tree in the back with a wooden swing. The tiny front porch sported two worn wood chairs and a table. He could see a bat and ball in one corner of it, along with a pair of metal skates. Danny had had a pair like that, he had strapped them onto his shoes and skated all over the neighborhood with his friends.

Dean took a deep breath. A child, a little boy, and Maggie, a single mother. *Was she divorced? A widow?* There was so much he didn't know about her. They had talked about books, commented on author's writing styles, and recited favorite passages. They had spoken briefly of his family. The pain had been so raw then, that it wasn't often. But how had they never spoken of her, or that she had a child of her own?

He paid the cab driver and turned toward the house. The screen door banged and a small boy, slight in build with light brown hair came running out of the house. He took the stairs in one leap, skidding to a stop in front of Dean at the end of the narrow sidewalk. A small cluster of freckles played over his nose. His eyes were exactly like Maggie's.

"Hi! Mama said someone was coming to dinner. That must be you. Unless you are a salesman. Are you a salesman? Mama said an Arthur was coming to dinner. Arthurs write books. Are you an Arthur?" This was uttered in a quick jet of speech, without any break or moment to take a breath.

Dean smiled. "I am an author. My name is Mr. Edmonds, what's yours?"

"I'm Teddy Aaronson. Nice to meet you." The boy stuck out a hand and they shook. Dean could feel dirt and stickiness covering the small digits. *Pretty typical for the age, all dirt and snails and puppy dog tails.*

"Mama is fixing dinner, she told me to be polite and talk to you." The boy eyed the bag in Dean's hand, "Whatcha got there, Mr. Edmonds?"

Dean handed the boy the bag, "Why don't you look and see?" He had picked out the candies at the corner market on Tenth Street, just down the block from his rented room. It had brought back memories of better times with June and Danny, when Betty was still an infant. After dinner, they would walk down to the neighborhood store and Dean would buy June a root beer and help Danny pick out a candy bar. The bag held Whoppers, a Rocky Road, and Pixy Stix. Teddy opened the bag and his eyes widened.

"Oh wow!" He ran away from Dean, tossing open the screen door as he ran into the house, "Mama! Mama! Look what Mr. Edmonds brought! Can I have one now?" The screen door slammed shut behind him and Dean was left standing on the porch. The smell wafting through the window was inviting.

"Theodore Aaronson you set that bag down right now." Maggie said, her voice ringing from the rear of the house. "And you had better not have left our guest alone on the front porch." Her voice held only the slightest amount of scolding tone. "Mr. Edmonds? Please come inside. I can't leave the kitchen at the moment, the meat might burn."

Teddy returned to the front door and opened it, a look of remorse on his face. "Sorry, Mister Edmonds."

Dean couldn't help but grin and wink at the boy, "Don't you worry one bit, Teddy. I remember how exciting candy and surprises can be." He followed the little boy into the kitchen and stopped dead in his tracks.

Maggie was hovering over the stove, a spoon in her hand. Her face was flushed from the heat of the day and the hot room. It felt at least ten degrees hotter in the kitchen than outside.

Dean was struck with her beauty, despite the simplicity of her appearance. She wore a cotton print dress with a full skirt, and it was covered with a clean, but worn apron. The edges of it were frayed from repeated washing. Her blond hair was pulled back in a long braid that hung low on her back. It was a deep golden blond, bordering on brown. He had never really seen it fully before today. In the hospital she kept it in a bun, hidden under her nurse's cap. June's hair had been curly, but Maggie's was straight.

She turned and smiled at him, "Good afternoon, Mr. Edmonds. You found us, I see. Did you come by taxi or bus?"

"Please, call me Dean. And I took a taxi, although it isn't far. I may walk back home."

She smiled, "Sorry. Force of habit, I guess. Can I get you something to drink? Perhaps some sweet tea?" Teddy danced around them, his attention fixed on Dean.

"That would be lovely."

"I'll do it, Mama." The boy hauled on the ice box handle and reached for a cut glass pitcher. Maggie intervened.

"Not a chance, my little man, that pitcher is going to end up on the floor. It's heavy!" Her tone was gentle, chiding, yet firm.

"I'm stronger than I look, Mama." Teddy protested, puffing up his chest.

"Of that I have no doubt, Sweetheart, but I really must insist. Here, will you hold the cups for me? I need a steady hand." She reached over him and pulled out the pitcher. A thick sheen of condensation covered the intricate details of the cut glass. She poured the amber liquid into three cups, one small and two larger and then placed the pitcher back in the ice box.

Dean took a small sip and grinned, "There's nothing like good old-fashioned sweet tea on a summer afternoon."

Maggie took a sip from her own glass before returning to the meat browning on the stove. She glanced over at Dean, "I hope you don't mind pot roast. We normally have it for Sunday dinner, but since I had it, I thought I would fix it for you today."

"What's your favorite dinner, Mister Edmonds? Do you like pot roast? I don't like pot roast as much as I like spaghetti. Spaghetti is my favorite!" Teddy nattered on between sips of sweet tea.

"I have to admit that pot roast is one of my favorite meals, Teddy. But I also am a fan of spaghetti." Dean said, smiling down at the little boy.

They sat down to the meal. The small kitchen had just enough room for the battered wooden table and three weathered and creaky chairs. Everything in the tiny house was clean, spotless even. Dean could see that all of the furnishings were second-hand, and there were several patched quilts in the living room on the back of the divan and rocking chair. A simple life, but one rich in love.

Maggie parented Teddy with a calm yet firm hand. When he began to slurp his tea, she raised an eyebrow and he stopped immediately, "Sorry Mama." His small face was quickly covered with the rich gravy from the meat.

There was a simple salad, consisting of lettuce and carrots, with a creamy dressing in a small pitcher. And Dean had brought a crusty French bread from a bakery June had always insisted was better than anything she was willing to bake.

Maggie had been grateful when she spied the offering, "Oh you chose well, I love this bakery!"

Hours later, in the gathering darkness, he couldn't help smiling. They had eaten dinner, crowded around Maggie's tiny battered kitchen table. Her young son Teddy peppered him with a wide range of questions.

"What kind of books do you write, Mr. Edmonds?"

"I have plans to write cross-genre, but..."

"Cross what?" The boy interrupted, "Cross like mad?"

"Son, don't interrupt Mr. Edmonds." Maggie admonished.

Dean laughed, "It's all right. Cross-genre means different interests. Say you like adventure stories and your mom likes romances." He said, winking at Maggie.

"Mama doesn't like girly books, Mr. Edmonds."

"How well I know that!" Dean said, smiling. "Back to your question, though, young man. *At Winter's End* is considered speculative fiction."

"Spec...spectacle...ative..." The boy struggled with the word.

"Speculative."

"Sort of like science fiction, Teddy, like Buck Rogers." Maggie said, looking at Dean for confirmation.

"Yes, exactly. It is considered a new genre, very similar to science fiction, but not completely. For example, *At Winter's End* is set in a country on Earth that does not actually exist and focuses on a time in history that never happened." Dean explained. "It could be considered science fiction, but that genre usually comes with the connotation of space travel, aliens and different planets."

"Oh." Teddy thought about that for a moment and then asked, "Do you have any dogs in your books?"

"I do, actually. I don't discuss her much, but she is very brave and completely loyal to her owner, despite his shortcomings."

After dinner, Dean volunteered to wash the dishes while Maggie dried them. He couldn't remember ever helping June with such things. Perhaps when they were first married? No, even then he had been far too busy with work at the plant. Their fingers connected several times as she passed him a soapy plate. Standing next to her, so close, he could detect more than just the pleasant scent of lavender, but another gentle smell he could not identify. It was familiar, however, *possibly a soap?*

Each time her fingers touched his he felt a small current of desire. Wrong or right, he was attracted to this woman. It was a feeling he hadn't allowed himself to feel in a long time. The sun had set as they watched Teddy playing in the yard.

"What is it?" Maggie's words brought him back to present, sitting on the tiny porch. The fireflies were out. In the yard, Teddy ran, his short legs pumping, as he followed the intermittent spots of light, eager to fill his empty mayonnaise jar.

"I was remembering what you said to me in the hospital," Dean answered, taking a chance and reaching out to find her hand. She tensed for a moment and then relaxed, curling her fingers against his.

"You said to me that it wasn't too late to follow my dreams. I sold my business and wrote the book. And here I am."

"I'm so happy for you, Dean." Dean felt her hand squeeze his.

"Do you remember how you said you had become a nurse because you wanted to make a difference?"

"Yes."

"Well, you made a difference in my life. And I'm a better man because of it. I just wanted you to know that."

Teddy had been busy filling his mayonnaise jar, and he bounced up the steps, eager to show them both his collection of fireflies. "Mama! Mr. Edmonds! Look! I caught five of them!"

Maggie leaned forward and hugged her son close. "Oh my goodness, yes you did, Teddy! That's one more than yesterday!" She took the jar and admired the boy's catch.

"I want to name them, Mama! And keep them. Can I keep them this time?"

Dean could see her shake her head. The street light illuminated that much, but not her face. Still, he could feel her smile in the dark.

"No, darling, we can't keep them. They die in captivity, remember? And we wouldn't want that."

"Oh." The boy sounded dejected, "No."

"I don't think there is any harm in naming them, is there?" Dean interjected.

Dean could feel Maggie's warm smile as she turned in his direction.

"Well, no, Mr. Edmonds has a fine idea. What would you name them, Darling?"

"Oh, oh, I'll name this one Corporal Rusty. And this one can be Major Swanson. This one here is special, so his name is Rin Tin Tin." The boy continued as Maggie and Dean laughed.

Later, after Maggie had put Teddy to bed, she joined Dean on the front porch. A moment of hesitation and then she slipped her hand into his.

"I guess I know what show Teddy watches each week."

Maggie sighed, "He's been begging me for months for a dog."

"Let me guess, a German Shepherd?"

She laughed then, "Why Dean Edmonds, I think you must be psychic!"

"A dog is just what a young boy needs. Danny begged for one every birthday and Christmas for two straight years. If I hadn't have been such a self-absorbed ass, I would have bought Danny a dog. It would have gotten him out from in front of the television and given him some responsibility." Dean said, tilting the last of the soda pop out of the bottle. It had warmed in the hot summer air.

"Well, we can't do that. Not without a fence. And besides, dogs cost money."

"I see." They sat for several moments and watched the older children called one by one inside. "So, about Teddy."

There was a long pause. Maggie finally answered, her voice clipped.

"His father isn't in the picture, hasn't been, since before he was born."

A longer pause followed. The cicadas began their steady hum. The wind shifted, and the humid air and dark clouds promised a break from the unseasonably dry heat.

"You aren't going to ask more?" Maggie said, her voice guarded.

"I was waiting for you. You'll tell me or you won't." He paused for a moment, "I am not judging you, Maggie."

She sighed, and pulled her hand from his. "His name was Conor Saronica. What can I say? I was in love. I fell for the wrong guy, I guess. I was young. It was my first year in college and I was studying art. He was studying to be a doctor."

She shrugged, "Or so he said."

"When we found out I was pregnant, he said he would marry me. He told me..." She stopped, took a deep breath and stared out into the night. "He said that he loved me. But the next day he was gone, no note, no message, nothing. We were to meet at the library on campus, but he never showed up. The next day, I went to his dorm room and his roommate said he hadn't come home that night."

Maggie stared away from Dean, biting her lip, her hands balled together in her lap. "I kept coming back, every day, for three weeks. It was the end of the semester and I didn't know what to do. When I returned home, my mother took one look at me and she knew. She didn't even let me stay the night."

Dean reached out for her hand. Her fingers were long and her nails cut short. He squeezed her hand gently.

"I was luckier than most girls in my situation. A letter came from the college, some family friend of Conor's. My mother forwarded it to the room I was renting. There was no return address. The letter was short, abrupt even. It said that Conor was needed back at home, family business, it said. It said that he would not be returning and that I was not to contact the family. And there was a check enclosed as well." She shrugged, her shoulders stiff, her eyes on the approaching storm.

"The check was enough to buy this house. It paid my medical bills and covered my nursing school costs. I returned to college after Teddy was born and switched my focus to nursing. I even had a little left that I set aside for Teddy for when he is older. My salary is sufficient. We make ends meet and in another year I hope to have enough saved for a car." Her head dipped down to stare at their hands, fingers entwined. "More checks have come, one each year. They stopped last year. I have put them all in Teddy's account for when he is grown."

Her hand twisted in his, "I know it is stupid, but I'm grateful not to get them. It felt like hush money...or worse."

"I have a good life, Dean. I may have made mistakes, but keeping Teddy isn't one of them."

"No, it isn't." He smiled at her, "He is a good boy, very bright and curious. And obviously well-loved, I can see that."

"You don't think less of me?" Maggie asked tentatively.

"Less of you?" Dean stared at her in astonishment. "*Less* of you? You had a child in the face of no small amount of adversity, and have cared for him well, despite being all alone. If anything, Maggie Aaronson, I think *more* of you."

Her eyes filled with unshed tears, "Thank you, Dean."

They sat there silent for several minutes. The wind was cool and refreshing.

Dean smiled, as the tiny drops of rain began to drip from the tin roof.

"I love the rain."

"Me too."

"I would like to see you again, Maggie."

Her voice sounded fragile, almost fearful, "I would like that too."

"This Friday? We could all go to see a movie."

"Teddy would love that."

He stood up, pulling her up with him. "It's a date then."

He leaned down and kissed her hand. "Until then."

As he left, she called out, "Wait! Do you need me to call you a cab?"

"No, I'll walk. Good night, Maggie!"

The rain fell around him in a light mist. And Dean felt his legs stretch and fall back into the rhythm he had adopted in Florida while writing his book. The long walks were just what he needed to get his thoughts in order.

The streets were quiet. Inside of his head, the words began to dance.

Closer

Friday, June 4th, 1954

The book tour had been slated to end next Monday. His agent, Scotty Abernathy, appeared to have other plans.

"Dean! The book is inching its way up the lists like a champ!" Scotty's voice blasted through the receiver. Louise Abney's eyebrows raised and she turned and walked away from the phone in the front entry. Dean held the receiver away from his ear, "You just edged out *The Bad Seed* by a camel's hair. You are on fire! We need to add some dates to the tour, my man. I need you on the next plane to New York, you can stay at my townhouse in the city. Y'ever been to the East Coast, Dean? You are gonna *love* it. People come to the big Apple and they never wanna leave. I'll take ya on a tour around the city. Show you the sights in between book signings."

Dean cleared his throat, trying to get a word in as Scotty kept on talking. "Scotty, I..."

"Look, you're gonna love it here, Dean. Be sure to pack light, the summer here is a scorcher."

"Scotty, I..."

"I swear to you, this city, it never sleeps, somethin's happening all the time."

"*Scotty!*"

Scotty stopped, "What?"

"I can't go right now."

"Of course you can. You come out here, the book will move up, up, up. Swear to God, Dean, you're gonna make it big, but you gotta haul your corn-fed butt outta the Midwest and come to New York."

"Not now, Scotty. Give me a few weeks and I can be back at it again, maybe do the European loop you were originally talking about."

"Europe's a goddamn mess, Dean. Y'know how many bookstores burned their books to stay warm? Y'know how many got bombed out of existence by the Nazis? Europe. Hell, that's where we send the folks no one gives a damn about. I'm telling you, ya gotta get out to the East coast. Listen to me. Right now, you're number twelve on the *New...York...Times...Bestseller...List.*"

The man enunciated every syllable, drawing it out.

"But you come out here, do some book readings, show them literate types you don't have straw in your hair and patches on your pockets. You come out here and I'm telling you that *At Winter's End* is gonna edge out goddamn Morton Thompson. He's been on that damn list for *twenty-five weeks*. That egotistical bastard has gotta go!"

Dean interrupted, "Scotty, I've got something scheduled for Friday. I'll talk to you after that."

"You got a *what*? Something scheduled? Is that prairie-speak for a *date*? Are you brushing me off for a *broad*? Dean, you come to New York, we got tons of broads here. Hot ones. I'll set you up!" Scotty's voice bellowed over the phone.

The crazy bastard is talking so loud the other renters upstairs will be able to hear.

"Talk to you later, Scotty," and Dean hung up the phone before Scotty could object.

Ms. Abney came back down the hall. Her mouth was pursed in disapproval.

"I'm sorry if that phone call was loud, Ms. Abney. Those long-distance calls can often have a bad connection. I apologize if it bothered you."

"You aren't a bother Mr. Edmonds, not at all. But that agent of yours. He could certainly benefit from some lessons on comportment and more. His diction when he tried to pronounce your name, it was so garbled I could barely understand who he was asking for. As for his dreadful nicknames. *Dino.* Does he think you are a dinosaur?" She sighed, "And is he deaf? Shouting that loud is simply inexcusable."

Dean grimaced, "He is a handful. New Yorkers, what can you do? Thanks again, Ms. Abney."

"Not at all, Mr. Edmonds. It is quite inspiring to read of your success in the paper. I have greatly enjoyed reading the copy of *At Winter's End.* Thank you for giving me a copy." Her eyes bored into his. "Your prose is truly delightful. I imagine that with your success, you will not be staying here for long."

"I assure you that I will give you plenty of notice, Ms. Abney. But for now, I have no plans of moving anywhere."

The next day, after an early morning jaunt to a Buick dealership on Truman Road, he pulled up to the small house. Teddy raced out to the car.

"Mister Edmonds! Mama says you are gonna take us to the movies!" Teddy was vibrating with excitement. "I've never been to the movies before! Can we see *20,000 Leagues under the Sea?*" His hair, recently washed, was breaking loose to form a jaunty cowlick on his forehead.

The boy suddenly realized Dean was in his own car. "Wow! It's shiny! It's brand new, isn't it? Wow! When did you get it Mr. Edmonds?"

"Just this morning, Teddy. I figured it was time to stop taking taxicabs and the bus everywhere."

"It's super, Mr. Edmonds! Are the seats leather? Can I honk the horn? Is it hard to drive? Will you let me steer?"

"Teddy, honey, try not to forget to breathe." Maggie laughed as she walked down the front path and laid a hand on her son's shoulder. "I'm sorry, he's been excited all day over going to the movies."

Dean sucked in a sharp breath. Her figure was flattered by the dress she wore, a crisp white cotton summer dress with lively yellow flowers printed on the fabric. Her arms, toned and tan, emerged from the short jaunty sleeves. The neckline dipped in a V-shape and the dress hugged her trim waist before flaring out in a playful skirt.

"Dean? Are you okay?" Maggie asked, a bemused smile on her face.

He had been staring, saying nothing, *again*. He shook his head, embarrassed, threw the driver's side door open and got out. He dug into his pockets, retrieving a small bag which he handed to Teddy.

"Forgive me for staring, you look beautiful in that dress."

"Mama makes her own dresses," Teddy piped up.

"Does she now? Well this one is very pretty." Dean looked at Maggie, doing his best to tamp down the desire he felt for her, one that she seemed to be returning.

"But not as lovely as the woman wearing it is."

Maggie blushed.

"Who are these for, Mr. Edmonds?" Teddy had opened the paper bag, which held two lollipops, along with several cabinet pulls and screws.

"Well, before we can see that movie, we have some work to do, young man. It's your job as man of the house to take care of things, and I noticed several cabinet doors in the kitchen are missing their knobs. Do you mind if I help you take care of that?"

Teddy's chest puffed up with pride, his face serious. "Yes, you may help me."

Maggie stifled a giggle, "But who are the lollipops for?"

Dean turned to her and winked, his face serious, "Why that is our reward, for later, of course."

Later at the movies, Teddy sat between them, his eyes wide with terror and excitement as they watched *20,000 Leagues under the Sea* in the packed theater.

As the credits rolled, Maggie leaned over and whispered into Dean's ear, "He will be re-enacting that last scene for the next *week*."

After the movie, Teddy had chattered with excitement as Dean led the way across the street to the local diner.

"And then Captain Nemo picked up the spear and stabbed the monster, *blamo*! And..."

"Teddy," Maggie interjected, "take a breath."

"This is tasty chicken-fried steak." Dean remarked, scraping the plate clean.

"I imagine you don't eat much home-cooking these days." Maggie noted, wrinkling her nose as she took a bite of overcooked green beans.

"I don't. Mainly I've been traveling on the book tour, and I'm staying in a little room for rent, so there really isn't much in the way of cooking to be done. Even if I had any idea of what to cook." Dean shrugged, "I honestly couldn't tell you a mixing spoon from a spatula."

Maggie laughed. "I wasn't much better off. We had servants growing up so it was a shock to be sure when I set out on my own."

Teddy was still talking, "And then when Ned killed the squid, I thought if they had a dog on board the ship, it coulda just barked and barked and that woulda scared off the giant squid."

Dean smiled, "Still set on getting a dog, are you?"

Teddy's face fell, "Mama says we can't have one."

Dean nodded, his face solemn. "Because there's no fence."

"Yeah."

"And because it costs to feed them."

"Yeah."

"Well, maybe someday things will change, son."

Teddy's mouth quivered up into a half-smile, "Yes sir. Someday."

They strolled to the car. It was still early, with several hours of light left in the sky, the air hot and humid. They had seen a matinee, eaten an early supper, and instead of heading for the Avenues, Dean turned the car north onto the Paseo.

"Where are we going?" Maggie asked.

"Have you been to Cliff Drive?"

"Not in several years, no."

"Do you mind?" Dean asked, reaching out to take her hand.

She said nothing, just smiled and shook her head.

The view of the city, the remains of the bluffs clearly in evidence, was inspiring. The city planners had moved vast mounds of earth in order to tame the land into the jewel of a city it now was. Dean slowed the car at the top of the hill and was rewarded by Teddy's gasp, "Oh wow! Do we live in the hugest city ever, Mama? Mr. Edmonds? I want to go there!" He pointed to one of the taller buildings in downtown.

"The one with the twin spires?" Dean asked, trying to see where the boy was pointing.

"Yes, the one with the blue green roofs!"

"That's the Fidelity Bank and Trust Building."

"It's so tall!"

"Yes, it sure is."

Dean's thoughts strayed to his discussion with Scotty a few days before. A day after the phone call he had received a telegram from Abernathy insisting that the book tour needed to be expanded. Ms. Abney had handed him a handful of notes, her mouth set in disapproval.

"Mr. Abernathy is quite persistent," was all that she said when he apologized on behalf of his excitable agent.

The truth was, he had no intention of going to New York right now. He didn't care if the book sold or not. Instead, his heart and mind were firmly here, with this beautiful woman and her young son. Here is where he would stay, for now.

Maggie's hand squeezed his, bringing his attention back to the here and now, "What are you thinking about?"

"My literary agent has been hounding me to go to New York for an extended book tour."

"Oh." She began to pull her hand away.

"I told him that I'm not going. Not for a week or two at least, maybe longer. Depending on how things go here."

He stole a glance at her face as the car moved down the hill. Soon they were lost in the shadows of the trees, surrounded by the green canopy. The temperature dipped and they all sighed in relief. It was cooler here in the shade.

The drive was empty, and Dean took his foot off the gas and let the car coast slowly along the winding road.

"Will your book sell more if you go on the tour?"

"Probably. But now isn't the time." He glanced over at her again, his fingers tightened around hers, "I have more important things keeping me here."

A smile ghosted past her lips.

"Is that a fishing pond, Mr. Edmonds?" Teddy bounced about the backseat, clambering from one side to the other, peering out of the windows, his hair disheveled from the wind. They had pulled back out of the canopy of trees and the body of water glinted green and blue.

Dean pulled the car off of the road and parked, "It is indeed."

Teddy wiggled in his seat. "Mama, can I go see the pond? Can I?"

Maggie nodded and as Teddy prepared to dash away, Dean called the boy back, "Here, you will need this." Dean reached into the trunk and retrieved a small fishing pole.

The boy squealed with excitement and hugged Dean before dashing off, the fishing pole firmly in hand, whooping with excitement.

An hour later, and a small horde of tiny fish, or perhaps just one very stupid fish, caught and returned to the water, Maggie shook her head, "How did you know he would like to fish?"

He snorted, "I didn't. But I don't know a single boy who doesn't."

"Thank you for this, Dean. You are so good to him, and to me."

Dean felt a stab of guilt run through him, "My son, Danny, he loved visiting this fishing hole."

"You must have taken him here often."

"See, that's the thing. I didn't. I brought him once. Afterwards, I always told him 'no' or 'later' when he asked. I was always too busy to go fishing." He sighed, "Too busy to do the simple little things with him. I never took him to the zoo, or the park, or even on a drive. I put off being with my family - being the father and husband I was supposed to be. And I would have kept doing it."

Maggie said nothing. She leaned over and kissed his cheek. He felt a flood of desire rush through him.

What kind of idiot walks away from a woman like this?

The drive back home was at a leisurely pace. The day was hot and they still had several hours of daylight left. Despite this, Teddy curled up on the backseat of the 1954 Buick Roadmaster and fell asleep, a glossy black arrowhead he had found clutched in his fist.

As they turned onto Maggie's street she leaned forward, confused, blinking in surprise.

"Dean? What in the world?"

There was now a sturdy picket fence enclosing the small yard and a large wooden crate on the front porch.

As the car coasted to a stop, Teddy woke up, his face flushed in the heat, sweaty strands of hair pasted against his forehead.

"Oh wow! Mama, we have a fence! How did we get a fence, Mama?" The boy struggled impatiently to open the heavy car door.

"Dean?" Maggie asked.

"I have one last surprise today."

The brand new gate squeaked and then slammed closed as Teddy charged through it, "What's in the box Mr. Edmonds? What's in the box?"

Dean got out of the car, walked around it, and opened the passenger door for Maggie. Her face was inscrutable and he felt a stab of fear.

Had he gone too far?

A scream of pure joy came from Teddy as he worked the box lid open. It was followed by a sharp bark from the fuzzy puppy inside.

"Dean, you *didn't*."

"I did." He waited a beat, "Please tell me I haven't overstepped my bounds."

Maggie watched her son dissolve into giggles. He had managed to lift the puppy out of the crate and was now being thoroughly washed. The puppy's pink tongue was moving so fast that it was blur. Teddy shrieked as he fell back onto the ground, the puppy licking him frantically.

"Overstepped? You have trampled the boundaries. But I have never seen Teddy so happy. I just don't know if I can..."

"He comes with a year of food. The account is already paid for at a local store. He's got two bowls, a collar, even a leash and ball."

"You thought of everything, I see." Maggie had noticed that her tiny garden was also enclosed and separate from the rest of the yard. A decorative gate, with a pair of gardening gloves, a metal pail filled with hand tools hung over one of the pickets. The puppy would not be able to dig into the soft ground or disrupt the delicate plants growing there.

"There's one more thing."

"Dean! No!"

"I insist. A big dog like that will need training. The breeder recommended a local trainer, and I've taken care of that as well. All you need to do is show up with Teddy and the pup and the trainer will take care of the rest. It is just a few blocks from here."

"I don't know what to say."

"You don't have to say anything." Dean took her hand and pulled her towards him. The soft lavender scent he had come to associate with her filled his senses. His hand held her hip and he kissed her gently, taking his time.

Teddy shrieked with joy, running through the yard as the German Shepherd pup bounded after him, nipping at his heels.

"We don't need to rush this, Maggie. Like you said. All we have is time." Her body shuddered in response.

Teddy rolled on the ground at their feet. "He says his name is Captain Nemo!"

Maggie laughed and shook her head. "Stay for dinner?"

"I would like that."

Breathe You In

Saturday, June 19th, 1954

Maggie was the first thing Dean thought of in the morning and usually the last thing at night. Teddy as well figured into this. The boy was friendly, enthusiastic, and well-mannered. At the same time it caused those ugly uncomfortable questions to surface.

If I had only stepped up, been more involved, would Danny have been a different boy? Less self-centered or belligerent?

As Dean pulled his clothes on, he did his best to push those thoughts away. Danny was gone. The pain of his loss was a dull ache in Dean's heart, as if a large piece of himself was gone from the world. No amount of wishing for a different outcome would make him suddenly reappear. This was the bitter part of the sweet he continued to feel each moment he spent with Teddy.

Dean heard the shrill ring of the phone downstairs and adjusted his shirt cuffs with a sigh. He heard Ms. Abney answer, then the familiar tread of her feet upon the stairs. A knock on the door confirmed it, "Mr. Edmonds? You have a phone call from that man again."

Dean suppressed a smile. After two weeks of daily phone calls she had ceased referring to Scotty Abernathy by name.

Dean opened his door, "Thank you, Ms. Abney. My apologies."

139

He followed her down the stairs. "He's quite persistent. You may consider doing whatever he is requesting, I fear none of us will get any peace unless you do."

"How well I know it."

At the bottom of the stairs he picked up the receiver, "Hello Scotty."

"Dino! For Christ sake, I'm a gonna come down to the boonies and fetch you myself. I've got folks calling all down the Coast asking if we can set something up and you are wining and dining some broad?"

Dean closed his eyes. "I know, I know, and the tour is important."

"Important? Hell, Dino, the books are flying off the shelves here! Every time you make a radio appearance the sales double. I hear Viking is authorizing another reprint and I got radio stations, *five of them*, askin' to interview you." His exasperation was clear even over the patchy connection. "But you are so damned busy playing Romeo to bother."

"I know Scotty, I know. I promise, it will be soon."

"You said that last week, Dino. I gotta have a date. I gotta have a *commitment* damn it, I'm trying to sell books here and you, my literary friend, are a real pain in my backside. *When* are you going to be out here?"

He couldn't keep putting off the inevitable. "I can fly out on Monday."

"This Monday?"

"Yes, Scotty, this Monday. I can give it five days."

Scotty began to swear loudly and Dean cast a glance around. Ms. Abney was out of sight, and he desperately hoped she was out of earshot as well. Scotty could swear worse than most. And the combinations he suggested, Dean was sure he had never heard such colorful and base words put together quite like Scotty could.

"Dino, damn you, now I gotta make calls and set it all up." He paused, "Be at LaGuardia by noon on Monday. How about eight days, no, *ten*?"

"Scotty, I'm giving you five days. Book me back to back, give me four hours of sleep a night, but all I can give you right now is five days."

His agent sighed, "Fine, fine. Five days. Damn it, Dino, just sleep with her, or marry her or whatever, but get over her soon. We got books to sell."

"I've got books to *write*, Scotty, *you* have books to sell."

Scotty barked out a laugh, "And damned if we aren't selling 'em Dino. Cha-fuckin'-ching! I'll see you Monday." He paused, "You know you are a goddamn pain in the ass, right? I'm gonna work you like a rented mule while you are here too."

Dean laughed and hung up. *I'll be lucky if I get a decent night's sleep in any of those five days.*

"Thank you, Ms. Abney," he called and walked back upstairs. He still had to take a bath and shave. This evening was special. Just him and Maggie.

Teddy was off with the neighbor, an invitation from months before to take the boy with the rest of the family and go camping. After seeing the two of them on a near daily basis, he and Maggie would finally be alone.

Just the two of us. He had picked the restaurant, a well-regarded one, and with a little trepidation and no small amount of hope, reserved a room at the hotel adjacent to it.

He had put the convertible top down, then up, then back down. He was standing there in front of the house when one of the boarders, a pinched-face girl barely out of her teens, came out onto the porch.

"Alice, isn't it?" He called out to her.

"Yes, Mr. Edmonds."

"Alice, I need a woman's opinion on this." The girl looked around, as if searching for the purported woman he was referring to before realizing that Dean was asking for *her* opinion.

"Oh, um, the top...down?"

He smiled, "You don't seem too sure."

"Well, if the top is up, the sun is off of her, but there's less breeze. Down and it will be bright, but airy."

Ms. Abney stepped out then, "It all depends on the lady, Mr. Edmonds. Is she very particular about her hair?"

Dean tried to think back. They had driven in the car, both with the top up and down, and Maggie hadn't seemed to mind in either case. *At least, I don't* think *she minded.*

Ms. Abney's mouth twitched in amusement.

"It looks very nice either way Mr. Edmonds," Alice offered, staring longingly at the car.

"It is for a nice dinner out."

"Definitely up, Mr. Edmonds," Ms. Abney said, and Alice nodded.

He tipped his hat, checking the time on his watch.

"Thank you, ladies, your advice has been invaluable." He slid into the seat and pushed the button to bring the top back up, used his handkerchief to mop his already damp brow, and put the car into gear, waving at Alice and Ms. Abney as he drove away.

The summer sun was still high in the sky as he cruised to a stop in front of Maggie's little house. Dean knew he had made a good choice when Maggie's front door opened. The pale blue dress was form-fitting. Around Maggie's neck was a string of pearls, at her ears was a pair of matching earrings edged with gold filigree.

"You look," Dean stopped, momentarily at a loss for words, "absolutely stunning."

Maggie blushed and looked nervous, "Is it too much? I could find something else. You said it would be fancy, but you didn't say *where*, so I wasn't sure."

He put a hand on her arm. "You are perfect, just as you are."

Touching her, he could feel the attraction between them and from her reaction, she felt it too. Her lips parted, and her beautiful blue eyes focused on his. Dean leaned forward and kissed her. It was full of promise and desire. Maggie reciprocated, pulling him close, mouth soft against his. The kiss lasted, intensified, and Dean stepped inside the house, letting the screen door swing closed behind him. The umbrella stand banging against the wall brought them back to present.

Maggie broke the connection first, licking her lips and staring at Dean with a mixture of desire and alarm. "That was..."

"Something I have wanted to do for several weeks now," Dean finished for her.

She surprised him by laughing. "Same here." Her fingers crept up to his lips. "But I think you have more of my lipstick on now than I do!"

Dean reached into his pocket for a handkerchief and wiped at his lips while Maggie turned away and used a small hall mirror to freshen her lipstick.

They walked to the car, Dean opening Maggie's door for her. She put a delicate hand on his as he started the car. The engine rumbled steadily, "So, where are we going?"

"How does dinner at The Savoy sound?"

Her eyes lit up. "I've never been, but I hear it is excellent!"

It was a short drive to the bustling restaurant. They entered and Maggie paused, entranced by it all.

"Oh Dean, look at those murals!" she pointed to one depicting a covered wagon with a team of oxen crossing a river.

"They were all painted by Edward Holslag, back in 1903. My parents collected some of his work and I still have one of them. Gloucester Harbor." Dean laughed, "Call it a childhood obsession, but all I wanted was to grow up and become a sailor. At least that was my life goal before I learned to read."

Maggie giggled and threaded her fingers through his. "Did you have a sailor hat?"

"How did you know?"

The maitre'd showed them to their booth and handed them both menus.

"Everything sounds fantastic," Maggie murmured, one delicate finger running down the list of entrees. "I don't know how I will make up my mind."

"They are well known for their steaks and lobster. However, if you are in the mood for something else, the Coq au Vin is especially good." Dean said, looking over his own menu. "I think I might indulge in a steak and some lobster bisque."

"The Coq au Vin does sound wonderful," Maggie commented staring at the menu, "Yes, I think I shall try that."

The green leather seats were surrounded by dark wood and the sun outside illuminated the art deco stained glass window above them. Maggie's eyes shone as she took in the tasteful decor.

Dean leaned forward and whispered, "I hear that President Truman sits in this very booth whenever he dines at The Savoy."

"*Really?*"

"Good evening sir, madam, welcome to the Savoy." The waiter wore a white coat and had a round silver pin with the number five embossed on it.

"I see you have water, may I bring you a glass of wine or a cocktail? Perhaps an appetizer to start with?"

"We will have some wine with our dinner. I'm particularly interested in the Crab Meat Ravigote for an appetizer."

"Excellent choice, sir. Are you both ready to order then?"

"Yes, the lady will have coq au vin with a Caesar salad and I would like the steak and some lobster bisque, please." Dean stared at the wine menu, "What would you suggest for a wine pairing?"

The waiter leaned over, "A burgundy would be an excellent choice for both entrees, and we have a bottle left of the 1949 Volnay. It was an excellent year."

"Yes, that will be fine." The waiter nodded, collected their menus and disappeared.

Maggie sipped water and glanced around. "I feel so out of place. I'm used to an apron, an overheated kitchen and a boy who hates eating his vegetables."

Dean laughed, "We could see if they have an apron for you to wear, but believe me, you do not look out of place. Not at all." He reached over and took her hand, gently squeezing her fingers. "You look absolutely stunning. If I don't keep your interest I fear that half of the men in here will swoop in and run off with you."

Maggie laughed then and her smile sent a warm glow surging through him. She was so beautiful. *More than that*, he mused, *she was intelligent, well-read, and incredibly kind. How had no one seen it before?*

The evening was humid and heavy as they left the Savoy, heading back to the Board of Trade garage where they had parked the car. The sun had slipped below the horizon and the orange glow of it was obscured by the clouds gathering, thick and billowing.

"It looks as if it is going to rain."

"Indeed," Maggie replied, staring up at the sky.

"Did you enjoy dinner?"

"Need you ask?"

"We men need our egos stroked often."

Maggie laughed, "Well then, by all means, consider your ego stroked. It was absolutely amazing. Thank you for sharing bites of your lobster bisque, it was divine. And the dessert," she sighed, "It was everything I had heard it was."

He squeezed her hand and they walked slowly towards the car.

"Maggie, I don't want this night to be over."

Maggie paused, stopped walking, and met his eyes, "Neither do I."

"We could, we could go back to your house. Or we are here at the Savoy."

Dean's stomach twisted with nerves as he said it. He shouldn't have called ahead and made reservations. Would she be angry? Insulted? Still, he would be damned if he would stand in a lobby and be turned away with Maggie on his arm.

"You made reservations, didn't you?" Maggie asked, tilting her head, assessing him.

"I did." His stomach did flip-flops. Had he screwed it all up? "That was very presumptuous of me. Is this the part in the story where you slap me, hard?"

A smile twitched at one corner of her mouth, her eyes steady on his. "I think this is the part in the story where the woman is rather modern and says 'Yes, I would like to go with you, Dean.'"

"It is? I mean," He blinked a moment, "Are you sure?"

She leaned close. Her lips on his ear, a whispered promise that sent waves of desire through him and he nodded, his mind and body full of thoughts of her and they turned back around and re-entered the building through a different door. Maggie's steps slowed as she gasped at the round dome of stained glass above them. They stood there, unmoving, and drank in the detail and workmanship in the glass.

"I love stained glass," Maggie murmured, her fingers entwined in his, "Such beauty coupled with utility."

"Indeed."

They continued to stand there looking up.

"Are they looking at us?"

"Who, the staff?"

"Yes."

"Don't worry." He slipped his arm around her and, finally tearing her eyes from the dome, Maggie walked beside him to the desk. "I reserved a room for my wife and I, it should be under Dean Edmonds."

The thin man in his impeccable black uniform with shiny buttons nodded, "Yes, Mr. and Mrs. Edmonds, we have you in Room 505." He did not ask if they had bags or needed a porter. "Please let us know if you need anything to make your stay more comfortable."

Hours later, in a well-appointed room, they lay close, spent. A sheet covered everything but one long, slender leg. Maggie's hair, so perfectly coiffed at the beginning of the evening, lay spread out in a fan behind her, the roots damp with sweat. Dean ran a thumb over her profile and she stretched, her eyes closed, a small, content smile upon her face. Outside the thunder grumbled and the rain fell in long, heavy sheets. The storm had cooled the air significantly, and a cool, damp breeze pushed its way in through the window, washing over them.

"You have be-spelled me, Dean Edmonds."

"I have be-spelled *you*?" he laughed, "I fear I must claim the same. You and Teddy both."

She opened her eyes, her face serious and troubled, "I don't do this. At least, not with anyone since, since…"

"Since Teddy's father?"

She nodded. "I just don't want you to think I'm easy."

His laughter echoed through the small room, "That is the last thing I would slander you with, believe me." He leaned close and brushed his lips against hers.

Painful Memories

Friday, June 26th, 1954

"Mr. Edmonds! Mr. Edmonds! Look what Captain Nemo can do!" Teddy was jumping up and down on the sidewalk. Behind him the puppy yelped with excitement and jumped at the fence in tandem with his young master.

Dean had just returned from a five day leg of the book tour along the East Coast. It was the only way he could shut Scotty Abernathy up and get some breathing space. After signing countless books at stores throughout the East Coast, he was wrung out, exhausted. He had visited five cities in five days before flying back to Kansas City. But the moment the plane's wheels had touched down his thoughts had been of Maggie and Teddy.

He had promised Maggie he would come by and see her as soon as he landed. Starting Saturday, she would be working night shifts for the next month. "Teddy will be with my neighbor at night, and I'll be so tired during the day I won't have much chance to see you," she had said.

"Hey Teddy. Give me a moment, son, and I'll get this old lady parked."

The boy bounced up and down on the sidewalk, "Can I help, Mr. Edmonds?"

"Well sure you can, get in and sit here, you can help me drive."

Teddy climbed in, settling his tiny body on Dean's lap. Dean's heart stuttered for a moment. Betty had been the same size the last time he had held her. He tried to hang onto the good memories, like how she had always smelled of strawberries.

"Mr. Edmonds?"

"Oh, sorry Teddy. I was a million miles away." He pointed to the side mirror. "Now you see this mirror here? We need to look in it and see how close we can get to the curb."

A few minutes later, he followed the boy in through the gate, Captain Nemo jumping up to lick his hand. The pup had visibly grown in just the few days he was gone.

"Look Mr. Edmonds, watch this." Teddy turned to the puppy, and said in a clear voice, "Nemo. Sit!" The pup ceased his bouncing and sat obediently, his big brown eyes fixed on Teddy.

"That's quite impressive, Teddy. Truly. I think you have a knack for it."

"Teddy has been working very hard with Nemo," Maggie said, a proud smile on her lips as she stepped out on the porch, wiping her damp hands on her apron. A spot of flour adorned the top ruffle of the apron, and there was another on her chin. Her blond hair was pulled back in an efficient bun and her cheeks were tan.

Dean smiled as he leaned forward and gently kissed her, "You have been getting some sun."

"Yes, the garden needed weeding. I had a few hours to myself yesterday and knocked it into shape. The salad and the baby potatoes are all home-grown."

She fanned herself, "It is a little warm in that kitchen. Summer is definitely here."

"You need a window unit," Dean said, immediately thinking of the one he had purchased for his room on Tenth Street. It cooled the room well, but was quite loud. Ms. Abney had ended up trudging all the way up the stairs and knocking on his door.

"That Mr. Abernathy called," she had said, her lips set in a thin, disapproving line. "He talked my ear off for five straight minutes. In the middle of his blathering there appeared to be one simple message."

"Oh?"

"Your book has now broken into the top ten, edging out *Bhowani Junction* by John Masters." She nodded curtly, "It is to be expected. I found John Masters book rather lackluster compared to yours. Has there been any movement on the screenplay adaptation?"

There hadn't been, but that was due to his reluctance to hand over the reins to anyone else. He wanted to do it himself and life had been so busy with the book tour. If only he could be left alone to write. Well, that and see Maggie and Teddy. The two of them had occupied his thoughts every waking moment, making writing, much less a screenplay adaptation, an impossibility. And every time he thought of them, memories of June and the kids entered the fray as well. It was hard, part of him wanted to commit fully to Maggie and Teddy, yet at the same time, it had been one short year. What would people say? What would they think?

Scotty had asked those very questions when he called Dean at the hotel in Atlantic City. Dean wished he had not mentioned seeing Maggie.

Maggie's voice jostled him from his musings, "Dean?"

He blinked, "I'm sorry. I've had so much on my mind with the tour and all that." He smiled at her, reached out and smoothed the flour from her chin, "You've been baking as well." The yeasty smell of fresh-baked bread permeated the house.

"Yes, I've made biscuits and gravy. It's tradition."

"For dinner?" Dean asked, amused.

"Yes, Mr. Edmonds!" Teddy bounced next to them, his curls dancing. "We have it every second Friday. Mama says that's when the sausage goes on sale."

Maggie turned pink with embarrassment, wiping her brow.

"Still, it is quite a bit of work to do in the heat of the summer. Whether the sausage is on sale or not."

"Summer or not, we still have to eat. An air conditioner would be nice, but I imagine the extra electric would cost a pretty penny."

"I could help..." Dean began, but Maggie shook her head sharply.

"No Dean, please."

The rejection stung. He tried to see it her way, even began to ask why she wouldn't let him help, when Teddy ran past, "Mommy, can I watch the television at Max Burkin's please? It's time for Captain Video!"

Dean was hit with a blast of deja vu. Captain Video had been Danny's favorite show. Just fifteen minutes of it, and so ridiculous.

"Mrs. Burkin has a TV Guide and it said that this episode they follied a plot to blow up the world but the mastermind gets away!"

"Did Mrs. Burkin read that to you, Teddy?" Maggie asked.

"No, I read it myself, Mommy. What does follied mean?"

"I think you mean *foiled*, sweetheart. It means that they stopped the bad guy."

"He's not just a bad guy, Mommy, he's a *mastermind*." Teddy corrected her.

"Right. A mastermind." Maggie's words were lost on her son. "Sure, go ahead, but then come right back home, you hear?"

Teddy yipped in excitement and ran out of the house, feet flying.

Danny had been like that.

"I can't believe it. I'll have to ask Mrs. Burkin if she has noticed him reading or not." Maggie was obviously excited over the news. "Imagine it, Dean! He's reading so young!"

Dean nodded, his thoughts on his own children. "Betty learned young, at four like Teddy. June thought it was because of her asthma. It kept her from running and playing with the other children as much. The cold, dry winters always triggered attacks, so she spent most of them inside."

Maggie's excitement dulled at the reminder of his dead children. "Oh, well, yes."

Dean turned to her, "I'm sorry, I shouldn't have brought her up, it's just..." He nodded as Teddy disappeared into the house across the street. "Danny was obsessed with Captain Video."

"I guess all boys are crazy for that silly show."

"I guess so." He couldn't help but relive the memories that continued to loop in his brain.

Teddy had pouted when the show ended and he had to come home.

The biscuits and gravy, normally something Dean would have expected for breakfast, was a welcome change from the endless string of greasy spoon cafes he had found himself dining at while on tour. Maggie was a good cook.

The domesticity he felt when he was here brought back rushes of memory. Danny and Betty at the table, sitting across from June. Maggie's house was tiny and quaint in comparison, but the food and shared meals reminded him of everything he had lost. Perhaps it was too soon. Perhaps he was rushing things.

"Dean? Are you all right?" Maggie finally asked, her pretty young face troubled. "You have been rather quiet."

Dean had been silent as he ate, lost in his memories, still decompressing from days of travel. Teddy had dashed from the table when excused, running out into the yard to play fetch with Captain Nemo, the call of the television traded in for an active back and forth with the pup.

They had moved to the porch, sitting down in the two metal chairs with scalloped backs. Dean's chair rocked back and forth.

"Sorry, Maggie. My thoughts are just..." His voiced petered off, lost in a sea of emotions.

He looked at her face. It was troubled. She stared back at him directly. "Dean, it has only been a year for you, you know."

"I am well aware of how long it has been." Dean snapped. He felt the sting in his words as they left his mouth, wished he could take them back.

"I just meant that..."

Dean stood up, "I'm sorry, Maggie. I shouldn't have snapped. It's late. I should go."

A moment later, as he drove away into the gathering darkness, his thoughts were not on his family, but that of Maggie, who had looked so lost and hurt as she stood at her gate, her lithesome figure disappearing from view as he turned the corner.

What was he doing? What was this?

In his rented room that night, Dean tossed and turned. There had been another message from Scotty, proposing an extensive tour through Europe, and a demand Dean call him as soon as he received the message.

Ms. Abney had written the note in her perfect flowing script, including quotation marks around Scotty's colorful speech.

Dean-call me, day, night, whatever. I sweet-talked the heavy-hitters in Europe and they are scrambling over each other to nail down a date with you. We gotta hop on this quick-like. I've wired tickets for the plane ride from Kansas City. Call me Dino.

Dean couldn't help but smile. Ms. Abney had no time for such extremes. Her view of the English language and speech patterns was like that of a drill sergeant.

His smile faded as he surveyed his rented room. He looked around, took in the single bed. The only other furniture in the room was the small dining table that doubled as a workspace and a tall dresser. A short, stout stove had been excellent at heating the room in the winter and serving as a cook-top for simple meals.

Here it was, a life beholden to none but his own whims. It was empty of responsibility and required no compromises.

Dean thought of Maggie and Teddy. It was a package deal, after all.

Teddy was a sweet boy. His mother was strong, independent, and hard-working. Alone, they would manage to eke by. Perhaps she would meet a nice doctor at the hospital, she certainly had the looks for it.

Dean had to wonder, was some of what he felt for this woman and this little boy some kind of white knight syndrome? Did he expect to ride in and save them both from a life of stretching the budget so they could afford a bit of meat once or twice a week?

Had he fallen from one frying pan only to jump into another? Was he looking at Maggie and Teddy as some kind of replacement family?

Dean sighed, slipped his shoes off, stretched out on the bed and closed his eyes. He could hear Alice trying to shush her wailing child. Susan, just over a year old, had been toddling about rather well until two weeks ago. Her mother had taken her swimming at a local lake.

Last week the news headlines had screamed *"Will 1954 Be the Year of Victory over Polio?"*

And then word had come of at least two dozen children sickening, all from the same lake.

Ms. Abney had updated him upon his return. Baby Susan's left leg was showing signs of weakness and it would not hold her weight. It remained to be seen how badly the child would be affected. Dean had heard Alice sobbing in the wee hours of the morning. The door that connected their rooms was bolted on both sides, but it carried sound better than the thick lathe and plaster walls.

If I feel compelled to be a white knight, better to help those two out. At least Maggie has the means to support herself. He knew Ms. Abney had been accepting partial payments from Alice for several months now. And even he had slipped a crisp five dollar bill under her door a week ago when he was sure she was gone.

He certainly could spare it, and she had enough to deal with at the moment.

Baby Susan's wails slowed and then finally stopped. Dean could hear Alice singing, her voice soft and soothing. Poor girl, she was scarcely more than a child herself. He had overheard Florence and Frances, the identical twin sisters in the double room apartment next to Miss Middaugh talking about her a few weeks ago.

Alice's husband had been struck by a car just one month after Susan was born. The tiny apartment had been all they could afford, and that was with Robert's job at the warehouse off of Hardesty. For now, Alice had a small stipend from Robert's employer, but that would run out soon.

Soon the song changed to soft sobs again. They invaded his dreams as he drifted off to sleep.

Dean woke early the next morning. The rest of the house silent. He sat down at the table and wrote a short note to Maggie.

Dear Maggie-

My agent has been asking me to extend the book tour to Europe. I will be gone for a few weeks. My regrets for not telling you sooner.

He then penned a note for Ms. Abney, and left his rent, along with an extra five earmarked for Alice and a short note asking Ms. Abney not to say he was behind it, before walking down to the corner market to call a cab. Once he was at the airport he would phone Scotty and tell him he was on his way.

A week later, in a bookstore with gilded wood and roughly patched plaster walls near Buckingham Palace, he read passages from his book, and then signed copies until his hand ached.

Maggie's face haunted his waking moments. He missed her, but he had to wonder, was he rushing into something out of guilt? Was he diving into a relationship in order to escape being alone?

"Mr. Edmonds?" The bookstore owner, a woman with frizzy red hair and thick glasses, stood in front of him. "Are you all right?"

He shook his head, "I'm sorry, did you say something?"

The woman gave a brief smile, her teeth crooked and gapped, "I was just saying that I had never seen such a crowd. Really, everyone is talking about your book. Have you started on your second one yet?"

Dean leaned back, massaged his stiff fingers, and shook his head. "Just some notes. I've been so busy traveling and lugging around a typewriter can be exhausting. I hope to start on it in the fall."

He looked around. The store was still full of patrons, despite the warm, sunny weather. He thought of Maggie and Teddy. The temperatures were soaring into the high 90s this week. He imagined the two of them in their tiny oven of a house and made up his mind then and there.

"Will you be heading south into Europe now, Mr. Edmonds?" The woman asked.

"No, actually. I need to return home." Dean said, gathering his hat and briefcase, "Could you please call a cab for me? I need to get to Heathrow as soon as possible"

He reached down, scribbled a short note and a phone number on a piece of paper and gave it to her along with a crisp bank note.

"And if I could ask you to just please send a telegram to my agent, Scotty Abernathy, and give him the following information, I would be forever grateful."

"Of course, Mr. Edmonds."

By evening he was on a plane that would take him back across the Atlantic Ocean. From New York, he connected to a flight to Kansas City. He arrived shortly before ten in the morning the following day. A note from Ms. Abney lay on the floor in front of his door, along with a small pile of mail.

He read Ms. Abney's note first...

Mr. Edmonds-

Your agent, Mr. Abernathy called. He sounded rather perturbed. He asked, no, demanded, that you call at your earliest convenience.

Yours,

Ms. Abney

He ignored it, started up his car and drove to Maggie's. The house was quiet when he arrived, Teddy and Nemo were obviously elsewhere and Dean cursed himself for forgetting that Maggie's shift had changed to nights.

She answered the door cautiously, a thin robe covering her. He could see her skin was beaded with sweat.

"Dean? What are you doing here?"

"I came back early from the tour, Maggie. All I could think about was you and Teddy and I couldn't stay away."

She said nothing, her mouth was in a tight line, her eyes apprehensive.

"I want to take you somewhere tomorrow. If you will let me. I want to show you this place, and get your opinion on it."

"I'm not sure that is such a good idea, Dean."

"Maggie," he took a deep breath, "I am so sorry if I hurt your feelings the last time I saw you. I've had some time to think, and now isn't the time or place for it, but I'm asking you, will you please come with me tomorrow? Say around noon? Or would one p.m. be better?"

She looked at him, obviously considering it.

"Please Maggie."

"Fine, yes. Be here at one p.m."

"Thank you, Maggie. I'll see you then."

Vows

Wednesday, July 7th, 1954

The next afternoon Dean pulled up at Maggie's house at precisely one p.m. The back of his collar was moist and the fabric damp, it was promising to be another warm, muggy summer day. He walked up the front steps, expecting to see Teddy and the pup come running out. Only Captain Nemo was in evidence, first barking and then leaping in excitement when he recognized Dean. With his free hand, Dean ran his hand over the dog's head and scratched his ears, ignoring the sloppy kisses the puppy doled out, his eyes on the front door.

Maggie stepped out of the house and shut the door behind her. The look on her face was guarded. Her hair was pinned in place and she was dressed in a summer frock with short sleeves that were cuffed. The fabric had delicate flowers in red, mustard yellow and cornflower blue which danced over a white cotton background. A matching belt was cinched around her tiny waist.

"Where's Teddy?" Dean asked, the present he had brought for him still out of sight behind his back.

"At the neighbor's, Ms. Burkin, why?"

157

"I found something at the airport and wanted to bring it to him." Dean put down the wrapped package he had bought on a tiny table there on the porch. "Well, perhaps later."

"Perhaps." Maggie's voice had a professional tone, the one he had first heard in the hospital. A stab of fear filled him, had he messed it all up, bolting like he had that last day?

He held the door for her, helping her into the vehicle before walking around to his side and starting the car.

"Are you going to tell me where we are going?" Maggie asked.

"I need to look at a house, I was hoping for your opinion on it."

"My opinion?"

"Yes."

She gave him a measured look, as if trying to understand what he was doing. The sun was beating down. It was early July, and the temperatures were soaring into the nineties already. It was going to be a merciless summer.

It took only a few minutes to drive to the house in Northeast. It wasn't far from his rented room on Tenth Street, another ten blocks to the north on St. John. They made small talk along the way, Maggie's guard lowered as he asked how Teddy had been doing training Captain Nemo.

"Well we have Sit and Stay down pat," she said, a smile creeping over her face. "He's been doing so well listening to the trainer. Teddy, that is, not the dog. The pup adores Teddy and does everything he says. You would not believe the racket that dog makes when I have to send Teddy to Ms. Burkin's house before I leave for work. You would think the dog's heart was broken."

"I found a book for Teddy I think he will like."

"It looked like a book. Which one?"

"Rinty. It's a Rin Tin Tin book and the dog on the cover is identical to Captain Nemo. I thought it might help with his reading."

"Thank you, Dean that was kind."

Dean turned left on Spruce, they were almost there.

"This is a lovely area," Maggie noted. There were children playing in yards and running down the sidewalks.

"Yes."

"Is this the house?" she asked, pointing to a smaller place across the street as they slowed to a stop."

"No, that one there, the brick house."

Maggie gasped, "Dean, that house is enormous."

He held the door for her and she got out, eyes locked on the house.

"The real estate agent tried to talk me out of it. It seems that everyone wants new these days. She heard I was a writer and insisted on showing me a half dozen newer homes before I insisted on something different. The house was built in 1901 so it is over fifty years old."

They walked up the front path to a large, shady porch. Instantly the temperature fell noticeably. "This porch is well-shaded, perfect for summer," Maggie noted.

The real estate agent had left it open for them and they entered through the set of leaded glass doors into a small entry, before they were faced with another set of large doors. The wide front entry was far better than the home he had shared with June and the children. She had preferred a more modern look, while he appreciated older homes, so their house, built in 1925, had been a compromise.

She turned to Dean, "You are asking my opinion on this?"

"Yes."

"Why?"

Dean smiled, "I just need a second opinion. I walked through it already, but I wondered what you would think of it. Is it a house you would ever think of living in?"

"Think of?" Maggie scoffed, "Don't you mean *dream* about living in?"

"Come on," he said, taking her hand, "Let me show you around." Her fingers stiffened, then relaxed within his grasp.

He led her through the house. She stopped and sighed, "Those stairs are stunning. All of my friends at work are obsessed with the newer architecture," she said, her eyes roaming over the carved banister of the stairs. "But none of the modern homes have any real class to them, no detail or workmanship. Just look there," she said, pointing towards the stained glass windows. "Such delicate roses. And the gold damask wallpaper is timeless."

Dean smiled, he had asked the realtor for just that detail, remembering Maggie's reaction to the stained glass at The Savoy.

There were four large bedrooms. By the time they had explored the second floor, Maggie was shaking her head.

"Dean, you can't possibly be considering this house."

He frowned, "You don't like it?"

"What? No, I love it, it's beautiful." She threw her hands in the air, "But houses like this, they need families. They deserve them. How many children did the owner have?"

"Seven, if I remember the agent right."

"Exactly, seven. You will just knock about in this place. It's too much."

"I never intended to live here alone, Maggie." He looked at her, his fingers running over the velvet covered box in his pocket. "You said I was kind, earlier, but that isn't what this is to me. You, and Teddy, you both mean more to me than some fleeting dalliance or interest." Dean reached out and captured her hand and then he bent down, his injured leg protesting as he balanced on one knee.

Maggie's eyes widened. Later Dean wondered if he hadn't have taken her hand at that moment if she would have fled the house.

"Dean, this is insane." She made as if to pull away.

"Hear me out, Maggie."

She stopped, her face a mix of emotions.

"You were just the person I needed in my life when I lay there in that hospital bed. You didn't sugar-coat anything, you didn't sing platitudes of my lost family, and you didn't let me lie there and obsess about what had gone wrong."

He pulled the box with the ring out, "You reminded me that I had the ability to make my life into a future that I wanted. That I could be a writer that I could dream."

He opened the box. Inside was a classical gold band. Three large round diamonds lay nestled within it, buried deep in a beveled edge. The diamonds sparkled, dancing prisms of light, reflected by the Edison lights overhead.

"You also helped me realize that, despite my mistakes as a husband and a father, I could be different, better. It took me some soul-searching. I went off to the book tour, wondering if I was somehow trying to play a white knight and ride in to save you. But the fact is, Maggie, that *I* need you and Teddy far more than you need me."

He looked up into her eyes, "You complete me. I love you, and I want to marry you, Maggie. I want to adopt Teddy, and spend the rest of my life with you."

He placed the box in her hand. "I want this house filled with a family. *Our* family."

"Dean, I..." Her hands were trembling, "Are you sure you are ready to take on a child that isn't yours? With your book, you are a public figure, this will end up in the papers. Can you imagine what they will say?"

"I don't care what society or convention says about us. Let them gossip about it being 'too soon.' I only know that I love you and Teddy and that being with the two of you feels natural and right. And if you feel the same way, then say 'yes.'"

He paused, "Or say 'no,' but one way or the other, I think you had better say it soon before I find I'm stuck here and can't get back up without help."

Maggie's lips twitched. "On two conditions," she said, trying not to smile and failing.

"You have conditions?"

"I do."

"Let's hear them then."

"I keep my job and you teach me to drive."

"That's it?"

"Yes."

"Done."

"You don't mind?"

"What, do I mind you driving? Maybe a little, you might be really bad at it."

The look of shocked amusement on her face was worth it. "No silly, me keeping my job."

He grinned at her, "Are you kidding me? I figure you are my backup plan in case the next book is a flop."

They both laughed, and Maggie leaned down to help him back up. "Then yes, Dean Edmonds, I will marry you."

Barely an hour later, and she sat in the car, staring at the department store across the street and refused to budge.

"I don't want a big to-do, Dean. People will talk."

"To hell with them. Besides, we are just going in for a dress. You deserve this, Maggie."

"But, it's..." She stopped for a moment, staring at the building with a mixture of excitement and dread. "It's *Harzfeld's*, Dean. It's so...*posh*."

He laughed. "You know what I mean, Dean Edmonds."

He took her hand, "I promise, they won't eat you. Sell you an expensive wedding dress, undoubtedly, but I've heard that shopping here is a fairly painless process, possibly even something that can be endured. I have also heard that some women actually *enjoy* it."

"It's too much."

"Please Maggie, let me give you this one thing," Dean had said in the face of her objections.

"You have given me far more than just this one thing, Dean," she said and proceeded to tick off the items on her fingers, "An enormous house, with no less than *four* window units, the dog..."

"That was for Teddy," he said smiling.

"The ring."

"I have never known a woman to argue so much against buying a pretty dress," he mused.

"It's too much! Harzfeld's is...well..." she stared at her feet, fingers twisting in her lap, wiggling her toes in her shoes. "I've never even stepped foot in that place."

Dean blinked, "*Never?*"

"Growing up, we had the money, I guess. Lots more than I realized. But my mother, she was raised to be frugal. She would never have allowed me inside that store, not if I'd been engaged to the king of Persia. And I've always wanted to go inside, not just look in the windows, but..."

"But what?"

"I'm nervous! I've heard how nice it is! They will take one look at me and know I didn't belong there."

"That's it, I'm taking you in there myself."

"You can't! The groom never sees the wedding dress before the wedding!"

"For you, my dear, I'm prepared to break some rules."

They finally had agreed to go into the store together, and after he walked her to the appropriate department Dean made his escape to the Men's Department, leaving her in the capable hands of a matronly saleswoman.

The next day he called Scotty and gave him the news.

"Well, damn, if Lucinda wasn't feeling so poorly, I would be on the first flight out." He paused, "The papers will have a heyday with this one. You know that, right Dino?"

"Don't the papers have anything better to gossip about?"

Scotty laughed, his voice loud and clear over the phone line, "Whether they do or don't, you can't blame 'em. Juicy stuff and all. Famous writer marries fallen woman and adopts her illegitimate son."

"Seriously? That's what they are going to write?"

"That and more, I'm sure." He paused for a minute. "But fuck it, don't you worry about it one bit, Dino. She sounds like one hell of a woman. Between this wedding and your abrupt departure from the tour, I'm going with the whole eccentric author angle. Your fans will eat it up. And it's sure to sell more books!"

Scotty had then put him in touch with a lawyer who, after trying and failing to convince him to get a pre-nup, had put together the adoption paperwork in record time. "Are you sure you want to do this, Mr. Edmonds?" He had asked.

"Yes, I am." Dean had said, his tone inviting no further questions from the attorney. The attorney had drawn up the paperwork to be finalized the day after the wedding.

The following week, they were married in a small, private ceremony. Maggie had chosen a simple, yet elegant wedding dress and her co-worker had done her hair for her. Dean's fellow roomers and Ms. Abney were invited on his side.

Maggie had one co-worker from the hospital and also her neighbor, Ms. Burkin, in attendance. Teddy stood stiffly in his new suit and took his ring-bearer duties very seriously, determined to make them both proud.

Afterward, the boy had flung his arms around Dean and whispered in his ear, "I'm glad you are my dad now, Mr. Dean."

"Me too, son, me too."

True Vision

Friday, August 27th, 1954

The typewriter keys tapped intermittently, starting, then stopping for long periods of time. Dean could not seem to get the words to come out right. He reached for his pencil and drew a line through the last two sentences.

"Dean?" Maggie poked her head through the mostly closed door.

"Hey, Sweetheart," Dean said, getting up from his desk. "How are you feeling?"

"Still under the weather," she managed a half smile, "Teddy's better, but my stomach is still convinced it is on a boat in bad weather."

He held her gently, lips pressed against her cool, clammy forehead.

Her face was pale and pinched. It had been three days since Teddy woke them up in the middle of the night, having vomited all over his bedsheets. A bath and a sleepy midnight cleanup had been in order. That morning, with the sun barely peeking over the horizon, Dean had woken to Maggie retching in the bathroom.

"Teddy was only sick for two days, but this seems to have hit me far worse," she said, leaning against him.

"Well, I tell you what. You go back to bed, and I will take that boy of mine fishing. We haven't been in over a week, and I am having a hell of a time working out the kinks in this manuscript."

Maggie looked relieved and concerned at the same time. She bit her lip, "Are you sure, Dean?"

"Are you kidding me? I *need* a break, the typewriter is winning this here staring contest."

Twenty minutes later, Dean kissed Maggie on the forehead. The poles were packed and he and Teddy would get a couple of sandwiches at the market on the way to the fishing hole.

"Is there anything I can get you before I go?" She looked so pale and miserable.

"No, I'll be fine, really." Maggie assured him, a wan smile upon her face. "I love you."

"Love you too." He kissed her again and left.

Teddy clutched the dashboard of the car while Captain Nemo sat in the back seat, the dog's tongue flapping out the side of his mouth as he leaned his head out of the window. Teddy talked a mile a minute. "Mr. Ed...I mean, Daddy..." The adoption had finalized three weeks ago, but Teddy still had trouble remembering at times. Dean was patient, it would take time, but the boy clearly adored him. The feeling was returned, in spades.

"Yes, son?"

"Are we going to the same place?"

"The one up on Cliff Drive?"

"Yeah, that one."

"Actually, I thought we might go somewhere different, somewhere we have never been before."

"Really?!" Teddy bounced harder. "Oh yes, please Mr...I mean, Daddy, yes please!"

The next few hours weren't filled with much fishing. Instead, Teddy, with his dog in tow, befriended another little boy and began splashing about on the edges of the lake. Any fish that might have been in the vicinity were certainly frightened away. This did not bother Dean. He watched Teddy and the other child splash and play along the edges of the water while he took notes, filling his notebook with pages full of looping script.

Stepping away from the typewriter, sitting here on the rock, it was exactly what Dean needed. He could feel the words rising within him, like a flood.

Clouds scudded across the sky, slowly building, and he could see the light dimming as the cloud cover increased. The wind had picked up as well, and it teased at the corners of his notebook, insisting he pay attention.

"Teddy," Dean called, "it's time to head back home." Captain Nemo had already tired of all of the activity and was curled up, fast asleep at Dean's feet. He raised his head when Dean called out, turning to look for his young master.

Teddy, it seemed, had worn himself out as well. He waved goodbye to his friend and jogged back to Dean, the German Shepherd pup jumping to his feet and meeting him halfway.

"You wore out yet, son?"

Teddy shook his head, but he looked done in.

"I'm going to sit in the back with Captain."

"Okay, son."

The drive back home proved too much, and at a stop sign, Dean looked back to see the boy fast asleep, his head pillowed into Captain Nemo's fur.

The clouds had fully formed and fat raindrops began to fall as Dean lifted Teddy out of the backseat and took him inside. The house was dark and quiet.

Upstairs, after putting Teddy in bed, clothes and all, Dean slipped the boy's shoes off and crept away down the hall to the master bedroom.

Maggie lay there asleep. And after a moment of watching her, listening to the steady sound of her breathing, he slipped into his study. He could feel the words inside him. They bubbled at the back of his brain, jumping about, jostling for position, and waiting for him to put them onto paper.

As the storm moved in, Dean began to type furiously, afraid that the spell would break, that he would lose the ideas he had done his best to jot down. They were there, inside his head and fully formed, just waiting to be brought out.

The darkness closed around him, only his desk lamp shone in the darkness, as he continued to pour the manuscript out on paper.

Two weeks passed this way, then two more.

Maggie continued to struggle with nausea, some days seemed worse than others.

The pile of papers had grown. It looked as if this book, *True Vision*, would be even larger than *At Winter's End*.

The weather had begun to cool in late September. The mornings held the chill of night and the days were noticeably shortening when Maggie slid into his office one evening. He had written pages that day, and could feel the end of the novel approaching. It wouldn't be long now.

"Dean, Teddy fell asleep before I could call you in to say goodnight. I hope you don't mind."

"He was playing all day with the other children in the neighborhood." Dean pushed back his chair and got up to stretch his legs and give his wife a hug.

"I think you are finally kicking this flu. You look much better this evening. Much better. There's even color in your cheeks."

He had worked straight through the afternoon, stopping only to nibble on a sandwich Maggie brought him.

She nestled her head on his shoulder. "I'm feeling much better today."

"Will you be returning to work soon?" he asked, not that he wanted her to. That had been a condition of her agreeing to marry him. She wanted to be independent, but he hoped she would eventually reconsider. He had several investments that were going well, and her income wasn't needed. She had been sick for weeks, and since she had transferred to the Infectious Diseases wing of the hospital, her manager had insisted she fully recover before returning to work.

"Actually, no."

"No?"

She pulled away, and met his gaze. "I finally realized, and I visited a doctor this afternoon to confirm it. I haven't been sick with the flu."

Dean, his mind preoccupied with his book, frowned. "Well what is it then, if not the flu?"

Maggie's eyebrows arched in amusement, "I'm pregnant, Dean." When he stood there staring, her smile turned down at the edges. "You don't look happy about it."

"What?" He blinked, "No, no, that's not it at all." His mouth opened and closed, "I was just so sure you had the flu, especially with Teddy being sick and..."

He stared at her, his mouth curving up into an enormous grin, "You're sure?"

Maggie nodded.

"Oh my love, that is such wonderful news!"

She smiled, her eyes dancing, "You are happy, aren't you, Dean?"

"Yes, of course I am!" He hugged her close to him, covering her neck and mouth with tender kisses before he pulled away.

"What?"

"I need to finish this book. Right away! Scotty will lose his mind if I make him wait until after the baby is born."

Maggie giggled, "Yes, he would."

"When are you due?"

"Late March, so you have a little time."

He pulled her close. "Don't you dare think for a moment that I'm not happy," he said, his mouth near her ear. "I'm over the moon, my love. A *baby*, my god," he smiled against Maggie's soft, lavender-scented skin. "You have no idea how happy that makes me."

She sighed, and leaned against him as he kissed her neck and nibbled her ear. "I should let you write a little longer," she began, "It's still early."

Dean reached over and flicked the desk lamp off, without letting Maggie go. He could hear her breath quicken as his mouth continued to travel, his hands moving over her body. "No, I think I'm done writing for the night. There are other far more pressing priorities to consider."

The walls rang with Maggie's laughter when he picked her up and carried her to their bedroom.

Little Sarah

Tuesday, March 15, 1955

Dean held his daughter, entranced by her delicate face with rosebud lips and the tiniest of birthmarks on her right cheek. Where Danny and Betty had both come into the world nearly bald, this tiny child's head was covered with a mass of thick blond hair. As it dried, he could see ringlets forming.

"Oh Maggie, she is absolutely beautiful." Dean didn't care who saw the tears on his cheeks as he looked down at his wife, her face worn, pale, and exhausted from hours of childbirth. An IV dripped fluids into her left arm and she held the baby with her right, lips brushing her newborn daughter's tiny forehead.

The nurse had come out first, their daughter in her arms, wrapped in a pink blanket and tiny pink knit cap.

"It will be a few minutes until you can see your wife, Mr. Edmonds, but here is your pretty little girl."

It had been a rush to get to the hospital in time. They had thought they had another two weeks, but the puddle on the floor of the kitchen right before dinner had changed everything.

The plate crashing to the ground had been Dean's first warning. It was accompanied by a pained cry from Maggie. "Dean!"

He had arrived to see her bent over, gripping her rounded belly, pain contorting her face.

"Mommy?" Teddy had looked terrified.

"It's okay, son," Dean said, his voice calm, at odds with his racing heart. He put an arm around his wife.

"Oh, Dean, we need to go to the hospital. The baby is coming quickly!" Her face held a fair amount of panic, and Dean held her close, feeling the twisting contraction run through her.

"Son," he said, turning to Teddy, "Get our coats and your mother's purse, quick now."

"I knew the baby had dropped, but I didn't expect this. I was overdue with Teddy by nearly a week." Maggie said, desperate to keep her mind off of the pain.

"Don't worry, sweetheart, I'll get you to the hospital," Dean reassured his wife, easing her into a chair so he could help Teddy with the coats. He could hear the boy scrambling in the closet.

A moment later they returned, a mess of coats and hats, as Maggie let out a muted groan of pain, her teeth grinding. "It came on so quick, Dean. I felt nothing and now..." She let out a full scream, her body convulsing, her stomach rippling.

Dean slipped her coat on, tossed one arm into his own coat, and picked up his wife up. Teddy followed, mute, terrified, and struggling to pull on his coat. They opened the front door to a whirl of snow. What had begun as a quiet, soft snowfall had intensified in the past few minutes. Fat, thick flakes of snow fell, obscuring anything more than fifteen feet away in an opaque white curtain.

"Quick, Son," Dean said to Teddy, "Climb in the back, while I get your mother into her side."

Teddy skittered over the seat, snow flying from his shoes. His face was pale and pinched, tears forming in his eyes. The plan had been for him to stay with a neighbor, but there was no time, not even to run him across the street.

"What about the neighbor?" Maggie asked, doing her best to recover from another contraction.

"No time. I'll call them from the hospital," Dean answered and kissed her. "Hang on, we're just ten minutes away, fifteen minutes tops."

"We will be telling this story for years to come," Maggie said, her face contorting with another contraction.

"Just as long as it isn't a story about our baby being born in a car," Dean said.

"Get us there soon, or I'll make no promises! Oh!" Maggie wailed.

The trip there had been terrifying. There was enough snow on the ground to ensure that the tires of the car could find no traction. In the last leg of the trip, Maggie's contractions were coming one after the other, and Teddy was huddled in a corner, his fingers stuck in his ears.

Once there, the staff had whisked Maggie away and Dean had called the neighbors across the street to come and get Teddy. As the hours ticked by he was thankful he hadn't asked them to stay. Just before midnight a thin wail had issued from the room. It had been another half hour before the nurse had emerged with the tiny pink bundle.

The doctor had come out next, looking exhausted.

"Mr. Edmonds, if I could have a moment to speak with you. Let's give the little mother a chance to hold her baby."

Dean nodded, handing the newborn to the waiting nurse and walked down the hall, out of hearing range. "Spill it, Doc, you are making me a little nervous here."

The doctor slipped off his glasses and rubbed his eyes. "Your wife had an extremely difficult labor and delivery, Mr. Edmonds. Your daughter was in the breech position."

"What position?"

"It is where a child comes out feet first instead of head first. Getting her out was quite tricky and unfortunately very damaging to your wife." The doctor looked away, down at the ground, "What I'm trying to say Mr. Edmonds is that I don't believe it will be possible or recommended for the two of you to have any more children after this."

Dean closed his eyes. She had wanted more, and so had he. They had lay in bed at night talking. Especially since she had realized she was pregnant. They had both been only children and wanted something different for their family. How would she take this news? Would two children be enough?

"Mr. Edmonds?"

Dean nodded, "I understand."

"I am sorry, Mr. Edmonds."

"Is Maggie all right, I mean, will she be all right?"

"Yes, yes. She will take a little extra time to recover, and I would advise against any, ahem, close relations for the next few months. But yes, she should be fine. We did give her a blood transfusion and she will need to stay in the hospital for a full two weeks to make sure there are no complications. Just to be safe, you understand."

"Yes, of course."

The doctor had shook his hand and left. Dean watched him leave, turned on his heel, and made a beeline for Maggie's room.

Sitting there next to her in the hospital room, and seeing how pale and exhausted she was, Dean was overwhelmed with a rush of emotion. What if he had lost her? What if the baby hadn't made it?

Dean remembered the first book Maggie had lent him there in the hospital, nearly two years earlier. "For life goes not backward nor tarries with yesterday."

Maggie turned her head up and he leaned down and kissed her.

"I think that is one of my favorite lines," she said, turning her eyes back to the baby.

"What shall we call her, my dear?" Dean asked, his eyes tearing up again.

"My mother had a younger sister," Maggie answered, eyes never leaving the baby, "Her name was Sarah Magdalene." I was named after her, but my mother never liked the name Sarah. She always called her sister Maggie."

She turned and looked then at Dean, "What do you think about Sarah? I've always found it a very pretty name."

"It means princess, if I remember right." He said, running a finger along the baby's delicate cheek. The tiny creature made a sound that was not unlike a kitten's delicate meow and then yawned.

"What about naming her Sarah Magdalene, just like your aunt?"

Her smile spoke volumes.

I Must See Them

Fyrsta Heim - The Cliffs of Behel

Zenobia gazed up at the castle, the bell signaling her arrival in The World uttered its first low gong, the note hanging in the air.

It had been a difficult journey. She had seen half a dozen Njerez on the road - with their dark hair and green eyes probing each car that passed with sharp attention. She had taken an enormous chance coming here. The bell rung again, the second note on the heels of the first.

But how could she stay away?

After two years of hiding, constantly on the move, she had only been able to return to The World twice. Each time, the cool salt air had caressed her face, a respite from the hot desert sun. A third gong from the bell. She could feel it in her bones, along with a low hum from the ground beneath her feet.

She was thinner, almost haggard in appearance now. Half a dozen times, possibly more, they had nearly been at her heels, the full force of the Primera Veu propelling the Fer Complir to hunt her wherever she went. Armed with farseers, Eryka Zradce leading them, Zenobia had been forced to move constantly. The village bell uttered its fourth gong.

She had prepared for the worst before setting on her journey to Rotterdam. She had hoped, after all, that they would be able to see that Conor was no longer a threat, even consider a more humane alternative to killing any newborn Bram, but it was to no avail. She smoothed her robes, composed herself, and began walking towards the dark castle rising up before her. The bell sounded again, announcing to all the arrival of a Protectorate in their midst.

She had hidden under the floorboards of the large produce truck - a trick from decades past when Prohibition had been in full swing and her mother had wanted a shipment of spirits delivered with discretion. A sixth peal of the bell. She had slid the boards aside last night, climbed in, and waited for dawn. The old farmer was as predictable as clockwork. The truck had been stopped of course, but none of them suspected the secret compartment.

Another gong rang through the air. That made seven. Then another.

No one had noticed the truck stop on the way back down. A small, insignificant road to the left, with a small stand of wind-worn knotty pine trees, provided just enough cover. Her limbs had creaked and popped as the old farmer removed the boards and offered his chapped hand to her, "Senora Saronica, here let me help you." He drew her up and she had groaned. Movement, after three long hours of immobility, was painful. "Are you sure you want to get out here, Senora? There is nothing here!"

"Thank you, Luis." She had sighed, sipped from the canteen he offered and then smoothed her hair back, and adjusting the pins that held the long tresses in place. "Yes, I am sure. This will be fine."

Luis had not seen the small building hidden behind the trees. Moments after his truck had rattled away she had walked the handful of yards to the small building, unlocked it, and backed the car out. As it turned onto the main road it then vanished with her inside, a sharp flash and crack accompanying her departure.

Zenobia came to a stop before the massive doors of the castle. She took a moment to stare at them, *who had made them? How old were they?* There was so much they didn't know about their own past. So much that had been lost in the Great Dissolution. She realized she was about to see something that none of her people in living memory had seen - a Bram manifesting his powers in The World. *We belong here. HERE. Not on Earth.*

She listened too, as the village bell continued to sound, nine, ten, eleven, and twelve. The ground thrummed beneath her feet, undulating with raw power.

It was time, after all, and she had been waiting for this moment for more than two decades. The bell sounded the final time, thirteen, and the notes died on the air as she waved her hand, murmured a command and watched the massive doors open for her. Zenobia stepped inside.

Conor had woken that morning feeling different. A deep, thrumming was rising up through the stone beneath. Here the ancient castle stood upon hundreds of feet of granite. The ramps and parapets hugged a tall cliff on one side, the mountain above disappearing into the mists.

On the other side was the ocean, a massive, roiling, ugly expanse of water. There was no beach, no gentle sands here. Not like the beaches in which he had grown up visiting often in Los Angeles.

Here the air was damp and cold. It smelled of fish and salt and it seeped into his bones. His golden skin had paled in his time here. He suspected too that time passed differently than in the distant world he still considered home.

He pulled his robes close around his body. He hated the obsequious nature and surreptitious stares of the castle staff. Seconds after his mother had disappeared from view, accompanied by a large crack of thunder, the immense glass wall had vanished. He had sunk to the floor, fury and misery battling for supremacy.

The servants had waited, held back from approaching, until he composed himself and stood. They had known he was coming. Zenobia had planned this, down to every last detail. The only fool here was him.

What had he thought would happen when he came of age? Unicorns would fart rainbows? World peace? He had read the histories of his people. It was required. A Bram could not be suffered to live. Once their powers vested at the end of their twenty-first year, the magic was wild and strong. Death and destruction always followed.

The people from the cliff village were ringing a bell. The first time he had heard it was seconds after arriving here in Fyrsta Heim. There had been only two other times since.

She was here then. He wasn't surprised. Whether time ran the same here or not, today had to be his twenty-first birthday. He could sense it. The World spoke to him, responded to him, and he could feel the power curling through his body.

He schooled his expression. He was watched constantly, after all. Their eyes followed him wherever he went, when they weren't busy scurrying about their tasks. He had quickly learned not to go to the village unless he was willing to magnify that staring many fold.

He had learned little since Mother had trapped him here. The village was the only pocket of humanity in the area that he could see. However, it was hard to tell, especially since his mother had given orders that he was to stay put. If there were a road out of the village, away from the castle, instead of towards it, he had never found it.

He thought of the baby. His and Maggie's child. He thought of Maggie, alone, frightened. Mother had promised that she would make sure that Maggie and the baby were taken care of. That had been such an empty promise. It should have been him. It could have been him if Mother had only listened.

The humans here would not have cared, and Maggie would have grown used to it. She would have been treated like a queen.

He paced the floor of his room. Beneath his bare feet he could feel the world vibrating from deep down. It was as the moldered texts in the library had described. He was sure that today was the day.

The room was more of a cavern than anything else. The walls were stone, carved and etched into columns, laurels, and wreaths. There were corbels, balusters, and even a mural, all etched in the hard granite. When he had first arrived, his tongue and limbs freed at last from his mother's influence, he had stared at these walls and more, for hours.

He had marveled at how long it must have taken the stone carvers to create this palace. The details were so intricate, so precise.

He wandered the levels of the palace, over twenty of them, his fingers tracing the carvings on each. The top five levels, where his room was, and where the highest echelon of castle inhabitants would have lived, were the most decorative. The tapestries on the walls were adorned with scenes of what the Njerez world looked like before it fractured, before the Great Dissolution. Lush forests transitioned to prairies and plains. Mountains meandered into desert. There were seas, oceans, and rivers scattered throughout, some labeled, most not.

Their world had never been as large as Earth, but it had been close in size. Conor thought often about the loss his people had suffered. To not only lose your homeland, but to have to exist outside of it, never returning, seemed difficult enough. But to live without magic, or not have full use of your birthright on Earth, well that was worse.

Mother had explained it to him when he was fifteen. The magic lay dormant within him, something he could only dream about, but that was more than any other of his particular kind could do. Mother had broken the law giving birth to him. And then she had broken the law every day of his life thereafter, keeping his true birth date a secret.

Just his thoughts dwelling on it made the ground quiver beneath his feet. Conor could feel the magic from Fyrsta Heim coiling and moving, slipping into his body. He wondered if the world had called to Mother because of it. Her job as Protectorate was to come when the World needed her, and if his magic was vesting, then it would most certainly do just that.

The World used to be full of Brams. At least, that is what Mother and the texts had told him. But with the fracturing of time and space, and the loss of not just an intact world but access to it, now most of the Njerez were restricted to Earth. Conor smiled. He was the only Bram in this world and now Mother would not be able to stop him.

She thought him broken, she thought that he had accepted his fate, but she was wrong. He might not be able to walk through the world walls like she did, but he knew that the way out was the way he had come in. He would use that, but only when she least suspected it.

The door at the far end of his chamber opened in a slow painful creak. It was heavy, made of a thick, carved wood at least six inches thick. The servant didn't bother to knock, someone would have to pound on the door to make themselves heard. It swung open, the thick cast iron hinges groaning in protest. The door itself had to weigh at least two hundred pounds, maybe more.

Alfriel, his back to the room and Conor, backed into the bedchamber, pulling a wheeled cart in with him. On the cart was a stone teapot and cups, along with a plate of various breads and fruits. Alfriel's greasy white hair obscured half of his face, and his frail arms struggled with the door.

Conor had railed against his fate for weeks, even months. The sun had risen in the west and then set in the east each day without fail. Yet another oddity of this fractured, broken world. The two moons, Grote and Min, had cycled across the night sky, unceasing. Eventually, Conor had recognized the truth of it all. If he wanted to get out of this place, he would have to pretend, and pretend well.

The feel of a pencil across paper had always calmed him, even centered him. He had begun to draw. First out of complete boredom, and later with intent. As a child he had sketched whenever he was frustrated, or angry, or alone.

The latter he had been a lot, his sister not a wanted playmate and no one else of his age around except for infrequent visits with Castor. His drawings had usually comprised of buildings, the low-slung adobe-style houses of the Los Angeles basin. But he had also been obsessed with imaginary castles, mostly from the stories he had read.

The Castle Behel was something beyond his wildest dreams. It wasn't just a castle, it was a monument to Njerez history. The tapestry that had captivated him that first day continued to morph and change. He had set up a table and a chair in front of it, and would sketch a part of it that lay unmoving. It seemed that the tapestry held parts of the world, perhaps all of the world, and all of its scattered pieces combined into one kaleidoscope of change.

Conor knew that the key to deception lay in maintaining a level of civility, of model behavior, that would serve to manipulate everyone around him. He slept in the chamber they gave him. He ate the food they offered him. He smiled and spoke to the servants in a polite and civil tone.

When Mother had visited the first time, it was to inform him of the birth. "They watch the girl, but I have my own spies. You have a son, by the way. She named him Theodore."

"And they are both healthy? And well cared for?" He asked, saying nothing else. It was better that way. She expected him to be upset.

"Yes, my son. I made sure that they are well provided for." Zenobia reached for his hand and Conor schooled his response. His skin crawled, the fury raged within him, but he smiled quietly instead.

"Thank you, Mother."

He had shown her the sketches then and she had admired them.

On her second visit a year later she had watched him, examining each reaction with a careful precision. He had asked after Maggie and the child again, then nodded when she reported that they were well.

As the power coiled within him, he counseled himself to patience. Today was the day. She was here, and he had his powers. Today was the day he would find Maggie and his child.

"My son," Zenobia passed through the door, Alfriel bowing low before her.

"Mother!" Conor turned to her, "Perfect timing, I was on my way to the village." He crossed the short distance between them and kissed her cheek.

Her brilliant green eyes regarded him, "Do you know why I'm here, Conor?"

"I would expect the world called you, Mother, isn't that the way it works?" He forced a smile onto his face. Mother missed him, wanted him to be happy, and so he would show her what she so desperately hoped for, even if it wasn't true.

"Yes," she smiled slowly, "of course it is." Her hand reached out, smoothing an invisible crease out of his robes. "It's your birthday."

He nodded, there was no point in denying it, "Yes. I can feel it. Is that why the world called you here?"

"I imagine so." A silence hung between them.

He smiled, and tucked her arm into his. "Come on, let me show you the project I am working on in the village."

He had begun it months ago, after stumbling upon some moldering tomes in the castle library. Careful to hide the one he was most interested in, he had filled one corner of his chamber with illuminated texts filled with forest scenes, stags, hunts and more. He had kept the small book hidden. It hadn't been easy.

He had caught Alfriel nosing about on several occasions, and had taken great pains to distract the old man by gushing over the other books. He had taken him by the arm and pointed out different aspects of the artwork within one that was crumbling along the spine.

There were so many books in the library that he had to wonder if anyone truly knew *what* was in them anymore. Many of the books crumbled at his touch, they were so ancient. But the small book, it had been hidden from the others, and his stumbling upon it had been such astounding luck that he still could not believe it. Spells written just for him, for his kind, so different from those crafted for the women. Here, in this slender tome he had learned his heritage.

Protectorates held their power in certain elemental magics - typically fire, air, water, and earth. Brams were supposedly wild magic, with no control, but this book clearly contradicted that. Brams held power over time and weather and crystals. It was something he had never been taught.

The Council and the Fer Complir, they are to blame, he told himself. *They twist our history, insist on murdering my kind, and manipulate the truth.* Once he had learned that, he had studied the book each night and began to memorize the words he would need - to gain control and his freedom.

"It is good to see you, Mother." Conor said, as they moved down one staircase after another to the Great Hall below.

"And you, my son." Zenobia answered, smiling. "I wasn't sure what to expect on this day, but it is very good to see you."

On the desk near the world tapestry, Zenobia paused, taking in the scenes depicted. One in particular caught her eye, "Well that looks familiar!" It showed the two of them there in the Great Hall, tall glasses within their hands. Conor hid a smile, it was as he had hoped.

"Well, far be it from me to interfere with the hand of fate," he said, and reached for the flask of wine. He poured a small amount into each of the two glasses, the deep red color bursting forth. "For you, Mother."

He handed her a glass and waited until she raised the glass to her lips before he sipped from his. She had not seen the two single drops of golden Majia wine present in his glass before he added the common red to it. He had read of the Majia wine in several tomes, but the slender book had gone into more detail.

To fully key a Protectorate with the world, a single drop or two of the Majia wine was consumed. Originally a rite of passage for all, it was now limited only to the women who made it through the world barriers. It connected the Njerez to The World and completed the magical link. Zenobia had mentioned it once in passing, describing it as the final step in

linking her to Fyrsta Heim as the chosen Protectorate for her fragment of
The World.

It had taken him ages to find it. Alfriel, his mother's seneschal had hid it
well in a box in the bowels of the castle. But by then Conor had become very
good at slipping through the halls of the castle unnoticed.

He swallowed the wine now, on the 21st anniversary of his birth, and
felt the drops slide down his throat. He had tasted the Majia wine before,
but it had done nothing. Today, however, was a far different experience. He
felt it building like an electrical charge as they continued on their way and
approached the tall doors that would lead out of the castle. It was just as he
had read of in the moldering book - the flow of power rose inside him, fueled
by the very center of their world, filling every part of his body with magical
energy.

His sip of the wine, combined with his birthright, bringing everything
together in a crescendo of power. The stone floor of the castle shook beneath
their feet and his mother, always so calm and collected, began to look afraid.

Conor smiled, and reached out his hand, encircling his mother's wrist.

"Conor? What have you done? How did you...why?"

Zenobia looked dazed, confused even, and he pushed his influence
through the crystal that hung at her throat, centering his intent on her, just
as she had done to him that day on the college campus.

"Really, Mother? Why? Do you really need to ask?" He smiled, baring a
row of gleaming white teeth. "After you took my love from me and prevented
me from being a father to my child?"

Her wrist darkened under his fingers, bruises appearing. His grip was
firm, but not tight enough to harm. However, the power seething within him
now was not a gentle thing.

"It is time I returned to Maggie. Time to meet my child and reclaim my
family."

"Conor, do not do this. You will tear a hole in time and space. You are
not meant to live there on Earth. Your power is wild, uncon..."

"Shh," he put his finger to her lips and looked deep into her eyes, still
smiling.

Zenobia whimpered, her throat closed as she found herself suddenly
unable to speak. He tilted his head, regarding her with indifference. With his

free hand he took the wineglass and drained it, emptying it of the last of the Majia-infused wine. He closed his eyes and felt the power surge again and the ground shake beneath their feet. The glass fell, dashing to bits on the stone floor.

Zenobia shook in his grasp, the line of bruises now traveling up her arm. He smiled broadly at her, "Come, Mother, it's time for me to find Maggie and my son." Around him he could see the castle servants appearing, looks of fear imprinted on their faces, terror in their eyes. They did not approach. They wouldn't be spying on him any longer, he was certain of that.

The car started of its own accord and he made sure not to let go of his mother for even a split second. By the time they were seated, her arm, from the shoulder all the way to the tips of her fingers had turned a mottled blue/gray. She shook in his grasp as if in a fit of palsy. Her eyes pleaded with him, just as his had with hers that terrible day she took him away from the woman he loved. Perhaps now she understood how it felt.

As they jumped through the World walls, he could feel every component of it. Before it had simply been a flash of white light and then the sight of this impossible place slamming into view. But this time he could see the world walls, a membrane through which they slid. As they reached the other side, the entire world seemed to tilt. They came out on the other side to a dark, predawn morning. Less than a second and the murky view of the pavement slid away as the ground began to roll and buckle, shaking mercilessly. It shocked Conor, and he released Zenobia's hand just as the passenger door swung open and she tumbled out into the crevasse.

There was no sound, no call for help, just a look of shock and horror on her face for that split second before she disappeared from view down the cliff face. Conor screamed, the sound lost in the enormous rumble of the earth splitting, calving, and chunks of rock flying past him from high above on the opposite side.

The Kern County earthquake would claim over fifty lives and shake for nearly two full minutes before the massive tremors ceased. Somehow, as he had forced Zenobia to take him back through the world walls he had also pushed time back. Instead of arriving back at the same time Zenobia had left - June 21st, 1953 - the clocks had rolled back to July 21st, 1951.

Conor was not aware of any of this. All that he had left was Maggie and their son. Mother was gone, a blink of the eye and the roiling ground had gobbled her up. *Had it been as she had warned? Had his power caused this?*

Conor felt a thick cord of fear rise up within him. He had to find Maggie and their son. If he could just find them, and then return with them to Fyrsta Heim, all would be well. Conor felt another massive surge of power coil and shift within him. He focused on the memory of Maggie's face, the smile on her lips, and he found himself in the dark. It was warm, humid and there was a driving rain. He looked around and realized he was standing on an unfamiliar road that was lined with trees, swaying and bending in the strong wind and rain. A glaring bright light lit up the blacktop and he looked up, staring into the headlights of a large truck bearing down on him. A bolt of lightning lit the sky and Conor was so close that he could see the driver's eyes flare in fear as the man wrenched the wheel to the left, into the oncoming lane.

There was the sound of a woman's thin scream as the truck impacted with a sedan carrying a family of four within it.

The violence of the crash shook the earth beneath Conor's feet, pieces of metal and glass flying past his face. He struggled to deal with the power that rippled through him again. If he could only find Maggie. His entire being centered upon her and he moved again, time bending in his path. Here on Earth, his power burned white-hot, as if a rocket where blasting from within, eating him up, and everything he touched.

Darkness again, but different, earlier perhaps, the sun's rays still lighting the sky in the distance. The rain poured down, soaking his robes, and they steamed. He saw the truck coming this time, and he crossed, striding across the road, his hair and face lit up in the bright beams of a baby blue and white two-door sedan. His heart pounded as he stared at the occupants in the car bearing down on him. A man, very much like the man in the Ford sedan, children in the back, and a familiar face. Older now, but still unmistakably her...

"Maggie?" Conor whispered. The driver swerved away from him, slamming into a tree and he watched the people inside, twisting, surging, the bodies flying like rag dolls. He reached for them with his power.

Schicksal Turnpike

Sunday, May 13th, 1962

"She's sick, Dean, and she isn't getting better." Maggie's face was pinched with concern.

"It looks like measles." She continued, nibbling on her lower lip and staring at little Sarah. Their daughter was asleep, her breathing rough and her skin flushed.

"But the doc gave her that new vaccine," Dean said, running a hand over Sarah's arm. "Jesus, she's *burning up.*"

"That's what I'm saying," Maggie said and then winced. "I'm sorry, that sounded far more like a snap than I intended it to be."

Dean reached out and squeezed his wife's shoulder, "You are worried about her. And if you are worried, then I think I had better be too. The wind and rain are really picking up out there, though."

He walked over to the window. Outside the streetlights were just flickering on, but they were almost invisible, impossible to see through the driving rain and howling wind.

"I just don't think we should wait any longer on this, Dean. She won't eat, and I could barely get her to sip the water. The high fever is the worst part of it. If it gets much higher..." Maggie's lips thinned in a tight line of worry.

Sarah twisted, turning her head away from them. Her blond curls were plastered to her head, her cheeks bright pink. She was drenched in sweat, her clothing damp and sticking to her skin. A swath of the ugly flat red rash had spread over her delicate pale skin all the way from her midsection down to her legs. It was now moving to her arms and neck.

"It has to be measles." Maggie said, reading from one of her medical textbooks. "See here it says, 'Initial signs and symptoms typically include fever, often greater than one hundred and four degrees, cough, runny nose, and inflamed eyes. Two or three days after the start of symptoms, small white spots may form inside the mouth, known as Koplik's spots. A red, flat rash which usually starts on the face and then spreads to the rest of the body typically begins three to five days after the start of symptoms."

She ran her hand across her daughter's forehead. "She's just so *hot*, Dean."

Dean stared out at the rain lashing the window. He hated to drive in weather like this. And tonight of all nights, he felt the fear crawling in his heart. Nine years ago today, and here was yet another storm. He thought of Betty, he couldn't help but compare it with Sarah being ill. There were too many reminders.

His eyes closed for a moment, remembering his family. What would it have been like, if they had survived? Would he have become a writer or just kept soldiering on, wretched and spreading his misery to the rest of them?

Danny would be a teenager now, possibly even driving. And Betty would have just begun diving into adolescence. She would have been a beauty, with her tight curls and big brown eyes. He would have had to beat the boys away with a stick!

He had visited their graves earlier in the day, when the air held the promise of rain and the wind had riffled his hair steadily. No one else visited, but Maggie wasn't the jealous, small-minded sort. Without a word, she had picked some flowers that morning, a huge bunch of iris in a riot of colors. Maggie had tied them with a piece of ribbon and set them in a simple vase for him next to the front door to take to the grave site. He had kissed her then, her thoughtfulness filling his heart. *How had he gotten so lucky?*

It was something the two women had in common - both loved flowers. June had overseen the establishment of multiple flower gardens in their old house, directing their gardener and poring over seed and bulb catalogs in the winter.

Her precise, well-defined landscaping choices had helped attract a buyer and sell the property in record time when he had decided to sell the house on Grand.

Maggie didn't have the same taste for well-manicured lawns and perfectly placed plants. Instead, her flowers were a riot of colors throughout the growing season. The yard was a jungle of plants, scattered paths, and a large green space for the children and the dog to run. Captain Nemo was feeling his age these days, and had slowed down significantly this year, the dog's hips an obvious source of pain. Teddy, now almost twelve, still spent time walking his beloved hound each day. But he now spent more time riding his bicycle and running through the wild spaces with the other neighborhood boys.

"Dean?" He opened his eyes to see Maggie watching him, tight little lines of worry around her eyes. "Would you prefer me to drive?"

It didn't matter what day it was. Sarah was sick. He shook his head. "I'll drive. You get her ready and I'll go start the car."

Minutes later, they eased out of the driveway. The water roared down, drumming on the car, the windshield wipers trying, and failing, to keep up. The water poured from the dark skies, night had come early, the gray-black clouds blocking any remaining rays. Dean focused on the road.

They would need to head down Benton to Truman and then turn towards the south. As they eased onto Benton, several sections of the road were awash, water rushing past the car tires and the overloaded sewers.

Despite the street lights, the darkness was overwhelming. Teddy sat in the back seat, holding a cold compress to Sarah's face, her head in his lap. Despite a gap of nearly five years, the two siblings were close. Two weeks ago, Dean had watched from his office window as Teddy stopped playing with his friends and ran over to help Sarah up after she had tripped and fallen while skating down the street. He kept an eye out for her wherever they went, conscientious and kind without fail.

Maggie looked back over her shoulder, obviously worried. "It's okay Mom, I've got her."

Maggie smiled, "Thank you, sweetheart."

"This rain, my god, it is as if the floodgates have been opened in the heavens." Dean gritted his teeth, his eyes glued to the road. A dull red light flashed in the street. A patrol car, its red dome light flashing, blocked the wide street. A police officer, covered in a poncho, held his hand out authoritatively. "What the...damn it, they've closed the road!"

The next ten minutes were a series of turns onto increasingly dark roads. Every time Dean found a road leading in the direction of Hospital Hill there would be an accident or flooding. Dean kept turning and turning, hoping to find a way south. Soon there was nothing to help them keep track of which way they were headed. A tremendous explosion sounded and the street lights, along with all of the homes in view, went dark.

"A power outage. That must have been the transformer that blew." Maggie said, peering into the darkness.

Dean's dread at being out on this night of all nights, on unfamiliar roads, in a storm, was settling into his chest, making breathing difficult.

"I'm completely lost. Do you recognize anything?" He asked.

"No, nothing. I can't even see in all of this. The blackout must be citywide, even downtown has gone dark." They turned again, and the trees, swaying and bending on the side of the road, closed in around them. "Could we be on Cliff Drive?"

In the backseat, Sarah sobbed, "It hurts Mommy, and I'm so hot!"

Dean stiffened. "Oh...god." The headlights of their car, combined with a sudden flash of light, had lit up their surroundings. He remembered this place, he remembered it far too well. His guts churned full of coldness.

"Dean? What's wrong?" Another burst of lightning, "The sign says Schicksal Turnpike," Maggie said, pointing to a street sign that was being buffeted about by the wind.

Dean's body felt as if he had just taken an ice water bath. "No, no, no..."

A brilliant flash of light illuminated the roadway before them. In the middle of the lane a young man appeared, his black robes streaming behind him, turned into the illusion of great blackbird wings in the wildness of the storm.

Maggie gasped, her eyes round with horror and shock, "Conor!"

She screamed as Dean wrenched the wheel to the right, rocketing off of the road, time measured in sound. The roar of the engine, the deafening crash, and the sound of breaking glass. Finally, there was nothing but the sound of the horn, the bark of thunder above them, and the steady stream of water from the heavens. Another strobe of lightning illuminated the car crumpled against the base of a large maple tree. Twisted steel, broken glass, and silence.

Dreams and Words

The blackness seemed absolute. Within it, Dean existed. He could not feel his body, nor any sense of touch whatsoever. No light penetrated, no sounds, save soft, indistinct whispers. It was maddening. He listened to the sounds just on the edge of his hearing, desperate to know what they were. Were they voices? Some clue as to where he was?

He tried to call out, move his hands, anything - but in the darkness there was nothing. The quiet whispers came and went and no matter how hard he tried, he could not make out what they were saying. There was no sense of cold, warmth, or even pain. Only a yawning nothingness in the void.

Trapped in it, his mind active even if his body was not, he tried to count the seconds that passed. But numbers had no meaning here, time did not exist.

It might have been mere seconds or a thousand hours before it all changed.

The darkness cleared, showing a clear evening sky unlike any he had ever seen before. Two moons hung bright and full in the sky above him, and he could feel the rough cobblestone road under his feet. There was a smell of salt and sea in the air and the wisps of fog eddied close. They slid by him, touching his skin with an icy, damp caress. To his left, a sharp cliff descended to the pounding surf below. On his right a looming cliff face stretched up out of sight, the top of it hidden in mist and darkness. Behind him, a bell began to toll. Thirteen deep, resonant tones before it stopped.

Dean stared at the narrow, cobblestone road before him. It ended, quite dramatically, in the largest castle he had ever seen. Constructed of stone, the walls stretched up, reaching for the moons that hung above in the sky. A set of tall wooden doors opened, groaning as they slowly turned on massive iron brackets. Dean walked forward, through the doors, his breath hitching in his chest as he stepped inside the enormous building. Inside was even more impressive than outside. The entrance hall was lined with lit torches, flames flickering, gyrating. Above them were perhaps twenty or more levels of floors - walkways, doors, and balconies - a dizzying array of space, capped with a stunning stained glass skylight. The beams of colored light danced on his face more than two hundred feet below, lit by the rays of the bright, full moons. *This isn't my world. It can't be.* Dean struggled to understand what he was seeing and experiencing. He tore his gaze away from the brilliant skylight and cast a glance around the echoing entrance chamber. On one wall was a tapestry that appeared to be moving. The figures shifted, changed, and as he watched, he saw the history of this alien place unfolding. A great cataclysm, fire in the sky, and people fleeing through a rift. He walked towards it, soaking in the details, desperate to remember every moment it showed.

The gasp behind him ripped his attention away. Standing there behind him, just out of reach on the rich carpet, stood Maggie. Her dress was soaking wet from the rain, plastered to her body. She didn't see him, her eyes riveted on the young man standing in front of her. Dean could see his face clearly. It was the same young man he had seen standing in the road - the one he had swerved to avoid hitting. His hair was raven black, straight, and settled at his shoulders. He turned for a moment and looked straight at Dean, his green eyes assessing and understanding the relationship.

Dean watched as the young man turned back to Maggie.

"Maggie, my love. I am so sorry. I wasn't given a choice. I know that it doesn't matter now, but I did try to return to you."

Maggie reached out her hand and touched his cheek, "Conor?"

"I messed this all up, so bad. And I'm sorry for that. Sorrier than you can know, Maggie." The young man had tears in his eyes. "I can't fix it all, but I can make sure our son is safe, that he survives to live his life."

He turned back to Dean, his face full of anguish. "The accidents weren't your fault, neither of them. Thank you for loving Maggie and our son. I will try to right things for you."

Maggie turned back, spying Dean for the first time and reached for him as she cried out his name.

The blackness that surrounded the three of them exploded with light. The road and castle vanished as the light burst forth from everywhere, bleaching out any other details. Dean reached out for Maggie, his fingers missing her and instead brushing against the fabric of her dress for a brief instant before she was gone.

Dean was utterly alone in the bright white wash of light.

In some ways, the light was more terrifying than the dark had ever been. In the dark, there was a chance that something, someone might be there. Friend or foe, the darkness hides everything. But now? Dean knew there was no one else there with him.

How long it surrounded him he couldn't say. It seemed like forever, an endless moment strung out where time had no meaning. After a while, small sounds began to pierce the bright white void.

He heard the voice first. Quiet, a bare murmur. He concentrated on it, all of his being set on listening to what it had to say. Listening for minutes, possibly hours or days.

"Dean, come back to me."

The white light never wavered, and it seemed infinite. Was he dead? Was this the afterlife?

Again, the voice...

"Dean? I'm right here, holding your hand."

Another voice, lower in pitch said, "Keep talking, Mrs. Edmonds, who knows what they hear?"

If he was in the afterlife, in heaven, where was everyone else? His heart skipped a beat as he thought of Teddy and Sarah. But they weren't here, were they? Did that mean that they had lived?

In the light he waited, suspended. Occasionally he heard murmurs, voices. Some familiar, some not.

There was no need for breath, for food, for rest. He couldn't feel anything. Dean tried wiggling his fingers, his toes, even turning his head. Nothing.

Was this it? Was he doomed to exist here, in this halfway place, stuck between life and death?

"Let's see if we can't get some response here, Mr. Edmonds." A male voice said. "Hm, the patient's pupils responsive. And I'm seeing standard nerve responses." There was a pause.

"His head wound has healed well. That was a nasty crack on the head he took, Mrs. Edmonds."

Dean waited, hoping to feel something. The doctor's hands on him, any small wavering from this bright, shadow-less light that surrounded him. There was nothing, he was nothing.

"Will he wake up? Will he...will he be..." her voice cracked. "The children are asking to see him."

Dean wanted to reassure her, tell her it was all okay, but he had no idea how. The children though, the children were safe, alive. He felt such relief at that news.

"Head injuries can be tricky, and they take time to heal. The children should wait until their father regains consciousness to visit." The doctor's voice was kind, yet matter-of-fact. "It is important that you are patient and keep a positive outlook. I've been studying coma patients for years. It helps to talk to them, tell them about your day, the weather, and their favorite foods. Anything really. Just be patient, Mrs. Edmonds, it has been less than two weeks. He was the most seriously injured of all of you."

She didn't respond, but he could hear her crying. Dean willed his mouth to work, to make even the most minuscule of sounds. There was nothing no matter how hard he tried. Held in this brightness, he was alone. He could hear everything, but say nothing. It was maddening.

"There, there, Mrs. Edmonds. Perhaps you should go home, focus on your children and come back tomorrow. You need to keep your strength up, I wouldn't want you back here in the hospital. Your children need you." The doctor reassured her, "Take the rest of the day, eat, and be with your children. You have a fine son and daughter."

"Yes, Doctor, I'll do that." She said, still crying. Her voice was muffled now, probably buried within a handkerchief.

Dean could hear the squeak of a nearby chair and her sobs faded slowly from the room.

The doctor's voice, so close to his ear, startled him.

"Mr. Edmonds, if you can hear me, I highly recommend you wake up soon." The doctor's voice was heavy with concern. "Your family needs you and your time is running out."

Dean could hear steps approaching, then a woman's voice, older, her voice rough and hoarse, as she said, "Good evening, Doctor. Any change?"

"No."

"Shall I note a prognosis in the chart?"

"Prognosis? Hm, yes. Prognosis unclear." The doctor sighed then, "Honestly? I give him less than a twenty percent chance of ever waking up. For all I know, the man might be a vegetable." The doctor sighed. "I can't bear to tell that pretty blond wife of his. She has barely left his side."

The doctor and nurse walked away, their voices fading.

Dean remained alone, frozen in a sea of white light.

A New Day Dawns

Wednesday, June 10th, 1953

The first sound Dean heard was a steady breathing. Someone close by, sleeping perhaps?

After a few moments more sounds joined in. The steady murmur of voices, which seemed to rise and fall over time. The grinding of a metal cart as it came closer, then receded.

Where was he?

The acrid reek of antiseptic, along with the insidious hint of sick mixed in told him he was in a hospital.

Dean forced his eyes open. It hurt. Everything was so bright and the figure before him was haloed by the beam of sunlight pouring in the windows from behind. He blinked, willing his eyes to focus.

The figure leaned closer, "Dean?" Her features resolved, into a mass of curly blond hair, and...

How was this possible?

"Dean?" She smiled at him, "Nurse! He's waking up!"

His mouth opened and closed. "Muh...Maggie?"

The squeak of shoes in the hallway signaled the arrival of another - a hand on his wrist, cool fingers against his skin.

"I've called the doctor, Mrs. Edmonds, he should be here in a moment." Her hand moved to his arm, "Mr. Edmonds? Can you hear me?"

The nurse had a rough, almost gravelly voice. She smelled faintly of cigarettes.

Dean blinked, struggling to adjust to sunshine that still poured into the room. "Wh-What?"

June leaned close, tears in her eyes. "Oh Dean, I have been waiting and waiting for you to wake up. The children..." she choked back a sob, "the children have been asking about you every day."

Dean croaked out the words. "June? Where's Maggie?"

"Who?" June glanced back at the nurse, "Is there a nurse named Maggie here?"

'On this floor? No, Mrs. Edmonds." The older woman shook her head, "Edna and I handle the day shift, and then there is a Laura and Delia on the night shift." More footsteps, and more. Blurry figures began filling the room. Their features were indistinct. *Where were his glasses? Had he lost them in the crash?*

The doctor, a tall, thin man with long, delicate fingers pushed past the others as he hurried into the room. He wore thick, horn-rimmed glasses. "Mr. Edmonds! What a pleasure it is to see you have finally rejoined us!"

He pulled up a wheeled chair on Dean's left, focusing on his watch as he checked Dean's pulse and then leaned close. "You took my advice, I see."

"Ad-advice?" Dean managed, his throat was parched, his tongue swollen and thick.

"Yes. I've had several rather one-sided discussions with you recently on the importance of waking up. You've been in a coma for three weeks, Mr. Edmonds. Do you remember why?"

"There was a man...in the road."

"A man in the road, you say?" The doctor glanced over at June who shook her head. "And here I thought it was a truck. Nevertheless, you are awake and that is a very good sign. I'm going to conduct some tests and then we will see if you are up to drinking some water and talking with your lovely wife, who has been by your side this entire time."

The doctor turned and smiled in June's direction.

"Practically starved sitting here waiting for you to wake up."

He reached out a hand and the nurse handed him a chart. He studied it for a moment and then plucked a ballpoint pen out of his pocket. The doctor nodded to the nurse as he eyed the crowd of people.

"Please clear the room."

He turned his attention back to Dean, "You have garnered a fair amount of attention it seems. Would you care for some water, Mr. Edmonds?"

"Yes, please."

The nurse and the doctor propped him up in the bed. His ribs hurt, as did his right leg. Propped up with pillows behind him he could see that it was encased in a heavy white cast with weights hung from the back of the bed to provide traction.

June was still crying, yet smiling at the same time. Dean felt confused, his head swam with questions that he could not seem to formulate. How was June here? Where were Maggie and the children?

A cup appeared with a straw and he sipped it, coughing, as the first liquids in weeks slid down his throat.

"Good job, Mr. Edmonds." The nurse also clucked her approval.

The doctor checked his reflexes on his left foot, peered into his eyes, and took his pulse. "Excellent, all excellent, Mr. Edmonds. Why don't we check just a few more things, starting with your age?"

"I'm thirty-six."

The doctor lifted an eyebrow. "What is your birth date, Mr. Edmonds?"

"September fifteenth, nineteen twenty-five." The doctor looked at the nurse and at June.

"And what year is it, Mr. Edmonds?"

"Nineteen sixty-two." Dean could hear June gasp.

"What is your address, Mr. Edmonds?"

"Three twenty-three Cypress Avenue, in Kansas City." June gasped again, tears forming in her eyes.

"I see, and you have children?"

"Yes. Teddy and Sarah."

June began to sob, the nurse patted her back.

"Mr. Edmonds, the year is 1953, not 1962." The doctor said, a look of concern on his face. "Your chart indicates that you live at 5900 Grand. And your children's names are..." He looked over at June.

"Betty and Danny," she said between sobs.

Dean's head hurt. The flood of memories of June, Maggie, all of the children, it whirled about, confusing him further.

"Mr. Edmonds?" Dr. Waterston pressed, "Do you remember Betty and Danny?"

"Yes, but..."

"But what, Mr. Edmonds?"

'They're...they're *dead*.' June's head and body snapped back, reacting to his words as if he had assaulted her.

Dean struggled to understand. Was this hell? Was the doctor deliberately lying to him? How could June be alive all of these years and him not know? He turned toward her. Her face was young, mid-twenties at most, her appearance had not changed in the slightest. She looked every bit of the woman he remembered before the crash. She hadn't aged, not at all.

"And you, June. You died in the crash, nearly ten years ago now. But here you are here. I don't understand." He said, looking around at the nurse and doctor, at June whose face was filled with horror and tears, "Are we all dead?"

June began to scream then. An orderly had come running. June didn't fight as they pulled her from the room. Her body was limp in their grasp. Her feet dragged as they hoisted her between them and disappeared down the corridor outside of the room.

Doctor Waterston beckoned one of the hallway nurses over, "Give her a sedative and put her in a bed to rest, poor woman."

"Where is my wife?" Dean asked, his eyes on the hallway June had disappeared into. He could still hear her cries, even though they had grown dramatically quieter. "Where is Maggie?"

Doctor Waterston, patted his shoulder, "Now, now, Mr. Edmonds, please, try to relax now. Mrs. Edmonds will be fine."

"I need Maggie." Dean felt his anxiety spiking. "Where is she?"

"Who is Maggie, Mr. Edmonds?" the doctor asked, "None of the nurses on this floor are named Maggie. Was it one of the candy stripers, perhaps?"

"No, no, *no*!" Dean was terrified now, "My *wife*. Maggie, her name is Maggie."

The doctor's face tightened with concern, "Mr. Edmonds, your wife's name is June."

"June was my first wife. She died. My children, Danny and Betty, they died as well."

The doctor nodded, "And when did this happen, Mr. Edmonds?"

"In a car crash in 1953."

"And it is what year?"

"You know what year it is!" Dean said, sitting forward, his leg and ribs spiking knives of pain, "It's nineteen sixty-two! What the hell is going on here?"

The doctor gave a nod to the nurse, who turned away to a metal cabinet and pulled out a small bottle and syringe.

"It is 1953, Mr. Edmonds. And your wife June and the children, Danny and Betty, they *survived* the crash. You were the only one seriously injured."

The nurse returned, a sliver of metal and needle flashed in her hand.

The doctor continued, "Now I know this is all quite confusing. There can sometimes be a bit of a mix-up between what is dream, and what is reality, after a head injury like yours. I want you to just try and relax now."

Dr. Waterston took the syringe from the nurse and gave the needle a light squeeze, a droplet of clear fluid emerging from the sharp tip.

Dean felt a deep chord of fear. He didn't understand what was happening, or why. He tried to pull his arm away as the prick of the needle descended. He was still weak, too weak to move away in time.

"I don't understand." There was a warm rush in his arm, "I lost June and the children and I saw their graves. I saw them!"

His words were slurring and Dean struggled to keep his eyes open. He fell back into the bed. The sensation of heaviness spread from his arm to every part of him, finally reaching his eyes. He tried to fight it, to tell them this was all some crazy dream, that maybe they were all in hell. The words stopped forming, thoughts were muddled, and then there was nothing.

"My God," Dr. Waterston said, his voice heavy with concern. "I've never seen anything like this." He looked up at the nurse, whose face looked troubled.

She shook her head, "I've seen men with shell shock who woke from sleep confused, but never anything like this."

"Hm, well, call the Psychiatry department and ask for an evaluation." He rubbed his eyes, "That poor pretty wife of his, did you see her face when he said she was dead? The absolute horror on it. Poor woman." He moved away from the bed, "Let me know once he's slept it off and had the eval, I will want to talk to the doc myself."

"Yes, Doctor."

The room grew quiet and Dean slept, lost in a medicated abyss.

Assess the Threat

Wednesday, June 10th, 1953

Castor Lagenfeld spied the two women from across the dimly lit restaurant. Gwen Verndari sat in the corner, back to the wall, her eyes already on him. Her long fingers curled around a glass of wine and she nodded to him.

She didn't blink as he crossed the room. The girl, her back facing Castor, was far younger, not yet a woman. She cast a glance over her shoulder as he approached, bright green eyes curious. The family resemblance was strong, and she looked more like Gwen's younger sister than her daughter. He bowed slightly to them both.

"Castor, how good to see you."

Gwen, when she smiled, gave him the chills. Castor could sense her power, it shifted and moved within her, dark gray storm clouds roiling behind the green of her eyes. Gwen was dangerous on so many levels.

"Gwen," he bowed politely, his eyes steady on hers, yet eager to break from her gaze.

He turned to the left, his eyes falling on the young girl. She was dressed in a simple gray cardigan and full skirt. Her raven-black hair was loose and fell in waves down her shoulders and back. She looked up at him, curious.

"My daughter, Elizabeth," Gwen said, sipping from her wine and nodding toward the girl, "She leaves for Europe tomorrow."

"Ah, Fer Complir?" he asked, eyes assessing her.

"Yes," Elizabeth answered for herself.

She stared back at him. Castor smiled quickly, taking her hand and brushing his lips across it. After her training and induction into the Fer Complir, the Arbre Genealogic would step in, and begin their own meddling. Eventually this slip of a girl would bear him a child. At the moment, thinking of it, he felt like a pederast even imagining that future.

Elizabeth blushed, just a tinge of pink warming her otherwise alabaster skin, and her gaze darted back to her mother.

Gwen watched them both, smiling slightly. "I haven't seen you since the trial, Castor, how are your studies?"

"Done and done," he replied tightly.

His studies at the human universities had netted him a doctorate in psychology, and his studies with the Fer Complir after that had ensured his place within the highest echelons of power that he, a mere Njerez male, could achieve.

Castor had tried to hide his discomfort at the subject. Of course Gwen would bring it up. Anything to keep him off kilter. It was the way she handled most interactions. If you weren't her lackey, then you were a challenge to her authority. He didn't wish to dwell on the trial that had shamed Zenobia, in absentia, and tried to implicate him as well. She was in the wind, and so of course their gaze had fallen to him and others.

He had grown up with Conor, they had celebrated their birthdays together. Whenever he thought of Zenobia Saronica's deception, passing Conor off as born on August 5th, instead of nearly seven weeks earlier on Litha, his thoughts turned dark. She had quite nearly taken Castor and the rest of his family down with her.

Had Zenobia had help? If she had, it hadn't been *his* family. But that hadn't stopped the whispers, the rumors and pointed looks and then the delay in his admission to the Fer Complir.

Just a few more questions, Castor.

The dark-robed women of the Council had said.

You understand our concern, our reticence in light of your past associations.

He remembered how his jaw had ached, not from being held shut, but from his pleasant smile, his nods, his *acquiescence* as he had been re-tried by a gamut of questions.

Did you ever suspect that Conor was born on Litha? Were your mothers close?

And on and on.

Their courts were not like human courts. The trials lacked lawyers or prosecutors, and the panel of judges' made decisions that were swift and unchallenged. If he had been found guilty of conspiring to hide a Bram in their midst, the punishment would have been death.

Tessa Verndari had come close. As Zenobia's closest confidante, they had convicted her of complicity simply by association. With no evidence, however, they could only strip her of her position of Protectorate and banish her.

Mona, Conor's younger sister, was now Protectorate of that piece of Fyrsta Heim, something the Fer Complir court had no real say over. The World chose the Protectorate, until such time as the Protectorate died, or the World chose another. And shortly after the Kern earthquake, Mona had been claimed by Fyrsta Heim. The girl was not like her mother, she had immediately reported to the Fer Complir assigned at the sprawling California ranch and sent a detailed report to the Primera Veu. It could only mean that Zenobia was dead. The role of Protectorate was a lifetime of service - only death could end it.

"Well, sit with us," she said patting the seat beside her. He sat. "I've taken the liberty of ordering for you."

Castor nodded, and poured himself a glass of wine from the bottle on the table. It was an older vintage, expensive, and he sipped from the glass, rolling it over his tongue.

The call had come early that morning, waking him up in his small apartment in New York. It had been remarkably abrupt. "We have reserved a flight for you leaving LaGuardia at nine."

"Where am I going?" He had asked, rubbing his eyes and trying to focus. The girl in his bed slept on, oblivious. Her bare leg, tanned and slim, strayed from the covers. Her bra and blouse lay tangled in a heap, and the rest of her clothes lay in a haphazard trail from the front door to the bed.

"Kansas City. Conor has resurfaced." A dial tone droned in his ear.

Shit. Why couldn't he have stayed in Fyrsta Heim? Castor swore softly.

He had run a hand over the woman, who burrowed her blond head under the pillow in response, moaning. He had leaned closer, running his lips along her shoulder blade, "I have to go."

"Mm, no," she had said, turning over, revealing a pair of small, tight breasts. "Wait, where are you going?"

She had reached out, captured his hand and pulled him back into the bed. A few minutes longer with her had almost made him late for his flight, but it had been worth it. He could still taste her.

"My, my Castor, you reek of her." Gwen's words cut through his reminiscence. "Who was she, anyway?"

He blinked, "No one. A waitress, no, a stewardess." He tilted his head and winked at Elizabeth, who stared in fascination. He poured some wine into the girl's glass.

Gwen ignored this, sipping again from her glass. Her blood-red lipstick, applied with precision, left no imprint upon the etched crystal. He could feel her eyes upon him as he flirted with her daughter.

A waiter arrived, a platter filled with an assortment of finger foods.

Gwen waited until he had left. "What have you been told?" she asked.

"Nothing. Other than the fact that Conor has resurfaced."

Gwen sighed, "Of course. They leave it to me." She slid an oyster off of the shell, tilted her head back, and swallowed it. "He's dead. That's the long and short of it."

Castor's chest hurt. It had been four years since he had last seen his friend. No matter what Conor must have thought of Castor's betrayal of him, he had hoped...

Hoped for what? That the impossible would happen? That they would see each other again and that Conor would let bygones be bygones? Highly unlikely.

Yet knowing his childhood friend was gone, that hurt like the devil. He thought of Conor's easy smile and dry sense of humor. Together they had hatched the plan to escape their overbearing families and enroll in the college in New York. Far from their influence, and interference, Conor had relaxed and enjoyed college life. But he had enjoyed it a little too much.

If only he hadn't fallen for that human girl. Castor shook his head, picking at the food on the plate before him. It was, despite his growling stomach, suddenly unappetizing.

Maggie had been Conor's downfall. He hadn't realized it then, obviously. Castor set his fork down, the ache in his chest a sharp stabbing pain that took away any desire to eat.

But really, it was only a matter of time, wasn't it? No matter if he had met Maggie or not, Conor was destined to be imprisoned in Fyrsta Heim. That would have been the only safe future for him.

He felt Elizabeth's eyes on him. She may have been lacking in years, but she was her mother's daughter, sharp, observant.

"I see," he sipped some of his wine, and forced himself to eat a petit-four, "And why is my presence required here?"

"A human family was caught up in the mess. Conor was seen appearing in the roadway. There is evidence of time manipulation."

"And you need me because..."

Gwen snapped, "Don't be obtuse. You could make an effort here, Castor. Or am I boring you? Are you in that much of a hurry to return to pursuing your dual agendas of loose women and quasi-scientific psychological experiments?"

So the Fer Complir *had* been keeping tabs on him. He was not surprised. All of his life he had felt their watchful gaze. His work within the New York City Lunatic Asylum was a front for his real work with the Fer Complir. They infrequently used his position as a psychiatrist to cast doubt on those who saw too much. It had happened a mere handful of times in the past century, but displays of magic, and any human observers were quickly silenced by any means possible. If they were bringing him into this it was because a human had witnessed Conor's abilities and seen him manipulate time and space.

He sat back, amused, "Forgive me, Protectorate. How could I have been so reticent? Hand me a sword and I will happily slay all dragons. I am," he bent his head in a bow, "at your service."

Elizabeth choked back a laugh, taking a sip of wine.

He rewarded the girl with a slow smile that promised her hours of pleasure...once she was of an appropriate age.

Gwen's eyes narrowed, her mouth settling into a thin line.

"You annoy me, Castor, more than ever before."

He blinked at her, a lazy smile playing over his lips, "Shall I flatter you instead, Protectorate? You are looking exceptionally beautiful today."

Gwen sighed, and handed him a small note. "Here is the name of the hospital and the patient. He came out of a coma today. And he remembers far too much for his own good. The family requested a private psychiatrist. They are expecting you."

She took a bite of food, swallowed and said, "Assess the threat. If it is possible to not have to commit or eliminate him, all the better. But do what you need to do, Castor."

He nodded, and rose to leave, "As it should be."

"Quod ut is mos persevero futurus," Gwen and Elizabeth murmured in response.

Castor bowed and strode away.

Remaking a Man

Tuesday, June 16th, 1953

"They're...they're *dead.*" June rocked back, reacting to his words as if he had slapped her.

The next few days were a blur. Dean soon realized that if he asked after Maggie, Teddy or Sarah - he was sedated. June just wept and Howard Jenkins became a regular fixture in his hospital room.

Another visitor came by at least once a day. Dr. Lagenfeld, a visiting psychiatrist who said he specialized in traumatic brain injuries. His raven black hair and piercing green eyes were vaguely familiar. What was it about the man? It was as if there were a distant memory echoing about in the back of Dean's skull, a sense of deja vu he could not seem to shake.

"Good morning, Mr. Edmonds," Dr. Lagenfeld said, nodding to the other occupants of the room. June, whose beautiful brown eyes held deep shadows under them nodded in return. Her voice wavered, "Good morning, Doctor Lagenfeld."

Howard stood up, and introduced himself. Dr. Lagenfeld shook his hand and then stepped back.

"Mrs. Edmonds, Mr. Jenkins, if you both would take a few minutes to get some coffee in the cafeteria and stretch your legs, I would like to speak with

Mr. Edmonds alone." He softened the request with a smile which sported a set of perfect white, straight teeth.

"Of course," Howard said, offering an elbow to June, who took it, moving slowly, her eyes never leaving Dean. Her expression held such hopelessness that Dean felt guilt in addition to the confusion he felt over the situation.

He knew that Maggie wasn't a dream or hallucination. He remembered her scent, the way her body had felt against his.

And Teddy, who had grown to such a fine young man. Just a couple of months away from turning twelve.

His heart ached too for Sarah. His and Maggie's beautiful daughter. They had just celebrated her seventh birthday a few months ago. She had been surrounded by her friends from school, beautiful in a pink chiffon dress and a lovely pink cake to match.

They wanted him to say she wasn't real, that she had never existed. That was the hardest thing to take.

Every time he tried to reconcile it all, he couldn't. It felt like a betrayal to lie and tell them what they wanted to hear. He knew it, beyond a shadow of a doubt, he had *lived* it.

The night before, when June had thought him sleeping, she had stepped out into the hall and spoken with Dr. Waterston.

"You asked to speak with me, Doctor?"

"Yes, Mrs. Edmonds, I wanted to discuss your options with you."

"My options?"

Dr. Waterston had coughed then, a raspy thick cough, "Well, Mrs. Edmonds, your husband is a few weeks out from being physically recovered enough to no longer need us here. However, mentally, well, Dr. Lagenfeld has suggested there may be a need for Mr. Edmonds to recover fully at an institute that specializes in mental illnesses and injuries such as your husband suffered."

June's voice had quivered, "You are suggesting I commit him to an asylum?" She sniffled then.

"I am sorry Mrs. Edmonds, here, oh dear, I am sorry to see I've distressed you."

Dean could hear June begin to cry.

"Please Mrs. Edmonds, come with me to my office. Where you can have a moment to collect yourself." Their voices had faded as they moved down the hallway and out of earshot.

An *asylum*.

What exactly did you expect they would do when you keep claiming your wife and children are dead when they are clearly not?

Dr. Lagenfeld closed the door to the hospital hallway and pulled up a chair. "Mr. Edmonds, how are you today?"

"The same as I was yesterday, and the day before that."

"And that is?"

"Confused."

Castor Lagenfeld nodded. "I see."

"I have lived in this world, lost June and the kids, and managed to move on. I fell in love, adopted Teddy." Dean spread his hands, "Don't tell me that Sarah doesn't exist. I had a seven year old daughter and everyone wants to tell me that it's a dream. Do you know how that feels? To know such love and happiness..." his voice caught, "to lose a woman and children you loved more than life itself and then be told it isn't real?"

Dr. Lagenfeld was young. So young that June had asked if he were still in school. Dr. Lagenfeld had laughed and said, "I'm told I look quite young for my age. I suppose I should take that as a compliment."

Despite his youthful appearance, and the strange feeling of *deja vu* that Dean felt in his presence, Dr. Lagenfeld's eyes held a maturity that seemed to exceed his years on earth. He leaned closer, "Mr. Edmonds. We have spoken daily for a week now. And each day I have told you that your wife June, along with your son Danny and daughter Betty, are all still alive. Have I not?"

Dean began to feel a thick coil of fear growing within him. "Yes."

"And every day you have mentioned this Maggie, Teddy and Sarah, insisting that they are not some dream, that this is not 1953, but instead 1962."

"Yes."

"You saw a man that night in the rain. Right before the crash." Dr. Lagenfeld said it as if stating a fact, instead of a question."

"Yes."

"What if both of these obviously conflicting realities were true?"

"I don't understand."

"What if June, Danny and Betty had perished, just as you said, and that you were now married to Maggie and father to Teddy and Sarah. And at the same time, your first wife and children had *not* perished in the crash and you did *not* meet Maggie?"

"That isn't possible. This isn't a science fiction novel. It has to be one or the other." Dean insisted.

Dr. Lagenfeld smiled, "Indeed. And if you look around, who or what do you see?"

Dean felt like screaming. It wasn't fair, it wasn't right. If he agreed with everyone, with this doctor, then it was as if he was turning his back on Maggie and the children. He knew what he knew. He could still feel her hand in his.

"Mr. Edmonds?"

"I see June."

Dr. Lagenfeld nodded, "And?"

"Everyone I see in here tells me it is 1953." Dean ground out.

The doctor nodded, his eyes intent on Dean.

"Sometimes, no matter how sure we are of the truth, no matter what our hearts tell us, reality is something entirely different."

Dean forced himself to nod.

"Occam's Razor, Mr. Edmonds."

"I'm sorry?"

The doctor smiled, "William of Ockham, he was a friar, scholastic philosopher and theologian. He proposed that, among competing hypotheses, the one with the fewest assumptions should be selected. It involves fewer assumptions for us to accept the hypothesis that June, Betty, and Danny are your family and that the year is 1953."

He leaned back in the chair and regarded Dean. The seconds ticked by.

"I want to sign off on this, Mr. Edmonds. I want to look your wife in the eye and tell her that you understand that all of this was merely a temporary, dissociative state due to your head injuries. An intense, incredibly real-seeming one, but also temporary."

He cocked his head staring at Dean intensely, "I want to tell them that you aren't a threat to yourself, or others. I want to tell them that you now remember that it was a truck, not a man that was in the road in front of you. That the year is 1953, and that you are *in love* with your wife and ready to return home to your children."

He paused for a moment, "Do you think that you can do that, Mr. Edmonds?"

There was something in Castor Lagenfeld's eyes, in the inflection of his speech that Dean couldn't quite read. A warning, perhaps? An unspoken threat?

Dean remembered the conversation between June and Dr. Waterston the evening before. If he persisted, if he continued to talk about Maggie, Teddy and Sarah, what would happen to him? What would this doctor *do*? Would he really be committed?

He realized in that moment that he stood at a crossroads. If he continued, if he argued, they could commit him, write him off as mentally unstable, insane even. He pictured Fulton State Hospital, remembering his mother, so despondent after losing the last baby. She had spent two months there. He remembered his mother pleading with his father to let her come home. His father had been a cold man, busy with business and his mistress, even he had eventually relented. Would June? After all of their fights, after all of the bitterness, would she sign the papers and leave him there?

The past nine years, it all seemed so real. But how could it be? How could he be right and everyone else be wrong? And did he really want to take the chance that his wife wouldn't agree to lock him away forever? When was the last time he had a kind word for her? Perhaps they were right, perhaps it had all been a hallucination caused by the injury to his brain.

I've wanted a different life for so long, perhaps it really is all in my head. I wanted something real, something different and my mind made up the rest.

"Yes. You are right, Doctor" he said finally.

His eyes slid away from Dr. Lagenfeld's and found a spot on the bed sheet, a bit of pilling on a field of otherwise pristine white. He picked at it, his fingernails were long and overgrown.

"Of course it is 1953. And my wife June, and my children, they survived the crash, and thank God for that."

"And the accident?" Dr. Lagenfeld pressed, "What do you remember of that?"

"The lights of a truck in our lane. There was no time for me to turn away. I'm lucky that June and the children weren't hurt."

He looked out the window, waiting for Dr. Lagenfeld to speak. His stomach twisted in fear as he waited, a long moment spiraling out between them. He could feel the doctor's steady gaze.

Finally, Dr. Lagenfeld smiled. "I'm so glad to hear it, Mr. Edmonds." He wrote in his notebook. "I think we are done here. I'll leave it up to Dr. Waterston to clear you for your medical release. I am sure you are looking forward to returning to your home and seeing your children again."

"Yes." Dean said. He didn't look up until the psychiatrist had left, the door clicking closed behind him. He was alone.

His chest was tight, breathing ragged and difficult. *I have betrayed them.* "Maggie," Dean whispered, his voice broken, raw, "Maggie...Teddy...Sarah."

When June returned, coffee cup in hand, Howard Jenkins wasn't with her. She came into the hospital room and eyed Dean with trepidation.

"Is your session with Dr. Lagenfeld already over?"

"Yes," he paused for a moment, "June?"

"Yes, Dean?" She stepped closer.

"I'm sorry. This was all so confusing. Dr. Lagenfeld, he..." He searched for the right words, the right lies to tell himself and his wife. "He explained that with brain injuries, dreams can seem like reality. He said, he said it was a dissociative state caused by my head injury."

He forced a small laugh. It sounded like an aborted cough. "Obviously it is 1953, not 1962. I know that now. It just felt so real...so..." He steeled himself. He had to pull this off, had to make himself believe it. "I am so happy you and the children were not hurt in the crash. And I am sorry for anything I may have said which might have hurt or frightened you."

June's eyes filled with tears. "Oh Dean, my darling, I had been so scared! I didn't know what to think, and you, I mean we..." She took his hand. "I know that things hadn't been good between us, right before the crash, and I..."

"I am sorry about that June. I feel as if I haven't been a good husband to you." Dean beat her to it, "I promise, we will have a new start." June hugged him then, her hair spilling against his stubble cheek. He could smell her signature scent, Chanel No. 5, and thought of Maggie's Yardley English

Lavender. His chest ached. He closed his eyes and pulled June against him. "I'm better now, I promise."

He felt her melt into him. It reminded him of their first dates. That blush of love that had sucked them in hard and fast. He had loved her then, and would have done anything for her. It was why he had bowed to convention and finished his degree in business administration, took leadership of the company as his father had expected, and bought that fine house on Grand Street.

That was what a man did. He grew up, he took the reins of responsibility and cared for his wife and children.

But as Dean held June, his hand traveling over her back, feeling the tiny nubs of her spine and realizing how much weight she had lost as she sat at his bedside day in and day out, he knew that he was different now. The dream, for what else could it be, had changed him. He was no longer the man that June had married.

He had the chance to be the husband he should have been, to be a father that Danny and Betty needed. But he had to find a compromise somehow, between the man he had been before the crash and the man who had woken up in this hospital bed with these memories.

Dean realized he needed to remake himself into a man who was the best of both.

Saturday Surprise

Saturday, July 18th, 1953

Four weeks later, Dean was at home. The stairs were still difficult with his healing leg, even though the doctors had removed the cast before he left the hospital. June had set the long sofa in the living room up as a bed, covering the rough gold tweed fabric with a sheet and she had made sure Dean had plenty of pillows.

The children had acted shy, nervous, and he wondered how much they had overheard when their mother returned from the hospital. Plenty, it appeared. The morning after he had returned, he awoke to Danny standing over him in the living room, staring at him gravely. "Mother said you were better now so you don't have to go to Fulton State Hospital. Is it true, Father? Are you all better? Or do you still think we are all dead?"

Dean felt a spike of fear course through him. He had come close.

I can't ever speak of Maggie, Teddy or Sarah again.

To do so could be incredibly dangerous. With that fear spike came a deep valley of depression. Was he doomed to live out his life working in a job that he hated?

"Dean? Danny? Is everything all right in there?" June's voice interrupted the silent tableau. Danny stood there, waiting for a reply, and Dean's face flickered with emotion.

"I'm fine. Just stiff, that's all." He swung his gaze to Danny, "Fetch me my robe there, son."

Danny did as he was asked and, question forgotten, went to turn the television on. It was Saturday, and there was a full lineup of shows. Dean remembered this. Given the opportunity, Danny would not move from that position for the next three hours, possibly longer.

The boy clicked on the television. It took a moment for the tubes to warm up and then the screen filled with *It's a Great Day* variety show.

Dean pulled his robe around him and followed June into the kitchen.

"I'll make the coffee."

June laughed. "You've never made coffee in your life, Dean!"

He ignored her and reached for the teakettle and jar of coffee. June stared at him. "Do we have any bacon?" Dean asked.

"Of course." June stood there, watching him as he prepared the cups. "I'll make bacon then." She turned away, then turned back and asked, "Eggs too? And toast?"

"If you don't mind."

June shot him another look and he wondered if he was *that* different from the old Dean. He tried to remember his weekend mornings before the first crash.

The only crash. Believe it, or you might slip and end up locked up in Fulton State Hospital.

For the life of him he couldn't recall ever standing with her in the kitchen and he doubted he had ever made coffee, until he was alone by himself all of those months.

He winced at the memory of his early attempts. It was either too weak, too strong, or filled with the grit of loose coffee grounds.

"My leg feels better today. I would like it if we could get out, all of us, maybe we could go for a drive."

The 1953 Ford Customline sitting in the driveway was brand-new. Dean had asked Howard to pick out a good, solid car and had been pleased to see the gleaming vehicle in the driveway when he returned home from the hospital the evening before.

"Are you sure you are up to driving, Dean?" June asked, her hands busy as she cut the bacon into thick slices. He wondered briefly how she had fared without a car in the past month. Probably with help from neighbors. June had never driven, she didn't even know how.

"Yes, but we could also give you driving lessons if you like." She stopped slicing and stared at him wide-eyed.

"Me? Drive?"

"Yes, you."

"But Dean, you..." June stood there, her lips quivering, "You said that women shouldn't drive."

"I said that?"

"Yes, right after college, when I asked you if you would show me."

Dean blinked and thought about it. She was right, he remembered it now.

A rueful laugh escaped his lips, "I am so sorry, June. My dad said it all the time and I thought he was a right old fuddy duddy. I can't believe I said that to you! And here I wondered why you were never interested in learning. What an ass I was!"

June's mouth twitched in a way that he remembered all too well. She was trying not to smile.

Dean remembered the early days of their courtship, and the first months of their marriage, when he couldn't tell where he ended and she began. Legs and arms entwined, skin slick with sweat, those endless kisses. How had they become so lost? How had their relationship dwindled to the rare dispassionate lovemaking, silent meals at the table, and angry words?

"Well?" he asked.

"Well what?"

"Do you want to learn?"

June smiled. It was a small smile, replaced a moment later with trepidation, "I don't know. Would I even be able to learn now?"

Dean made a show of thinking on it hard. "I don't know. It can be pretty hard to teach an old dog new tricks."

The response was immediate. She gasped and he felt the kitchen towel smack his arm.

"Dean Edmonds, did you just call me a *dog*?" Despite her outraged tone, her lips curved into a bright smile.

"Daddy, Mommy is not a dog." Betty stood in the kitchen, sleepy, her blond curls in disarray. She said it as she scowled up at Dean.

"Of course not, Sweetheart. I was teasing Mommy." Dean reached down and lifted the child up into his arms gingerly, his ribs aching.

"Daddy, you never tease Mommy."

"Well, I guess there's a first time for everything."

Later over breakfast, during which June complimented Dean on his coffee-making skills and Danny sulked over his lineup of shows being interrupted for the meal, Dean made an announcement.

"After we are all dressed, we are going for a drive."

Danny immediately began to whine, "But *Abbott and Costello* just started and then there's *Big Top Circus* and..."

Dean cut him off, "We are going to spend time together today, as a family. Besides, I have a surprise for everyone."

"A surprise?" Betty immediately perked up. She had been pushing her eggs around her plate, uninterested.

"Yes, a surprise, now finish your breakfast."

"What's the surprise?" Danny asked.

"If I told you it wouldn't be a surprise." Dean replied, winking at his son. "Now go and get dressed."

The boy disappeared upstairs, taking them two at a time. Betty was a moment behind him, having shoveled the last of her eggs into her mouth and headed for the stairs, still chewing.

"Dean?" June queried, looking apprehensive.

He shook his head, "Nope, I'm not telling you either. It's a surprise for all of you."

Half an hour later, they pulled out of the driveway, easing the large car onto the street. Dean loved the smell of it. The leather was rich and soft to the touch. It was brand new, driven once by Howard, who had handled the transaction and delivery according to Dean's precise instructions.

"Where are we going?" Danny demanded, bouncing in the back seat in excitement.

"Downtown. I have a stop to make and then we will proceed directly to the surprise." Dean answered. His son's foot connected with the back of his seat. "Sit still, son, or I'll pull this car over and we won't go anywhere."

Danny settled down and both children fell to whispering in the backseat. Dean could hear them discussing what the possible surprise would be. It was too early for a movie, and they hadn't seen any fishing poles or picnic basket. He smiled as he heard them agree that it had to be a candy store.

As they pulled up to the General Typewriter Company on Grand, June looked at him askance, a confused and somewhat guarded expression on her face.

The children appeared confused as well. "This doesn't look like a fun surprise," groused Danny under his breath.

"Dean, they can't possibly be open on a Saturday."

He didn't answer her. Instead he parked and left the car running. "I'll be just a moment." He reached for his walking stick, and gingerly made his way to the front door.

The door swung open, the owner had been waiting for him. "Mr. Edmonds, so good to meet you. Mr. Jenkins said that you had a special order for us?" The man mopped his face with a handkerchief. It was mid-morning but already the heat was oppressive.

"Yes, I heard that you are stocking a new electric typewriter, the new IBM model. I will need one delivered to 5900 Grand today, and the other ten delivered to Edmonds Manufacturing on Monday. Can you do that?"

"I...uh...yes, yes, of course!" The man looked overjoyed. The electric models were a hard sell due to their higher prices. A sale of eleven of them was well worth the man's time to open for Dean on a Saturday. He bustled about, preparing the paperwork as Dean filled out a check and signed it. He took the receipt from the man, tipped his hat, and left.

June looked at him questioning, "Dean?"

"Just some business I needed to take care of." He turned and looked at the children, "Is everyone ready for their surprise?"

"Yes!" Danny and Betty chorused.

"Excellent, here we go!"

A few minutes later, having turned to the right onto Twelfth Street, they coasted to a stop in front of Kansas City Pet Shop.

June gasped, and Danny looked as if he were set to go airborne at any moment.

"A pet shop, Dean?" June asked, her eyes wide.

"We talked about getting a dog and never did it. No reason not to. We have a nice sturdy fence and plenty of room."

Betty let out a shriek of pure joy. "Rin Tin Tin!"

The two children bolted out of the car, feet flying as they ran to the front door of the store.

"Ah, ah!" Dean admonished them both before they could push it open. "You will be calm and quiet, you hear me?" The children quieted, although Danny looked rebellious. Dean leaned down, putting his hand on his son's shoulder, "We don't want to scare them now, do we?"

Understanding dawned in the boy's eyes and he shook his head, "No, Father."

"Good, good. Quietly now."

An hour later, the family emerged with not one, but two new pets. Danny clutched the small collie pup to his chest in a delirium of joy and Betty held a tiny orange and white striped kitten, a fiercely protective smile on her face. A store clerk followed, his arms weighed down with additional packages. There were collars, a leash for the pup, bowls, food, toys and more inside of several large bags.

June's face held a mix of bewilderment and amusement. She kept giving Dean sidelong looks as well as nervous smiles. He felt oddly ashamed.

We always see ourselves in the best light. I thought I was a little abrupt, distant, but was I this bad?

As they settled into the car, Dean could hear Danny whisper to the puppy in his lap. "I don't care if you don't look like Rin Tin Tin. You are perfect."

Dean smiled back at his children. "Betty, have you thought of a name for your kitten?"

She looked back at him, her face serious, "He says his name is Aslan, and he's a *lion*, Daddy, not a cat."

Dean matched her serious tone, holding back his laugh, "Of course, he is. Nice to meet you, Aslan."

He reached over and shook the tiny kitten's paw. It didn't stop purring for a second, the steady rumble vibrating under his fingers and the kitten's claws contracted with pleasure. It butted its head against Betty's palm, demanding she pet him more.

"And Danny, what about your pup? Have you thought of a name?"

"Cassie," the boy said without any hesitation. "Like Lassie, only better."

Dean nodded and the children happily held their pets all the way home.

What Has Gotten Into You?

Saturday, August 1st, 1953

"What has gotten into you, Dean?" June finally asked two weeks later.

It was a Saturday afternoon and Dean had been typing away for hours now. The typewriter had been delivered on a Monday, along with a box filled with reams of creamy white paper, and Dean had set up his office in the mother-in-law quarters above the garage. He had come here straight after breakfast and had been steadily filling page after page, stopping only to eat, and to wrestle with Danny and the puppy in the back yard.

Cassie's training was going well and she had quickly learned to go outside in one corner of the yard. She also could sit on command and Dean was impressed with how well Danny had handled the responsibilities of dog ownership.

Dean had shown Danny some tricks to training the dog, distant memories from his childhood days when an uncle had brought him a Labrador Retriever when he was eight, just a year older than Danny was now.

Dean stopped typing and looked up. June looked nervous, even scared.

"The driving lessons, the animals, and this typewriter. It's..." Her voice died away.

"I thought you liked to drive," he said, frowning slightly. "I mean, except for that one curb, you've done so well. You are a natural."

"It's not the driving."

"I wanted to get Danny out of in front of that television. Teach him some responsibility. The puppy will keep him occupied and get him out and about more."

"It's not just that, Dean." June sat down in a side chair and stared at him. "The fishing trips, the shopping, even helping with meals. *You* are different."

Dean leaned back in his chair. His leg was aching today, more than usual. He shifted it to a more comfortable position.

"Is that a bad thing?"

"No. Just...different." She seemed to be struggling for the right words. "Like it used to be, maybe, when we first met."

Dean stood up, walked around the desk and sat down in the small chair near hers, and took her hand. "And would that be so bad?" He asked it gently.

June looked down at her hands and said nothing for a moment. When she looked up, he could see tears in her eyes.

"No. It wouldn't. It's just that, you and I, we had grown so distant and now, with the accident." Her voice broke and she looked away again.

He gave her a moment to compose herself, waited to see what she would say next.

"I sat there in the hospital, Dean, all those weeks. I was so scared. I wanted you to wake up, and, sometimes, sometimes I also *didn't*."

"I see."

She pulled her hand away, brushing at her eyes.

Dean handed her a handkerchief.

"God, just saying it out loud, it sounds *awful*. What kind of a horrible person am I to feel like that? But it hadn't been good. Not for years. You know it's true." Her tone was defensive.

"Yes, it's true."

"Sometimes I felt as if you would be happy if we weren't around. Me, the kids, even the company. You hated it. You sometimes talked to me with such," she dissolved into sobs then, "such *disdain*."

Dean tried to take her into his arms, "Oh June, I am so sorry."

June sobbed for a moment, then pulled away. "I'm not done."

"All right." He leaned back, fear growing in his gut.

"I was just as bad. I know I was, Dean. I wanted a good life, an easy one. So I pushed you, all the way back in college. I pushed you into this. You hated it, you told me that going to work for your father's company would kill you. And I pushed you into it all the same."

He tried to comfort her, but she shook her head, pushed away his hand. "I didn't want that uncertainty that I had grown up with. I didn't want to be poor like my parents had been. Always struggling, never able to catch up. So I pushed you to do the responsible thing and join your father's business. Like *he* wanted. I knew I would never have to worry about money again. And we haven't, Dean, but at what cost?"

Dean said nothing for a moment. June sobbed, her thin shoulders shaking, her eyes red with tears.

"I actually hoped you wouldn't wake up. That I could start over, just the children and I. And then you were so confused, so sure you were dead, that the children were dead. That *I* was dead. I actually inquired about having you committed to Fulton State Hospital!"

She shuddered, her voice hitching, "But you got better, and you came home, and it's been so wonderful. And yet..."

Dean felt the hard knot of dread forming in his chest, "And yet, you don't love me anymore?"

"What?" June looked up, astonished. "No! That's not it at all!"

She burst into more tears then, "I don't deserve you to be kind, to be this amazing man that has come home to me. Not after I've pushed you and manipulated you, and..."

"What? Because it's okay for me to take out my frustrations on you, but you aren't allowed to do it to me?" Dean laughed. "So we have both been wrong and hurtful, but why can't that change? Isn't it changing now? We have both changed, are changing, right this very minute."

He seized her hands in his, "Why can't we start over? Why can't I be the husband that you deserve and still be happy? I've been thinking and I've been working on something, a plan of sorts, would you like to see it?"

He didn't wait for her to answer. He jumped up and opened up a desk drawer, retrieving a legal tablet from within.

"Take a look at this. I've called around and my parents' house is just sitting there, vacant. We could sell it. I had a realtor stop by it and look it over, he sent me this report and suggested an asking price." He pointed to a figure on the page.

"That much?" June asked, wiping her tears away with his handkerchief, "Are you sure?"

"The housing market is *booming* right now and prices for the bigger places like that old mausoleum are skyrocketing. The realtor may have underestimated the amount."

"This second number, what is this?"

Dean took a deep breath. "That would be a fair market value for the company."

June stared at the number, and then stared at Dean, "*That much?*"

Dean nodded and smiled. "I might have hated working there, but the worth of the company has doubled over the past six years. And we have had several lucrative contracts come in the last two months thanks to Jimmy Tannenbaum."

"Who?"

"That young fool who lost a couple of fingers working the line the day of the crash? He recovered and Howard put him to work in a sales position. Turns out he's a crack salesman. Damn, if I had known that, I would have had him bringing in the big bucks from the get go. He landed us a contract with *Boeing* in his first week."

June's attention was back on the notepad, still taking in the figures. "Dean, this amount of money, it's, it's..."

"Enough to last us for decades. Yes."

She said nothing. Seconds stretched into minutes. Dean could feel his concern mounting. June didn't have to agree. He could do this, without her approval. It was 1953, for crying out loud, and none of it was in her name. Still, the more he had thought about it over the past few weeks, the more he had wanted her approval. He imagined her standing beside him on this new adventure and being willing, eager even. For once, he wanted their marriage to be a true partnership.

She finally broke her silence, "What would you do?"

He smiled, "I thought you would never ask." He stood up, walked around to the front of his desk, opened a door, and retrieved a stack of loose-leaf papers. He cradled them against his chest for a moment and then gently placed them in her lap.

June stared at the top page. "Schicksal Turnpike? That was the road that we were on, when..."

He held up a finger. "Just read the first few pages. I'll get us some iced tea."

He walked down the stairs, into the kitchen, and pulled open the icebox door. It took him a few minutes to locate and fill two tall glasses with June's sweet tea, then balance a small plate with cheese and meat on top of one of them.

When he returned, still favoring his right leg a few minutes later, the tall glasses beading sweat in his hands, June did not look up. She read each page, her lips moving as her eyes scanned each of them. He set the glass of tea down next to her, watching her as she continued to read. The finished pages were set neatly on the corner of his desk, facing down. She continued to read past the few pages he had asked of her, never pausing or looking up, until she had come to the final page.

Her eyes met his. "You wrote this? That's what you have been in here typing for the past two weeks?"

He nodded.

"But what happens next? How does it end?" Her eyes were intense, captivated. His mind flashed back to sun-drenched Saturday mornings, the two of them lying side by side, reading books, exchanging them when the other had finished. He remembered how her hair had smelled of lilacs and the way it splayed out around her head in a halo on the narrow bed. Or the other moments, in winter, their bodies spooned, sharing a book as other couples would share a dessert.

He smiled. "You like it?"

"Like it? No. I don't *like* it. I *love* it. It's, it's *haunting*. It is so beautiful. So..." She stood abruptly. "You need to finish it, Dean. Now."

There were tears in her eyes again. "Dean, I never, I mean, I had no idea you could write like this. It's, my God, it's beautiful." She looked back at the stack of papers, "You need to finish it."

Her words washed over him, a sea of warmth and his smile stretched his face until his cheeks hurt. He pulled her close, tight against him and breathed in her delicate smell. So familiar. "We can start again, June."

Her arms crept up around him, encircling him, nestling her head on his shoulder. "Yes. We can."

A Familiar Voice

January 19th, 1954

The phone rang in the front hall. Dean called to Danny to get it, but the boy was out with his dog, playing fetch, or having some kind of dog-friendly snowball fight with Cassie, who was now chest-high on the boy and full of long-legged hyperactivity.

Dean had just ambled down the stairs and into the kitchen for more coffee. His leg felt stiff that morning, especially now that the weather had turned so cold. By the fifth ring, he had made his way to the bottom of the stairs, just as June, still dusting flour from her hands, managed to answer it.

"Hello?" she said. There was a short pause and her eyebrows raised, "I beg your pardon?"

"Who is it?" Dean asked her as she handed him the receiver.

"Some guy who just asked if I was the 'dame of the house,'" June said, sniffing in displeasure.

Dean smiled, he had a sneaking suspicion he knew who was on the other end of the line. "East coast accent?"

"How did you know?" June asked.

"Lucky guess." He put his mouth to the receiver, "This is Dean Edmonds speaking."

June stood there, hands on her hips, scowling. She had a dusting of flour on the tip of her nose. Dean wondered if she was trying the beignet recipe he had asked her about. Whatever she was doing, the heavenly smells originating in the kitchen were making his mouth water.

The voice on the other end was unmistakable, "Dino! You don't know me, but whatever you do, my man, do not hang up! I gotta tell ya that Viking Press is gonna screw ya if you don't take me on as your agent. What I lack for in clientele I make up for in contracts."

Dean repressed a smile and nodded at June. "It's okay," he mouthed quietly to her. She made an annoyed harrumph, turned on her heel and headed back to the kitchen.

"Hey, Dino? You still there? Have I got the right number?" The receiver crackled.

"Yes, I'm still here."

"Good to hear. Never can tell when I'm callin' the armpit of the world, or...Oh hey, I didn't mean you, I was talkin' about those damn fools down in Tennessee." The voice paused, "I'm diggin' myself in deeper, aren't I?"

Dean laughed, "Sort of. So, what can I do for you?" He knew who this man was. He had spoken to Scotty Abernathy on a monthly basis for close to eight years. Well, eight years in another life, if that made any sense. Part of him wanted to say it out loud. The memories that he had were so real, even now. He couldn't explain it, and it wouldn't make sense to anyone else. It simply was what it was.

Dean had spent the last six months reconciling himself to that fact. Somehow, he had seen into the future and in some way, experienced it. But Maggie? And Teddy? No matter the amount of surreptitious sleuthing he had done while June and the children were out, he had found no trace of them. Nothing that corroborated their existence.

The tiny house on Twenty-Seventh Terrace near Hospital Hill had been occupied by another family. The woman had been red-haired and fat, her two children equally red-haired, and her scrawny henpecked husband had stared at Dean with a mixture of awe and resentment when he had driven by in his shiny new car.

"Well, damn, you have to be wondering who I am by now." The jocular voice on the other end of the line said, his words running together as only those rushing from one point to the other can manage. "My name is Scott Abernathy, but everyone just calls me Scotty. I'm calling to tell you that I'm your new best friend."

"Are you now?" Dean couldn't make it easy for him. He had learned, albeit after the first book was out and an exclusive contract signed, that he hadn't negotiated as low a rate as he could have. Perhaps this time around, things could be different.

"Why yes, I am. Y'see, I was over at Viking Press the other day and they were talking you up amongst them. I overheard what they are offering you, Mr. Edmonds and let me just say, I can get you a far sweeter deal than that."

Scotty's voice continued, running through what was word-for-word the same discussion Dean remembered having with him before.

Dean half-listened, making small, noncommittal noises at all of the appropriate moments and thought about the past six months.

With June's support, he had sold his parents' house, along with Edmonds Manufacturing.

Doyle Laurel and Howard Jenkins had jumped at the opportunity. They had both started out on the ground floor, one of the company's first employees, and steadily risen up through the ranks. They had been indispensable by the time Dean had graduated from short pants, and both had worked hard to make the company the success that it was. The three of them had sat down and negotiated an even better figure than the one Dean had conservatively guessed at for June, and signed the papers a week later.

Dean and June had enough funds from that and the sale of his parents' house to keep them comfortably for the rest of their lives. It would even pay for Danny and Betty to go to college. Just over a month ago, Dean had bet on the underdog, the Detroit Lions, in the NFL championship game. The odds had been overwhelmingly in favor of the Cleveland Browns, but Dean had insisted on betting a stunning amount on the Lions, and won a pretty penny on the game. He had turned around and used the winnings to invest in two companies - Pfizer and IBM - which had both been showing a steady profit by 1962. He had nearly eight more years to wait on those results, but Dean had a good feeling about the investment.

The rest of the manuscript for Schicksal Turnpike had burst forth in a gush last fall. By the time the leaves in the trees were turning red and gold, he had gone through two edits, with June by his side. She had read the final pages and addressed the envelope to Viking Press herself, insisting it was ready.

"No Dean, don't you dare do another edit." She had insisted, her spirited side showing, "I mean it. Turn it in. It's perfect."

They had mailed it together the next day, her driving the entire way to the post office. Three weeks later he had received a letter from Viking Press.

The driving lessons had gone well. Well, almost. June had managed to dent the right corner of the rear fender, edging too close to a street sign. The look of mortification on her face was evidence that she felt bad enough over it.

Scotty's voice interrupted his reverie, "So I'm gonna send you some papers, Dino. I think you will find that six percent is more than fair. You won't get a better deal than that."

"Hm, well, I'm not sure about that."

There was a crackling pause, "Have you spoken to any other agents yet? I could possibly negotiate that down half a percent."

"Make it three percent and you've got a deal," Dean returned, grinning wider. "And you'll negotiate an extra four percent from Viking in exchange for that."

"*What*? Jumpin' Jehoshaphat, man! Does the Midwest breed some kinda poker players from hell? Three percent! You're killin' me here!" Scotty sputtered.

"Scotty, you know this book is going to climb the charts. You read it. Get me the deal with Viking, take the three percent, and send me the papers." Dean insisted, "You'll make it up in sales. Besides, I've got three more in the wings that I'm working on now."

June leaned out of the kitchen and raised an eyebrow at him. She knew he had all of three pages of notes on *one* book, not three. Dean had showed them to her yesterday morning.

"I'll get back to ya." A dial tone sounded in Dean's ear.

He smiled, "I'll take that as a 'yes.'"

"Who *was* that?" June asked. Dean walked over to her, reached up and wiped the smudge of flour off of her nose and kissed her.

"A literary agent. His name is Scotty Abernathy," Dean answered, "I've heard he is very good. Rough around the edges, but good. He will get me a better deal on that manuscript than Viking was willing to offer and I made him cut his rate by half."

"Is he going to take that?" June asked, perplexed, "I mean, can you even *do* that?"

"Everything is negotiable, my love." Dean said, slipping his hand around her waist and nuzzling her neck.

"Dean Edmonds, you stop that right now, I've got a pie in the oven!"

"Mm, how about a bun in the oven?" He murmured, his lips on her ear, nibbling, as he pulled her closer. She was wearing the new perfume he had bought her.

He laughed as she smacked him half-heartedly with her towel. She giggled and kissed him before pulling away.

"You are incorrigible! Now let me go, we have Howard and Doris Jenkins coming for dinner and I have a pot roast to get started!"

Dean made his way upstairs. He had a couple of hours left before the Jenkins arrived. He might as well get some writing done.

A week later he received a large envelope in the mail. There was the Viking Press contract and his agent/author contract, both from Scotty Abernathy's office. Scotty had given him everything he asked for. His book, *Schicksal Turnpike* would be published in February of the New Year, with a country-wide book tour to follow.

Call Her Sarah

Tuesday, March 15, 1955

"Oh, Dean, drive faster." June gasped in pain, stretched out on the backseat of the car, her hands on her distended belly, her pretty face twisting in pain.

The snow fell in thick, fat clumps from the sky. Dean could barely see the end of the street, the wind sweeping the snow sideways and around in heavy gusts of white.

"Damn this snow!" The flakes clung to the windshield, clotting as the wiper blades tried to clear a section of glass and only succeeded in smearing it. "I don't dare, June, I'm all over the road as it is."

Dean thought of his son and daughter's faces pressed against the panes of the living room window, waving half-heartedly as the car had pulled out of the driveway and down the street. They had looked rather frightened, despite Mrs. Wilcox's reassurances. A matronly woman who lived just three doors down, Ethel Wilcox had raised eight children of her own, the eldest of which had left for college the year before. She had volunteered to take care of the children as soon Danny knocked on her door in a panic. June had dropped the serving dish from dinner, still half full of tuna as her belly had twisted in a sharp, agonizing contraction. And the following handful of moments had been chaotic. Dean easing her onto a chair and barking at Danny to get Mrs.

239

Wilcox, while Betty cleaned up the mess on the kitchen floor. Mrs. Wilcox had arrived seconds later, puffing and red in the face.

"Don't you worry about a thing, Dean, you just get on to the hospital with June and I'll see to Danny and Betty." She had bustled into the kitchen, intent on tidying the mess and possibly baking up a storm. Ethel's husband Larry had passed away three years ago, and June had befriended her, especially after the youngest departed for college.

"She's all alone over there, Dean, and I can't imagine how hard it must be for her, especially after having a houseful for so long." June had said last summer. Since then, the widow had become a fixture at Sunday night dinner.

"The baby shouldn't be coming for another three weeks, maybe four," June said, gasping in agony as another contraction hit. "What if there is something wrong, Dean?"

"Hang in there, honey, I'm getting us there as quickly as I can."

He headed for Hospital Hill, paying careful attention to the road, his eyes straining to see through the thick snow and gathering gloom. It would be night soon.

The snow was accumulating, thick and slick on the pavement. It fell, filling the sky and the ground below with interminable white. It had been a long winter, this made two brutal winters in a row now, and Dean could feel the car slide, fishtailing from side to side. He didn't dare drive fast, nor could he pull over or stop, out of fear that the car might become stuck in the deepening snow.

The year had passed like a blur, and 1955 had been ushered in with *Schicksal Turnpike* at the number two slot on the New York Times list. He had spent most of the year traveling, attending book tours throughout the country. During the summer, June and the children had joined him. It had been marvelous. After months of working with Danny and Betty, and Dean schooling himself to be patient yet firm with them, they had been the perfect models of well-behaved children and enjoyed the plethora of zoos and museums throughout the cities on the east coast.

When school had begun in the fall, so had the startling, yet exciting news that June was pregnant. Dean had been overjoyed, and June had grown more radiant with each day that passed. Dean found himself reaching out to caress her belly, holding his breath and the baby had quickened inside of her, kicking and moving.

Their relationship had grown closer with each month that passed. June had served as his editor, critiquing his writing work and suggesting possible plot developments along the way. Each day of writing, when he could fit it in between stops on the tour, it had ended with her reading his draft, and scribbling comments in the margins.

He turned onto the last road, a wide one, and began to skirt a mass of cars that were twisted and turned, scattered like bumper cars throughout the intersection.

"Dean! Get me to the hospital! Now!" She screamed, panicked, in his ear.

He jumped in his seat, the wheel turning to the left and then the right as the car spun out of control. The heavy machine slowly slid of its own accord, not unlike a drunken ice dancer. He pumped the brakes, but it was of no use. It was fishtailing, moving inexorably closer to the patrol car and a patrolman standing next to it a mere fifteen feet away.

The officer looked up, his eyes widening as he scurried and slipped in the snow to get out of the way. He managed, and just in the nick of time. The two cars connected, metal grinding, denting the side panel of the car slightly. The slow speed had helped, but the bump was still a small shock.

"Dean, the baby is coming!" June screamed, a gush of liquid drenched the seat.

The police officer, ready to launch into a tirade as he closed the distance to Dean and June's car, took in the scene and jumped into action. Between him and Dean, they managed to lift June up and carry her the rest of the way to the entrance of the hospital fifty feet away.

Two hours later, Dean paced the waiting room. Despite her water breaking, and her screams which echoed down the hall, June was still in labor. Dean couldn't think. He was beyond terror.

Danny had taken a while, for sure, but Betty had been an easy birth.

"A walk in the park," the doctor had said later, when he brought out Betty. Her skin had still been red and her face had held a tiny scowl, as if she were unimpressed by this strange new world.

"Excuse me, Nurse," he said, stopping the first white uniform he spied walking by. The woman turned and he lost his breath for moment. Her hair was perfectly straight, and blond, her eyes blue, just like Maggie's. But it hadn't been Maggie.

"Yes, sir?"

"My wife, June Edmonds, are there any update?"

"I'll check, sir." The nurse smiled, "But babies take their time. Is this your first?"

"No, we have two at home, ages five and eight."

"Oh well, then you know how it is." She beamed at him and when he didn't return it, nodded with understanding, "Let me check then."

A few minutes later she returned. "Mr. Edmonds? It seems that there are some complications. The baby is, well, a little stuck at the moment." The nurse gave him a professional smile, "The doctor is working on it. The breech position can be rather, problematic, but we hope it will be soon."

Dean stared at the nurse and began to stride toward the closed door.

"Mr. Edmonds, you can't go in there!"

"Damned if I will stand outside here and do nothing!" Dean said, pushing the door open as June screamed in anguish.

On its heels was the thin wail of a baby.

Dean rushed to his wife's side, pandemonium ensuing as the nurse followed him. He took in the scene before him, blood stained the sheets, dark red, gouts of it, and his wife was a dreadful shade of gray.

June's eyes tore away from the baby to stare at him in exhaustion. "Oh Dean, look at her, she's so beautiful." Her eyes then rolled up in her head, her body going limp. The room erupted in a frenzy of movement.

Dean felt two sets of burly arms and steel-hard fingers grab his arms. "Sir, you will need to come with us." They lifted him off of the ground, pulling him backwards out of the room. As the doors swung closed, he could see the doctors swarming over June, her left arm, limp, hung over the edge of the bed. The screams of his infant daughter pierced the air.

It took three orderlies to fully subdue him as he struggled to return to June's side.

Hours later, he held his wife's cool hand. Her face was an alabaster white. Her lashes, black feathery fans against gray, sunken eye sockets. Seeing her there, so still, it drained him of all of his earlier fight. He imagined Danny and Betty waiting at home, scared for their mother, alone with only Mrs. Wilcox for company.

It was late, after ten now. Were the children in bed? Were they struggling to stay awake, waiting for him to come home to them? He needed to call them.

The doctor had been terse in his update, "We performed a full hysterectomy. There really was no other choice, Mr. Edmonds."

No more babies.

"She will be fine, Mr. Edmonds." The nurse lay a hand on his arm. "She's resting now and she lost quite a bit of blood. But the transfusion helped and the doctor says she will be right as rain in a few weeks."

"You're sure?" Dean asked, his chest constricted, staring at June's still form.

The nurse smiled and patted his arm, "Yes. Now come and meet your daughter. She's quite the beauty."

Another nurse entered the room carrying a tiny swaddled bundle of pink. She placed the baby gently in his arms.

Looking down at her delicate face with rosebud lips and the tiniest of birthmarks on her right cheek, he felt tears sliding down his face. Words failed him and he dug for his handkerchief with one hand, overcome by the familiar, and beloved child in his arms. The one he had wondered if he would ever see again.

"Oh...oh my. But of course it is you. My sweet little Sarah." His lips trembled, tears coursing down his cheeks, a faucet of emotion. "Of course it is you."

"That's her name? Sarah?" The nurse asked, smiling, "What a lovely name. I have a cousin named Sarah. It means princess. Did you know that? Have you decided on a middle name?"

Dean stood there, silent. He cast a glance at June, lying so still in the bed. *What would she think? Would she be upset?*

"Her middle name is, um, it's Magdalene."

"So lovely. Should I put that on the paperwork then?"

Dean nodded, his eyes riveted to the baby's face. How could she look exactly like Sarah? Down to the very birthmark. *How?* The old familiar ache spread in his chest. He was happy. He loved June. Since the crash, had dedicated himself to his wife, to Danny and Betty. And they had all thrived, grown closer, more than he had ever dreamed possible.

He loved his family. The baby in his arms had been conceived in love. Her birth had been anticipated, dreamed of, and would soon become family lore.

Despite this, Dean could still feel Maggie's pull on his heart. The loss of her, the memory of their time together, it felt as if two ships were colliding. How could he love June and Maggie both? How could he love what was surely a dream, yet also love the woman lying in the bed just a few feet away?

He couldn't understand it. He only knew it as his reality.

June stirred, her lips moving, eyes struggling to open.

"Dean?" Her voice was a mere whisper. Her eyelashes fluttered, reminding him of a butterfly's wings at the end of its life - so weak and tired.

"Hello my darling," he said, leaning over to kiss her cheek. "She's so beautiful. I can't even tell you how perfect she is." He placed their sleeping baby in June's arms.

A tiny wash of color pinked her cheeks and she smiled then, her lips curving up, tears in her eyes. "Oh my, she is perfect, isn't she?"

"Forgive me, I named her. We," he struggled to keep his voice even, to remove the longing from it, "We can name her something else if you want."

"What do you want to call her?" she asked, her soft brown eyes taking in the tears still drying on his cheeks.

"I, that is, could we," He stopped for a moment, desperate to gain his composure. "I was hoping we could call her Sarah Magdalene." The name came out in a rush, his fear of her reaction etched on his face.

June studied him for a moment and then turned her gaze to the tiny child in her arms. She smiled at her infant daughter, drinking in the delicate sleeping face.

She looked back up at Dean, held his gaze and then said, "Sarah Magdalene. It is a beautiful name, Dean." She touched the small birthmark on Sarah's cheek, and reached up to gently wipe his tears away before turning her gaze back to the child swaddled in her arms, "Hello, my darling Sarah. You are so loved."

Call Me Theo

Saturday, December 22nd, 1973

"I can't believe this will be our sixth Christmas without Danny," June said as she looked out of the wide picture window.

Behind her, the television muttered, the sound now turned down. The skies outside had grown progressively overcast throughout the day. The weatherman on WDAF-TV was predicting more than three inches.

It had been an overcast day like this one when they had learned the terrible news. Six months after Danny had been drafted, he had perished in the fighting outside of Khe Sanh on Valentine's Day 1968.

"It looks as if it will start snowing any minute. When will they get here?"

"Mom, for goodness sake, looking out the window won't make them get here any sooner." Betty said, jiggling the baby in her arms. Junior, Dean's namesake, was teething and quite cranky. Betty had cut her hair short last week, but it wasn't short enough. The natural curls of her blond hair, inherited from June, were an undeniable attraction for Junior. He reached out and yanked, hard.

"Ow!" Betty snapped, and the baby started to cry. "Jasper, take him for a little while, would you?"

Her husband took the baby, a dissatisfied look on his face. The rest of the family ignored him. Dean fought down a wave of frustration with his son-in-law.

"He's on my last nerve," he had confided to June the night before. "His writing is beyond terrible. He seems to think that everyone is deluded, and that we can't see his true genius."

"Perhaps he needs a good editor," June suggested, smothering a laugh.

"*Editor*? Hell, he needs to hire a ghostwriter!" Dean had scoffed.

Jasper's uncle was none other than the well-regarded J.D. Salinger. And while J.D.'s book Catcher in the Rye had been a runaway success when it was published, Jasper's dreams of literary magnificence were far from being realized.

Jasper seemed convinced that writing was an inherited talent and continued to deluge first his uncle, and now Dean, with manuscripts so awful Dean had a difficult time being kind.

June interrupted Dean's musings, "I'm worried, that's all. Sarah said she would be here by three and it's almost two now."

"Yes, almost two, she's not even late." Betty went over and hugged her. "You worry too much. She's fine. She's driving here with her boyfriend."

Junior struggled in his father's arms, his face screwed up, reddening, and an epic screaming fit mere seconds away.

June harrumphed, "Boyfriend, yes, I've heard." June's tone was frosty, disapproving.

Jasper jiggled the baby, his face twitching at the effort to hide his own frustration.

He had plenty to be frustrated over, Dean mused, the editor at the paper where Jasper worked kept refusing his proposed articles. Dean had gotten Jasper the job with an old friend, James Ford, a former classmate at William Jewell who had worked his way up from copy editor to head honcho.

James had called Dean the week before. "The kid hasn't got a lick of talent, Dean, he's in the wrong field." James had sighed, "Apparently the ability to write is not genetic. And from what I've seen, he's unwilling to learn. I'm going to have to let him go if things don't turn around soon. Perhaps you can talk to him, convince him that he would do better somewhere else. I know he's a family man, but I can't keep paying for someone who isn't pulling their weight."

Dean had thanked him, got off the phone and shook his head. Betty had sure had her head in the clouds marrying this one. But with a baby in the picture, divorce wasn't so simple.

The baby started wailing. Jasper looked at his wife, who ignored him. Dean suppressed a grimace.

Apparently the shine is off the rose.

Or as Scotty had commented after flying in for the baptism, "Dino, that boy is a fat-head, you shoulda seen the drivel he sent me last month. I think he's got it in his head that writing is like pennies from heaven. But damnitall, if he sends me more of that shit, I'm gonna tell him it's below my pay grade. When is Betty gonna wise up?"

Dean had shook his head, "I think it is far too late for that now, Scotty."

From the look on his wife's face, he had to wonder if she wasn't thinking the same thing.

"I just don't see why you are all in a dither right now, Mom."

"Your mother is worried Sarah won't finish her studies," Dean said to Betty, ignoring the angry screams of his namesake.

"Well, she wouldn't be the first one," June said, casting a glance at Betty. She had dropped out after the first two years, having achieved her "Mrs. Degree" and was now working as a waitress, supporting Jasper and the baby, while her husband stared at the dingy white walls of their cramped apartment and waited for the writing muse to magically descend.

That was how Betty had described it, bitterly, a few days earlier.

"Thanks, Mother." Betty sighed heavily. Junior continued to scream in Jasper's arms.

"Hand that boy over to me, Jasper," Dean said, holding out his arms. He tried not to think about his first grandchild alone with his son-in-law in the cheap apartment south on Benton while Betty worked at the diner. Jasper, relief written all over his face, handed the baby over. Junior calmed, his sobs subsiding into hiccups that rocked his small body. Dean reached for a teething toy, settling it in his grandson's hands while tucking his warm, tiny body into the crook of his arm. He leaned back, rocking contentedly.

"He adores you, Dad." Betty said, smiling for the first time that day.

Dean reached down and tickled his grandson, "And I adore him." *If only I could say the same for your daddy, Little Man.*

"Oh, I think I see her little car! Thank goodness! I was worried the weather would turn bad." June turned from the window, her mouth in a small frown, "I wonder if she drove the speed limit?"

"Oh for crying out loud, Mom." Betty groaned. "First you worried over her not getting here before the snow, and now you think she might have been speeding. Is there no middle ground?"

June looked affronted, "Betty, I worry for good reason, one of the biggest killers of people is car crashes. And this family has had their share of bad luck, if you ask me."

Dean levered his way out of his easy chair, the baby contentedly gnawing on a toy, his chin wet with drool. He looked the spitting image of his mother, and Dean was thankful for that. He stared out of the big picture window that overlooked the driveway, a happy smile on his face. He had missed his youngest child far more than he was willing to admit.

As if on cue, the sky began to spit out huge fat flakes of snow. The cream-colored Volkswagen Bug pulled into the already full driveway. Sarah's lithesome figure and blond hair were hidden under a knit cap and large woolen coat.

She clambered out of the driver's seat. On the passenger side, a tall young man, carefully unfolded himself. He was far too tall to be riding in such a small car, and Dean suppressed a smile at the thought of him crammed into the silly thing for the several hundred mile trip.

Why do kids want those silly little cars, anyway?

The snow had gone from nonexistent to a heavy flurry of activity in less than a minute. The weatherman had said it was going to be a doozy, and it looked as if he was right for once.

"What was the boy's name again?" Dean asked.

"He's not a 'boy' Dad, he's a good five years older than her." Betty admonished.

"Is he a slow learner?"

"What?"

"He's still in college at the age of twenty-three, so he's got to be slow."

Dean said it to needle Betty who had already jumped to the defense of her little sister's boyfriend and also so he could get a reaction out of Jasper, who *had* gone for five years and still not graduated.

Perhaps less partying or attending peace marches and more time paying attention to teachers might have helped.

"Dad! He's a *graduate* student!"

"Dean," June warned, "you be nice."

"I'm always nice, dear." Dean replied, smiling cheerfully. June rolled her eyes and tried to smother a smile.

The front door flew open and Sarah burst in, "Oh my gosh, that snow, it could have waited just five more minutes before turning into an avalanche, don't you think?"

One bag was slung over her shoulder, and her crayon-blue eyes sparkled above rosy-pink cheeks. Behind her stood a tall young man, over six feet, loaded down with bags filled with presents and his own suitcase.

Dean took one look at him and felt as if the world had fallen away.

"Oh wow, everyone, I see the family has gathered en masse. Teddy, don't you dare let them intimidate you." Sarah reached out and hugged her sister, "Hey Sis!"

A flurry of hugs ensued and Dean stood there, saying nothing. No one noticed, except for the tall man with black hair and brilliant blue eyes, who stared back at Dean in between introductions and hugs.

Dean could not believe his eyes. After looking for so long, in every possible way he could think of, here he was. All grown up, towering over them all.

"Dad? Hey Dad?" Sarah's fingers snapped in front of his face, startling him. Her face was puzzled, and beyond her Dean could see June frowning in concern. "Are you okay? You are a million miles away!"

Dean came back from the long-buried memories of the past, and smiled as he looked into his youngest child's eyes. "Hey Sweetheart," he pulled her into a tight hug, Junior squirming as he was suddenly squashed between them. "I sure have missed you."

She smelled of patchouli. "I missed you too, Dad."

Dean held his hand out, "Teddy, is it?"

"That's Sarah's nickname for me," the young man said, grinning, "You can call me Theo. I grew up just south of here, in the town of Raymore."

There was no recognition in his face for Dean. It was clear that Teddy, *scratch that, he said his name was Theo*, had no memory of ever meeting him. *But then again, he wouldn't would he?*

"Really? So you have family in the area, then?" Dean asked, hope rising.

Theo shook his head, "Not anymore sir, no. Well, a cousin, twice removed, Bearl Dean. He owns a farm and I lived there with Cousin Bearl and his wife Maxine after my mom passed away."

Dean's heart thumped in his chest, hope crashing at the young man's words. Maggie was gone then.

"For goodness sake, Dean, move out of the way, and let these two inside, the snow is getting inside the house!" June shooed Dean back.

She ushered Theo and Sarah inside and closed the door to the snowstorm outside before turning her sights on her youngest child's boyfriend.

"Well, we are so glad you are here Theo! We can put you up in the guest room upstairs on the left." Sarah and Theo looked at each other, and there was a bright flash as Sarah pulled off her gloves.

Betty shrieked, "Oh my God, Sarah!" She grabbed her sister's left hand and stared at the ring on her finger.

"Sarah, what is this?" June stepped forward to examine the ring on her youngest child's finger. She did not look happy.

"I'd give a guess and say that's a wedding ring," Dean offered dryly.

"Dean Edmonds, you are not helping," his wife snapped. She stared into her daughter's eyes, "Sarah, now would be a good time to tell me that this is an *engagement* ring." She used the measured tone that mothers have when standing at the edge of the abyss. Sanity a thin, easily lost thing.

"Actually, Mrs. Edmonds, it *is* a wedding ring." Theo said softly, "I didn't have enough for both and what with time being an issue, we..."

"Why was time an issue, Sarah?" June's voice held a barely disguised panic.

"Oh wow, shotgun wedding!" Jasper began to laugh.

Betty glared at him, "Shut up, Jasper."

June's face was a mixture of horror and fury. "Sarah Magdalene Edmonds..."

Dean handed Junior back to his son-in-law, "Here Jasper, make yourself useful for once." He put a hand on Theo's shoulder and an arm around Sarah and headed for the stairs, "June, please start dinner. I'm going to talk to these two in my office."

June sputtered, "Dean, I..."

"Please my dear, let me handle this."

Betty took her mother's hand, "Come on Mom, I'll help you."

Minutes later, the door to the office firmly closed, Dean sat down behind his desk. "Well, that didn't take long to come out."

Sarah sat hunched in her seat, her face buried in her hands. "I had this planned so much better in my head. I swear, the front door wasn't even all the way closed before the Inquisition started."

Dean suppressed a smile. Theo watched him, uncertainty written on his handsome young face. Dean couldn't help but feel a surge of joy run through him.

Of course they would have found each other.

The young man cleared his throat.

"Sir, I..."

"Considering you have married my daughter, I think you can call me Dean. Later, given time, we can graduate to 'Dad.'"

"I...uh, yes sir, I mean, um, Dean. I imagine you find us impulsive, but I assure you, I have the best of intentions, and..."

"I suppose we should just cut to the chase, Theo," Dean cut in. "Are your plans to return to school after the Christmas break, or stay here?"

"I've actually completed my Master's in Education and I have already been offered a job at William Jewell College beginning with the winter semester."

Dean sighed audibly, relieved. "I'm glad to hear it." He stared at his daughter, who had sat up in her chair and was staring at him in surprise.

"You aren't going to yell?" She asked, her tone hesitant.

"Would it do any good?"

"No, but..." her face crumpled, "I don't want you to be disappointed in me, Daddy. I plan on going back after the baby is born, I promise."

"I know you do, Sweetheart."

"Mom looks really mad."

Dean smiled. June had been nineteen when Danny was born. She had never gone back to college, and from her reaction it was obvious that there were regrets there.

"I imagine she is, but she will get over it. We all will. Go talk to her, try and work it out. I'll keep Theo here for a few minutes so that she thinks he's getting a stern talking to."

"Oh Daddy, thank you for not being mad."

Sarah jumped up, throwing her arms around him and kissing his cheek. He hugged her tight. She was still his little girl and Dean tried to wrap his mind around the image of a child growing inside of her.

Sarah wiped tears from her face, steeled herself, and gave Theo a quick hug before she left the office.

Dean turned to Theo, "Tell me about your family, Theo. You said you grew up here in the area?"

"Yes, sir, uh, Dean. I was born here in Kansas City, but my mother and I moved down to Belton when I was young, maybe four or five?"

"Really, why there?"

"My grandmother passed away. Mom was her only child so we moved down there and lived in her house. Well, at least until I was twelve."

Dean knew that Theo was twelve years old on May 13th, 1962. Could that have been when Maggie passed? "What happened then?"

"My mother died in a car accident in May of 1962." He gave a small shrug. "A truck came over into her lane and she didn't have time to get out of the way."

"I'm so sorry to hear that." Dean said the words, his mind reeling. There would be no reunion with Maggie, no way to see if she carried the same memories he did. She was gone forever.

"It was hard. It was just the two of us, so I really missed her."

"What happened then? Who did you go with?"

Theo smiled, "Just when I was about to be put into foster care, this guy showed up at my mom's funeral. It turned out he was a distant cousin who lived there on the edge of Raymore, on a farm. He took me in until I came of age," Theo answered. "Sir it might seem like I'm penniless and more, but I do still have a fair amount of money from my grandmother's estate. It's enough for us to get a decent start. My grandmother's house was sold when my mother died, but Bearl and Maxine, they wouldn't take anything for caring for me, so I was able to pay for college and even graduate school. I won't be saddled with loans."

"You have really thought things out," Dean commented. "We could see about finding a nice starter house for you two nearby."

"Actually, I have that covered as well," Theo said. "The house my mom owned before my grandmother died. It isn't far from here. She kept it and rented it out. It was occupied by tenants until last month. I held off on getting new ones until I would be back in the area and then, well, Sarah told me she was pregnant. So it worked out well. We can take it over and fix it up before the baby comes."

Dean had a feeling he knew exactly where that house was.

"And when is the baby due?"

"The second week in July."

Dean nodded, stood up from his desk and walked over to Theo. The young man stood and Dean pulled him into a hug. "Welcome to the family, Theo. It will take June a while to get used to it, but she'll come around."

Theo relaxed, "Thank you, sir."

Unexpected Attention

Wednesday, June 9th, 1982

"Dino," Scotty Abernathy's grip was strong, his round face as jolly as ever, "So good to see you. How was the plane ride?"

"Not too bad. A little bumpy for the boys here, but nothing they couldn't handle." His grandsons were staring at the front entry of his agent's apartment, their mouths gaping.

Scotty's penthouse was a-glitter with gold lame, gem-studded lampshades and mirrored walls. The floor was covered with a burgundy shag wall-to-wall carpet. It reminded Dean of an odd mix between a disco and a porn star's boudoir. A happy scream emanated from the kitchen, and a blur of blond hair and a hot pink spandex pantsuit barreled towards Dean and the boys, "You're here! And you brought the boys!" The owner of the spandex enveloped him in a tight hug, sending a wave of Aqua Net crashing over him. Gina's nails were dagger-length and ornately decorated with multiple coats of shiny lacquer and sparkles.

"Hi Gina, good to see you again." He hugged her back and watched with bemusement as the boys endured bone-cracking hugs from Scotty's girlfriend of over ten years. She simultaneously smothered them in her impossibly large and quite obviously amplified breasts.

Scotty's wife Lucinda had been a mouse of a woman in comparison to Gina. She had also had better decorating taste.

"For Christ sake, Gina, you'll give 'em an overdose of that damned hair spray, you keep it up. It's gotta be like Agent Orange, stunt their growth or somethin.'"

"Oh shut it, Scotty," she released the boys and adjusted her helmet of hair, "It takes a lot of work to be this fashionable." She pouted and gave Dean her best come hither look. Beside her, Junior had a dazed grin on his face. Now nine years old, and closing in on ten, he couldn't take his eyes off of the ample breasts that had cut off his oxygen supply mere seconds before. Next to him, eight year old Michael appeared just as dazed, with a horrified expression frozen in place.

Dean took in the dizzying array of gold, metal, and mirrors. It replaced the primarily orange and yellow hues the front entry had once been painted in. He couldn't see a single familiar piece. June would be joining him next week for the book tour, and he couldn't wait to see her face when she took in the latest transformation of Scotty's apartment. "I see you have been redecorating, Gina."

Her expression turned from coquettish to hopeful, "Oh Dean, what do you think?" She pouted again, "Scotty says it is too much. He says it looks like a gold mine made babies with the seventies." She cast a hurt look in Scotty's direction. "I've been following Liberace. The man isn't just a musical genius, he's got *style*."

Dean smiled at her, "Liberace is certainly a trend-setter."

Gina beamed, apparently taking his response as affirmation of her decorating skills.

"Oh, for Christ sake." Scotty's eyes rolled, "Gina honey, take the boys and feed them something fabulous, I gotta talk with Dino 'bout the book."

Gina looked rebellious for a moment, but if there was something she enjoyed more than decorating, it was cooking. And she was excellent at it. Scotty had once confided that her cooking had gotten him past any horror he felt over her bad taste in fashion and decor.

"I just close my eyes, Dino, and take a bite of cannoli. Food of the gods, I swear to you." He had laughed then, *"Between the fireworks in the bedroom*

and the masterpieces she cooks up in the kitchen, I figure I can live with Elvis, Liberace and disco."

Gina waved the men off and grabbed the boys by her dagger talons, "C'mon boys, I got some zeppole waiting."

Michael cast an apprehensive look back over his shoulder at Dean as Gina dragged them towards the kitchen, her ample spandex covered rear swaying from side to side. Dean had a difficult time not laughing out loud. Instead he followed Scotty to a set of large doors now covered with a thousand tiny mirrors.

As the doors closed behind him in the office, Dean stared at the ceiling, "Is that...?"

"Yeah," Scotty said with a sigh, "It's the bloody fucking Sistine Chapel."

"How did she...?"

"Dino, I swear to God, that woman drives me nuts. All this damned decorating. She gets done, finds a new muse, and next thing you know I got God reaching out to Adam on my goddamn office ceiling."

Dean couldn't take his eyes off of it. "She had you made into God, I see." The face was indisputably Scotty's. "So who is Adam, then? He looks familiar."

"The doorman." Scotty let out an exasperated sigh. "She said he had a 'classic beauty' or some such bullshit."

Dean chortled as he took a closer look, "I visited the Sistine Chapel a few years ago with June. I don't remember Adam being quite that well-endowed."

Scotty sighed again, "So help me, Dino, I swear that woman is doing her best to kill me. Can we please talk about your book now?"

Dean tore his eyes away from the ceiling, his lips twisting as he smothered a grin, "Sure, *God*, what do you want to talk about?"

Scotty let out an exasperated roar as the door opened, Gina's stiff helmet of hair brushing the bottom of the tall door frame. "Dean Honey, I brought some zeppole for you." Her eyes rolled over Scotty, her lips pouting as she ignored him, and deposited a plate heaping with the sweet treats directly in front of Dean.

"Thanks Gina."

"The boys love them, they're scarfing them down."

Dean picked one up and put it in his mouth and sighed with pleasure. He tasted the ricotta hidden in the pillow soft dough, the sweet sugar melted on his tongue.

"These are fantastic, Gina. Thank you. You make the best zeppole ever."

Gina preened for a moment, "I'll let you get back to business. Don't let Scotty scalp you for any extra percentages, he's a shark." The door shut behind her, leaving an overwhelming wash of Aqua Net and Giorgio perfume hanging heavy in the air. Dean tried not to breathe through his nose.

Scotty leaned over the desk, pulled the plate closer and grabbed one of the treats, popping it into his mouth. "Christ, that woman sure can cook. Between her authentic Italian recipes and those enormous jugs of hers I'll put up with the doorman having a baby's arm for a cock and gold sparkles in my sheets. By God, I will."

Dean choked on his zeppole as he laughed. "Whatever you say...*God*."

Scotty chortled, his mouth full of another pastry. "Ah Dino, I have missed you! Two years is too damn long!"

Dean nodded, "Same here, my friend. This book, it took on a life of its own."

Scotty leaned over, pulled out a copy, and set it on the desk in front of Dean, snagging another zeppole. The book was neatly bound, its dust jacket glowed with the tall jagged cliffs, the castle and village below it just as Dean had described to the artist. The title *A Life Relived* spelled out in rich gold letters.

"I gotta say, it is a sharp departure from your normal work, Dino." He tapped the book, "Don't get me wrong, it is absolutely fucking amazing. Just different. I just don't want you to be surprised if it doesn't appeal to your usual readers. They can be fickle, always wanting what they just read, only different, but not too different, if you know what I mean."

Dean did. Not all of his books had been bestsellers. A couple of them had been criticized as "repetitive, worn-out refrains that only an author's mother could love." That criticism had stung. No book had been a failure though, and all of them had gone to multiple reprints.

He shrugged, "We will just have to see how it goes."

Scotty nodded and stuffed a third zeppole in his mouth. "So the tour dates for Europe are already being set up. It's gonna be gorgeous there, Dino. June is going with you, and the boys?"

Dean nodded, "Yes. It will be the boys' first trip to Europe. We treated their parents to stays in Bali and the boys will have a great time with June seeing the sights."

"Get 'em to Pompeii and some of those European castles." Scotty advised, "They aren't too old to think about valiant knights are they?"

"Who knows, we can try."

Scotty's fingers were now coated with sugar and he sucked them clean, nudging the plate of zeppole closer to Dean, "Eat up. If they aren't gone, Gina will convince herself you don't love her cooking and then she'll set her sights on reproducing the goddamn Roman Coliseum in our front entry. Y'gotta help me out here, Dino."

Dean took another one from the plate, "So what are the numbers looking like?"

"On *A Life Relived*? Well for now, they are good, damned good. We go to a second reprint next month. Hell, for all I know, you just wrote yourself into a whole new fan base. Which is all money in the bank, cha-fuckin-ching, Dino!" He leaned over, and pulled out a box filled with letters. "Oh yeah, I got some fan mail for ya. If ya want, I could have Gina go through it for you, but I also got a telegram askin' for you to interview with someone in Rotterdam."

"Rotterdam, Netherlands?" Dean asked.

"Is there some other Rotterdam I don't know about? Yeah, the Netherlands. I guess you musta hit a nerve or gotten someone interested in your new book. They want to interview you for some magazine article or somethin'."

"Huh. Well, by all means, set it up." Dean sucked down another zeppole and smacked his lips. With Gina cooking, he would be lucky if he didn't gain five pounds every day of their visit.

Scotty reached out and set the book upright, staring at it. "It is quite unique, this story. What made you write it?"

Dean shrugged, "Call it a dream, I guess. It's more complicated than that, but such is the life of a writer."

Scotty quirked an eyebrow and leaned back in his chair. It creaked under his weight. "Well, whatever works, my friend. It's different, but I enjoyed it. More important, we are moving up in the lists. Keep doing what you do, Dino."

Thousands of miles away, deep below the ground in tunnels carved in stone, a group of women met. Raven-haired, with vivid green eyes, each wore elaborate embroidered robes. If one looked close enough, the scenes appeared to shift and change with each movement. The figures outlined in a copper thread, moved, adjusted themselves, just as the large panel of tapestry on the wall did, the cliffs of Behel in Fyrsta Heim in sharp focus.

Anna Verndari nodded to a younger woman at the far end of the table, "Read it again, Protectorate Saronica, for the official record."

Mona Saronica stood, picked up the book, adjusted the slipcover with the rich gold letters and read aloud.

"*It was a world not unlike ours yet indisputably different. The sky was overcast and gray and two moons hung bright in the evening sky. The air was damp, chilly, and everything smelled of salt and fish. On one side a sharp cliff descended to the pounding surf below. And on the other, a rock face stretched up out of sight, the top of it hidden in the mists. It was the castle, however, which drew my attention and set me to walking on the narrow path.*

Behind me I could hear a bell toll. I counted thirteen deep resonant tones before it stopped and the walls of the great stone castle stood before me. As I entered through the tall wooden doors, they groaned, slowly turning on massive iron brackets.

What lay inside them took my breath away. Beneath my feet was a thick carpet, above me, however, were many levels - walkways, doors and balconies hung above me, at least twenty levels, more than any castle on our world, and at the top, a massive stained glass skylight. The beams of colored light danced on my face more than two hundred feet below.

A tapestry on a far wall shifted and changed. I saw a rush of what could only be the history of this world in the ever-moving landscapes. A great cataclysm, many dying, and the survivors fleeing through a rift of sorts."

Mona paused and looked up, "And this line, a few sentences later, '*They speak of white lights, of loved ones who have gone before waiting for you. I saw none of this. Instead, I saw the cliffs of Behel, a brief glimpse of another world just beyond the veil of our own. And I will never forget it.'"*

There was a murmur among the seated women.

"Thank you, Protectorate Saronica." Anna Verndari nodded and Mona sat down.

"How is this possible?" One of the women at the table asked, "Travel through the world walls is limited to Protectorates."

"Yet my mother was able to imprison my brother there for over two years." Mona responded, her green eyes flashing. "You have all read the reports from the 1949 tribunal."

"No one has been able to repeat this. Not even you, Mona." The woman tilted her head, "Unless there is something you aren't telling us."

Mona bristled, "I have always been loyal. My mother's crimes have *nothing* to do with me. I have remained faithful to my duties, always."

The woman persisted, "What is that human saying? Blood is thicker than water? You would not be the first to choose family over your duties as Protectorate."

Mona's face twisted and the air crackled with a dangerous, dark energy.

Anna Verndari slapped the table. Now in her late 60s, she appeared no older than forty, yet her new position as Crone within the Council carried weight. "Enough! Protectorate Saronica's loyalty is not in question here. Instead, we are pointing fingers and dancing around a very real concern. How is it possible that a human, this Dean Edmonds, was able to describe Fyrsta Heim, the cliffs of Behel, and the oldest and most majestic castle of our world so precisely? More importantly, what are we going to do about it?"

The air still crackled, Mona's eyes snapping. The women on each side of her pulled away slowly.

"Are we sure he saw it himself?" An older woman asked, "Is it possible that it was described to him?"

Anna turned on her with a cool gaze, "Are you suggesting a Protectorate shared our deepest held secret, that of another world past this one, with a *human*?" Her tone was measured, but several others winced and the woman withered under her stare.

"My apologies." She whispered, her hands pulling at her robes.

Anna stared at the woman a moment more, long enough to make her shift in her seat, and sink lower in it, before Anna turned back to Mona.

"You have arranged for a meeting?"

"Yes, through his agent. He believes it is for a magazine interview."

"And he is the one who saw Conor back in 1953?"

"Yes."

"I want Castor here as well."

"He is in transit now."

"Good. I will conduct this interview myself."

Welcome to Rotterdam

Friday, June 11th, 1982

"Shall I come with you, Darling?" June asked. She sat at the desk in the hotel room, brochures spread out in front of her. She twisted a lock of her lustrous blond hair in her finger, staring at one brochure of a medieval church with no small amount of interest.

Dean finished buttoning his shirt and leaned over and kissed her.

"I'll meet you after. It shouldn't take long. What is on the agenda for today?"

"I've heard amazing things about Laurenskerk," she replied. "Did you know it is the last remnant of the medieval city of Rotterdam? It was damaged in the Rotterdam Blitz and they considered tearing it down until Queen Wilhelmina interceded and insisted it be saved."

Dean smothered a smile, "Are you taking the boys?"

June sighed, "Junior has already tried begging off, but Michael seems interested. Perhaps he is just humoring me."

"Oh honey, it just isn't Junior's thing. He's like his dad. Take Michael and let Junior stay here. He'll be fine."

"Dean Edmonds, you can't be serious!" June stared at him, aghast, "He is sure to head for the red light district and who knows what else!"

"Would you prefer that I take him with me to the interview?" He reached out and patted her hand. "Go on, take Michael and I'll take Junior. I promise to keep him far away from the red light district and any other evils."

"You are humoring me, aren't you?"

"My darling wife, I would never do such a thing."

June shook her head, "You would, you terrible man. But fine, yes, take Junior. Shall we meet back here for a late lunch?"

He smiled and hugged her, his lips brushing her forehead in an affectionate kiss, "Sounds perfect. I'll see you then."

An hour later, he approached the low-slung mid-century modernist building on Jan Evertsenplaats with his grandson Junior in tow. The building consisted of two stories, although the upper one appeared to be a recent addition. In its entirety, the building consisted of dark tinted glass and concrete and a small sign out front read Fyrsta Heim Associates.

This had to be the place.

They entered through the glass door and approached the receptionist. Other than the girl, whose raven black hair was cut short and whose emerald green eyes were complimented by a matching green suit, there was no one else in sight. A heavy wooden door to one side hid the rest of the building from view.

"Goedemorgen." The girl looked as if she were only a few years older than Junior. "Kan ik jou helpen?"

"Um..." Dean tried to pick the words apart. *Had she asked if she could help them?*

Junior whistled under his breath, and the girl blushed, two spots of pink appearing in her face. "Oh, you are American, yes?" Her English was heavily accented, yet understandable. Dean found it delightful.

He nodded, "Yes, do I have the right place? I'm supposed to be interviewed for my book by..." He consulted his note, "Anna Verndari?"

"Ja. I mean, yes, I will page her for you." The girl pressed a button on a small box and spoke quietly into it. There was a whisper of a response in return, "She will be here momentarily, Mr. Edmonds. Would you like tea, water, or perhaps coffee?" She asked as she motioned to two chairs next to the door they had entered.

Junior spoke up, "Do you have any pop?"

Her eyebrows knitted together, "Pop?"

"Soda pop? Coke? Pepsi?"

"Oh, ja. Coca Cola! I will see." She began to turn away, stopped and swung her gaze to Dean. "Would you like ze Coca Cola as well, Mr. Edmonds?"

"Water will be fine, thank you."

She bowed slightly and disappeared through the heavy wooden door, reappearing a few moments later with two glasses. Junior sucked his down in a matter of seconds, the straw sucking air loudly as the large wooden door opened yet again.

A tall woman with jet black hair, piercing green eyes, and clothed in an expensive silk business suit locked eyes on Dean. She seemed oddly familiar, but Dean could not place her. Something about her hair, her eyes, and the way that she carried herself - as if she were...

She closed the gap between them and Dean rose to meet her.

"Mr. Edmonds. I'm Anna Verndari, it is a pleasure to meet you." A smile ghosted across her lips but didn't settle there. "Please, if you would come this way."

Junior stood up and her gaze shifted to the boy, saying nothing. Dean felt a shimmer in the air as she pressed her cool hand into his, almost as if her intent had taken form. Junior sat down as quickly as he had stood up. "Actually, maybe I'll just stay here, Gramps."

Dean looked over at his grandson, the boy's face had glazed over slightly. "You sure, Junior?"

"Yeah Gramps, go ahead and do your interview."

"Sarah," the woman said, still staring at Junior, "please make sure our young guest has more to eat and drink."

"Yes, ma'am." The girl answered, moving towards Dean's grandson. "I will get you more of ze Coca-Cola and a slice of spekkoek. It is quite good."

Dean allowed himself to be led away from Junior, through the heavy wooden door and a stone hallway and stairs beyond that. The hallway was narrow, yet wide enough for them to both walk side by side. The stone beneath their feet was smooth and as they descended the thick steps, the walls changed from smooth concrete to a rich stone etched with designs that appeared quite old. Some of it appeared to be runic, and there were scenes from Paleolithic times combined with different, unrecognizable symbols. "Is that Aramaic?" He asked, reaching out to touch one of them.

Anna's cool hand on his arm stopped him. "My apologies, Mr. Edmonds, but if you would refrain from touching the walls please. They are quite old."

"Oh yes, I'm sorry."

Anna watched his eyes move over the walls. "The building above is quite new. It was rebuilt after World War II as most of Rotterdam was destroyed in bombings. The catacombs below, however, well you can see that they are far older."

"I've never seen anything quite like it."

"We were proud to preserve some rich history," she said, pointing to a door on the left. "Here we are."

The door opened and Dean could see it was a conference room of sorts. A simple long table with leather club chairs occupied the center of the room and along the walls were several tapestries. For a split second, he was sure one of the tapestries had moved. More specifically, although impossible, a *figure* on the tapestry had moved.

Anna Verndari spoke a word under her breath, barely audible, and Dean blinked. It was a tapestry, after all, the breeze from the door had caused it. As he sat down he tore his gaze away from the larger one, which displayed a narrow rope bridge over a deep chasm, with a roaring river below. At the end of the rope bridge was a dark slit of an opening in the rocky stone wall, and the image of a sentry standing at the ready. At the other end of the narrow bridge was a thick, impenetrable forest of trees, their trunks red and brown and creatures, monsters really, were partially hidden within the leaves.

Dean studied the different panels. One showed a medieval stone house, another a village. Within each scene were fruits of impossible shapes and colors, combined with simple cottages and odd creatures hiding in the shadows. His eyes kept coming back to the first panel, however, the one with the rope bridge, churning river, and tiny entrance. Overhead, there were two moons in the sky. One was full and round, a hunter's moon, bloated and yellow. The other was a sliver of a moon.

"What a fascinating piece you have here."

Anna Verndari nodded, a glass of water in her hand was extended towards him. "Indeed. It is quite old."

"You don't see many pieces that are made from pure fantasy from the Middle Ages," Dean said, sipping the water absently as he sat down in one of the comfortable chairs, his eyes still fixed on the tapestry. "They tended to be more religious, at most ecumenical in nature." The water was sweet and there was an almost cloying aftertaste. He drained the glass as Anna sat in a chair across from him. She leaned forward, her lips shaping words that he couldn't quite make out. Her eyes reminded him of...

"Dean?" June's voice broke through memories of tapestries and stone walls. "You are a million miles away."

Dean blinked and looked around, noticing where he was for the first time. The tall windows of the hotel restaurant were clad in thick drapes, closed against the fiery rays of the setting sun.

"Sorry, dear. What were you saying?"

"I asked how the interview went. What magazine was it for again?" June asked, reaching for her glass of water. "I think I'll have a glass of wine. Would you like one? We could get a bottle."

"I, uh, wine would be fine." Dean managed, shaking the last of the cobwebs from his brain.

"Are you coming down with something?" June asked, her pretty face furrowing with concern.

"No, sorry, dear. Just distracted."

She smiled at him, "Okay, if you are sure. I hope you don't mind me insisting on dinner with you, just the two of us. The boys seemed happy enough to order room service. Michael and I had such a lovely time at Laurenskerk. The guide showed us the difference between the old and new construction but honestly, if she hadn't, I would have never known. The work was absolutely masterful."

Dean listened with half of an ear to June's words. *How did the interview go? I don't even remember it.* It was as if it had happened to someone else.

"Dean?"

"Some literary magazine that I can't remember the name of now." The words fell off of his tongue.

June laughed, "Honey, I asked you if you wanted an appetizer."

"Oh, yes. Yes, go ahead and order one."

"Well what do you want?"

"Surprise me." He managed a smile. "I'm famished."

"All right then. So how was the interview?"

If only he could remember. "It, uh, oh, you know, the standard questions and all that."

He shrugged and lifted his glass of water to his lips, the cold liquid slipping down his rather dry throat. His throat felt soothed, but the water tasted different. Not as sweet. He turned and stretched, as if trying to release a tension he hadn't realized was there.

"Nothing to write home about, I guess. I've already forgotten what she wanted to know."

June reached out and squeezed his hand. "Well then, let's have a nice dinner and you can help me plan some outings with the boys as we head south. Both of them sound quite interested in touring some castles."

Dean nodded and turned his attention to the menu.

Deep underground, the Primera Veu met, Anna Verndari at the head of the table, her business suit exchanged for robes intricately embroidered in metallic filament and richly colored threads. Around the table were three women and one man, all clothed the same. On the walls the sconces flickered, flames weaving and smoking.

"I questioned Edmonds at length," Anna Verndari said in the expectant silence, "And I am sure that he knows nothing more about our people. Our secret is safe."

"So how was he able to describe the cliffs of Behel and the entry point of Fyrsta Heim so specifically?" Castor's voice rang out.

"It seems that Conor's last act was bringing Mr. Edmonds and Magdalene Aaronson through the World walls temporarily." Anna answered.

"So it *is* possible." One of the women spoke, her voice little more than a whisper.

Anna shook her head. "It was an aberration."

"We should explore this further," Castor added, his eyes alight with excitement. "To be able to return, all of us, to our World after all of these centuries. This is..."

"Silence." Anna's voice was a sharp knife, cutting off the excited murmurs of the other two women. "It is impossible. This has been tried, over and over."

"And two have succeeded." Castor spoke again, ignoring the wrath that appeared on Anna's face. "We must..."

"Must I remind you of your place, Castor?" The youngest woman shuddered at the tone in Anna's voice. "You are here at our behest, but you do *not* have a voice in this Council."

Castor stared back at her. "Perhaps, Madame Crone, you should remember our most ancient history. In the World, male and female Njerez had equal power and equal vote."

Anna bent her slender fingers into claws and leaned forward, her jaw tensed, "And shall I remind *you* Castor Lagenfeld of how the actions of *your* gender brought us here to this place?" They locked stares until Castor broke first, staring at his lap, his own hands clenched tight.

"We are safe. This was an aberration. Mona Saronica does not share her mother's and her brother's powers. There is no one left who can do what Zenobia and Conor were able to do. This discussion is now *over*. We are here, we are safe, and we will continue as we have for more than a millennia."

There was silence as she turned to each of the others, daring them to object. "As it should be." Anna said, leaning back in her chair.

"Quod ut is mos persevero futurus," The others answered in unison.

An End to All Things

Saturday, May 10th, 1997

"Hi Mom, hey Gramps." Dean and Sarah looked up from their coffee to see Michael standing there with his dad. He was tall like Theo, but he favored Sarah in looks. His blond hair and crayon-blue eyes a certain giveaway that he was her son.

"Michael! Oh Michael, you made it!" Sarah jumped up from the table, her coffee sloshing on the chipped wood, and ran to hug her son. "I'm so sorry I missed your graduation. I wanted to be there more than anything, but..."

Michael hugged her close, "Don't sweat it Mom, really. Dad made sure to take a lot of pictures." He leaned back and looked at her face intently. Dean could see the concern in his eyes.

"How are you holding up, Mom?"

Sarah shrugged, her thin shoulders sharp against the fabric. She had lost weight, Dean could see that now. Too much worrying.

"As well as can be expected," she answered.

"And how is Grandma?"

Sarah's voice was thick with emotion, "Not good, baby, I'm glad you got here when you did." Her lip trembled, "The hospice nurse will be back in a few minutes. She says..." she took a deep breath, "They think it will be today, tomorrow at the latest." Michael hugged her tight.

"Michael! You made it!" Betty emerged from the basement bedroom with Jasper in tow.

Sarah stepped back, reaching out instead for her husband.

Betty wrapped her arms around her tall nephew, "It's been far too long!"

"Hey Auntie. I'm glad I got home in time."

Jasper leaned close, kissed his wife and clapped Michael on the shoulder, "Good to see you, Michael. I'll try and make it back before noon." He straightened his tie and nodded to Dean before he left

"Jasper has to head to work for a few hours," Betty explained as the door shut behind her husband. "He made General Manager last week at the Ford dealership, and there's some emergency meeting going on, so..." Jasper had finally found something he was rather talented at. Selling cars instead of producing stilted drivel had turned out far better for him in the end.

Michael made his way to Dean's side. "Hey Gramps, I've missed you." He leaned down and hugged Dean.

Dean hugged him back, his arms strong around his grandson's broad shoulders. "I have missed you too, kiddo. Congratulations, I heard you have your Bachelor's now."

"I do."

"And you are heading to KU for medical school in the fall?"

"Yep, that's the idea at least." Dean detected something else in the boy's voice. *Perhaps medical school is* not *in the future, after all.*

"Well, I'm proud of you, Michael." Dean nodded to his grandson. He felt a thousand years old. The last few weeks had been rough.

He sat sipping his coffee and listened as Sarah updated Michael, both of them walked towards the stairs.

"Can I get you some food, Dad?" Theo asked. "Maybe a fried egg or some oatmeal? Maybe an apple?" Dean watched as Michael walked up the stairs to see his grandmother.

Dean shook his head and gave his son-in-law a brief smile. June had stopped eating over three days ago. It was to be expected, but Dean had found it hard to eat anything either. The kids had been too upset, too preoccupied to notice, except for Theo.

"Are you sure?" Theo pressed. There was concern in his eyes.

"Maybe later. Coffee is all I need right now."

Theo turned to Betty, "Have you heard from Junior?" Junior, Dean's namesake, was still finishing his classes at Penn State, where he had a full-ride football scholarship. Despite plenty of tutoring and help from pretty coeds, Junior's progress had been delayed. His lack of scholarly aptitude saved only by his performance on the field. If he graduated this year, it would be by the skin of his teeth.

Betty grimaced, "He has finals, and you know Junior, I imagine he cracked his textbooks open for the first time last week, just in time to cram for his tests."

Dean shook his head.

Dean sat at the same table that he and June had raised all three of their children at. And after that, their grandchildren as well. Betty and Sarah had stayed close, and that had been a blessing, having the boys regularly in the house as they grew up.

The table was chipped, worn, and in dire need of refinishing. In every stain, Dean could see the evidence of countless meals, laughter, jokes, sibling fights and tantrums, birthdays, and holidays. His finger, bent with arthritis, sprinkled with liver spots, traced the stains, remembering it all.

In the hall, the phone rang. "Dad? It's Scotty," Betty handed him the phone, her hand straying to rest on his arm.

"Hi Scotty."

"Dino?" His agent's voice was nasal and loud, "How is my future wife? Have you told her I'm taking you both dancing? It's a goddamn party twenty-four seven 'round here. You tell Junie she's gotta hang in until New Years, go out with a bang and all that."

"Hi Scotty." Dean felt a lump forming in his throat, "She's uh, she's not good, Scotty. They uh," He fought to keep his voice even, "They think she might go today, tomorrow at the latest." He didn't sugarcoat it. Of all people, Scotty got it. He had lost his wife Lucinda back in '68 to ovarian cancer.

That had been a difficult year for them both. Danny had died on Valentine's Day, in fighting around Khe Sanh. Learning the news had nearly destroyed Dean and June. They had buried Danny a few weeks later, only to have to leave a month after that to attend Lucinda's funeral in New York.

"I'm heading out there, Dino. I'll be on the next flight out. You tell Junie to hang on, no need to rush things." Scotty's normally ebullient tone was muted.

"I'll tell her. Give the house a ring when you have the arrival info and I'll have Jasper pick you up."

"Will do, Dino. Stay strong, my man," Scotty didn't wait for a reply before hanging up.

"Dad, she's asking for you." Sarah's face was gray with exhaustion. Dean knew that she had spent most of the night at her mother's side.

He nodded and made his way slowly up the stairs. Every one of them felt like a mountain. He entered the last room on the right and walked towards the bed.

June had always been slim. Now, however, she was emaciated. The cancer had run through her body like wildfire, leaving her gutted and hollow. Her once lustrous blond hair was dull and brittle. Her skin had sunk into hollows, pooling in loose folds around her bones. Her brown eyes were clouded.

"Dean," she whispered, her voice a shadow of what it had been.

"Hi, Sweetheart."

"I talked to Maggie earlier." She said it so matter-of-fact. Her eyes were closed, so she didn't see him pale in response to the name.

"*Maggie?*"

"Yes," she smiled gently, "The same Maggie you told me about. All those years ago, do you remember? She came and introduced herself. And would you believe it? Danny was with her. It was so good to see him. I have missed him so."

Dean felt his heartbeat increase. He willed his mouth to work, to ask June what she meant, but nothing came out.

"She's beautiful Dean, inside and out. I can understand now how hard it was for you to let her go."

Dean's throat closed up, his tongue swollen, his thoughts a blur. He stumbled as he pulled up a chair next to his wife and took her hand.

"Thank you, Dean."

"For what, Sweetheart?" he croaked, his voice cracking.

"For falling back in love with me. Every day since, it's been," her voice was a weak whisper, "It's been wonderful. You were wonderful - to me, to the kids. I couldn't have asked for more."

Dean wanted to ask her about Maggie. He wanted to understand how or why June had thought of her and what she meant when she said she had talked to her. But it was too huge, too large a wound, even after all of these years, to open up and examine.

"You have been wonderful too, June." His voice sounded rusty, underused. "Thank you for giving me three amazing children. For supporting me in my writing. For everything. I love you."

She smiled at him and patted the bed. "Stay with me a moment, will you? Until I fall asleep?" Dean climbed into bed beside her and took her hand gently. When Sarah came to the doorway of the room, he beckoned her in, wrapping his arm around his wife, his body close to hers. She was so cold.

Slowly, the rest of the family gathered. Long moments passed. An hour later, June's breathing changed, rattled, and finally stopped. Her head was pillowed against Dean's chest, while Betty and Sarah held her hands.

Dean felt her body stop, and her energy rise up above them. A feeling of peace stole over him, her breath in his ear and hands over his heart, and then he felt her leave.

This Can't Be

Wednesday, May 13th, 1997

"Our Father, who art in heaven, hallowed be thy name. Thy kingdom come, thy will be done, on Earth as it is in Heaven..." The minister droned on as the casket was set in position. It was comprised of a burgundy lacquered surface, brass filigree, and brass handles. Dean stared at it. Scotty Abernathy's girlfriend, Gina, had picked it out. He hadn't had the heart to tell her how gaudy June would have found it. *Besides,* he reasoned, *funerals are for the living.*

The sky above was patched with clouds. The air was heavy and thick, rain was certain to arrive by evening. Dean sighed. The past few days had been a haze of grief along with waking and dreaming of a woman whose vivacious smile he had tried to forget for more than five decades. It felt wrong to think of Maggie in a time like this. Dean wondered if he wasn't betraying June as he mourned both of them. How could the loss of Maggie feel so fresh all over again? It was a sharp ache, a pain that ran through him, slowing his movements.

The church service had been well-attended. June had spent a decade before her illness working for a charity that helped to get homeless families off of the streets and into homes of their own. Dean had lost track of how

279

many had come up and given him hugs, telling him about her kindness and generosity. The news of her passing had spurred many to attend the service.

Why today, of all days?

Dean couldn't help but wonder. The crashes, both of them, had happened on the 13th of May. Now that he was here, at the end of his life, he could acknowledge it again and not fear the repercussions.

What was there to lose, after all? Maggie had existed, Theo's arrival in their lives had proved that. And then there were June's last words to him. She had said her name! Had she actually *seen* Maggie? At the crossroads of life and death, had June truly seen Maggie for the first time? How he had wanted to ask her that in those last moments. With his family surrounding them, he had held back and given her those last moments of peace. She had earned it.

A hand fell onto his shoulder, and Dean was pulled into a hug. "Dino, come visit me in New York. Gina's been redecorating again and she's got some damn Taj Mahal theme going on in the spare bedroom. I'll take you to the Met, show you the sights, and at night you'll dream you're some goddamn Persian prince. What do ya say?"

Dean smiled at Scotty. He was tired. He had slept ten, eleven hours each night since June passed, but it never seemed to be enough. Watching her fade away had been hard, but living without her steady presence was even harder.

Sarah, who had stayed by her mother's side, barely sleeping and coordinating everything in the days since June's death, looked as bad as he did.

"I'll have to get back to you on that, Scotty."

"Of course, Dino," the man paused, a flash of sadness crossed his face, and "She was a good woman." He leaned closer, "Probably better than you deserved."

"Without a doubt."

Gina, who had been a short distance away swooped in, her hair streaked with blond and brown highlights, her eyes still bloodshot from the tears over the service. She hugged Dean, her overabundance of perfume washed over him, a cloud of fruity and floral notes filling his nose.

"Oh Dean! I am so sorry!"

She began to sob again, and Dean patted her back. Gina and June, as different as they were, had bonded over coffee and baked Italian desserts years ago during a visit to New York. Dean smiled as he remembered June's assessment of her.

"She decorates in a style that fluctuates between a bordello and Liberace, but Dean, that woman can *cook*."

Theo stepped forward, "Scotty, let me give you and Gina a ride to the airport." Scotty nodded and beckoned Gina over.

Dean watched Scotty and Theo walk away, and felt a wave of dizziness wash over him.

"Daddy?" Sarah's hand wrapped around his arm. Beside her stood Michael.

"I'm fine, Sweetheart."

She kissed his cheek and took the opportunity to whisper in his ear, "I'm so sorry about the coffin, I had no idea she would pick *that*."

Dean managed a small smile, "I doubt your mother would have minded. She loved Gina and I think she secretly loved every tacky gaudy over the top part of her as well. If she is looking down on this, I'll bet she is having a good laugh."

Sarah smothered a giggle, "You are probably right, Daddy."

The line had been long, but now it was done, the people dwindling, moving away to their cars, and on to the reception back at the house. By now, Betty and Jasper would be opening the doors, inviting people in, and directing them where to put the endless casseroles and dishes. Some things, it seemed, stayed the same.

"Daddy?" Sarah asked, "Shall we head back now?"

He wasn't ready to return to a house without June in it. He missed her, he missed Maggie, and he missed Danny. All of them. His body ached from it, his skin felt old, stretched over bone, worn out. The words that marched through his mind, the ones he carried a notebook with him at all times to capture, had fallen silent.

"I just need a few minutes alone. Get some air, stretch out my legs." He patted Sarah's arm, "Borrow your keys?"

Sarah reached into her purse, "Are you sure you don't want me to stay and wait for you?" She handed the keys over, reluctantly. "I don't have to head back now, Betty and Jasper are handling things at the house."

Michael spoke up, his eyes steady on his grandfather, "C'mon Mom, let's give him a little time on his own. He's had nothing but our company for days now."

Sarah's expression spoke volumes, but she allowed Michael to take her by the arm and lead her away. "We will see you at the house soon, right Daddy?"

Dean nodded and watched them walk away. Nearby, the cemetery attendants stood waiting to lower the coffin into the ground. They stood a distance away, quiet, watching the last of the mourners leave.

Dean reached out. His fingers traced the filigree on the coffin. "I miss you, June. So much."

He backed away and nodded to the attendants. They hesitated for a moment and then got to work. It didn't take long for the coffin to be lowered into the ground, the ropes creaking slightly as it settled into place and then the dirt smacking against the glossy rounded surface of the coffin.

Dean turned away. It was done. She was gone, the earth settling in close around her.

Since the crash, all those years ago, Dean had taken up the habit of walking. It was when he got his best ideas, ones that spurred on books which rose to the very top of the New York Times bestseller lists. There had been ten in all that had made it to the number one spot. Books he had written. Those had been heady times.

There had been valleys as well. Books that were not lauded or recognized, despite a loyal following of fans.

As Dean walked along the spongy grass, still damp from the brief morning rain, his thoughts were on June, on Maggie, and all of his children and grandchildren. He didn't notice as the trees enveloped him, and closed in tight. His body ached as he entered a tiny grove encircled on all sides by trees. Standing outside it, the greenery was so thick that he hadn't expected the clearing.

Within the circle of trees in one shade-dappled corner, was a bench. He was tired, the weariness inside him something that no amount of sleep would ever fix. He sank onto the worn stone bench. The paper in his pocket crackled and he took it out. He hadn't been able to bring himself to share the words on it with anyone else. Perhaps June was listening right now, perhaps Maggie was as well. He unfolded the paper and read the words aloud. Around him, the birds fell silent.

You would know the secret of death. But how shall you find it unless you seek it in the heart of life? If you would indeed behold the spirit of death, open your heart wide unto the body of life. For life and death are one, even as the river and the sea are one...like seeds dreaming beneath the snow your heart dreams of spring. Trust the dreams, for in them is hidden the gate to eternity...For what is it to die but to stand naked in the wind and to melt into the sun? Only when you drink from the river of silence shall you indeed sing. And when the earth shall claim your limbs, then you shall truly dance.

He finished reading. His voice sounded old, fragile even to his ears. He looked around and saw for the first time a handful of gravestones in the shadows. They were covered with vines, honeysuckle, which wrapped around them, covering them in a forest of green. The flowers would be blooming soon, but right now, there were only the green vines, twisting, obscuring. The one on the far left was broken, pieces missing. The other three were intact, but covered in the honeysuckle, which had spread over their surfaces, obscuring the names below.

He stared at them. They weren't terribly old. Some parts of the cemetery harked back to the mid-to-late nineteenth century, but these stones were far more recent. He leaned forward and pulled the vines off of the last stone. What he saw took his breath away.

"Sarah Magdalene Edmonds," he read softly, "Born March fifteenth, nineteen fifty-five, died May thirteenth, nineteen sixty-two."

His heart began to beat an irregular time, and his pulse pounded in his ears.

He cleared away the next stone, "Theodore Aaronson Edmonds, born August tenth, nineteen fifty. Died May thirteenth, nineteen sixty-two."

A deep aching pain began to radiate from his chest. "How is this possible?"

He cleared the third stone and tears obscured his vision, "Magdalene Aaronson Edmonds, born June second, Nineteen thirty one. Died May thirteenth, Nineteen sixty-two."

By now the pain had spread from his chest down his left arm, his fingers felt numb in response. He gasped for breath, reaching for the last headstone, and slipped down onto his knees, sinking in the damp soil.

"Dean," the dizzying scent of Lavender Yardley perfume surrounded him. He looked up, shocked to see her.

"Maggie?" his eyes moved across her, taking it all in. All the years fell away.

"I've missed you, Dean," his wife said, her hand brushing his cheek.

Pain and pleasure intertwined themselves inextricably within him. He could feel his heartbeat, now sluggish, pulsing in his ears. It seemed his heart was unsure of whether to continue or stop altogether. The pain was excruciating, but his eyes were filled with the sight of Maggie standing in front of him. She wore her favorite dress, a smoky blue sleeveless number and she smiled at him, her magnificent blue eyes filled with tears.

His heart stuttered, stopped, and he could feel his body falling, his limbs folded up, and limp, unable to hold his weight any longer. His hand, caught in the honeysuckle, pulled up to his chest reflexively, taking a swath of vine with it. He could see the broken edge of that final headstone. The first name was obliterated, but the last name, Edmonds, and the dates, "Born September 15th, 1925 and Died May 13th, 1962," were etched deeply into the stone.

His birth date, his stone.

He collapsed, rolling onto his back, the view of the green leaves and tall trees a canopy above, and the faces of his family just feet away. Dean smiled. He had lived a long life, filled with love and happiness and success.

He closed his eyes, his mouth shaping words that remained silent, unspoken. *And when the earth shall claim your limbs, then you shall truly dance.*

In the distance, thunder rumbled low and slow, shaking the air. A storm was coming.

Dear Sarah

Sunday, June 29th, 1997

"Do you, Michael Dean Aaronson, take Julie Ann Geneser to be your lawfully wedded wife, to have and to hold from this day forward, for better or for worse, for richer, for poorer, in sickness and in health, to love and to cherish: from this day forward until death do you part?"

Listening to the words, Theo's hand holding hers so tight, Sarah had felt happy, yet bittersweet, tears coursing down her cheeks. Her son, so tall, so handsome, stood with his back straight and said his vows proudly, his voice carrying in the crowded sanctuary.

And Julie, her lithesome figure flattered by the beautiful wedding gown, had uttered her vows with a clear voice, her eyes steady on Michael.

A month after her dad's funeral, a letter came in the mail. It was postmarked with a New York address and addressed in Scotty Abernathy's sharp scrawl. She loved the old coot, but Sarah had set it aside. She would read it when she had a moment to cry and feel sorry for herself.

There had been a wedding to prepare for, after all. She had lost a mother and a father, but she was also gaining a daughter-in-law. *I need to focus on the living right now*, she had told herself.

The house was quiet, all of the excitement, all of the preparations and the flurry of people dashing about in those last harried moments were now

285

just memories. Sarah sat down and stared at it before she slid a small knife under the flap of the envelope. Inside was a short note from Scotty along with a hand-written letter from her father. She recognized his penmanship instantly. Three pages of thick, rich paper. Her heart panged, missing him again, the loss of his steady presence was still a shock. She hesitated for a moment. What kind of answers would these letters hold? Had Betty received one as well?

Sarah -

I've held onto this letter longer than I should. I'll admit, the enclosed letter from Dino was the first thing I thought of when you telephoned me that evening after your mother's funeral with the news that your dad was gone. Coming back home, I can't tell you how I felt hearing that message on the machine.

It all made sense, and yet, it didn't at the same time. Your father lived, wrote and dreamed in a world of words. I just knew how to sell them, so my old brain can't take all these damn twists and turns of fate.

That's what his first novel was all about - fate and our never-ending struggles to change it. "A seminal work" the critics called it. And Schicksal Turnpike *was amazing, I must have read it twenty times over the years.*

Your dad asked me to send this to you, and only you, in the event of his death. I'll admit it, I read it and thought he was crazier than a shithouse rat. I've known Dino a long time, and according to him, he's known me eight years longer than that. Damn confusing, if you ask me.

I've lived a long time, girl. Long enough to know that sometimes, things don't have to make sense. They don't have to follow logic, but that doesn't make them any less real. If this happened to your dad like he said it did, well, hell, it hurts my brain to think of. I know that in all the years I spent with him, he always had a tiny touch of the blues. You had to really look for it, you know? But it was there.

I got to wonder, if his books and his writing weren't his gift to all of you, especially this Maggie he mentions, along with Theo and you.

In any case. End of an era. This old dog is packing up. I got no time for these foolish youngsters with visions of fame and fortune in their damn starry eyes. Your dad and the way he wrote, he ruined me forever. I'll never accept less.

I'm retiring. Hell, maybe I'll finally get around to marrying Gina and making an honest woman of her if she'll have me.

You know where to find me.

Yours,

Scotty

Sarah stared at the note from Scotty Abernathy and at the other, far thicker letter in her hand. She felt as if she were standing on a precipice, the fall might not be far, but there would be no going back once she made the jump.

Maybe it would be the answer to everything. Or maybe it would just give her more questions.

She wasn't sure, but she figured it was time to hear the rest of the story.

Dearest Sarah -

If you are reading this, well, you know how that line goes.

Know that I have loved you, your brother, may he rest in peace, and your sister. Most of all I've loved you, though. A father isn't supposed to have favorites, but I am only human, and you were always my favorite. Perhaps it is because you were conceived in love, in both of my memories of you, and you have grown into an amazing woman in one of them.

When I woke up in the hospital the second time, I didn't understand. I couldn't. Losing Maggie, you and Teddy, it was too much. I nearly lost my mind, and I know June was inches from committing me.

Sarah stopped. "What is he talking about?"

"Is everything all right, dear?" Theo had come in, rubbing sleep from his eyes. "Damned if a nap doesn't solve all my ills. I can't wait to take naps with those future grandkids, how 'bout you?"

He nuzzled her neck, his cheeks rough, stubbly.

"I have the strangest note here from Scotty, Theo. And a letter from Dad. He's talking about losing a woman he calls Maggie, Teddy and me in a crash. It sounds a lot like that crazy story Betty told me back at Dad's funeral."

Theo looked curious, "My mother was called Maggie, and when I was small, everyone called me Teddy. Man that was hard to outgrow. Can you see me heading into college with the nickname Teddy Bear?" He nuzzled her neck again, hand sliding under her arm and traveling up her ribcage.

"Stop it that tickles!" Sarah smiled at him, then turned back to the letter in her hand. "Now seriously, Theo, read this with me, because I see your name mentioned later on."

"Okay, okay," Theo focused on the letter and stopped teasing his wife. They moved to the couch and began to read.

Dearest Sarah -

If you are reading this, well, you know how that line goes.

Know that I have loved you, your brother, may he rest in peace, and your sister. Most of all I've loved you, though. A father isn't supposed to have favorites, but I am only human, and you were always my favorite. Perhaps it is because you were conceived in love, in both of my memories of you, and you have grown into an amazing woman in one of them.

When I woke up in the hospital the second time, I didn't understand. I couldn't. Losing Maggie, you and Teddy, it was too much. I nearly lost my mind, and I know June was inches from committing me.

But I knew you were REAL, Sarah. And Teddy, sorry, Theo, was as well. When you were born the second time, with your perfect little face, those lips that looked like a rosebud, and the small birthmark on your right cheek, I knew that somehow, everything I remembered, everything I knew to have happened, WAS real.

I remembered him then, the man I saw in my coma. The one who spoke to Maggie. Really he wasn't much more than a boy. He said that he had messed it all up, that he was sorry. He promised to fix it as best as he could. I won't pretend to understand the conversation. Perhaps he was Conor Saronica, Teddy's father, but I can't be sure. I only know that he kept his promise. He saved June and Danny and Betty, and he saved you too, Sarah. I think that, in a way, he brought you back to me.

In truth, it was Scotty who returned first. When he called me on the phone, I recognized his voice immediately. I knew then that I hadn't hallucinated or dreamed it. He was real. Call me crazy if you like, but I knew who he was because I had known him for eight years.

Sometimes forewarned is forearmed, because I managed to negotiate a hell of a better deal the second time around!

As I moved through life, that second time around, through the years of 1953 through 1962, I knew things I couldn't have known. Some carefully placed bets on who would win the World Series netted us some extra change, something your mother June never even knew about. I knew Eisenhower would be re-elected, despite many folks disagreeing, and I knew John F. Kennedy would be a shoe-in.

All of that prescience stopped after May 13th, 1962, however. After that, it was a blank slate. The future was unfinished, malleable.

Not everything was the same. My books weren't. Perhaps because I was the variable in all of it. My heart, my mind, they remained independent of the different lives.

I searched for Maggie. For years. It wasn't until you brought Theo home that I understood. There he was, little Teddy, grown up, turned into a man. I was so proud of him, so full of joy. I wanted to know everything about him! He had been my son for eight years and losing him was as devastating to me as losing Maggie and you.

Learning too that his mother, Magdalene, my beautiful Maggie, had died in a car crash on May 13th, 1962, was something I had suspected. My deepest fears come true.

Of all the emotions or fears this letter might stir in you, reading that Theo is, in my memories, both your brother and your husband might be disturbing to you. Believe me, it took me by surprise, and yet it also made absolute sense. It felt as if the world was put right again in some way by Theo's return to our lives. Perhaps your souls sought each other out, reuniting that which had been lost.

Sarah, if you are reading this and think that I didn't love your mother June, you couldn't be more wrong. It took time for me to let go of Maggie's memory enough to fall back in love with your mother. But I did. I loved her for every minute thereafter, and I will until the day she dies. Which will be soon. The doctors have given her a month, maybe two.

How can a man love two women? I wish I had the answer to that. I don't. I weave my words, dream in prose, and long for answers that will never come.

Theo, if you are reading this, and I imagine you are, you have always been a son to me. I was proud to adopt you after I married your mother. I loved you as my son then and as my son-in-law now.

I imagine you as you were the moment I first met you. You will not remember it, but I do. You were four, full of energy, curiosity, and joy. I sat with your mother at that little house on 27th Terrace, near Hospital Hill, and we watched you catch fireflies in an old mayonnaise jar.

When you returned to me that Christmas in 1973, I asked a few questions. Just enough to understand how I had missed you, and your mother, all those years ago.

What would I have done differently? If I had seen Maggie and you there at that house? If I had known that you were just inside, playing with your cousins who were visiting?

I suppose that life turned out just as it was supposed to. You may have grown up without a father for those first few years, and lost your mother in 1962, but you had money, relatives who cared for you, and a decent home. You are a fine man, a good husband, and you have in turn raised a son you can be proud of.

As for me? I fell back in love with my wife, raised three wonderful children, two of whom have survived me, and I have lived a rich and full life.

If there is a heaven, or an afterlife, I hope that Maggie, June and Danny are in it. And God, I hope they all get along! I think they will. I have been so lucky, and so well-loved. I wish that for you, my daughter. I wish it for Theo, the man I will always think of as my son. For Michael too, may he find the love of his life and never let her go.

All of my love...in whatever life we live in next...

Dad

Theo and Sarah sat in silence. Finally, Theo spoke up, "Does this mean we are related?"

Sarah looked at him, "Really? That's the question you ask first?"

Theo's face fell, "I'm sorry, that was a poor attempt at humor." He took the papers, paging through them again. "Sarah, seriously, how is this even possible?"

She shrugged, "I don't know. Maybe it's like Scotty said, sometimes things don't have to make sense. Maybe we can never understand it."

"And who was this guy he talks about, Conor Saronica, who he thinks he saw during his coma?" Theo asked, pointing back to the spot in the letter. "That he could be my birth father? It's all absolutely insane."

"I have no idea. Whatever happened, it was real to him, and Dad wasn't a head case, not at all. You know that about him, Theo, and he was always so good to you." She tilted her head and assessed him, "More than that. I thought it was because he missed Danny so, but he sought you out so often. He took time to spend with you, just you." She shook her head, "To think I was a little jealous of it, but now, the way he looked at you Theo, with such pride!"

"He was good to me, Sarah, he was." Theo gnawed on his lip, "I remember thinking that very first day that we met that he was everything I wished I could have had in a dad. So many times it felt like he *was* my dad! But my god, this letter, I don't know what to think!" He shook his head, "That he knew my mom that he was in love with her, *married* to her, and had *you* with her. Is that what you would have me believe?"

Sarah shrugged again, "Honestly, I have no idea. Who knows," her lips curved up into a broad smile, "perhaps I need to write a book about it."

Theo smiled in return and pulled her close. "Perhaps you should."

Outside of the small, cozy house, two women stood. One was older, heavyset, and wearing a worn and faded house dress. Her hair was silver, just a few strands of black left.

Next to her was a younger woman, thin, with raven black hair and a hawkish nose. Both had bright green eyes. "The Fer Complir will receive a full and complete report on this, Martha."

The older woman sighed, "Of that I have no doubt, Elizabeth. But as you can see, they are causing no trouble."

Elizabeth Verndari's lips thinned into a disapproving line and her brilliant green eyes flashed, "And if she *does* write a book?"

Martha couldn't help but laugh, "What if she does? It's known as *fiction.* Really Elizabeth, it's *over.* Conor is dead, as are Edmonds and his two wives. Who is left, really, of any consequence at all?"

"Theodore."

"You know as well as I do that pairings between our kind and humans produce *normal* offspring. He has no gifts, therefore he is the same as any other human. He is irrelevant."

"The child in your house," Elizabeth asked, swiftly changing subjects.

"Liv?"

"Yes."

"What about her?"

"There have been questions."

"Her mother was my niece. Her father is human. I care for her. But she knows nothing." Martha answered.

"She was born on the solstice."

Martha laughed, "Yes, I know. But her father was human. Humans are born on a solstice too, you know. It just doesn't have the same consequences."

The younger woman stared at Martha, "Are you absolutely sure?"

"Short of digging his parents up from their graves and interrogating them? Or watching him leap from his mother's womb? Yes. Besides, the Arbre Genealogic already investigated Larry Parker's family history shortly after Liv was born. You know this."

Elizabeth sniffed, as if unconvinced. "And you will apprise us if anything changes?"

"Of course," Martha sighed.

"As it should be." Elizabeth noted, still staring at the house.

"Quod ut is mos persevero futurus," Martha answered.

As one, the two women turned and walked away, disappearing into the night.

I hope you have enjoyed this book. You would make this author very happy if you could take a moment on Goodreads or other favorite place to learn about new books. Reviews help others decide whether to take a chance on a book and I want to share my writing with as many people as possible.

A Note from the Author

All of my fiction books occur within the same universe, known as the Kapalaran Universe. They transcend genre and they are interconnected, tracing family lines for decades in either direction.

The story you have just read is a stand-alone novel, however, as I'm sure you have noticed, there is another storyline here. Perhaps you have been left with questions? Answers to those questions, dear reader, will be explored further in my upcoming fantasy series, *The Chronicles of Liv Rowan*. Here is a chapter from Book 1 of *The Chronicles of Liv Rowan*. A sneak peek, just for you!

The Chronicles of Liv Rowan
Book One: The Glass Forrest

Excerpt: Dreams with Sharp Teeth

Brilliant light. The kind that dazzles and disorients you and leaves your pupils aching, blinded, for a moment. That, and the abrupt stutter of the engine as it stopped, the vehicle drifting to a halt.

Defining moments. That first terrified leap off of the diving board at the local pool. The day I got my first period, in gym class, *of course*. A train ride in Germany and the scant number of seconds in which my family went from three to just one. And now, in this moment and time, another defining moment, and one that made no sense, whatsoever.

The creature levitating next to my car was impossible, completely so. It hovered a scant three feet off the ground, at car window height. Which seemed completely impossible given its undersized stumps of wings. Although they moved at a fast blur, they did not seem capable of sustaining flight. Especially when you took into consideration the size of creature's round, rather protuberant belly. As I struggled to process what I was seeing, my befuddled brain could only produce a quote I had heard once.

Aerodynamically, the bumblebee shouldn't be able to fly, but the bumblebee doesn't know this so it goes on flying anyway.

I blinked, reached up and rubbed my eyes before I looked again.

Nothing had changed. There was still the same impossible creature before me. It was slightly larger than Widdershins, Aunt Martha's aging and decrepit rat terrier. Like Widdershins, it had a narrow, rat-like face. That was where the resemblance ended, however. I couldn't think of any living creature that had this creature's shade of shockingly orange skin. When paired with its potbelly, small feet and short, ineffective arms - the combination seemed impossible. And yet here he was - not just defying my understanding of physics but flaunting it. He looked like something straight out of a movie or fantasy novel.

I miss reading. I miss it so much. I used to tear through stacks of books as a child. Mom once said, "The library sees you coming and shudders in fear like a refrigerator does when faced with a teenage boy."

Which really, if you think about it, seems rather silly. Refrigerators are made for holding food, and libraries are made to hold books for readers, so why...never mind. I am being over-analytical.

As I continued to stare, the creature reached out and tapped politely on my car window. Its delicate fingers, all four of them, ended with sharp claws that flexed into what could only be interpreted as a welcoming wave.

I sucked in a breath. "What... the... hell."

And if that were not enough, it now leaned in, bared its teeth in what I could only interpret as an attempt at a smile and called out a cheery "Hello!" through the thick glass.

The creature's mannerisms were human-like, and I found my hand raising in response. To do what? Wave back? I caught my hand in time, stopping it from automatically waving in response, my head dipping slightly in response. I felt silly. What was I responding to? A hallucination? Its human-like behavior was at odds with its impossible appearance.

I blinked, rubbed my eyes again, and tried to clear my head. Perhaps if I ignored it, the strange vision would disappear. My mind felt muddy, as if I were emerging from an intense dream. My thoughts came slow, thick and plodding. *I feel like I'm full of molasses.*

The creature said something else, but its words were muddled and indistinct through the window glass. I cocked my head, trying to hear his words more distinctly, but it was as impossible as the creature before me.

Despite its bizarre appearance, something that I was still struggling to comprehend, along with the sneaking suspicion that I had to be dreaming, the thing seemed to want to *talk* to me. It was now pantomiming rolling down the window. Occasionally it stopped to cast quick, glances at the tree limbs overhead. I might have been trying to read too much into it, to ascribe human characteristics to it, but it appeared to be nervous, even afraid of something there in the forest.

The old car's engine was dead. I tried it once again just to be sure. Not even a click when I turned the key. This had seemed to coincide with the blinding flash of light. One minute I had been driving down a wooded lane, listening to Pink Floyd's *In the Flesh*, then a burst of static and a blinding flash had filled my vision. It left my eyes hurting and they were still obscured with large spots.

As my eyes recovered, I could see that the road was gone. In fact, there was no trace of it remaining. Had I turned the wheel? Driven off of the road? I turned to look behind me. There was nothing, no tarmac behind me, not even a rutted country road. Everywhere I looked there were trees. And it was so *green*. Had I entered some evergreen forest?

No amount of pumping the gas or turning the key would induce the vehicle to start again.

I missed my Mazda. Unfortunately for me, the Mazda's transmission had failed and now I was stuck driving Auntie's ancient 1976 Dodge Dart until I could afford to have a new transmission put in. The Dodge Dart, built in the dark ages before computers or cell phones, relied on quaint concepts such as actual handles for rolling down windows. Without power to the engine, there would have been no way for me to roll the window down in my little Mazda. But the engine on this car had died upon arrival to this strange place, the machine slowly coasting to a stop, leaves and sticks crunching under the tires. It now showed no signs of starting back up no matter how many times I tried turning the key. The engine would not turn over, heck, I couldn't even get a dry click out of the starter.

This has to be a dream, I thought. The creature was insistent, tapping again on my window and again pantomiming that I should roll down the window. It had become overwhelmingly hot in the car. Sweat trickled down my brow, my winter coat was heavy; perhaps it would be cooler with the window rolled down anyway. I eyed the creature cautiously and rolled down the window a few inches.

The air outside was hot and humid. It smelled of summer and something else. A thick, cloying spicy smell. It was lovely, actually, and felt like home had been neatly boxed up and handed to me. A home I had never smelled before, yet knew, in my bones, was where I belonged.

"Greetings Mistress, welcome to Fyrsta Heim." The pot-bellied creature executed a half bow, no mean feat when you are pear-shaped with midget dragon wings and hovering three feet off the ground.

"Uh, hi?" I didn't know what to say to this strange creature. My body was beginning to bead with sweat; it was even hotter *outside* the car than inside of it. My brain still felt like it was filled with thick molasses – where was I? What was this place? Had I hit a tree sliding on that ice? Was I hallucinating? Was this a dream?

"Mistress, I am Pernicious Pert and I am your dragoman while you are here in the World."

"My... *what*?" I rolled the window down the rest of the way, blinking at the heat. How had it turned from winter to summer so quickly? I knew Missouri was given to abrupt changes in weather, but this was ridiculous.

"Dragoman... mm," His hands flapped expressively, and included a very human-like shrug of the shoulders, "Escort, interpreter, if you will. I am summoned whenever you enter Fyrsta Heim and I will remain by your side throughout your stay here." I noticed he had violet eyes, which continued to shift from gazing at me to keeping a watchful eye on the branches of the trees surrounding us. Now that my window was down, I could hear strange hissing sounds. There was also rustling, as if a large body or bodies was moving overhead. The occasional creak of branches betrayed the presence of something large, as if something were walking on them or jumping from one to the other.

This had to be a dream, it just had to. Nothing else made sense. *I'm asleep, in my own bed, just* dreaming *that I went to work today. I haven't actually woken up yet.* I smiled, decided to roll with it, "You have perfectly purple eyes, Pert Pernicious. Did you know that?" The p's felt rather delicious as they rolled off my tongue. "I'm Liv Parker, by the way."

The creature bared its sharp teeth in what I hoped was Pert's attempt at a polite smile.

"Why, thank you Mistress." He bobbed again in midair before casting another nervous eye to the trees that surrounded them. "If we could perhaps leave this particular area for, ahem, safer accommodations. The forest is not safe, even during the day, and night will be here soon."

"It's barely noon. I think we have a while." I said, and then remembered it had to be a dream. The sky was noticeably dimmer than it had been a few moments ago. "Well, perhaps not."

The hissing from the trees seemed to be growing and I craned my neck outside of the car to stare up into the dark branches overhead. The trees were strange, like nothing I had seen before. Dark brown, with a high sheen to them that made them look as if encased in glass. As I stared, a large shape zipped past, leaping from one branch to the next.

"What was that?!" I leaned out further, staring up at the branch it had crossed. The oily red leaves still trembled from the creature's passing. I craned my neck, leaning out of the car window in an attempt to see better in the growing gloom.

Pert emitted a distinct whine of distress, "Mistress, it would be most advisable to leave now." The hissing was increasing markedly. The lower branches on a massive tree to the right waved frantically as creatures flitted through them, hissing and whispering. I was sweltering. I pulled my coat off, setting it aside on the front seat, and then removed the keys from the ignition. These I tucked into my purse, before I slid the purse straps over my shoulder.

Pert's gaze flitted from me to the trees, and back repeatedly. The whites of his eyes showed, rolling in growing fear. "Mistress, please, I must insist we leave this area immediately." Before his voice had seemed concerned, but now there was a distinct panic in it.

This is such an amazingly clear dream, I thought as I opened my door and slid out. God, it was hot even without my coat. The air was thick, heavy with moisture. The dry winter air had been replaced with the humid wet of summer. I hitched my purse closer on my shoulder and stepped gingerly out of the car, my heels sinking into the spongy forest floor. I glanced down and stared at the thick humus, a dozen unfamiliar plants along with a creeping ground cover, all jostled for space and light. Something swooped past me, a mere flicker in my peripheral vision. The activity in the trees was increasing, the creatures within were becoming bolder and bolder. I stared up into the canopy of trees, trying to glimpse the source of the noise. There was little to see past branches moving and waving, sometimes rather wildly. I caught a glimpse of a patch of red, then yellow, but the creatures moved far too quick to be identified properly.

"Mistress, please, we must leave *now!*" Pert's panicked voice registered somewhere in the background as a creature the size of a medium to large-sized dog flew towards me, its wide, leathery wings partially bent, its elongated beak extended. My eyes widened as I saw the sharp row of teeth set in garish yellow with red splotches on its leathery bat-like skin. As it flew towards me, I stared at it with incomprehension. What I saw was impossible. Everyone knew that dinosaurs were extinct. Despite that small and rather incontrovertible fact, here one was. It hissed again, its mouth open, and it looked *hungry*. I screamed and dove out of its path, nearly face planting into the spongy ground, my hands digging into the loamy soil and breaking my fall. The creature, its flight path determined, could not maneuver away. It slammed into the old Dodge and then fell, its wings flapping. A loud, angry screech issued from it as it cartwheeled through the open car door and window and toppled headfirst into the armrest that rested in the middle of the bench seat. It righted itself quickly, looking disgruntled, casting about in the front seat of the car for something to attack.

"Please Mistress, if we could go into the woods now." Pert's voice definitely held panic and he was edging away from me, eyes on the trees above. I could see him wrestling with the option of leaving me here.

I picked myself up off of the forest floor. A coating of pine needles from the trees that stretched above them smelled like lilacs and they clung to my clothes. "Right, let's get out of here!"

Pert zoomed before me, his wings a blur, one small hand pointing towards a small, overgrown path nearby.

"This way, Mistress!"

I scrambled after him, clutching my purse as I ran. Behind me, I could hear the beast snarl and rip into the car. As the trail turned to the left, I had one brief glimpse of the Nova. The creature was now in the middle of the front seat, ripping savagely at the ancient radio. I could hear the ripping and crunching fade behind me as I ran out of sight. I stumbled then, my heel catching on a thick root, and, cursing my high heels, I focused on following Pert into the darkening, glassy forest.

For a dream, this sure felt real.

Ahead of me was thick underbrush, and Pert zigzagged as he cast glances back over his shoulder to check on me. If I didn't hurry, he would easily disappear from sight. My hair was already straggling out of the neat bun I kept it in for work, damp rivulets of sweat trickling down my neck and back. A thick wall of trees and underbrush lay ahead, a small ragged and narrow trail just barely visible. Pert disappeared out of sight.

Just before I made it to the safety of the thick underbrush, another creature dove past, hot rancid breath on my cheek. I had a clear view of rows of sharp, pointed teeth. It turned, hissing, and angled upwards. I bit back a strangled scream. I could run, or I could scream, but I couldn't do both. *Was it turning back around to attack?* I stopped trying to understand what was happening. There was no time to ask questions or try to quantify what I was seeing. Instead, I ran for my life.

Interested in reading more? The Glass Forest *will be available for sale soon!*

About the Author

Fueled by homemade coffee ice cream, a lifelong love of words, and armed with strong female (and male) characters I cross genres like the Ghostbusters crossed the streams in pursuit of the question.

"What is the question?" you ask.

The question is simple. It asks, "What would you do, if..."

What would you do if you were fifteen years old and the world as you knew it fell apart? Would you run? Would you fight? Would you survive? – Meet Jess and her brother Chris in War's End[1].

What would you do if you had a chance to live your life over? Not just once, but twice? – Meet Dean Edmonds in Fate's Highway[2].

What would you do if everyone you loved was lost to a terrible virus and you faced the real possibility of the extinction of the human race in the dark void of space? – Meet Daniel Medry in G581: The Departure[3]

What would you do if hitmen were after you and you had no idea why? – Meet Lila and Shane in Hired Gun[4]

If I don't keep you turning pages late into the night, desperate to know what happens next, then I have failed at my job. I'm a Taurus and born in Missouri. That makes me bull-headed and stubborn to boot. I don't believe in failure or mistakes, only learning opportunities and clever conversation. There's not much I won't do to make you burn the midnight oil reading my words while you suffer sleep-deprivation the following day. It's my secret superpower.

---

1.   https://books2read.com/u/bwYNpY

2.   https://books2read.com/u/bPJG5Y

3.   https://books2read.com/u/4jDgPl

4.   https://books2read.com/u/bP0dOj

Born in flyover country, I've also lived in Arizona and northern California. I am an eclectic mix of snark and oddball humor. My colorful metaphors would make a fishwife blush. I'm an incompetent gardener, a dreamer and doer, in love with old houses and shooting pool, and chief organizer of all thing's household and financial. Feed me tiramisu and I'm yours forever.

Follow me, find my books, and more by going to: https://christineshuck.com

All Published Works

Christine writes cross-genre and her books can be found in e-book and in paperback through most book distributors.

<u>Non-Fiction</u>:

Get Organized, Stay Organized
The War on Drugs: An Old Wives Tale

<u>Fiction Series</u>:

War's End
     The Storm
A Brave New World
Tales of the Collapse
<u>Gliese 581g</u>
G581: The Departure
G581: Mars
G581: Earth (Late Summer 2021)
G581: Zarmina's World (Spring 2022)
<u>Chronicles of Liv Rowan</u>
Fate's Highway a.k.a. Schicksal Turnpike
<u>Benton Security Services</u>
Hired Gun
Smoke and Steel
Broken Code (Fall 2021)
<u>Children of Ruin</u>
Winter's Child (December 2021)

Don't miss out!

Visit the website below and you can sign up to receive emails whenever Christine D. Shuck publishes a new book. There's no charge and no obligation.

https://books2read.com/r/B-A-BOLF-DXRQ

BOOKS 2 READ

Connecting independent readers to independent writers.

Also by Christine D. Shuck

Benton Security Services
Hired Gun
Smoke and Steel
Broken Code
Benton Security Services Omnibus #1 - Books 1-3

Chronicles of Liv Rowan
Fate's Highway

Gliese 581g
G581: The Departure
G581: Mars
G581: Earth
G581 Plague Tales
G581: Zarmina's World

War's End
War's End: The Storm
War's End: A Brave New World
Tales of the Collapse
War's End Omnibus - Books 1-3

Watch for more at christineshuck.com.

Made in the USA
Monee, IL
20 September 2024